The First Sandcastle

A Novel

THE FIRST sAndcAstle

M. E. Delgado

Barrio City Press

San Francisco

From shore to shore,
a castle is built
and never more…

PART I

☼

Fallen Skies

1

Stained images of perfect pictures and *tideless* dreams tell not of worlds I've painted…of sandcastles I've built. Even when I was young, when truly I was innocent, I knew not why things were the way they were—or why I was chosen to grow up in such a desolate place with a unique gift that would forever overshadow my days. Somehow, I imagined things just happened because they happened—and what would have seemed normal and accepted in a most uncertain world, would only be a molding of delicate sand never to be touched—but only shaped by high tarnishing tides.

I could always feel the walls around them begin to tremble whenever an argument brewed in the shadows of our small three-bedroom home overlooking Hawthorne Ave. It was enough to frighten any young kid to death, including my baby sister, Tamara, who often went neglected during these shaky moments.

"La Sulema from the salon asked for help on Saturdays," Mother said just before dinner.

Dad stayed silent. His dark beaming eyes swept over her in bitter animosity, as this had been the topic of many arguments in the past. He had just come home from work, unbuckling his tool belt and letting his heavy muscular frame fall onto his favorite chair. Tamara climbed onto his lap as he sighed deeply and switched channels on the television. The Monday Night game was on, and the *Dolphins* were playing.

"La Sulema wants help on Saturdays," Mother's polite tone pushed on. "For a few hours."

She had always been a housewife; never had to work—a rarity around our lower-middle class neighborhood. Dad, a successful contractor, was a builder of inner-city homes in Miami, which many claimed could withstand any magnitude five hurricane. Even during hard economic times, he managed to keep our finances in check and took pride in making sure Mother was supplied with enough money to buy everything she and our house needed.

"How many times do we need to go over this?" Dad asked as he minded the television. Tamara rested quietly over his soiled cotton shirt, not seeming to care that her favorite cartoon show had now been tuned to the game.

Thunder outside roared like an angry mountain lion, and flashes of lightening took over the darkening skies as trickling rain streaked down our front windows. Monstrous winds possessed our garbage cans, making them tumble and roll up and down our front driveway.

His voice grew louder, his patience never an elongated fuse to carry him through the day. "You don't need to be walking around waiting to see which man's attention you can get." He leaned forward and put my sister on the floor, next to her dolls and squeeze toys. She immediately started to wail, throwing her little arms up in protest.

"You're so ridiculous," Mother snapped, daring to challenge his strong demeanor. "It's not about that at all."

"I see the way you are! I see how you go around teasing every man to look your way. You have your son and daughter, and they need you here at home."

I remember not understanding the logistics of jealousy but knowing it was everywhere—especially around them. Mother was a very pretty woman, hair light brown—almost blond with lips the color of ripened raspberries and skin as white and fair as fresh fallen snow. Despite having two children, her figure still swerved curvy attributes. Every time we were at the supermarket, men (strangers) would smile and pay her compliments on her flowery sunshine dresses and smile. Some would even be nice enough to let her cut in front so she wouldn't have to stand and wait in line. I'd only look on in silence beside our cart, studying their glued smiles and wondering why Mother was oftentimes treated like royalty. She wasn't even a very good driver. When stopped by police, more than half the time she was let go without being fined. Just as in the supermarket, I'd notice the same quirky smiles. Only when stopped by female police officers were her poor driving skills made obvious.

It didn't bother me having such a pretty mother, but it did seem to disturb Dad profusely, who quite often seemed governed by internal conflicts—a complicated twisted cynicism that triggered a meanness and coldness most would misunderstand, even me.

Externally, he was a simple man—yet very strict and traditional considering the times we lived in. At age thirty, Dad had never had a drink or even thought of smoking—nor found the need to stay out late with friends or co-workers. At family get-togethers, he'd distance himself when many of my aunts and uncles raised their glasses to say *salud*. "Why are you out here by yourself?" Aunt Trinidad would ask him, as often he'd be out in the back alone. "I don't like the smell of poison brew," he'd respond.

He wasn't into speaking to neighbors or accepting their invitations to backyard cookouts or barbecues. He didn't involve himself in my art or play with Tamara regularly, nor did he like to be seen or talked to by individuals outside the realm of his successful contracting business. He did, however, like to keep Mother happy and tried to give her everything she desired, including providing my sister and me with a stable home environment. We never had to move from place to place or go from school to school like so many kids I had known. The friends we made at school were the same ones we'd keep the rest of our lives—and our bedrooms were our own, never having to share them with other family members or outside visitors.

Dad's bitter anger followed me as I got up from the sofa and made my way to my room. I turned to look at him, as it was only his figure I now saw sitting in his chair. Strong and powerful he appeared, his voice dominating anyone who got in his way—like a king resting peacefully high above on his gallant throne. He was the only thing I knew back then, and although there was this indirect closeness between us, I would have given anything to be like him. For I wanted to be strong and forceful like he was—to be fearless and certain of this world which seemed so uncertain.

I slammed my door, hoping their anger would focus on me and not each other. Desperately I tried blocking everything out of my mind so I could dwell in a fantasy world where only splendor existed. Closing my eyes, I took deep breaths and concentrated on visions of darkness and emptiness that roamed everywhere. Often, my mind would drift and indeed venture into different worlds. Some were pleasant, happy, and peaceful—without shouts and screams…without rain and wind.

But not always was I able to survive in never-never land. Their loud voices and Tamara's wailing kept me in the present, forcing me to open my eyes to this universe I would always question. My small room was another world full of pictures and drawings of my own design. Elaborate depictions of animals, superheroes, sea monsters, and spaceships cluttered every inch of wall. Even back then, at age six, it was evident I had an extraordinary talent. I could already sketch detailed pictures from magazines, encyclopedias, television cartoons, and even real live landscape settings I had seen long ago on field trips or on drives up to

Abuelo's house. Vivid freehand portraits depicted our mailman, garbage man, and even those officers who thought Mother was too pretty to be a terrible driver. And though this would have impressed most people considering I had not yet taken a drawing or art class, my artistic ability became more of a silent vehicle into another reality far away from my present.

I rushed for my coloring books and began sketching the pictures that were meant to be colored in. I hoped for something new to pop inside my head, anything positive I could draw and replicate—anything to escape this bitter part of my reality.

"I'm not asking for the world," Mother cried out in a broken voice. I felt her tears over me as the blistering heat within the house made sweat run down my face.

"You'll be old and gray soon enough," Dad shouted. "Maybe then, with your beauty gone, can you walk these streets."

My sister had stopped crying momentarily, and it seemed as though the rain had even subsided. "I hate you and everything you stand for," Mother's muffled voice fired back, piercing the deafening pause protruding throughout the house. She then wept past my room and into hers, slamming the door behind her. Even with both our doors shut, I could still hear her cries.

Dad soon entered my room. I immediately jumped up, dropping my crayons to the ground. He rarely came in, and when he did, I always looked for any attention he could spare—good or bad it didn't matter. "You don't need to run off every time your Mother gets mad at me," he said, his broad figure nearly rubbing both sides of the doorway. His dark etched face turned to my drawings above my dresser. But his gaze soon slipped away, failing to acknowledge even one of my works—as though they were not really there.

"I just wanted to draw," I said as I sat on my bed, my voice hiding behind a need to be seen and heard.

"Let me tell you something," he said. "Women can be the hardest things to understand. I guess that's why God created them. *He* had to give man some kind of challenge. Do you know what I'm talking about, Marlo?"

"No," I replied softly.

"That's good. You're too young to understand anyway." He sat down next to me. The rain outside beat down on my window harder than ever, the wind whipping its fury through trees and rooftops. He continued to talk aimlessly, not looking down at me as he spoke and ignoring my sister's cries which carried from the other room. "Girls can cause a lot of pain, son. Don't ever rush getting involved with them. I may be sounding a little hard on them, but that's the way I was brought up. You sure as hell can't live with them—or overpower them. They can say, do, or be anything they want, putting the blame on men as a species for all their problems and misery—and even getting away with it. Giving women freedom is like giving them everything the world has to offer. No one can have everything...I guess that's why women are women. They want everything, and when they get everything, they aren't even satisfied... and then they want more, and *more* sometimes doesn't even exist. That's why they're always so damn miserable."

He seemed like he knew what he was talking about, though it wasn't quite clear what he meant. He appeared in control and so sure of himself—an attractive trait in the eyes of a little boy who daily stared fear and uncertainty in the face. He wasn't as weak as Mother was, didn't cry or complain he was afraid of mice or spiders. He wasn't tender, clingy, or afraid to say what he thought. He was the kind of Dad everyone at school would like to have had. He was young, tough, arrogant, and apparently, very wise. I could go to school and tell all the kids I had a Dad that knew everything—and that felt good.

Tamara staggered up to my doorway and braced herself against the molding of the threshold. Her eyes were full of tears from apparent fear and lack of attention, her nose a runny mess.

"Whatever you do, Marlo, don't ever trust girls. They're only out to milk what they can off you, and don't think they can't 'cause they have their ways." He stood up and headed for my sister. He paused for a moment as he picked her up. She immediately threw her arms around him and held on tightly, not wanting to ever let go. "Remember...the more you love them, the harder it is to forget them." He disappeared into the darkness of the hallway. Everything grew quiet. Even Mother's room was as silent as could be.

What did he mean? As always, I was left with so many questions. I didn't know of any pains a girl could bring me. Back then, no girl could beat me up at school. What did he mean about girls doing anything to get what they wanted? What was all this about women using their bodies to bring harm? On a similar occasion he'd said girls could cause terrible things to happen with their bodies. I couldn't understand, and I didn't want to understand because I had nothing to do with girls. There was Mother, but she was usually nice. I hadn't seen her hit Dad or use her body to bring any harm. The men at the supermarket and police officers were just being nice, and I know they didn't go home with any cuts or bruises—just smiles. There was also my younger sister, but

Tamara was too young to beat up on any boys or use her body to bring harm (whatever that meant).

Oh, how I wanted to reach out and talk to Mother about all this, but I was scared of what she might say. Would she get mad at me for talking with Dad, or would she make me understand more clearly—perhaps even say he was wrong? But then I thought to myself: *Men can never be wrong. Women are the ones who are wrong all the time. They're the ones who cause all the pain.*

Dad was all-powerful, a symbol of ultimate emulation. Mother seemed the sissy, and I saw this as weak, convinced in some way that anything she would tell me would keep me from being like him—and eventually bring me down to her level to live in weakness and misery forever.

Each time she locked herself in her room after a fight, we grew further and further apart. Whatever relationship Mother and I had up to that point dwindled into a simple unconditional love with no spark of interpersonal acknowledgement. I soon felt I could no longer approach her about anything, my trust in her all but gone. She couldn't understand any of my problems or be right about anything, could she? If she yelled or punished me, I blamed her because she was a woman. If a fight broke out between her and Dad, then it was always her fault because she was a woman—the cause of all pain, the instigator of all controversy and imperfection. It was all as simple as that.

Oh, Mom, I thought back then, *I love you a lot, but why do you have to be a girl?*

She came out of her bedroom later that evening and acted as if nothing had ever happened. It was Dad who approached her first with a simple smile and sweet voice. The next thing I knew, the rain had stopped, and I saw her and Dad hugging and kissing each other. She did most of the kissing, sitting on the arm of his throne, holding his head tightly against her big bosom, caressing his head and brushing it with those gentle kisses that always seemed to weaken him. I wondered if at that very moment my father was thinking about what he had said to me not more than a few hours ago.

By the following week, Mother had gotten her way and started work at *Sulema's Salon* on Saturdays. Since Dad too worked those days, a babysitter was hired to watch over my sister Tamara and me. As mighty as Dad seemed to be, Mother proved a little powerful herself.

My school was unique in that it was situated in a district surrounded by an affluent part of town which, at the same time, bordered an

impoverished area of Miami. I was in class with kids whose parents were millionaires as well as with kids whose parents were poor refugees from Cuba and Central America. The racial and economic make up of the school made for a diverse student body. I was considered one of few neutral kids, having far less than the richer kids—but at the same time seeming to have much more than those from the poorer sections of town. It was difficult for me to relate with kids who were dropped off every morning in a Mercedes, while still relating with kids who walked to school at age five or six because all family members had to work to help pay for a one bedroom apartment where ten or more people lived at one time.

I followed my timid ways and ventured from one group of kids to the next, speaking very little and only playing with kids when asked to.

Ms. Varian was our kindergarten teacher. She was thin and frail and liked to eat lots of tuna—and oftentimes walked around smelling like fish. She was a young teacher who really did not know how to control her class. We were usually loud and unruly. There were times our principal had to come into our class because Ms. Varian wasn't firm enough to keep kids from fighting or climbing up on tables and chairs—or from food fighting on rainy days. She always threatened everyone with timeouts or with reduced recess time. But in many instances, there would be too many kids with timeouts, and a large group of kids with timeouts only meant more disruptions and chaos.

"Can anyone tell me why no one wants to be Keliana's friend?" Ms. Varian asked us one day. A new girl named Keliana Rubia had just transferred in from another school. She had thrown a tantrum and was out in the hall, crying as one of the aides tried comforting her. Being told that no one wanted to be your friend was a very big deal for most kindergartners. Ms. Varian was forced to stop our lesson on shapes and colors.

I stood silently as did everyone else around the table full of scissors, colored craft paper, and markers. One of the most boisterous kids in the class spoke up, "I don't want to be her friend 'cause she's a girl, and she's got boogers coming out of her nose."

Everyone laughed except Ms. Varian. "Now that isn't a very nice thing to say, Ivan." She looked at the rest of us—especially at the boys and said, "We must all learn how to get along, and it does not matter if you are a boy or a girl. Keliana's new in our class, and we need to be nice. Now who wants to go out first and make friends?"

Nobody moved. Everyone was glad they were not the ones isolated and in the spotlight. One girl eventually did step forward. Others followed—enough for Ms. Varian not to notice the group of us boys who had no intention of following through. Something inside begged me to step forward, an internal tug of war that said it was okay to be friends with a girl—that not all girls were bad…But I was too shy and quiet to be any kind of leader or rebel. Instead, it felt safer to stand ground with the group of boys like this Ivan kid who appeared strong, who took pride in showing how tough he was—always valiant against consequence and never showing anyone he knew how to cry.

There were other boys who did step out. One of them was the fastest runner in the class—faster than some fifth graders even. His name was Danny, and unlike Ivan, I envied him not for his running ability, but for possessing a genuine side of himself I was often too afraid to act on.

Art period was the only time I let my guard down to expose a bit of my individuality. When asked to finger paint, I'd grab paint brushes and paint lions, bears, and space monsters. When asked to draw a picture of my family for homework one night, I came back the next day with fully sketched portraits of Dad in overalls, with his tool belt over his shoulder—and one of Mother dressed in her favorite pink flowery dresses holding my sister Tamara.

"Wow," Ms. Varian said. Her eyes remained fastened to my drawings. "This is very good, Marlo. Did your mom or dad help you do this?"

"No, I made them myself."

She smiled. "Are you trying to kid me?" She looked deep into my eyes to see if maybe I would give in and say I was lying.

"My mom doesn't know how to draw, and my dad doesn't care about drawing. He's always at work. And alls my sister knows how to do is break things and play with dolls."

"How on earth did you ever learn how to draw like this?"

"I draw and use paint brushes all the time in my room when I'm alone," I told her.

I was glad Ms. Varian was my teacher that first scary year of school. She was an art lover and really appreciated all of our work—especially taking notice in my ability to draw and paint more so than anyone ever had up to that point. Other teachers I'd later have would look past my talent, and some wouldn't even give time to express oneself artistically or even acknowledge art period as an actual grade on report cards. Everything would later be geared towards math, science, reading, writing—and computers.

"You're a very good artist, Marlo," Ms. Varian said as she patted me on the shoulder. "I hope you'll keep on drawing and painting. This is a gift."

I didn't comprehend the gift part, but she quickly put things into perspective. "It's like having special magic powers that no one else has," she said. "You must use it so you can touch people, like a magician who can make you smile when he makes a dead flower come back to life… Look, everyone." The class turned around as she held up my drawings. "Let's take a moment to see what Marlo's drawn."

I hated the spotlight, but welcomed a bit of the fame. It gave me a chance to break the ice with some of the other kids. After all, I could not run fast—and I certainly was not boisterous.

Dad may have been a great builder of homes, but he was not a magician when it came to sandcastles.

One Sunday proved to be like no other. Rain had not fallen for weeks. The joy that was the sun beamed everywhere, and the skies that whispered everlasting promises were void of all clouds and haze.

"C'mon," Mother said. "You've been watching that all morning." Tamara rested in her arms still drowsy and woozy from her recent nap.

"Hey, I was watching that," Dad's voice lashed out. He reached for the remote and turned the set back on. "Can't you see the game's on?" He didn't make eye contact with her. His attention dove right back to the action on the screen.

"You've been watching football all morning. You got up to watch the pre-game highlights, then the game, then the post-game highlights, then the pre-game highlights of the next game—and now another game? We want to watch stuff too. Marlo probably wants to watch something different also."

It made no sense to me why Mother had to fuss being that there was another set in her bedroom which got even more channels. I was sitting on the floor playing with some clay, occasionally taking a bite to see if the yellow tasted any different than the blue or green. I hated football but was always glad to be around Dad. Sundays were the only days he was ever around.

"You wouldn't understand if I tried to explain," he boasted, his attention still distracted from Mother. "Right Marlo?"

"Yeah," I said not really knowing what his point was. Mother gave me a quick look of disappointment, as if expecting me to be on her side. She didn't say anything else and turned and walked into the kitchen with Tamara. The door swung back and forth behind her.

Moments later, Dad switched the television off. I wasn't sure if he was either satisfied with the outcome of the game or just felt guilty about not letting Mother have her way. "Okay, hun, it's yours." He got up, but before he took a step, he banged his toe against the corner of the coffee table. "Hhhh, damn it," he shouted as he grimaced.

"What's wrong?" Mother said as she rushed back into the room.

Dad raised his knee and grabbed onto his foot as he hopped up and down on one leg. "I banged my foot on the table."

She laughed but stopped when she saw his pain was not subsiding. "You're such a damn baby," she said, walking back into the kitchen. "The worst part is you're always trying to act like Mister Macho."

Dad's grimace left him as he looked down at the table. In a fit of rage, he kicked it with the side of his other foot, knocking our family picture to the ground. "Well I don't see why we have to buy so many tables," he hollered. "It's like a maze in here." He grimaced again as he continued to massage his foot.

"You okay, Dad?" I asked softly.

His face still squished, he nodded, "Yeah. Let's just get out of here."

Mother came back with a bag of ice. She put Tamara down on the couch. Without any hesitation, Tamara slid off the couch and headed straight for my modeling clay. "Don't you want any ice?" Mother asked.

"No," Dad flared, "I'm supposed to be Mr. Macho, remember? Marlo and I are taking off. Too many women around here." He opened the front door. I jumped up and let the remaining clay fall to the floor, happy that I had a chance to leave with him. Once in his truck, he said, "See what I'm talking about, Marlo? Do you really think we need so many tables in the house? This is something your Mother doesn't understand. You ask her, and she just doesn't see things the way you or I would." He shook his head to himself.

I never had noticed the tables, so I couldn't say I'd seen anything. But I had hit my foot several times. And now that I thought about it, we had a heavy wood and glass coffee table in the center of our living room. We had three matching end tables around our sofas, two tables in the dining area, a table with a vase near our front door—and a table in the hallway under a portrait of the Virgin Mary. They all did seem to make our home somewhat cluttered. So maybe yeah, the house was a maze. Yeah, we didn't need so many tables. Yeah, Mother didn't have to go and waste our money on so many tables. Maybe buying driving lessons would have been a better idea.

"I don't know," he said. "Your Mother is a good woman, but she can make me madder than hell sometimes."

He drove to the beach, and we spent much of the day there. The water was so blue it reflected on the white sands, making the shoreline sparkle a delicate aqua teal. The cloudless sky nearly matched the water, turning the horizon into one big patch of crystal blue. Waves broke in and out, revealing a neat virgin layer of sand.

We took off our shoes. Dad's toe was feeling better. He bent down and tore into the immaculate sand. I copied him, feeling a bit of the perfect aura surrounding the day. He began piling the mud, and I did the same.

"It's a big chocolate mud cake," I said, giggling as I splattered more mud on top.

"No," he said. "It's gonna be a castle."

"A castle?"

"Yeah, a sandcastle. We can build one with a king, a dragon, lots of soldiers, and a huge wall so nothing can ever destroy it."

I was immediately lost in his words, spellbound by the way he put things. "Can we really build one that lasts forever?" I asked him.

"We'll try."

We spent an hour trying to erect a mound of sand that never took on any familiar shape. It was just one big glob of sand, with another shapeless mound on top to represent a deformed, meshed tower. That whole moment we spent together was enough to change me in many more ways than one. I could feel a passion begin to build, my artistic side touched as nothing had ever touched it before. My fingers tingled in the sand, my soul enriched by the warm soothing encompassing water. I felt a stream of electrifying energy wash over me as I floated away into a far off land. Something about the sand and the idea of a magical sandcastle standing for all eternity conquered my everlasting imagination.

I looked up at Dad before we left that day. "Will it really still be here tomorrow?"

"Yeah," he said, confident this castle was like the many homes he'd built throughout the Miami area. "If the tide stays away," he added.

I would never dream a grander dream. Whenever I made it back, I always searched for signs of what we had built. Many tides have come and gone since then. Dad and I never spent another day on the beach as we had that day—and it was not because he and Mother never quarreled again.

2

Societal inconsistency, Freudian realizations, and inescapable taboo grappled me as it would during most of my younger days. Strange it seemed to spend my days in front of a mirror wondering what my tiny image's sole purpose for being here was. In the midst of a large hideous world, a scared little boy seemed to perpetuate among all that was fear and certainty. Not even Descartes could have explained the simplicity of it all. Silent in my ways and discreet in my thoughts, I spoke out in many more ways than one.

It was rather ambitious for Ms. Varian to organize a field trip to the museum of modern art within the first two months of school. Several kids didn't even make it into the building when we arrived. One kid lost his shoe as he exited the bus. Another girl was too bashful to let anyone know she needed to go potty and ended up wetting her pants on the bus. And once outside, one kid jumped into a fountain after he had thrown his money into the water. All were later sent home.

Those of us who made it into the museum followed a guide who took us through an array of strange, brightly-colored rooms. He was an older man with pale white skin and a set of sun-stained yellow teeth that seemed to bite at you as he smiled. His voice was dry, and his eyes never blinked as he rambled on and on. "And this," he said as he pointed to a large picture full of brilliant orchestrated triangles, squares, and circles, "is our most prized piece of work, a glimpse of futuristic art in the making. It's been fully designed and created on computer. Notice how exquisite the circles are and how they blend in and become part of a square which at the same time becomes a triangle."

Nothing in the room appeared to be colored or painted as Ms. Varian had us do in class. How odd to think of finger painting on a computer or drawing without a pencil—or painting without a brush. Still, the artwork did look enticing as it drew our attention to a precision of spectacular shapes and colors—colors I'd never find in a crayon box or among the set of assorted watercolors I had at home.

The guide turned our attention to an object in the center of the room. It resembled a dog and was made of tin cans. "Now this artist's genius is found in the unique way he has chosen to display an everyday image using soda cans. Notice how he has chosen to scrape away the labels on some of the cans but has chosen to leave the labels on others."

The Ivan kid who stood behind nudged me just then. "Hey," he whispered. "Danny and I are going to the bathroom. No one's looking. C'mon."

Ms. Varian and her aides were busy listening to the guide. I hesitated momentarily. I wasn't one to step out of line. Something, however, told me I should follow along. For Ivan was the leader I always wanted to be, and Danny's sensitivity appeared free of all restrictive influences which to that point had invaded my everyday life. Slowly, they stepped backwards and disappeared through the heavy red drapes leading to the main hallway. I followed and sunk through the curtains. Once out in the hall, we were free—feeling as though we could do as we pleased. Who cared about going to the bathroom? We ran up and down the main hallways and avoided the main entrance where other guides gathered to greet incomers. We came to other doorways with similar red velvet drapes. More unusual figures and computerized artistry invaded the interior rooms. In one room, a quiet statue immediately stole our attention. Solid gray and headless it stood, limbless with simple breasts exposed for all to see.

"You think they're real?" I asked as we walked in.

"I bet you they are," Danny said.

"Ah, hell no," Ivan said. "It's a statue, dummy. It doesn't even have a head or arms. How can they be real?"

"I dare you, Marlo," Danny said giggling. "I double dare you to go up and squeeze 'em."

"No way," I replied, smiling. "Someone might come." I looked right at the red velvet rope tied from one post to another, clearly telling us to stay away. I felt Danny push me forward. Even in kindergarten the peer pressure was immense. This was not like playing in the yard and being asked to jump off the highest monkey bar or pour sand over some girl's head. The stakes were higher. I actually took a few steps of my own, almost ignoring all inhibition.

It was Ivan who saved me just then. "Forget it," he said. "They're probably no different than Barbie doll boobs. Let's get out of here before Ms. Varian finds out we're gone."

They darted out of the room, but I remained transfixed with only my curiosity to keep me company. Surrounded I stood, as more computerized artwork and other deformed figures and sculptures bombarded me from all angles. Almost ashamed by my curiosity, my attention swayed back to the statue. Why didn't it have any clothes on? Our guide mentioned nothing related to the nudity of art or the splendor of nature as it related to our feelings and perceptions of our then limited life experiences. Why were breasts suddenly left open for all to see and yet head and arms gone? Even Barbie dolls came with clothes to conceal that which seemed forbidden. I pondered over the realization of everyone who wore underwear, and for a moment wondered what it would have been like if we all stood headless and naked—in silence, and in our bare essence of humanity for all to see.

"*Te tienes que ir,*" someone voiced. "*Voy a limpiar.*"

Startled, I turned immediately, imagining that I had been caught and would get into trouble—not so much for venturing away from the class, but for being caught in what seemed like shameful bewilderment. A man dressed in white overalls split open a set of curtains from a different doorway on opposite side of the room. His head was pointy with a small bushel of hair resembling a smooth mountaintop with a peak of black melted snow. He rolled in a bucket and mop as he entered. I was not fully fluent in Spanish but understood well enough to know he was telling me to leave. Dad often spoke Spanish in the house when *Abuelo* came down to visit from Daytona, and there were also Cuban peers in class whose only language was Spanish.

I said nothing as I backed my way through the curtains. Ivan and Danny were nowhere to be found. The room where we had left the class was empty and not one guide was seen near the main doors. Through the huge glass windows I finally spotted my entire class out in the center of the courtyard, next to the great big water fountain. Ms. Varian was doing a head count. I rushed out near tears as I thought I had been missed.

I had made it back just in time for lunch.

"I really want to go with you guys," Mother told me on parent teacher-night. "But Tamara's not feeling well and has to go beddy-bye. I'm sure you're doing well. Your dad will let me know everything when you get back." She hugged me and placed a kiss on my cheek, reassuring me that she cared. I couldn't find the words to tell her I wanted her to come, couldn't find a way to say, *I love you mommy.*

Dad had never been to my school before and relied on me to show him around. I was proud to be seen with him, for he was tall, muscular, and walked with a poised arrogance not seen by most. He wore his usual work jeans, T-shirt, and big black heavy boots. His waist was smaller than his upper body, his hair cut very short, and his face clean-shaven and smooth despite rough, callused hands. His skin radiated a dim-dark complexion from all the sun he took in daily at construction sites, making his appearance look all the more like that of a man who preferred the outdoors, as well as one who wasn't afraid of a little hard work.

"It's a pleasure to have your son in class," Ms. Varian said as she shook my father's hand. She seemed tiny in comparison to Dad's big, burly figure. She looked him up and down, seemingly struck by the "macho" image he seemed to carry. "I'll be right back," she let us know as she made her way to the back room.

Dad looked around the room to find lots of cut out images of animals, trees, mountains, and an ocean full of fish, whales, and sharks. A brightly colored alphabet with pictures representing each letter was pasted along each of the four upper walls. Toys, games, and activity puzzles lay piled mountains high, while ten small round tables and chairs stood scattered throughout the room.

He awkwardly sat in one of the tiny chairs until Ms. Varian returned dragging in a different seat.

"Try this one," she said.

"Thank you," Dad acknowledged as he grabbed the heavy chair with one hand and positioned it to his liking. "So, how's Marlo doing?"

"Well, his social skills are not as evident as some of the other kids, but he is liked and well-behaved. It's probably just a personality trait."

I understood only the part about "well-behaved." She took a seat behind her desk.

"We don't really live in an area with other kids Marlo's age," Dad let her know. "I've tried getting him to play some little league, but he hasn't had interest."

"It's nothing to worry about. Like I said, he seems to be liked by the others, and I'm sure he'll break out of his shell as the year wears on." Ms. Varian got up and opened up a filing cabinet behind her. "There is something you might want to take a look at." Out of the cabinet came one of my art projects. She unrolled it to reveal a landscape picture of our schoolyard. It included the basketball courts, the benches, parts of the school building, and a garbage can with various pieces of trash scattered throughout the yard. "This is something Marlo painted a few days ago."

She gave my father a few moments to look it over. I felt a bit uneasy given Dad had never talked to me about my interest in art, nor had he ever acknowledged any of my work. "Oh, yeah," he said as he leaned back casually in his chair. "Marlo does like to paint and draw. He's always in his room drawing away."

"I must say though," Ms. Varian responded with a smile. "This is not the usual six year old you have here. The detail in this work is amazing, and he did it mostly from memory. He didn't sit outside or have a picture in front of him to guide him. I know that I, as an adult, could take a dozen art classes and never in a million years be able to do anything that comes close to this."

I remained silent and picked up the building blocks on the floor and awkwardly stacked them one on top of the other until they all collapsed.

"I hope that you encourage him. I think he has something really special."

"I will," Dad said. Then Ms. Varian showed him the family portraits I had drawn. They were pinned up next to the chalkboard for all to see. But he said nothing; rather, he looked expressionless, as if he had no way of determining or identifying my inherent talent. He looked down at me. I knew his smile would be short-lived.

Back in the truck, he said, "I'm glad you're doing well in school, Marlo. Looks like Ms. Varian really likes you." But he failed to mention anything related to my artistic ability or any of the works he had just seen. Disappointed, I shrugged lower into my seat and wondered what Mother would have said or done had she been there. Would she have hugged me and told me I was a good artist and said she was proud of me, or would her voice and smiles have expressed the same kind of apathy?

But then I thought it wasn't Mother who really mattered. It was Dad who seemed to hold my identity and all that was certain around me.

I later smiled only because he took me to eat ice cream at the nearby ice cream parlor, where I was able to be drawn away from my disappointment and discontent.

Were women truly evil? What was the definition of evil and how could anyone really define what it meant?

"You probably suggested her because she's young and beautiful," Mother said shortly after Daisy's interview. She really wasn't looking for a fight, just one of those complicated jealous kind of remarks to let Dad know she really loved him.

"Oh, please," Dad said as he smirked. "You said you wanted someone fast, so I got someone. Besides, she's just a little girl. She doesn't compare to you." Mother seemed satisfied with his response and quieted.

Daisy was hired the very next day to watch over Tamara and me on Saturdays while Mother went off to work at *Sulema's Salon*. Daisy lived down the street from us and was the daughter of one of Dad's foremen. But she wasn't the little girl Dad had suggested. She was sixteen years old and in high school, seemingly old and mature back then.

I paid little attention to her long blond hair or her pretty facial features and marveled more over all the money she got to carry. For Daisy had dollar bills and debit cards in her pocket, while I carried only marbles, army men, and loose change. And she was also free to stay up as long as she wanted, already dating and oftentimes returning home late on Friday nights. Sometimes, when I was able to fight off my sleep, I'd sneak a peek out my window and see her with older boys in fast expensive cars. I couldn't understand why these boys wanted to go out with her—or why they would ever want to give her candy and flowers. She was just a girl, a young and beautiful one as Mother had said…Maybe it had something to do with all those warm goodnight kisses Daisy often gave her dates at the end of each night.

I couldn't care less about flowers, sweet chocolates, or kisses. Oh, how I dreamed of staying up 'til the lonely hours of the night so I could draw and paint to my heart's content—or until I was lulled asleep by peaceful images of quiet open fields or far off cities up in the clouds I often imagined in blank picture books. Being Daisy's age also meant I wouldn't have to be afraid of the dark or be frightened of whatever I thought lived inside my closet at night. I could breathe freely and need not live under my blankets night after night. Shadows of trees that beamed through my window would now only be pleasant silhouettes—and not some giant octopus trying to suck me away into the darkest reaches of the sea.

Daisy proved to be most fun. She liked board games, hide-and-seek, and watched all the cartoons I liked to watch. She didn't mind singing my sister to sleep or changing her diapers when needed. Whenever I was hungry, she'd take me into the kitchen and fix me popcorn, cereal, or waffles with lots of syrup. It didn't seem to matter that she was a girl. From time to time, I'd even forget she was a girl…that is, until that one Saturday when she popped into my parents' room wrapped in only a towel. Her clothes were in hand as she headed straight for my parents' bathroom.

"I'm going to take a bath, okay?" Daisy said. I rested atop my parents' large king-sized bed, watching television as I often did before dozing off. I did not know why seeing her in only a towel should have mattered, but the overwhelming feeling that flowed through my small body said that it did.

Water splashed into the tub as she peered her head out the door. "Your sister's asleep. If she wakes up, just stick the bottle back into her mouth. I won't be long."

I nodded and wondered the reason for her bath. She always looked fresh and clean, her hair bouncy and sparkling—her skin always dabbed with sweet scented rosy perfumes. Mother had even asked her to stay out of this bathroom and only use the one in hall. Then it dawned on me...I'd overheard a conversation she'd had over the phone with one of her friends. She had described my parents' bathtub and mentioned that she had never bathed in a seashell shaped tub. Dad had installed the large exotic tub to Mother's liking shortly after the bathroom had been remodeled.

Daisy closed the door only halfway. She had no idea the mirrors on the walls and door gave me a clear view of everything inside. For just a split second, I had a clear view of her bare body as her towel dropped to the floor. My curiosity again had me chained. I dared not turn my gaze or cover my eyes as Mother often had me do during kissy lovey-dovey scenes on satellite television. The only naked female I'd seen to date was my sister during her nightly baths. There was definitely lots more to Daisy than Tamara's flimsy little body—much more. Unlike the headless statue at the museum, her breasts were real and appeared tender and alive. They moved as she moved, her curvy figure quickly blurring as it dissolved into the misty steam now encompassing every inch of the interior.

I waited to see if the mirrors would clear, hoping to see more of Daisy if I could. But when she was done, she shut the door. All I could do was imagine her naked body as she put her clothes back on. I had fallen asleep before realizing I was back in my own room. Everything was dark, and it was very late.

The following week, Daisy bathed again. But this time I was in the living room. I walked into the room when I heard the water. She stepped out of the bathroom fully clothed. "You can't let your mom know I take baths here," she said as she knelt to make eye contact with me. Her face was so much younger than Mother's, her skin without blemishes and seemed incapable of ever pruning like *Abuelo* or Aunt Trinidad's face.

"I know," I said. "I haven't said anything."

She went back into the bathroom. She left the door slightly open once again, but by now, the hot steam had invaded most of the mirrors. I saw nothing.

I rested on my parents' bed, already tired and dreary-eyed. I tried to wait for Daisy to come back out, but I soon found myself in the middle of a dream. I was on the beach, surrounded by thousands of naked mermaids who all called my name, wanting me to come into the water and swim away with them to the deepest parts of the ocean. They assured they meant me no harm. But I refused, waking shortly thereafter, shaken by the thought of being underwater with no air for me to breathe. Quickly I raised my head from the pillow. The bathroom lights were still on. But the sound of water was no more, and the condensation on the mirrors had already dissipated. Only the fan hummed harmlessly throughout the quieted room. Someone was in the living room, certainly Daisy who had long since finished her bath and was straightening up the front room before Mother arrived. But to my surprise, Daisy popped out from behind the bathroom door and rushed out in only a purple brassiere with tiny matching underpants small enough for my sister to wear. Her face was in disarray as she tried squirming into her blouse. I was still confused but quickly realized what was going on as soon as Mother's voice called Daisy's name.

She tried desperately to get her clothes back on, but to no avail. Mother walked into the bedroom and found her with blouse and pants halfway on.

"What are you doing?" Mother uttered as she set her package on the dresser.

"Oh, hi Mrs. Clemente," Daisy sputtered in an ill-fainted voice. "You're home early. I...just finished taking a shower, that's all. Tamara's already in bed, and I figured I had enough time before you guys got home."

Mother looked at her suspiciously. "I told you that you were not to use this bathroom."

"I know but—"

"And how dare you undress in front of my son." Her voice was deep and direct.

"I didn't mean any harm Mrs. Clemente, honest." Daisy looked over at me, as if I had something to say in the matter. But I remained quiet and waited for a chance to get out of the room. I wanted no part of this.

Mother's eyes grew narrower. "You have no right to impose yourself on my son's innocence. Please leave as soon as you're finished getting dressed." She grabbed me by the arm and forcefully pulled me into my room. I wailed, as I thought she was going to hit me. I'd only been hit by

Dad, and that had not happened in quite some time—way back when I'd been caught playing with matches out in our backyard.

Whatever harm Daisy inflicted upon me I did not know. It did, however, make my mother very upset. She yelled at me for not having told her of Daisy's secret baths. But I just as well have been hit, because she'd never yelled at me before—and that seemed to hurt more than any slap could. We'd always kept ourselves distant, and I always respected her as I did distant strangers. How did I go about telling her that Daisy had done nothing to hurt me—that I did not mind seeing Daisy naked or in her underwear? I was in tears as she made it seem like it was all my fault. "You never keep anything like this from me or your father again! Do you understand me?"

I cried and didn't respond. She finally calmed and hugged me tight, telling me she loved me and never wanted anything bad to happen to me. It felt good to have her affection, but I could do nothing more than hate her just then, unconvinced that she could be concerned and still yell at the same time. I soon told myself it was okay—she was my mother and she was also a woman who could not help but cause me pain. She finally finished by calmly asking me if Daisy had touched me on any of my private parts. This totally blew me away like the many winds which toppled over trees during the grandest of hurricanes—or the many tides I'd later see wash over my sandcastle dreams. *Why would Daisy ever want to touch my private parts?* I thought.

I told her the truth. No.

When Dad got home, Mother blamed him for having hired her. They fought and fought. She swore in Spanish and called him awful names I'd never heard before—even threw and broke dishes in the kitchen. Of course Dad defended himself and seemed the more logical of the two, returning the blame.

"Oh, for Christ's sake," he yelled from the living room. "You're the one who wanted a job in the first place, and now you act like such a victim." Another dish smashed against the sink. Dad paid little attention to her rage. "You act like she's killed the kid or something. It's not like she was doing anything to him. Hell, the boy's got to learn what a real woman looks like sooner or later."

"Oh, shut up," Mother screamed from the kitchen. "*Cabrón que eres.* She's not a woman, and you are nothing but a dirty pervert to think what she did was appropriate." I heard more dishes smash into the kitchen sink. I hid and cried alone under my blankets, wondering if this would ever end. "I bet you would have loved to be in Marlo's shoes as his innocent eyes watched her bathe in our own bathtub."

"Yeah, right," said Dad calmly.

A new babysitter was hired the following week. Instead of pretty Daisy, Mother insisted on a fat girl with greasy hair from the local high school. I wondered if Mother had done this on purpose. For looking at this babysitter's naked body was the furthest thing from my mind.

3

The world became more of a puzzle I'd never solve. For things weren't any less complex or any more certain than the fiercest tempests to strike down on scariest of nights when all I could wish for were long bright summer days. Despite the physical and emotional realities of this world which appeared would never comprehend me—or I it, I continued to dream of castles that would never fall, of sunsets that would never fade into deceiving moonlit abysses…of never-never lands that would never vanish beyond my waking dreams.

I hated geometry and everything Pythagoras tried to prove. I hated to write in ways I did not always speak or feel, or read books and plays I did not always understand—or which told stories far different than those I had lived or wished for. I hated to memorize dates, names, and events—especially those which saw men become slaves, of golden lands lost or stolen by those in search of wealth, and of cultures long since forgotten in the depths of a history made to look glamorous…More than anything, I hated teachers who made me think as they did—who never gave me freedom to wander off into the fathoms of my own ingenuity.

My sophomore year at Beach High School proved most grueling, though somehow I managed to remain the quiet, observant student who did what was required of him in the average realm of predefined academia. Of course, the only class I enjoyed and excelled in was art. For art was still the only vehicle I used to search for my true identity, the only class where teachers took notice and accepted this somewhat complicated me. Always was there something to be sketched, something to be painted—another stepping stone laid forth to answer questions I had not yet learned how to ask. It did not matter if I painted dark images of torrential storms crushing cities or green pleasant pastures revealing a peaceful side of life's paradoxical paradises. I would have rather suffered the most torturous of pains than see an empty page go unblemished or a plain sheet of canvas go bare.

Mr. Parlante was Beach High's last true remaining art teacher, a lover of music and philosophy with a passionate taste for classical and traditional art. Many artists had come in and out of his art classes during his many years at Beach. He was widely known throughout the school district and highly respected among his peers. Computers played no part in his classes, and the only technologies found in his room were the latest innovations in paintbrushes and finely textured canvases. "You're of a dying breed, Marlo," he said before school let out that year. "There are very few of you left, and the ones who are like you don't even know it. They're lost in what is now a world of little or no imagination, with a large dependence on machinery to create beauty which can only truly be created from mind and spirit."

Like Ms. Varian before him, Mr. Parlante really appreciated my talent, and I loved him as a teacher. It was sad, however, that the art department at Beach High only offered three traditional art courses, most of which had been eradicated to make room for high-tech graphics and drafting courses. Other traditional art teachers had long since been replaced by teachers of limited artistic backgrounds, devoted computer technicians whose sights and sounds were limited by a dependence on machinery and gadgetry. My ability and I were left on our own now, for I had already taken Mr. Parlante's drawing, painting, and advanced sculpting and ceramics courses. His art history class was done away with the year I had entered Beach. Like him, no one could convince me that micro-technology would ever replace the paintbrush. Rather, it would only prove to help those who knew not how to decipher the ultimate possibilities and passions of this encompassing world. I too felt true artists could not be made. We simply were.

I followed his advice and enrolled in philosophy courses rather than subject myself to computer related art courses which laid claim to the future of artistic creativity. "Philosophy will help you battle all those impossible questions we as artists sometimes face," Mr. Parlante said when I voiced my concern about taking computer arts. He rarely ever made eye contact with me or anyone else for that matter. Though this time his pale gray eyes and long gray hair swung my way. Everyone else had already rushed out of the room and headed to the end-of-the-year picnic out on the Green. "You just keep painting and creating what is deep in your heart. Don't listen to those who continue to wave their hands in front of computer screens or projections. Critics will tell you your art is outdated, archaic—old school. But those who ponder this world will be touched. It's not easy to hide the power you hold."

And as I battled to find my true identity, I also came to question: *What is true friendship, and is there really such a thing?* Mr. Dupaoli's *Intro to Philosophy* course introduced me to Aristotle. After reading up on his concept of ethics, Aristotle's writing struck an inspiration. *No one would choose to live without friends, even if he had all other goods.*

Since the day of our field trip at the museum, Danny Skies and Ivan Cantón became my very best friends. I guess right from the start we were drawn to each other for reasons only Aristotle could have surmised. We were different, coming from three different worlds, yet sharing a passion of being separate from the rest of humanity—of possessing God-given "gifts" and sharing them with the rest of the world the best way we knew how.

For the remainder of our kindergarten year, Danny, Ivan, and I spent our time together in the yard during lunch and recess. When we got to grade school, we walked home together and spent our afternoons at the park, near Ivan's house. Later, we would spend the night at each other's homes and spend our weekends at the mall, hobby shops, novelty stores, arcades and at the movies. Instead of going our separate ways when we entered Beach High, we kept to each other and made our friendship grow even stronger.

Were we special? Was I special? Did we really hold this mysterious world in our hands, waiting to take everyone by storm?

"Hey, fill this up," I said as I handed Danny the bucket.

"Sure." He grabbed the bucket and dashed closer to shore.

"Is this one gonna have a moat?" Ivan asked, not really interested as his gaze made its way to the water.

"No way," I replied. "A moat takes too long. Besides, the last time I built one the whole thing nearly fell apart."

"Here," Danny said.

"Thanks."

"So what's up, you gonna stick around here all day?" Ivan inquired.

"I guess so, why?"

"Let's hit up the mall and hang out," Danny said. I used my shoulder to brush some of the sand off my face. I stared up at Danny's tall figure as his shadow shaded both Ivan and me from the hot blistering sun. He was the handsomest of us all. His evenly proportioned figure, rich-hazel eyes, wavy blond hair, and great big smile contributed to Danny's good looks. He was generally soft-spoken and a bit reserved. His emotional and sensitive side was still a constant—as constant as the many proofs I encountered in geometry class.

"Why the mall?" I asked, pouring some of the water onto the drying mud, then shaping the pile into a little mountain—forming what I imagined would to be an impenetrable plateau. "It's boring going up there everyday. Besides, I don't have a lot of money on me."

"C'mon, Marlo," Ivan said as he got up from the sand. "You know we don't go down there to shop. It's all about the females—cute ones." His hair was longer than Danny's or mine back then, and it whipped across his pale-white face like a dangling flag in the delicate summer breeze. His cutoff shorts were torn and faded, his discolored T-shirt displaying the name of some ancient-old rock n' roll group I'd never heard of before: *Def Leppard*. Unlike Danny, Ivan was never afraid to say anything like it really was. He was often loud and obnoxious—much like Dad. He could be very serious about certain issues and less complicated in his ways, never letting his sensitive side get the better of him. He was often predictable and strong and decisive in his decision making. Wisdom followed him like his own shadow, and his flamboyance and cunning nature made for a strong, recognizable image in my heart.

"Are you just gonna stick around here all summer and build sandcastles?" he demanded. His tone expressed a bit of resentment, as if something had been building for quite some time. "Don't you ever think about girls?"

His question didn't surprise me. It had been asked before. There was always the need to prove my manhood around my friends, as well as with others at school. I avoided the topic of girls like the plague, not wanting to admit I was still the virgin all other guys at school claimed they were not. Back in locker rooms, all guys talked as though they were rulers of their own sexuality, rulers of women—something Dad had always said was impossible.

I could feel both their stares beaming down hard on me, just as the cloud-free sky and bright sun beamed on the entire white sandy beach. I ignored his remark and continued to pour more water onto the pile that was now beginning to take shape.

"I don't get you, Mar," Ivan added. "There's lots of girls that dig you at school, but you never bother to do anything about it. I'm seriously beginning to think you're going gay."

I hated when Ivan made such suggestions. No, I wasn't gay. I thought about women, and I was certain I had a handle on my sexuality. In fact, the older I became, the more exciting it seemed to have had a babysitter who used to undress in front of me. Couldn't he understand there was just something about girls that frightened me? Didn't he know girls were only out to get me in the worst of ways, and for this reason it was better not to have any part of them? *No girl could ever make a difference in my life. They caused the worst of pains that made a guy want to die—the kinds of pain that made your heart ache more than any heart attack could.*

Instead of lying and trying to become one of the many fake studs at school, I remained quiet and let the world, including Ivan and Danny, think as it pleased.

This time Danny interjected, "Are you coming or what?" He too liked to put me on the spot just as much as Ivan, and he pissed me off more than Ivan at times. He was no more a stud than Ivan.

"No, you guys go on without me," I said finally as I continued molding what I could of the mud.

"I guess we'll see you around then," they commented with a touch of sarcasm in their voice. "Have fun."

I tried not to pay attention to their smart, drifting remarks and laughter as I continued work on my sandcastle. But what they said stayed glued to my mind: "What a little bitch. Just leave the little homo lover alone."

After a while, I stopped. I looked at the ocean, the sun, and the spotless blue sky. I took a deep breath and took in the salty aroma of the gleaming water which appeared more like liquid silver. It was a beautiful day—the kind of day printed on postcards and traveling brochures. Umbrellas covered the white sands as far as the eye could see. People walked along the shore hand in hand, with gleaming smiles, enjoying a world I didn't seem a part of. Others raced to the water with boogie boards and beach balls. The hotels were filled with life, and life in turn made the hotels come alive...I couldn't believe I was here, soon feeling as though I should have been with my friends, being normal and having a good time.

But how did I hold onto my sandcastle dreams and still find a way into social arenas? The day I turned thirteen my parents had allowed me to venture out of my neighborhood alone, mostly on weekends and during summer when school was out. From that point on, Miami Beach and sandy edifices became my life. It was a sense of independence and a home away from home. People around the beach were attracted by my work, and many would even take pictures.

Neither Danny nor Ivan could understand my talent even though they were the ones who acknowledged it the most. To them, what I did was sad. I was the creator of beautiful things that eventually were destroyed by high tides and sullen rain. I was the builder of sandcastles, the sculptor, the painter...I was the artist. They, on the other hand, did things which seemed everlasting. For they were the athlete and sports hero—the popular musician and electrifying rock star. They made people cheer and scream, and they were the ones to be worshiped and glorified.

Danny's stature as an athlete went far beyond stardom. He'd always been the fastest sprinter among all kids our age or older. He had dozens and dozens of trophies and ribbons, competing in running events at age eight, when all others were ten or eleven. His biggest dream was the Olympics, and this kept him very focused. He made the starting varsity track team his freshman year and led Beach High to its first state finals in only his sophomore year. He was famous, and many at school flocked his way after meets and rallies just to congratulate him. If you didn't know of him, then you would have been one of few not in the bleachers as everyone cheered, *"Danny Skies stands tall. Danny Skies will never fall."*

Ivan always had a natural ear for music. Back when Ms. Varian was still our teacher, he surprised the entire class by sitting in front of the grand piano in the school auditorium. He played the theme song from "Charlie Brown" and also "Nadia's Theme"—and this after never having taken a single piano lesson. He claimed it came naturally, that all he needed to do was listen to a certain song and, with little practice, he'd find the right piano keys. We were all amazed, including Ms. Varian who had him perform at our first school play where everyone gave him a standing ovation. As Ivan grew older, he grew fonder and fonder of the guitar. He talked his father into buying him a used electric guitar for his tenth birthday—and with his allowance paid for lessons. I don't think there was one person at Beach High who didn't know Ivan by his guitar playing skills. He was the school band's lead guitarist his freshman year, beating out some of the most talented guitarists the school had ever known. He could play anything, including Beethoven and Mozart, and usually had everyone on their feet at football and basketball games, sending chills and thrills down everyone's spine.

I never stuck around to watch the tide come in, was never around when the rain fell. Maybe Danny and Ivan were right. I shouldn't have been wasting my time trying to build something that wasn't going to be around a very long time. For what I did seemed never to be worshiped or glorified. I was only a creator of things which made people wonder, ponder, and perhaps even flounder. My ways were subtle—my beauty seen in spark images of a moment's time…What I did could never last forever.

I got up from the sand and picked up my bucket and skateboard. Depressed, I walked up to the sidewalk and rode my skateboard home.

4

It was so appropriate for the rain to come when it did. For the rains which fell upon Miami Beach during the second week of summer drenched in me a reality I was beginning to overlook. One last castle I would build, as I now promised to lay off my sandcastle dreams and spend the rest of the summer with my friends. I hadn't seen or heard from Danny or Ivan in over a week and wondered what they were up to and why they hadn't come over or even called. Had I angered them so much that they'd now chosen to forget our many years of friendship?

The heavy summer rains left Dad jobless. Bids and job requests were either canceled or postponed for later dates. Although it was a great chance for him to catch up on the administrative side of his business, he was still left with plenty of time on his hands—and lots of time to be at home.

Mother was now working part-time during the week at Sulema's Salon. This made her happy. She had more freedom to do as she pleased, something she never had being that she'd always been home with Tamara and me. She worked rigorously to keep her liberties by trying to make Dad as happy as possible, aware he would not have tolerated a messy home or uncooked meals. She never hesitated to ask about his day when he got home, never failed to have on her nicest dresses with her nails done and hair curled, always smelling fresh and pretty. And she never refused to take off his shoes when he complained how much his feet hurt or massage his back on his hardest days.

Still, as much as Mother tried her pampering, Dad's pride and continuous ridicule would not allow things to stand at bay. He really did not like her working—especially during the rains when he'd wake to find her gone. Things grew worse when Sulema's began servicing men. The salon had long since grown in popularity, and the owner had bought the adjacent building over and combined both places into one large unisex facility. Mother was now cutting men's hair as well as styling and perming women's.

Dad was incensed when he found out. I guess it reinforced his worst fears and insecurities. He had always accused Mother of wanting to work so she could be closer to other men. By now, she was in her late-thirties and still very attractive. Her waist narrowed her hips, keeping her figure well-defined and bottle-shaped. Her face exposed not one fine wrinkle, and her hair was the same light shaded-brown color I had always known it to be—not one trace of gray or discoloration.

"I want you to quit," he raged at her.

"I can't just quit."

"Why not? Why must you hurt me the way you do? Why must you make me look like a fool and disrespect everything I am, everything I do for you? Don't I give you everything you want?"

She did not answer. She finished setting the table and went back into the kitchen.

His voice grew in intensity. "Haven't I made you happy? Don't you know what you're telling me by doing what you do?"

She came back out with silverware in her hand. "No, I don't know what I'm telling you," she replied in a much lower pitched tone.

"Haven't I pleased or satisfied you in all these years that now you gotta be with other men? Is that what you want, to leave me and your kids behind?"

"Is that what you think?" Mother's screechy voice now snapped. She was more focused and now on the same wavelength as Dad. "Is that what you see me as—some tramp? After all these years, if you can't see that I love you and that I've always been right by your side, then you never will."

"You're not by my side," Dad responded forcefully. "You're out feeling on other men's hair, servicing them—making them feel like they're important to you...Maybe you are—"

"What am I?" she shouted as she slammed her hands down on the table. Some of the silverware went crashing to the floor. The air stiffened as silence mirrored not what at other times could have been quiet peace. "What are you really saying?"

He didn't hesitate. "Maybe you are a tramp."

I got up from the couch and headed for my room. Although their fighting no longer seemed as threatening as it once was, it still bothered me, and I know it bothered my sister who by now was old enough to feel our parents' continuous and complicated turmoil. Tamara was no longer the small-thin twig girl I'd always known. She was already nearing her teens, her body beginning to shape curves much like Mother's—her breasts growing out like swelling mosquito bites. Her room was wide open as I walked by. She rested on her bed as she listened to music with her headset, always trying to block whatever realities roamed through our house—always hiding and avoiding in her own little way, just as I always had.

Rain streamed down the streets in endless rivers. Water spilled from our rooftop ever so hard, causing our front yard to flood over and join the flowing streets. Mother screamed and shouted, crying—always crying. Ritual called for her to head for her bedroom. She uttered not one word to me in the hall. A look of desperation plagued her face. The house shook as her door slammed behind her.

Still sitting at the table, Dad rested his head over his hands in silence. He never wanted her to have her way, never wanted to give up his stubborn ways—at least not until she came out of that room and acted as though nothing had ever happened. That was when Dad's weakness took over, a weakness he'd always said could only be brought on by women…a power only they had, a spell only they knew how to cast.

"Money, control, power, heartache—that's all they ever want," he said to himself. There was no need for me to stick around and hear more of his wisdom. In my room I hid, as I'd already heard it all before… Besides, his talk of women played no importance to me. There were no women in my life that could manipulate me. Mother and I were simple strangers—and my sister a mere pain in the neck I could lock out of my world whenever I chose.

Later, Tamara knocked on Mother's room. The door opened and closed behind her. Their quiet voices went unheard for hours. I assumed they spoke of men as a species. I assumed Mother taught Tamara how to control her feminine powers so she too could one day cast her own spells over men…No doubt Tamara took Mother's side on everything, just as I had always found reason to make Dad my hero. For indeed he was still everything to me—the only constant and permanent force leading me through this dreary cold world of uncertainty.

Watching Mother and Tamara later come out of the room together almost made me shed tears, especially when Danny and Ivan weren't around. Never had my questions or desire to reach out been greater. Never had a need to be nurtured been more evident. Questions and emotions I did not feel appropriate to express to Dad fluttered throughout the deepest reaches of my persona. A yearning to cry, and a yearning to be heard screamed within. To tap in seemed almost impossible.

She replaced the last of her tears with her seemingly real smiles and soft-spoken voice. That's when I felt it better that we remain outsiders. For I could decipher Mother's games, knew how to recognize her spells. "Have you eaten yet?" she asked as she approached Dad.

"I'm sorry I yelled," he said, ignoring her question. "You know how I get out of hand sometimes. I didn't mean to say what I said. It was awful. I know I wouldn't want those things said to me." He pulled her closer to him. Mother then followed with a forgiving kind of talk, except she wouldn't say sorry as much. Everything seemed Dad's fault in her eyes, and Dad was willing to accept that—or so it seemed. Then there were her kisses as she fell on his lap. Dad never resisted those soft kisses, never turning away from her warmth and gentle nature. She hugged him close and squeezed his head closer to her big bosom. He didn't move for a long moment—apparently cherishing the attention and assuredness that she did love him. After making up, he swore there would never be another argument in the house again. I don't know why he liked to say things he knew would never come to pass.

Mother would get her way yet again. She didn't quit her job. Though Dad reluctantly accepted the situation, it caused him such anguish that it was impossible for him not to blow up the very next week—and in weeks following. As much as I looked up to him, I also hated his seemingly weak and hypocritical ways. And as much as I longed for a better relationship with Mother, I also hated her for casting spells and using her powers on Dad to make him contradict what now held true in my heart. It made everything seem inevitable, and yet so helplessly uncertain.

After a week of continuous rain, the sun lazily raised its charm over the calm ocean's horizon. Remaining clouds seemed only scraps of uneaten popcorn ready to be gobbled up by an upcoming scorching afternoon. Humidity filled the air and stuck to you like sand over wet, moist skin. Temperatures soared to a constant eighty-five degrees, and winds died as they often did following a huge torrential rainstorm. With bucket, shovel, Dad's shaving blade, and camera in hand, I skated through the still damp city streets. My skateboard skidded over puddles of water like a surfer riding the largest of waves. Signal lights blinked on and off. Some didn't even work, as power had disappeared throughout most of Dade County.

It was still very early. Not a single bird or plane conquered the skies when I reached the outer part of South Beach. Hotels appeared dead, and shops and cafes alongside Ocean Drive were still gated and as quiet as a forgotten ghost town in the middle of the Wild West.

Soggy sands made it easier to keep structures in place. What had been a muddy abyss of sea-covered shore cleared and ensured that walls, towers, and dreams would not sink, slime, or slump…Just perfect for building my last sandcastle of the summer, I thought. I would not have to build so close to shore.

Buckets and buckets of sand I piled. The hot, spicy sun soon dried outer layers of sand already mountains high. I kept the bucket constantly filled with water, adding appropriate amounts to moisten and shape. As I carved, scraped, and smoothed with one of Dad's putty knives, I soon found myself swallowed by instinct—something I could never explain when later asked how I went about creating my art. My eyes shut, letting go of familiar surroundings only consciousness could have mistaken for certainty. In my head I counted its many walls and towers. All senses and perceptions of reality dwindled into a black abyss of unconsciousness, dipping deeper into another world. For a moment's time, I felt myself become the sandcastle and somehow felt as though the sandcastle became me. It was perfect; and for a moment, I was perfect. A tiny prince I imagined in the midst of this great awesome spectacle. Its towers pierced the skies and seemed to disappear into space, its architecture flawless as delicate pillars held up corridors surrounding a second level. A hundred steps leading to an intimidating doorway spoke of great wizards with magical powers ready to unleash mystical forces to protect their prince. The tallest tower was a turret where I saw a damsel awaiting rescue before being fed to dragons that were the epitome of the castle's stronghold.

It was inevitable for my solitude to be invaded. What first appeared to be a deserted wasteland had now turned into an inhabited arena of endless white sands encompassed by a vast ocean of teal-blue water. Crowds of people inundated the shore—pretty native girls in bikinis and muscular guys in swimsuits and tans. Stores were open and filled with tourists, hotel lobbies hectic and alive again, and sidewalks packed with people bicycling and rollerblading.

Confidence soon soared, enough for me to let go of all flaws and imperfections. In the past, there had always been something to improve or perfect. Today, however, all was perfect. Precious were these moments when I was struck by my own talent, instances when I'd look at one of my paintings or castles and be completely overwhelmed—times when there was no need for anyone to acknowledge…moments when my creations spoke for themselves. If a picture really could tell a thousand words, then this one told a thousand stories of a sandcastle that would never fall. Even I could not help but marvel. Astonished, I stood up and stared. *Me, I created this? It seems so unreal, but it's gotta be real—'cause if isn't, then I wouldn't be real.*

I snapped a picture, noticing through the lens that Danny and Ivan were approaching the site. Weary and hungry, I sat back down on the sand, finally catching a deep sigh I'd not had in hours.

"Didn't I tell you?" said Ivan as they came nearer. "I knew we'd find him here." He was eating an ice cream cone. Danny had a peach which he devoured in two bites.

I was so hungry I could have eaten a whale. Their food made me feel all the more hungry and weak.

"So what's up, my man?"

"Nothing," I said as I put my camera and Dad's putty knife into my bucket.

"Don't even tell me you've been out here since that last day we left you here." Ivan laughed and could barely keep his ice cream from melting onto his hand. He finally got to the cone and bit into it.

"Yeah, right," I said.

Danny was first to take notice of my work. "Woah," he remarked, "nice job. You must've been out here a week."

"I started early this morning." I stared out at the ocean. It was difficult to make eye contact when admitting I'd been wrong. Twelve hours on Saturdays and sometimes on Sundays was a bit long to be playing with sand. Friends just had to be more important. Nothing like this should have ever come in the way of our friendship.

"What's the matter?" Ivan asked.

I took a deep breath and said, "I've decided this is gonna be my last sandcastle of the summer."

"Are you serious?" asked Danny.

With enough courage, I turned to face them. "Yeah. You guys are right. I can't leave you guys hanging all summer."

They met my eyes in silence, seemingly surprised by my sudden change of heart. Big smiles soon replaced their expressionless faces.

"Now you're talking," Ivan said cheerfully as he gobbled up the last of his cone. "Working this hard could be bad for your health. You could go blind—or lose your mind."

"I could use a vacation," I agreed.

"Damn right you can," said Danny. "I'm not even running as much this summer."

"Hey," Ivan acknowledged, "I didn't mean to act like such an asshole last time we were here. I just didn't get what you got outta coming here day after day, spending so much time building sandcastles. I have to admit though, this is nice—the best I've seen you do."

It seemed we had parted for years rather than weeks. But in no time, it felt we hadn't parted for a single minute.

"What've you guys been up to?" I asked as I picked up my skateboard.

Ivan took a look around the beach, as he too seemed pleased with the bright sunny day. "Not a hell of a lot," he replied. "It's been really dead with the damn rain and all."

"I know what you mean," I said. "I couldn't even get out of the house. It was all about watching cartoons and rerun videos on the music channel. And it's been nothing but hell with my sister and parents locked up in the same house."

Danny's attention still focused on the sandcastle which seemed to overtake all of the water and the shore. "Man," he said, carefully encircling its five foot perimeter. "You should really enter one of those contests like on TV. I bet you'd win. Ivan's right, this is the best one you've ever built." He stared a bit longer. "I wish I could do this."

"And I wish I could run as fast as you can. This is really nothing."

"Yeah, but shit," he added, "I'll be old one day and won't be able to run as fast. What will I have then?"

It felt good hearing him say that. And to hear Ivan be so positive was a joy. It really was like winning the hundred meter dash in a big track meet—or better yet, like playing everyone's favorite tune on a guitar and having everyone dance and melt away. Yes, I could make people's eyes dance, emotions sing, and minds marvel…Yes, my sandcastles could last forever.

"Ah, Christ," Ivan said, his attention glued towards the water. "It's Kelly and her friends—and I look a mess."

"You always look a mess," Danny said.

"Shut up. This ain't funny."

I turned around and saw Keliana Rubia heading our way with three other girls. A far cry from the quiet little girl who had no friends her first days of kindergarten. Keliana was one of the most popular girls at Beach High, a cheerleader and an active participant in student government. Her good looks made all the guys wish for a date, and her amiable personality attracted many friends and acquaintances. She had obsessed Ivan ever since his hormones started kicking into overdrive in the seventh grade. Often he claimed she was the star of all his wet dreams, but little did he recall how he'd been one of the mean little kids who wanted no part of her friendship back in kindergarten. Little did he remember how he'd always seen girls as poisonous to a boy's utter well-being.

Certainly I was not crazy over her or had insatiable fantasies whenever Kelly's name came to mind. She had always been nice to me—and I nice to her. We'd always talked in art class, and sometimes I'd help her out with some of her art projects. Yes, she was pretty, tall, with sandy blond hair and an athletic figure much like Daisy's years ago. She was also very rich, living in a much more upscale part of town than I—or even Danny did…But she was just another girl, never one to play a part in any of my dreams—wet or dry.

"Hi, guys," she said as she approached with her three companions.

"Hi," we replied back.

All held towels and all wore two-piece swimsuits underneath shorts and cut-offs. Two of the other three went to Beach High. The third, behind the other two, I did not recognize. She didn't appear to be from these parts, at least not in my eyes. Her white cut-offs were not worn as snug over her slender figure as was the case with the others, and her red low-cut T-shirt displayed not the rest of her two-piece. Her brown shoulder-length hair gleamed in the sun, perhaps from a swim in the sulky waters of the Atlantic. Her smooth tanned skin was rich and stunning, difficult to tell whether her tan was a natural one. She too had the prettiest face, free of acne with a matching flawless mocha-cream complexion—and slanted narrow-green, cat-like eyes that were almost intoxicating, enchanting me with the kind of inspiration I often got just before painting or sketching on loneliest of nights. What made her different? What made her speak when in fact she uttered no words? Could it be the way her wild eyes silently glowed upon my sandcastle, or the way they seemed to beam through every ounce of my being?

Girls were supposed to be bad news, the evilest of all creations and the cause of all pain and hardship on men. I was supposed to keep my consciousness and good judgment from being invaded—never to wake, never to soar or adore…and never to keep me from focusing in on what was supposed to be definite reality. An unfamiliar sudden rush of adrenaline flowed through my veins as my eyes grew fixated by her presence. A feeling of warmth followed, blanketing every part of my body—just as the infinite ocean beyond covered the shoreline, near my sandcastle. Perhaps this was what had inspired countless poets, songwriters and storytellers of the past to speak of funny smiles love forced over one's eyes, cheeks, and heart. Perhaps this was the spell Dad would call love at first sight.

Oh, how I wanted to forget all of Dad's warnings and simply muster up enough courage to say something to her, anything—it didn't matter. My attention shifted back towards Kelly, trying my hardest to keep my stares at bay. It wasn't easy though. My eyes and neck seemed strained.

"What are you guys up to?" Kelly asked.

"Just kicking back," Ivan replied.

She looked down at the sand. "Now this is a sandcastle. Did you guys build this?"

"Marlo did," Danny announced.

The spotlight beamed. It seemed even brighter than the sun. I shook inside, not knowing what to say or do—especially when the girl with the wild green eyes looked my way. I hid behind my modesty and kept quiet in the midst of my seemingly perfect creation. After all, I had not won the hundred-meter dash or played any kind of magical melody on a guitar. And as much as I would have liked to be Danny or Ivan for even just one second, I certainly wasn't one to readily accept such attention or admiration. I could even say I dreaded to think of such moments. For it wasn't common to find a guy who spent an entire day at the beach on what he considered to be a work of art. *What's this girl think of me now—a guy my age building sandcastles like a child of six?*

"This is awesome, Marlo," Kelly acknowledged.

"Thanks," was all I said. I glanced back at the dreamy girl. Her gleaming eyes still gazed my way. I immediately pulled mine off her. Uneasiness swayed me as her stare seemed to overpower every inch of me, sensing she could undoubtedly spy right through me and read my most personal thoughts and secrets—secrets I myself had not yet learned how to uncover.

"I didn't know you could do stuff like this," said Kelly. "How come you've never done anything like this in class?"

"I never thought it would fit in."

"I bet Mr. Parlante would love it."

"I don't know," I responded. "He might—I guess."

Kelly looked at the castle some more. "There's no way of taking it home. How can you possibly bear to see it go to waste?"

I held up my camera for everyone to see. "I just take a picture of it and then leave. I don't really stick around to see what happens."

"I bet you always come back and hope it's still here," she commented.

I didn't respond. I looked back at the girl with the enchanting eyes. Her attention was fixed on the sandcastle. She stared at it deeply until finally she looked up and caught me looking at her. Again, eye contact with her intimidated me, and I did nothing more but turn my attention back onto Kelly.

"Any of you guys got Day on the Green tickets?" Kelly asked.

"Ah, hell no," Ivan said. "I wasn't about to wait in line at two in the morning."

The upcoming Day on the Green concert was a two-day spectacle which had sold out a year in advance, a once in a lifetime extravaganza with the hottest rock 'n roll, pop, and alternative bands gathered together to play over a two day, two night period. People were traveling from all over the state and other parts of the country just to be a part of it. Tickets had been scalped at ten to a hundred times their face value—and at one point even ceased, as the event became too priceless to pass up. Even those with enough money to pay skyrocketed prices could find no available supply lines.

"A cousin of mine has tickets," Danny said. "He's thinking of selling."

"How much?" Kelly inquired. "Oh, I'd give anything to go."

"Probably a lot."

"What day you thinking of going?" Ivan asked.

"Day Two. Oh, I want Day Two."

"Day Two?" Ivan blurted. "Why Day Two? That's when all the bubblegum groups are playing. Day One's where the shit's gonna slam. You got *The Screaming Blades, Erectile Dysfunction, Spit in Your Eye*, and *The Crushing Melons*."

"Yeah," Kelly replied, her eyes widening as she spoke, "but Day Two will have *Empty Charms*, and I heard he takes his shirt off on stage. Plus you also got *Casual Lullaby, Party on Tuesday*, and *The Summer Boys* all on stage that day. Day Two is where I want to be."

"*The Summer Boys? Empty Charms?*" Ivan hurled. "That's pretty boy stuff. Only guys wearing pink shirts and purple shorts'll be there. I wouldn't be able to survive in a crowd like that. Besides, that kind of music kinda tickles—if you know what I mean."

Everyone laughed, even the girl with the eyes. I stared at her for as long as possible. Her attention drew back to the sandcastle, appearing captivated—as though the castle had been a new discovery, an eye opening experience witnessed only once in a blue moon. *She must like it*, I told myself. Our eyes met once more. Her deep green gaze bit deep into my body and soul, making me soft and weak all over. I hesitated, but again I broke off contact. A bit of insecurity lashed out to reinforce that maybe she didn't like me or my sandcastle. Desperately I held strong though and told myself that she must like me, at least a little—as a friend. My insecurity eased when I found her staring down at the castle yet again.

"My parents said I can have tickets for my birthday," Kelly said. "You'll ask your cousin, won't you, Danny? Ask what day they're for, and if he says Day Two, tell him I'll give him a stack of money a mile high."

"I'll see what he has," Danny said. "But I wouldn't have him sell them to you for a stack of money. I'll talk him down."

She smiled. "Thanks, Danny. You're such a sweetie." His face turned tomato red as she gently stroked his cheek with her hand. Bashfully, he smiled back.

"See you guys later." Kelly and her friends walked away. I longed to pursue so I could somehow have a chance to talk with this girl with the eyes. But that was far too ambitious for me. I didn't have the courage, and I knew Danny and Ivan would never let up if she were to reject me. There was also the realization of facing up to this indescribable weakness she was making me feel. How could I deny Dad and everything he'd warned about women? I saw how much he did for Mother and saw how much Mother took his love for granted by going out to work and feeling other men's hair—ultimately causing Dad the worst of anguish. No, I couldn't. I couldn't let this love thing complicate my life. Life was far too complicated as it was.

She made no attempt to look back or say anything. All I could do was watch in a daze as she treaded through the sand behind Kelly.

"What's your problem?" Danny asked me.

A few seconds went by before I responded, my attention still transfixed. Weakly, I pointed. "Who's that girl with the eyes?"

He followed my hand, taking a closer look in their direction. "Who?"

"The one at the end," I said in the same dead tone.

"Oh, you mean her—Desiree?"

"I guess," I answered, unsure if that was the girl he was referring to.

"She's new here. She came down from New Mexico a few weeks ago. She's kinda cute, I guess—but she doesn't say much."

"How do you know her?"

"Why, do you like her?" Ivan butted in. He gave my body a hard shove, nearly toppling me over the sandcastle.

"You would've already met her," he added, "if you'd come down to the mall more often—like you used to."

I ignored him. The image of this girl named Desiree seemed to transform my mind. Her pretty little face with her wild looking eyes became inscribed into my every thought.

Ivan went on with his meaningless words, "Besides, Kelly is way cuter than her. I mean, what wouldn't you give to have a girl like Kelly?"

"Desiree," I uttered softly to myself, not realizing I had answered his question.

5

Reality...was there anything more difficult to come to terms with? It seemed better to imagine myself a prince in a fantasy world than go on and face things as they really were.

I sat on the sand, mystified by an overwhelming awareness I had never experienced before. Every inch of my body and soul laid touched by this girl named Desiree—and every thought focused only on her. I felt like a hopeless victim, awestruck by her pretty features and tantalized by the thought of being closer to her in some way, of somehow connecting with her immaculate aura. It was definitely more than a physical attraction. *Her eyes*, I reassured myself. *There's something about her eyes.* The way they'd looked at the sandcastle and the way they'd glanced right through me pleaded not to be frightened—told me she was a different kind of girl, told me she was nice.

Danny and Ivan spun a Frisbee they had taken away from a little kid. The kid cried, but Ivan silenced him when he flung it into the water and dared him to go after it. I had little energy to do anything else, as I had still not eaten lunch or breakfast. As I got up and shook the sand from my clothes, I saw the water begin to surround the sandcastle. The sky was just beginning to dim, suggesting the afternoon was all but over. The lower walls of the castle slowly blended in with the rest of the shoreline and the incoming tide. A large wave smacked against the main foundation. One of the towers gave. It too began to blend. Soon the stairways melted, and the pillars eventually cracked and collapsed. The castle and all its majestic vitality was all but gone; its beauty and promise laid to waste.

This was the first time I had ever witnessed any of my castles fall. It was a sad sight, sad indeed. "Let's get out of here," I told Danny and Ivan. "Let's go and get something to eat." I wanted to leave so badly, not because of my hunger so much. For so long I had dreamt, dreamt of a day my castles would never fall. Always there had been hope. Always there had been pleasant memories. Now, I wasn't so sure.

I kept my promise and avoided the beach, spending most of my days with Danny and Ivan. The days grew hotter and muggier. You couldn't stay outside too long without having to drink gallons of water just to keep from dehydrating. Although it was more comfortable to stay indoors, we continued our summer days out in the hot scorching sun. We had more time on our hands than we knew what to do with and would not accept being trapped indoors a single minute as we had during the rains.

We took the bus up to Fort Lauderdale a few times and spent most of our time at the mall, the music store, and the arcades. Wherever we went, I kept a close eye out for Desiree, hoping we'd run into her again. But she was nowhere to be found. The parks, the swimming pools, and even the streets and beach spoke only of her void. Had she gone back where she'd come from? Maybe she'd been visiting a relative for the summer and had already headed back. Danny and Ivan had mentioned they had only seen her once before at the mall. She'd uttered no other words except to say hello.

When the county fair arrived during the Fourth of July weekend, we ran into Kelly, but there was no Desiree. Though the fireworks cried her name that night, she did not answer, nor did her face appear in the crowded walkways of the fairgrounds. As days wore on, it seemed Desiree had only been someone I'd dreamt up, someone who presided only in those dreams from which you never wanted to wake. I kept my feelings to myself and continued to be possessed by all thoughts of her stunning eyes and perfect sweet-looking face. I could think of no other thoughts more pleasant and satisfying to get me through some of the longest and hottest summer days I could remember. Yes, crushed I was, and I didn't quite know how to talk to anyone about what I felt. Ivan was not a reliable source despite our longtime friendship. Guys just didn't talk to their friends about such feelings. It was just simply understood that you had to like girls and that was it. There was a definite fine line—nothing in between. If I brought her up, I knew he'd bring up sex, and I just didn't want to think of her like that. And Danny, well I knew if there was anyone I could talk to about falling into instinct and emotion, it would certainly be him—but he could never keep anything to himself. I knew if I told him anything, he'd only tell Ivan and I'd be exactly where I didn't want to be…out in the open with feelings that were far too foreign to feel safe or comfortable. So I kept whatever I thought and felt to myself, almost bursting in frustration as this Desiree girl became more of a rare apparition that would only appear once in a lifetime.

I was home in time for dinner on most evenings. I'd rush to eat just so I could lock myself in my room and play my stereo and continue with the large array of paintings I had started working on long ago, when Ms. Varian had inspired me to keep on with my "gift."

Dad turned his attention to me before I left the table. "You should be working rather than wasting your days away."

"Leave him alone," Mother said. "He's still a boy and needs to have his summers free. Isn't that why you've spent your entire life working so hard for—so your kids wouldn't have to work like you have?"

"Yes, but he must learn how the business works, so the day I die, someone will be able to take over and continue the tradition. God knows that day'll be soon."

"Oh, don't talk that way," Mother replied.

Things had never been better at home since the rain had stopped. Dad was working full time again, and although he still despised Mother working and "servicing" other men, they were both busy and well enough away from one another to eventually miss each other at the end of the day. These were happy nights when not one loud voice would be uttered around the house, when both my parents would retire early to their room and lock the door behind them.

Tamara would sometimes come out of her room and knock on their door, but neither of my parents would answer.

"What are they doing in there?" she'd ask me.

"Leave them alone. They're sleeping."

"If they were sleeping they wouldn't be making any noise and banging on my wall. It's annoying." Her room was adjacent to theirs. I'm sure she heard more than I ever did.

"Would you rather they be yelling and arguing?" I whispered.

"No."

"Then give them their space."

With my parents in a more loving and caring state, I thought the world would continue on like a picture perfect piece of artwork, an everlasting sandcastle. Nothing else in mind could have been considered more perfect, since it had always been their anguish and aggression towards one another that had always been at the center of our dysfunction.

It was my friend Danny's turn to fall. And hard he did fall.

On days that were just too hot to venture anywhere, we'd sit and talk outside the shady surroundings of his home while listening to music and drinking some ice tea. Danny's two-story home was surrounded by a white picket fence and great big palm trees which shielded it from the hot Miami sun. Hardly a car ever sped down his street, and the only noise you'd ever hear was a neighbor's lawnmower on a Sunday afternoon—or the wind briskly ruffling leaves and hedges warning of an incoming storm.

"She goes to Beach," he said smiling, his eyes gazing into the street beyond the spatial reality of his peaceful neighborhood. "She's gonna be a junior. I'm sure you guys have seen her. She's like the finest thing, honest. And she's really sweet too." He held nothing back and didn't think twice about revealing his innermost feelings. I listened intently to his enthusiasm, certain I could now relate.

"I don't know any girl named Gracie," Ivan interjected. "You sure she's got style?"

"Guys, you just don't know. She's got this smile—this smile that makes me smile every time she smiles." Danny now focused back on us, giving us a quirky smile while still projecting a trancelike state. "And she's got this touch that makes me dizzy and makes me want to spin and fall."

"Yeah, right," Ivan said, "you've only talked to her once. How can she make you feel all dizzy?"

I didn't expect Ivan to understand. He was of course the realist, the one I never imagined ever feeling the way Danny felt, or the way I now felt about this girl named Desiree. He'd always made his attractions to girls known but never let on to feelings that were mushy-mushy—not even for Kelly whom he was so attracted to.

"Let him go on, Ivan," I said, taking nothing away from Danny's enthusiasm. "I wanna hear more." Perhaps Danny could now help me come to terms with my own feelings. Perhaps now I could be free to speak what was innate and learn how to verbally reveal my feelings about Desiree.

"You've got to believe me when I say she's hot," Danny went on. "She gave me her number and wants me to call."

"I'd call," Ivan said as he sipped his tea, "but I'd stop the moment she gave me the slightest hint she wouldn't be down with letting me in her pants."

"It isn't like that," Danny said. "I don't want to think of her like that."

"You've got to. It's only natural."

"Do you really think sex is the only way a girl can make you feel good?" I directed at Ivan.

"Right now it is. Why would we want to think a girl could give us anything else?"

"I mean…" Trapped was how I felt suddenly, daring to question his wisdom—and at the same time, compelled to leave him unchallenged, just as I always had with Dad. "There's got to be more to loving a girl than sex," I said.

"Yeah," Danny agreed. "My feelings are not of sex even though my body says it wants sex. It's these same feelings that tell me she's great—these feelings that tell me she can give me more. All of a sudden, sex just doesn't really matter that much."

"I'm almost afraid to think what you'll feel if she does let you get in her pants," Ivan said. He nodded to himself, realizing it was impossible to get his point across. Or perhaps he questioned his own wisdom just then being that he had never let himself fall as Danny or I had.

The subject was dropped until later on when Ivan and I saw first hand the extent of Danny's attraction to this Gracie girl. For days to come, Gracie was all Danny spoke of. It was Gracie this, and Gracie that. He seemed different when he talked about her, much happier and more talkative. He claimed spending hours on the phone with Gracie and had even gone out with her for ice cream. It didn't surprise me that such a girl would move Danny. He was for the most part a quiet and lonely individual. His father had died at a young age. He was an only child and lived with only his mother in the estate his father had originally inherited from his deceased grandparents. His mother was never home, being that she was an airline stewardess. All Danny had was his running and our friendship. Although he was an attractive guy and popular athlete, girls sometimes stayed well away. Some were intimidated by his success and stature, and some never even had a chance to speak to him. He was seldom around main campus as he spent most of his time after school out on the track field.

At first, Ivan and I ignored his continuous talk of Gracie. We thought it was a passing thing and expected him to forget about her and turn his attention back to us, or perhaps to some other girl. As the days went by, however, we saw more changes. Danny no longer wanted to spend his days with us or consider us in his plans. A number of times he stood us up when we were all supposed to meet at the local pool for a swim. This was definitely not a common trait we had come to know. He later admitted it was Gracie who was taking up his time, saying he had little time for anything else. He even claimed to be sick a few times—or used his running as an excuse to further distance himself. "C'mon. You guys know I have to be in shape for school in September. I've been lagging on my running."

We couldn't argue with that. After all, he was a star athlete, and in my mind being a big-time jock couldn't compare with spending hours on the beach building sandcastles. We soon lost contact entirely. He went from being our close friend to an unknown stranger.

"What should we do today?" I asked Ivan one day. We were still in July and the greater part of summer was still before us.

"Let's go rule the world."

"What about Danny?"

"What about him? He's married, remember?"

I didn't feel as betrayed as Ivan did at first. Something deep down told me it was okay to fall for a girl, to let her rule and somehow change you. I still had not stopped thinking of Desiree and wondered what it would have been like to spend nights on the phone with her—or spend an entire day eating ice cream and talking about whatever came to mind. I tried not losing faith in Danny. I tried contacting him on several occasions, wanting him to know that it was okay—that I could still be his friend even though he had met this wonderful girl, the girl of his dreams—this girl who made him dizzy every time she touched him, the one who made him smile every time she smiled. I tried looking for him on my way to Ivan's house each morning, but he was never home. When I tried calling, he never returned my calls. And when I checked the park, he was nowhere to be found.

No, Ivan and I didn't rule the world in any sort of way that summer. We both continued to hang out at the pool, the mall, and South Beach where all the action seemed to be. Weeks after Danny's change became evident, Ivan and I stood on the outskirts of the beach, near the railing separating the sand from the pavement. It was still very hot, and every part of our bodies could not help but perspire salty oceans. The beach was beyond crowded. We couldn't walk through the sand without stepping on someone's feet or towel. Ivan headed for the hot dog stand across the street. As I turned around and looked out towards the water, I spotted Danny walking with a girl. They were heading off the sand and onto the sidewalk.

Ivan came back just as they approached. "Hey," he shouted as he bit into his hot dog.

Danny was startled, surprised to see us—as if explaining why he had become a sudden outsider was something he'd rather not do. But he didn't have to explain. He grasped her hand tightly. "What's up?" he said.

"Just hanging out like always," answered Ivan as he sipped from his soda.

"This is Gracie," he said as he let go of her hand. "Gracie, this is Ivan and Marlo, my two best friends in the whole wide world."

"Hi," she said in a tight squeaky voice. She held out her hand for us to shake.

She did look familiar. I'd seen her at school many times. She was not quite the dream girl Danny had described. Her hair was as white as a fresh gallon of pasteurized milk—and teased and knotted like an overused mop. Her face displayed pigments of dried acne, making me play connect the dots in my imagination. She had very high cheekbones which made her appear more like a skinless boned cadaver. Her eyes were flint black, her teeth twisted and crooked, and her nose small and pointy. She was heavy, but her curves loomed straight through her tight blue sundress and grabbed at you like a mob outside a rock concert. She appeared too much for Danny to handle all by himself. From what I'd noticed, her friends at school were very much like her, always concerned about their looks and very selective with whom they dated, spoke to, or admitted into their little cliques. I was surprised to see Gracie take an interest in Danny. I would have never imagined her with a guy as sensitive and as quiet as he was. Back when we were freshmen, I recalled walking through the crowded gymnasium at our first high school dance. I happened to be near her when one of many shy boys had asked her for a simple dance. Gracie had turned him down. It wasn't unusual for girls to reject guys at dances. But what struck me was the manner by which she replied. This guy too was a freshman, slightly overweight and not too confident. She looked him up and down before she spoke. Even through the blaring music kept all conversations to a minimum, her distinct high-pitched voice penetrated all those who stood around. "No way. I wouldn't be caught dead dancing with a beached whale like you." Her friends who stood around laughed and snickered. She seemed mean, and from then on knew she was one I'd never associate with.

Gracie leaned up against Danny's solid body and pasted on a phony politician kind of smile, looking as though she would have rather moved on. I should not have judged her so definitely, but there was just something about her that made her seem so fake. Politeness didn't seem to fit her style even though she uttered no words of interruption and simply waited patiently for Danny to finish his hellos and good-byes. I guess I really could not help but visualize that first image I'd gotten of her that night at the dance.

For a moment, Danny appeared his old self. He laughed at Ivan's jokes and inquired about his guitar playing. He even asked about my sandcastles. But eventually Gracie whispered something into Danny's ear. Just like being under a hypnotist's hex, he snapped back into his prior trancelike state. He became hesitant—almost speechless, dropping our conversation immediately. I knew we'd be like strangers again. "Uh, all right," he complied. "I guess we better get going now. We were just about to get something to eat before we ran into you guys."

I wasn't quite sure just who to blame when I saw Danny show glimpses of his old self and then turn back into a dormant, controlled zombie. Of course, I wanted to blow up and put the blame on Gracie. She was the female. She was one who controlled the book of spells all women had access to. Danny couldn't be looked down on for not noticing his own transformation. Couldn't this girl see we were best of friends? Couldn't she see we had always been a part of his life, and to accept Danny would have been to accept us?

Gracie gave us another display of her crooked teeth. "Bye," she said as she gave us a dead wave. "Nice meeting you."

"I'll see you guys," Danny said flatly.

I returned the same dead wave as they walked away. Ivan only nodded goodbye.

"Danny," she said, "remember that bracelet? I saw it at the mall. Oh, it was so beautiful the way it sparkled in the light…" Her irritating voice finally faded across the bright sunny day.

"What do you think?" Ivan immediately asked.

"I've seen her be really mean before," I said, "but it seems she really likes him."

"Yeah, but he looks a little bit too blind if you ask me. I know who she is. I've seen her at school." He tapped some ice out of his cup and into his mouth. "I don't like her. I've heard a lot of bad things about her. She does have some booty though, and I don't blame Danny for wanting some of that. But I don't think Danny's after that—and that's what's scary. I bet she could get him to do anything she wants him to, and he wouldn't even think twice. He thinks she can give him what he wants, but she can't. No girl can."

"Why not?" I asked. "Why wouldn't she be able to give him what he wants?"

"What Danny wants doesn't exist. Smart guys know that. You actually think that in that classic old movie, *Titanic*, Jack and Rose would have lived happily ever after had they both gotten off that boat alive? A nice thought. But no. They would have fought—and if love wouldn't have gotten the better of old Jacky boy, then he would have been left cold, as she would have come to her senses and went on to marry some rich guy like she was meant to—like all women were meant to. Poor Jacky boy would have gone back to France to a reality of cheap women and cheap beer. Reality says life is a bitch. Movies don't portray that."

He stopped and waited for me to react. I hadn't seen *Titanic*. Always thought of retrieving it off of our old digital archives at home, but I never made the time. A part of me would have rejected Ivan's ideology had I not heard Dad's voice inside me warn, *All girls have fake hearts, son. Don't ever let yourself be fooled by the way they light your fire. Don't ever let yourself be tricked by falling into this weakness they make you feel.* I never quite knew what he meant all those times he said it. Did Gracie have a fake heart? It looked like she liked Danny the way she held on to him. And she did not appear to be quite as rude as I had remembered years back. I was sure Danny was only being overly humble because he liked her. He wouldn't be tricked. He was smarter than that. The first signs of pain or heartache would surely send him running just as fast as he ran around the track field. It would be impossible to be fooled. There just had to be some kind of allergic reaction to such pain—a kind of repellent to protect guys from the kind of heartache Dad had always said was worse than death.

"She did look a little fake," I told Ivan, admitting what I could not deny. But in the back of my mind, I was just hoping that there could be a girl who was different—a girl who could make a guy happy—a girl like Desiree. "She does appear to like him though."

"What happens when she stops liking him?" he asked. "Boy, I just know she'll crumple him up and throw him away. I don't think she'll have any problem doing that. Danny doesn't even know what he's getting himself into."

"Let's wait a while and see what happens," I suggested. "There's nothing we can do now. If anything does happen, we can always shed the light."

"I know what you're saying," he added. "But I don't think shedding any light's gonna help. You'll see—watch."

6

No more than a day had gone by since we'd last seen Danny's eyes and heart lost in love. I'd taken the scenic route to Ivan's being that I was insatiably drawn to the shoreline in foolish hopes of finding any one of my many sandcastles still left standing. The sun had long since climbed behind me, and the ocean along with calm winds and spotless blue skies promised many more sparkling days ahead.

I stood up to have a better look but could not deny it was her all right. Her thick-white kinky hair was like no other, and her curvy body protruded straight through her tight skirt and blouse, always grabbing at anyone who dared look. I too couldn't help but continue to play a game of connect the dots with her face—even from afar.

She smiled up at him and leaned her head against his shoulder, just as she had with Danny. He held onto her waist as he walked alongside her, emanating a poise and grace that would have reminded me of Dad had it not been for his thin tall frame and perfectly placed hair that glimmered in the sun like a pair of finely polished dress shoes. He was definitely older—out of high school and free. I'd never seen him around town and thought maybe he could have been her brother or some close relative. But he was too dark to bear any resemblance. A tight black T-shirt gripped his body to reveal a well defined torso. Dark pleated slacks matched the rest of him.

They stopped in front of a black speedy sports car. It too sparkled and shined like his hair. She gave him a tight hug and buried her face against his chest. He only smiled, his dark skin and sunglasses making his teeth appear whiter than they actually were. Politely, he opened the passenger door, never once letting go of that poise which made him seem attractively calm and in control. She stepped in. Stereo music thumped loudly, and the sidewalk underneath me shook as they cruised away down Ocean Drive.

A thousand thoughts rushed my mind as I raced my skateboard to Ivan's, though none of this should have felt like the heaviest of summer rains or the most ponderous of ocean surfs. For this was exactly the kind of thing Dad had always cautioned, a particle of his most certain world.

If this was what he'd always meant by evil, then Gracie was just that. I could not convince myself otherwise. No girl could be trusted. No girl could avoid causing the worst of pains. Not even dreamy Desiree, who'd whispered colorful, pleasant dreams, could hide past me dreary nightmare images of her being no different—that in reality she too could break hearts. It didn't seem to matter that maybe Gracie had already dumped Danny, just as Ivan said she would—or that maybe…just maybe, Danny himself had chosen to break up with her.

Up the stairs I flew as I entered the stucco-decayed building on 78th street. Ivan lived with his mother and father who both worked full time just to make ends meet. Both had very little time for him—and with no brothers or sisters around him, Ivan grew up alone and often hung out in front of his building where he developed a toughness and a strong sense of street smarts Danny and I did not have.

Paint chips fell off the door as I knocked. Mr. Cantón's familiar smile greeted me as the door swung open. He was much older than my father—rather stout and with gray-white hair which had already invaded most of his head. Ivan's mother sat quietly at the kitchen table, peeling potatoes and chopping onions. She too had the same color hair. Though much older than Mother, her face was well defined by smooth delicate skin, preserving much of her pretty features. She smiled, "Ivan's in the back." Her Spanish accent was still heavily imbedded in her speech despite her many years in the States.

The only sunlight found anywhere in this two-bedroom flat emanated from a pair of old garden house windows situated in the front room, overlooking the narrow alleyway down below. Tables cluttered most of the hallway. Like Mother, Mrs. Cantón too seemed a collector of needless tables. On them were an array of family photos, ornaments, religious caricatures, and vases full of artificial flowers. I turned back and looked at both Ivan's parents. For a moment, I wondered if they were truly happy— if they by any chance lived in happiness as portrayed in fairytale storybooks…Had they had their share of torment and endless arguing and fighting over the years as my parents had? Had Mrs. Cantón ever caused Ivan's father the worst of pains, tearing at his heart and sending him off crying as Dad had said all girls were capable of? *Oh, of course*, I thought bitterly as I headed through the hallway and into the back room where I heard loud screechy guitar play blare away strange, erratic tunes.

"Are you sure?" Ivan asked as he put his guitar into its carrying case. He'd just finished his guitar lesson. His instructor, a college student in ragged clothes with thick sideburns, quietly slid his way out of the room.

"Yeah."

"You're sure it was Gracie?"

I nodded. "Yeah, I got a really good look at her."

"And you're sure this guy wasn't her brother or cousin or something?"

"Not the way he had his arm around her—and not the way she held on to him."

He asked for no further details. This was, after all, reality. He remained silent, calm—didn't show the slightest bit of worry. "I guess we should go and straighten him out before things get worse for him."

The whole way to Danny's I could not help but wonder how things could possibly get worse. Things already seemed worse. Of course, it had only been Dad's words I'd always heard mentioned. I had not yet fallen in love or truly experienced this degree of certainty which mindfully plagued and shackled my every veracity. Danny's love life should have been neither of our business, but these worst of pains seemed all the more reason to get involved and help our friend.

The sun melted away as it descended behind tall trees and giant, pointed rooftops. Shadows toppled over the front lawn and the many pretty flowers that surrounded this elegant white two-story home. A paved brick walkway led us to the front porch. Just below was the small manmade fishpond with dozens of goldfish swimming about. A tranquil splash filled our ears with pleasant melodies. This had been the same pond we'd foolishly fished when we were younger. Though our hooks were always too big for these tiny goldfish, we'd spend hours having so much fun pretending we were at the Everglades waiting for "the big one" to bite.

"I'm willing to put down any money Danny doesn't suspect a thing," said Ivan as the doorbell chimed several times.

Danny finally came to the door. His confused eyes seemed to match his displaced hair as he focused in on us. "What are you guys doing here?" He half yawned and stretched his arms up as far as they would go.

"Just coming by to see what's up," I said.

"I'm so tired." Again he reached to stretch. His back cracked, and every muscle in his body seemed to tighten to a perfect squeeze. Not one ounce of fat hugged his body. Not one inch of his figure seemed flawed, as he couldn't have cared less who'd seen him walking around in only his underwear.

He said little as he led us up to his room. White walls matched bright white carpet. Lighting fixtures all around collided to match the same luster of brightly polished brass. Expensive tables and furniture decorated most of the five bedrooms within, expressing different decors from all over Europe. Genuine paintings livened up the halls—real oil paintings from well-renowned artists of France, Portugal, and Spain. His mother was very well-traveled and expressed an exquisite taste in art. I marveled, as this was one house that did not accept new revolutionary forms of digital artistry.

"I was taking a little nap," he said as he fell on his bed. His double closet doors were left wide open to reveal forgotten piles of dirty laundry. Running shoes were thrown to one side, and the smell of dirty socks inched every corner of the room. Many of his trophies were also on the floor and knocked off shelves. Old sports magazines lay everywhere. Most were still in their protective plastic wrapping, many having gone unread. All this was surprising to see, as he had always been very neat—disciplined, taking after his mother who worked so hard to keep the house in such pristine conditions.

On the dresser, stuck between the edges of a fancy mirror were pictures of Gracie, all shot in different poses, as if she'd been posing for a modeling shoot. She looked so much different, her face sparkling and without any flaws, her hair as fluffy as freshly baked bread and styled like that of a brand new Barbie doll. *Makeup can do wonders*, I thought.

We chatted a bit—nothing related to Gracie. Certainly I would not be one to break any kind of ice. Patience would soon get the better of Ivan, for he never liked to waste any time. Straight to the point was how he liked to be. "So how's Gracie?" he asked finally.

Danny smiled. "Oh, she's fine—you know, sweet as honey." His eyes seemed to beg us to inquire more, eagerly wanting to further divulge how wonderful she really was.

I picked up one of the magazines off the floor and sat down on the windowsill that overlooked the front yard. The sun was all but gone now. Many homes began to light up their windows. Kids we'd seen playing in front of homes retreated back indoors. I turned my attention back to the magazine and quietly flipped through the pages.

"I guess you weren't out with her today," Ivan remarked.

"Nah, she had to stay home and take care of her grandmother who's dying of cancer."

Ivan noticed Gracie's photos and studied them for a moment. He then reached down and grabbed something I had not noticed. "Wow, where did you get this?" He whistled as he dangled up a shiny gold bracelet. Diamonds glittered in all directions.

Danny raised his head off his pillow. "Oh, that's just a present I bought at the mall for Gracie. Isn't it nice? It's gonna be our one month anniversary tomorrow."

I walked over to have a closer look. "Very nice," I said over Ivan's shoulder, almost thinking it was too nice. Was he crazy? It looked very expensive and seemed a bit much considering they'd just started dating.

"It must have cost a fortune," Ivan commented.

"I know you guys think I'm crazy—you know, spending this much on a girl."

"Isn't this a little bit too much?" I asked as Ivan put the bracelet back in the box.

"Not for her. I haven't felt like this about any girl. She's the best thing that's ever come my way. For the first time, I see there's more to life than just running and school."

We remained quiet as Danny told us more about how great Gracie was, how special and sweet she was to him—sweet as honey. His smiles never left him, and his trancelike state seemed ever more permanent. It was upsetting to think a girl he thought to be different was actually playing him like a fool. He seemed in an ocean mirage, caught somewhere in the middle of a vast, dry desert. He had no idea what she was really like—much less any other girl for that matter. For he had never been told about women and their evil ways. More of Dad's words came back to me: *Don't let yourself be fooled by any girl. Know when to get out while you still can, before you fall into their inescapable power.*

"Danny," Ivan said. He turned from the dresser, "We have something to tell you about Gracie. And we're only telling you because you're our buddy."

Danny sat up on his bed. "What?"

"First of all, is she really your girlfriend?"

He hesitated for a moment. "Yeah, of course she is." His eyes jumped from me then back at Ivan.

"We hate to tell you this, man," Ivan went on, "but Gracie's taking you for the longest ride of your life."

Danny half laughed. "What are you talking about?"

"She's not all you think she is," I interjected.

"You're just a way of getting what she wants," said Ivan. "You know, like money, bracelets—that kind of thing. You really mean nothing to her."

Danny's smile all but disappeared. His eyes turned up to the ceiling as he stared off blankly, as if ignoring what we were saying, shutting away our accusations. "You can't say that about her," he said slowly. "How would you know? She's the sweetest thing I've ever met, like honey. You don't even know her. She wouldn't use me."

"Oh, yeah? Well Marlo says he saw your little honey with some other guy today."

"That's a bunch of bull," Danny replied. He stood up and shifted his attention my way. "She was with her grandmother all day long. She even called."

"It's true, Danny," I said. "I saw her with this guy at the beach, and he had his arm around her. She even got into his car."

He knew I wouldn't lie to him, but he still protected her for reasons I could not understand—I guess that inescapable power Dad had always said all girls were capable of wielding. I sensed his hurt. His stare looked the other way. "No!" he bellowed, shaking his head. "It's not true. She wouldn't do this to me. I know her. She's too nice."

"Danny," Ivan said calmly. "Face it. She's a fake—nothing but just another bitch, a slut. You should know that."

The silence in the room echoed familiar sounds, the kinds often heard at home just before Dad yelled or Mother went weeping to her room.

His eyes narrowed, and slowly they began to water. "Don't say that about her," he cried out in anger. He stepped closer to Ivan. "Don't ever say that about her again! I swear, if you ever say anything like that again, I'll—" The anger in his voice couldn't hide how much he liked her. "Just get out," he bellowed. His tears flooded the room. "I don't wanna have nothing to do with you guys. Stay away."

"Come on, Dan," Ivan uttered calmly. "Learn when to stop. She's no good for you."

Not since grade school had any of us gotten into a scuffle. I thought certainly they'd fight, as I knew Ivan would begin to take Danny's anger personally. I wanted no part of this. Danny was the stronger of the two, but Ivan had a worse temper and was by far the better fighter. I'd get killed breaking them up. For this would be no brawl over a ball or who'd pushed whom. We were older now, more complicated in our ways. Words hurt more than fists, and feelings were oftentimes more difficult to put into place or come to terms with…As it was, I had always gotten the worst of it whenever anything got rough.

"Leave! Get out!"

Silence broke as I dropped the magazine and headed to the door. Relieved I was when I turned to find Ivan had followed my lead.

"I don't know," I said as we walked off the porch, "maybe we shouldn't have said anything. What if we're wrong about her?"

"No way," Ivan protested. "Danny's being stupid as it is. Did you see that bracelet, hear how he was talking all lovey-dovey? Blind is what he is."

"Yeah, but what if..."

"What if what?"

"Nothing," I replied. We couldn't have been wrong about her... Certainty demanded it.

Danny wasn't one to be gripped by pride. Big dark rings encircled his eyes, his face not seeming to have known the sun, as his complexion had turned corpse white. Head held low and voice in faint whispers, he told us, "I'm really sorry guys. I should have known you were just looking out for me." The mall was not as crowded as it normally was. The heat kept most people near the shore, as the water was the only relief in sight. He paused before going on, seemingly distraught and with very little confidence. "She dumped me. I thought I treated her best I could. I gave her everything she wanted—even my heart." Not once did he mention anything about there being another guy. Not once did he make her out to be a demon. "She just all of a sudden told me she needed her space. She told me to stop calling or coming over. I feel like everything's my fault, that I messed up—that I did everything wrong."

"Hey," Ivan said, "don't apologize to us. Apologize to yourself. We were just trying to help. First off, it wasn't your fault you couldn't see through her. A girl like that can do that to a guy, ya know. Look at what Eve did to Adam and the rest of humanity of now and forever...Adam was fine 'til Eve gave him that apple. Blind, but not really blind."

"You didn't do anything wrong," I said. "She's the one who was wrong."

He cried—almost like a baby. The worst of pains was upon our best friend. It seemed there was nothing Ivan or I could do. He dwelled in a quiet trance for most of the day. Ivan told some of his sickest jokes as we walked him home, but even that ceased to force a smile on his face.

"C'mon," Ivan said as he lightly punched him on the arm, "it's not the end of the world."

"I know," Danny responded flatly.

"Let's meet up tomorrow," I suggested.

"What do you guys wanna do?" he asked as we led him to his front door.

"Anything—as long as we hang for a while," Ivan responded.

"Sounds cool, I guess." He shrugged, still frail. But at least he was smiling—a sign that perhaps his heartache would soon cease.

"Whatever you do, Danny," Ivan advised as we walked off his porch, "don't call her. And don't take any calls if she decides to call. Don't go backwards, man."

Danny must have really liked Gracie not to have noticed or accepted her heartbreaking ways, I thought as I strolled home. In all, Ivan seemed right. Danny was not to blame for being blind. Gracie could have done it to anyone. Danny just happened to be the fool to fall in the way of her flattery and sweet smiles. By now, she was probably doing the same to that other guy with the black hair and speedy car.

Tamara didn't see me as I stepped to our front door. She was standing behind our neighbor's tree with a boy from down the street. I could have easily gotten her in trouble. Dad had made it very clear she was not to even think of boys until she was at least sixteen. She hadn't been causing me any trouble in recent days, so I decided to let it slide and use this against her later, if need be.

"I got good news," Danny said when I called him later that night. His voice was not as sulky as it had been earlier that day. Had his healing begun? Were men able to overcome even these worst of pains so easily—a gift from God being that Adam had screwed up so badly? "I got a hold of two tickets to Day on the Green—Day Two. My cousin pulled through. Do you know how much these babies are worth?"

"I guess I wouldn't be able to pay for them if I broke open my piggy bank, would I?"

"Try breaking open a real bank. This show's gonna smash. I bet Kelly's really gonna be happy when she finds out."

"She's gonna totally love you for life," I replied.

I didn't know her number. I did, however, know that she worked at the mall, inside the cookie shop.

"You gotta go down Marlo and let her know. Day One's tomorrow. If she wants Day Two tickets, she's gotta know as soon as possible."

"Hey, I thought we were gonna hang tomorrow," I told him. "Why don't we all go down tomorrow?"

"I can't. I forgot I have to help my mom with something. Besides, I really need to get back to practicing. I haven't run in weeks."

Kelly's face lit up when I told her about the tickets. "No way," she responded. "Are you serious? Day Two?" She nearly dropped the batch of cookies she was emptying into the glass cabinet underneath the register.

"Yup, that's what he said last night."

"Where is he?"

"He couldn't come down. He wanted me to get a hold of you." I smiled somewhat, trying to share in her excitement even though I wasn't going to the concert. I would have asked about Desiree right then and there, but she was too joyous to have our conversation go astray. And besides, I could not let her know I too, like Danny, had a weak heart for dreamy girls.

"Tell him to come down, or...wait." She pulled out a pad and pencil from one of her front pockets. "Here's my number. Tell Danny to call me tonight. I can have my brother drive me to his house."

"All right," I said as I glanced at her pencil perfect writing.

"Day Two. Oh, my god. No one's gonna believe me when I tell 'em."

"I'll tell him to call you right when I see him."

"You better," she replied jokingly.

She offered free cookies, but I wasn't hungry.

7

Shiny summer days made it impossible for one not to ever see the sky's light that was so bright. For darkness was what I thought all people who could not see saw.

"You what?" I asked fretfully.

"I gave the tickets away."

"Why'd you do something like that for? I already told Kelly you'd sell them to her." I paused a short moment, not knowing what else to say. "She was really happy when I told her, Danny. And now she's counting on them. The concert's tomorrow."

"I was hoping you didn't get a chance to go down there. I'm sure she won't take it too bad. It's not like she was really planning on going anyways. Besides, I can just say my cousin didn't pull through."

"I guess you can. But she was offering you money for them! Why would you give them away?"

He didn't answer.

"Who's gonna pay your cousin now?"

"I guess I'll have to."

"Danny," I said, running my hands through my hair. My patience had all but run dry. "Who the hell would you give Day on the Green tickets to?" I don't know why I asked. I should have known.

He was reluctant to go on at first. When he finally said, "Gracie," I knew not whether his familiar impulsive side had gotten the better of him—or if in fact, he was the victim of devious spells.

"Man," I said softly. "That's so screwed." I turned away. Magazines and dirty laundry still cluttered the floor. His bed was a mountain of sheets and covers, and his dresser and shelves displayed not his usual orderly array of trophies, medals, and ribbons.

"Wait a sec…you don't understand," he said with that familiar short laugh—the one that said everything was okay, the one that said there was really nothing to worry about. "She came over earlier today and said she was sorry about not wanting to ever see me again. She heard I had tickets and knew I wasn't into going. She asked me if she could buy them 'cause she had a cousin who was dying to go to Day Two. I couldn't charge her, so I—"

Just as I thought. He never believed my story about her and that other guy, and she wasn't about to mention any other guy either, knowing very well she could connive him anytime she pleased. I was so disgusted I headed for the door.

"Wait!" he pleaded.

I stopped, but I didn't turn around.

"C'mon," he said, "trust me on this one. She says she really cares."

"You should have trusted us," I said bitterly as I walked out of the room.

How quickly things seemed to change. I was so angry I couldn't have cared less whether we ever spoke again. I thought surely Danny would have tried hard to forget about Gracie and go on with his life, accept no calls or even think of answering the door when she came knocking. This had been no unexpected visit. It was probably Danny who decided to call her and plead her not to break up with him. He likely mentioned the concert and of course she'd come crawling to his house and used him to get her way—all part of her power and control over a helpless, handicapped fool.

I obviously could prove none of this, but it was evident he was blind, caught up in a web of her power and deceit. Oh, why couldn't he see the light?

My mind struggled all the way home. Even if Gracie did care for Danny the way he claimed she did, even if there was just the slightest possibility that Ivan and I were wrong about her—that everything I had been led to believe by Dad was wrong, he still shouldn't have backstabbed Kelly. He had promised her the concert tickets, and she had her heart set on going. What on earth would I tell Kelly now…that Danny was so blind as to lose sight of all that was real versus all that was fantasy? That would be the last thing I could do. I felt no choice but to lie and cover up for him, knowing very well he would never contact Kelly. Maybe it was a mistake to do so, but deep down, I knew it was all beyond his control. I realized I could not really stop speaking to him. And deep down, as funny as it sounded, knew Danny would have also done the same for me had I been just as blind. He was my friend, and I still continued to have faith—faith somehow everything would work out for the best.

I stopped by the beach on my way home. I wanted to lose myself in the sand—to blend in with the beauty of the shoreline and the dancing waves which always seemed to call my name. But I didn't know if building a sandcastle would ever be worth the trouble again. For it too would eventually fall like most things around me always seemed to fall. Oh, how I hated to think there were no exceptions to certainty—that somehow there was a predefined fate that held us prisoner in a definite aura of predictable occurrences. When it really came down to it, I guess there really was no reason to dwell—no reason to be bothered. What was happening to Danny was unavoidable and meant to be. My father had always laid out things in simple step-by-step instructions. All I had to do was accept and absorb his wisdom. Women were evil because God made them that way. It was God's way of making life more challenging for man. And if you became a victim of a woman's "inescapable power," then you simply became a blind fool like Danny. It was all as simple as that, so simple to see.

I felt a little better when I got home—though still very confused. I found Mother cooking in the kitchen. "Hi," she said.

"Hi," was my reply, and then everything went quiet as she turned around and minded the boiling pots and steaming pans. It was not an intentional silence, just something that had grown over the years. Simple words and a couple of phrases here and there was generally how we got by. I could never find it in me to do or say anything else, and it appeared neither could she. Even calling her "mom" became burdensome at times.

I observed her while still in that annoying silence, watching her as she stood there looking so pretty in her white dress with matching shoes and necklace. Despite always believing that separation was the best way of surviving this world filled with a cruel opposite sex, I wanted so much at that very moment to open up and tell her I felt sorry for all those times Dad had made her cry; wanted her to inquire about my life, about Danny and Gracie—about this dreamy girl named Desiree and to have her understand and be proud of me and my artistic ability. Most of all, I wanted her hugs and her love and affection that had been vacant for most of my life.

But how? How did I wake something that by now had grown so dormant, impossible to wake? How did I go about expressing what was seemingly too foreign and unfamiliar? Did I simply let go of everything and run up to her and put my arms around her—hug her tightly without saying a thing? Or did I simply just tell her I loved her so very much, tell her there was something missing in my life I so badly needed?

My eyes watered for just an instant, insisting there was something definitely missing, something so natural and too necessary for me to go on and feel good about who I was and who I would become. My throat twinged, as I now struggled to hold back my tears. It was just then that I felt my pride tap me in the back—that impenetrable barrier which had always kept me safe and sound from all pain this world had to offer. It was back…hiding and masking me from the kind of courage I could never muster up, a vulnerability that told me to be careful—that things were dangerous.

My eyes soon dried and thoughts of opening up left me as easily as they had arrived. Again I was protected. Again I was safe. *I really don't need her*, I told myself. *I have my wise father, and that's all I need.*

She soon looked over at me. "What's wrong?"

"Nothing," I replied. "Just seeing what's for dinner."

"Tell your sister to get her butt in here and do the dishes."

She never had to ask for anything twice. Defiance was never in me being that I'd always feared further dialogue that may come from my disobedience. Respectful and cooperative was how I was towards her. For that's how she'd always been with me. She walked by me and headed to the garage. I heard our noisy washing machine give its usual rumble and shake as it vibrated through the kitchen walls. I felt my tears come back only because the yearn I had felt was way beyond me now. It seemed I had blown yet another chance.

"Tamara," I yelled at the door as I wiped at my eyes. "Mom says to come in and do the dishes."

"All right," I heard her respond. "Tell her I'll be right in." She popped out behind the same tree I'd seen her the previous day. Her same little boyfriend followed.

"Who's your little friend?" I asked as I opened the refrigerator and poured myself a glass of juice.

"You mean Timmy?" She emptied some left over food into the garbage disposal. "He's just a guy. He says he wants to marry me. Can you believe that?"

"That's dumb," I said sipping from my glass.

"No it isn't. He says he likes me a lot. I think it's kinda cute."

"You're gonna get your ass kicked by Dad," I warned.

"Dad doesn't need to know," she shot back.

A knock came from the back door just then. Tamara looked out the kitchen window and in a flat voice said, "It's Ivan." She had never been too fond of Ivan, being that Ivan's pestering and teasing usually got the better of her. She still had not gotten over the time Ivan had locked her inside our attic during the big power outage. He'd been telling a frightening story about a lady with a white gown who had no face and who glided throughout the floors of our upstairs attic. Tamara and I, along with Danny, were sitting with only a candle in the middle of the living room floor.

"She's still up there," Ivan had announced as the candle flame viciously made our huge shadows prance along each of the living room walls. "Sometimes, I hear her call your name even in Marlo's room."

Danny and I didn't take Ivan seriously. Tamara, however, trembled as she hid her face behind Danny's shoulder.

"You're gonna wake up one night for some strange reason," Ivan went on as his eyes bulged out towards Tamara. "And when you do, you'll notice your door knob begin to turn slowly, and she'll come floating in with no face."

"Stop it," she pleaded as she stood up and raced for Mother who was somewhere in the kitchen. Ivan got up and chased her, moaning out eerie cries. A door then slammed as Tamara's frantic screams faded. By the time Danny and I made it to the kitchen, Tamara was frantically pounding the insides of the attic door. Ivan laughed hysterically. When Danny unlocked the door, Tamara rushed out in tears. She grew frantic. I can't say that I blamed her. The narrow staircase leading to the attic was one of the scariest places I'd ever known—especially if there really was a floating lady with no face living upstairs. Tamara couldn't sleep alone in her room for weeks. She spent her nights in our parent's room and wouldn't speak to Ivan for the longest time—even after hundreds of apologies.

"How goes it, little sis?"

"Don't call me that," Tamara voiced. Water splashed in and out of the sink as dishes clanked. "I'm not your sister."

"Ain't we touchy today," said Ivan as he joined me at the counter. "Hey, I thought we were gonna hang with Danny today."

"He said he had to help his mom out," I let him know.

"I just came back from the mall. Everyone's down there shopping for Day Two tomorrow. It's pretty wild."

"Must be packed," I said.

"Is it true Danny got Kelly tickets—Day Two?"

"Yeah," I said as I finished the last of my juice.

"I was just talking to her at the cookie shop. She sounds pretty excited."

I debated whether or not I should come out and tell Ivan what Danny had really done with the tickets. As wise as Ivan was, I also knew he was not as understanding. He didn't question things like I did or ever give things the benefit of the doubt. He wouldn't forgive Danny for not staying away from Gracie—much less for trashing up on Kelly. Oh, how I wanted Danny not to be wrong in trusting his instincts. How I wanted him to prove that you truly could love a girl and express your innermost feelings without ever getting hurt—lovey-dovey feelings I'd always found to be incomprehensible…And how I too wished I could be as strong witted as Ivan was—immune from all doubt and confusion, so sure and certain of everything.

I played it off and said nothing more about Danny. I set my glass beside the sink, knowing it would irritate Tamara.

"Hey! I'm not your slave," she spouted.

"Just wash it," I stated. "And wash it good. I still found soap in a glass the other day."

"Yeah, do what your brother says," said Ivan, "or I'll tell your dad about all those guys you're always trying to flirt around with."

"Shut up, Ivan!"

"Tamara, what's all the yelling?" Mother voiced as she entered the kitchen with a basket of clean laundry in hand. "Why are you acting like a snob? I could hear you all the way in the garage…Hello, Ivan. How's everything?"

"Pretty cool."

"That's good. I haven't seen you in a while. Where's Danny?"

"Helping out his mom, I guess. I haven't talked to him today."

"I saw his mother at the salon not too long ago," Mother commented. "She came in to get her nails done. She said Danny has a steady girlfriend. Do you have a steady girlfriend yet?" She smiled.

"Sure I do." Ivan put his arm around Tamara who had her back to us all. "It's your daughter here. We're crazy about each other."

"Stop it," Tamara wailed as she shoved him away.

Mother offered dinner, but Ivan refused. "My mom's already cooking," he explained. "I just stopped by to say hi to Tamara."

"Yeah, right," Tamara responded.

"Talk to you tomorrow, Marlo," he said. "I better get going. I'm gonna try and hit up the stadium on my way home just to see who's at Day One. Good-bye, Mrs. Clemente. Bye, little sis." He closed the door and tapped on the window. He pressed his face against the glass and stuck his tongue out at Tamara.

"I wish he'd stop bugging me," she remarked. She picked up the dishwashing liquid and nearly emptied the entire content into one glass. "Do I have to wash Marlo's glass, Mom? He just dumped it on me. He should wash his own glass."

"Washing the dishes is your job," Mother confirmed. It wasn't the first time she had to explain. I only smiled in the background, knowing it would annoy her more.

"What about the garbage? It's overflowing—that's Marlo's job."

"Oh, stop complaining," Mother's voice swelled. She then looked over at me. As usual, she didn't have to ask. I jumped up from the counter stool and snatched the trash can underneath the sink. It wasn't even as full as Tamara had suggested.

"You're such a little bitch," I said soon after Mother faded into the living room.

"MOM!"

Mother came back in, but I had already stepped out to the back.

Later that evening, I called Kelly. It wasn't easy telling her she wasn't going to the concert. She sounded so excited when she heard it was me. "Where's Danny? Why hasn't he called? Where're the tickets? How much is he charging?" She must have asked a thousand questions before I even had a chance to make all her questions pointless. I hated doing Danny's dirty work and didn't see why she had to be the one to end up with the short end of the stick. Again my mind went back and forth, defending Danny's better judgment and at the same time condemning his blindness. I lied and gave her a last minute fluke story about Danny's cousin changing his mind and giving the tickets away to some long-lost friend. From the tone in her voice, I could hear her let down. Danny had been her last hope of ever going to the concert.

"It's okay," she said. A great big sigh followed. "It was too good to be true anyways. None of my friends believed me when I told them I was going."

Why did everything always seem to be filled with such broken dreams?

Dim morning rays crept through my bedroom window ever so slowly as faint sounds of a bicycle rattled over our front lawn. It could have been the paperboy I thought as I wiped the sleep from my eyes, but I remembered Dad had long since canceled his subscription being that he now got his weather forecast online. Quietly, I made my way to the living room. It was still rather early for a Saturday. No one was up. From the front window, I saw Timmy make his way off our porch and back onto his bike. A bouquet of wilted daisies rested at the edge of our doorstep. A note read:

> *Dear Tamara,*
>
> *You're the prettiest girl I've ever seen, even prettier than these flowers. Don't ever stop liking me. Being around you makes me happy.*
>
>

Love always,
Timmy

How foolish to leave flowers right where Dad could find them, I thought. If this had been Dad instead of me, Tamara would have really been in for it. I put the flowers back only because I was certain Mother was fully aware of Timmy, sure it was she who permitted Tamara to secretly have a boyfriend. Certainly Dad would eventually find out. There was no need for me to be at the center of eventual storms. For already, I'd weathered many.

Ivan was busy with his usual Saturday morning guitar lesson. With only my imagination for company, much of my time was spent dangling on new ideas to paint—new worlds to explore. Every disk jockey in town broadcasted how successful Day One of the concert had been. Promotions soared high for Day Two later that day even though the concert had long since sold out. A last minute contest was held for a lucky one thousandth caller. I tried calling for the pair of winning tickets, but it was impossible to get through. Frustrated and with little spark of artistic inspiration, I rode my bicycle out to the stadium just to experience some of the hype.

Streets were blocked off for miles, congesting the inner-city area with bumper-to-bumper traffic. I saw many from Beach High cruising by in souped-up cars, all polished and chromed as they rolled by thumping the loudest of funky beats. All were individuals such as myself who were unable to go to the concert, but who found the occasion another excuse for adventure. Surrounding streets near the stadium were covered with trash and debris from Day One. Merchants surrounding the area were booming with business. Those who had closed for the day had their windows broken or doors and windows graffitied with spray paint. As expected, thousands of people formed tremendous lines hours before Day Two even let in. Most were girls, and the guys were just as Ivan had assumed—many dressed in pink-collared shirts and purple corduroy shorts and pants. All screamed and yelled to be let in. Although this was supposedly a tamer crowd than that of Day One's, some threw bottles out into the streets. Others tossed food and empty cooler containers. Some even lit fireworks, while others got into fist fights for their place in line.

One girl was even pulled from her spot and tossed into the middle of the street by a group of boys as she fought, kicked, and screamed. Security guards dressed in long yellow-neon windbreakers were overwhelmed as they tried keeping whatever peace they could, but to no avail. There were just too many people and too many things going on all at once. Police cars even lined crowded parkways, every officer standing quietly as they clutched long heavy batons. They tried controlling traffic and the cruising best they could, but they too appeared overwhelmed.

As I rode away, I faintly heard someone call out, "Hey, Marlo." I stopped and turned every which way, but there were too many people to distinguish anyone in particular. Again I heard, "Marlo." Across the street, I spotted Kelly as she waved me down.

"What are you doing all the way out here?" she asked as I rode up to her.

"Just checking out the scene," I said, trying best I could not to think why she was out here rather than in line. "I heard it was gonna be pretty wild."

"I thought I'd check out the scene too," she said. "Some of my friends are waiting to get in."

Immediately I thought of Desiree. Was she somewhere out there waiting to get in? Was this another chance to see her again? I followed Kelly's stare through the swarm of people. I would have asked about Desiree, since this was a better time than any. However, I was distracted by something else she said, something I would not have noticed had she not made mention of it. She pointed at the crowd. "I feel sorry for Gracie over there. She's all the way at the end."

It was Gracie all right—Danny's *Gracie*. She was leaned up against the surrounding fence, entwined in someone else's arms. But it was not Danny who held her; rather, it was *him*—that same guy I'd seen her with before! He was leaned up against her, caressing the sides of her body and kissing her emphatically. She eagerly accepted his tongue and sucked it down like a giant gulp of cherry-flavored Jell-O. She soon broke off the kiss and accepted his embraces, leaning her chin on his shoulder, smiling and appearing so very happy as she displayed to the entire world her crooked, embedded teeth.

My stomach turned. Another bite of reality I received yet again, reinforcing what Dad had always said to be true. Was this supposed to be Gracie's cousin, the one Danny had said was dying to go to the concert? There was no further doubt in my mind she was evil. Danny's plea to trust his better judgment was laid to waste, and I felt so badly for him. There was nothing I could do for him now but hate her...

Oh, how could I ever think of doubting Dad? *Forget about dreamy girls with pretty faces and delightful eyes. Forget about how nice they can be or how innocent their smiles appear. Forget that every situation's different, every girl different—or every guy in charge of his own destiny…In the end you'll be bitten with the worst of pains—a venom that'll travel through your eternal veins and make you cry a thousand rivers. There is no escape. There is no hope. Love is just something a guy pays a dear price for.*

"I can't believe this," Kelly said glumly. "Even Gracie gets to go to the concert."

"I gotta go," I said, not hinting in the least that I was steaming inside and wanted to explode like a giant volcano. I rode home as fast as I could, holding back most of my anger and confusion. I glided through red lights and nearly hit several pedestrians along the way, my hair whipping back in the warm, moist Miami breeze. *All girls have fake hearts. Don't be tricked,* Dad's voice continued to echo in me. *Even if she is sweet and kind, she'll stomp you dead in the end, bite you like a poisonous snake.*

I could have stopped by Danny's and told him, *You see, you screwed up. You're an idiot. Why couldn't you listen to me? Gracie's a fake and you mean nothing to her—nothing.* But I imagined Danny not ever believing me. He didn't believe me before, why should he believe me now? He'd think I was crazy or jealous that he had a girlfriend like Gracie, and I didn't.

"What's the matter?" Mother asked when I stormed through the door, letting it slam behind me.

"Nothing," I replied, figuring she wouldn't understand. She was probably just like Gracie back in her younger days. She probably tricked guys and used them to get what she wanted, and when she felt she had nothing more to gain by tricking and biting boys like prey, she decided on marrying Dad so she could feel secure about everything. She probably had him on the side the whole time, fooling him and using him to see which guy could give her more.

"Marlo, you come right back here," she said sternly. "How dare you come in here…" She rambled on but soon stopped when she heard my bedroom door slam shut.

This was my safety net, the only place I knew where I could escape this wretched world, a giant, scrambled jigsaw puzzle covered over with paintings and drawings I had sketched long ago. Hung above my bed was one of my most prized works, a piece I'd painted shortly after starting high school. Its background was black with many small sparkles of hope and wisdom. Towards the center was the Earth with its various people standing alike—together, each different but all acting as one. The upper right-hand corner revealed a full moon…and there I was, stranded on this small, lonely wasteland with nothing there but me and everything I was made to believe. Alone in body, spirit, and mind I sat—desolate in my own little world. With hand raised and extended, it opened to reveal a handful of gold-tarnished sand which fell between my fingers and into the deepest reaches of space where no hope or wisdom lay. My eyes were set upon my hand and the falling sand, not realizing this cold forsaken land (and its sand) controlled the most mysterious and treacherous tides found throughout each and every sea.

In one empty corner near the window stood my easel. It was surrounded by old paint-stained rags. The wastebasket was usually filled to the top, sometimes two feet past the rim. Old sketches, paintbrushes, and bottles of all shapes, sizes, and colors lay scattered throughout the tops of my desk and dresser. Stuffed desk drawers overflowed with scratched sketches I no longer wanted but refused to throw away. The dresser beside my bed was in similar condition—clothes spilled out and hung over the sides of opened drawers. Covers on my bed were awkwardly tossed to make it look as though the bed were made.

One other object claimed my walls, though it was nothing I could draw, paint, or sketch. Just to the right of the closet was a huge mirror that appeared to be a part of the wall itself. It was as tall as the closet door and extended to the other end of the wall, near the room's entrance. It was the only one in the house that reflected one's entire image. Dad had mentioned the mirror was already embedded in the room when *Abuelo* bought the house decades earlier. It watched me grow and become older with each passing day, always showing me something different—telling me more about myself than anyone else ever would. It never lied or exaggerated, and everything the mirror spoke of was crystal clear and as plain to see as the clearest of days.

"Mom," I had said as I sat on the edge of my bed looking into the mirror, my voice younger and softer, "why do I have such a big mirror for?" I was still trusting towards her and still dependent on her for everything.

"For very special reasons, Marlo," she had answered as she tied my shoes.

"Special reasons?"

"Yes, special reasons...It tells me when you're being a bad boy. The mirror knows everything. It sees everything you do, and it tells me. So be a good boy and don't get into any trouble only the mirror would know about."

How different I looked and saw myself then. So many events, secrets, and revelations. Sometimes I liked what I saw. A lot of times, I hated what I saw. I stood nearly six feet tall now, my body full and much more developed than I'd been at six. My hair had grown lighter, like Mother's—but kept short like Dad's. My cheeks were much more deflated and not as irresistible as they were when I was six. No longer did family members insist on giving my cheeks those annoying squeezes. Hair began to grow above my lip, and sometimes annoying pimples populated my face. My eyes were smaller and surer about things, not surprised to see things like beggars, drunks, or addicts laid out on city streets—or shocked when fights or riots broke out on corner stores or buses. I thought I'd seen it all, no longer looking into this mirror to find a small hopeless little child having to have his shoes tied by his mother…or coloring in flawless coloring books—or pretending to go places he'd never been to on electric train sets.

I remained in my room for the remainder of that day and next, hoping to paint anything that would alleviate my confusion. My window became a picture frame which saw the sun rise and fall into dark shadows. On and on I closed my eyes and hid in darkness as I often had as a child, back when Dad and Mother had their worst fights. I even plugged my ears to block away my parents' loud voices and my sister's noisy music. Calmly I dipped out of reality for just a mere instant in time, just enough to dig deep into my unconsciousness and imagine a perfect little world where nothing seemed to matter, where all perplexity and uncertainty was laid to rest.

But I grew frustrated as my concentration broke away and went back into my real existence. I tore up the piece of partially stained canvas in front of me and commenced the same routine over and over again—hoping, just hoping this once I could somehow capture a perfect world.

I stopped work only because I felt weak from not having eaten all day and part of the previous day. I finally exited my room and headed towards the kitchen. It was rather late at night. Dad's snoring suggested he and Mother were both sound asleep. Tamara's light was still on. That was not unusual being that she'd always been afraid of the dark. I would have continued my way to the kitchen had I not heard her stereo. I tried the doorknob, but it was locked. When I knocked, I got no response. Something didn't seem right. An old school ID card proved to be the perfect tool against our home's old-fashioned lock mechanisms. The lock gave in a matter of seconds.

Her room was empty, the stereo left on auto play. I opened her closet, but all I found were clothes and an assorted collection of stuffed animals and shoes. On her pillow were more of the same kind of wilted daisies I'd found the other morning. At the edge of her bed was a crumpled piece of paper. It was another love note written by Timmy. As I turned off the stereo, I noticed the window wide open. The wind smothered my face as I poked my head out, forcing my eyes shut and nearly stripping my hair from my scalp. There were no signs of Tamara anywhere. Only the neighbor's tree stood alone as its branches whipped back and forth across the dark, ominous skies. Another storm was headed our way. Where on earth could my sister be? And how long had she been playing this off?

I stood quietly in the darkness of the hallway, thinking I'd heard something coming from the porch area. But it could have very well been the wind or the neighbor's cat. I listened for a moment. There was only humming as the wind grew in intensity. Silhouetted trees swayed back and forth as I approached one of the side windows. I kept my distance from the see-through curtains and remained still. After a moment, I heard soft whispers. I peeped through the curtains and caught a clear view of Tamara and a boy. They were both kissing on the far left bench. I would have left and minded my own business now that I knew she was safe, but I noticed she wasn't with Timmy, the same boy I'd seen her with all along. This boy's hair was dark, and he appeared much heavier—older. I'd never seen him before.

Something in me cringed. Just the thought and sight of having someone like Gracie for a sister made all my hate and anger explode all at once. Was Tamara treating Timmy the way Gracie was treating Danny? I reached for the front door and furiously swung it open. Startled, they both broke off their kissing. The boy didn't even turn to look at me. He immediately dashed off the porch and stumbled onto the front lawn before running off.

"Get away from me," Tamara shouted vigorously. She too headed for the lawn, but I managed to grab hold of one of her bony little arms.

"Come here you little slut!" I yelled, not caring who heard or how loud I yelled. She screamed, punched, scratched, and kicked, but I still held on and pulled her into the house.

By now, Mother and Dad had come out to see what was happening. Mother's hair was undone, and she looked quite pale without her makeup. Dad had on his usual pajama bottoms and no shirt. "What the hell's going on out here?" he asked. "It's one o'clock in the morning."

"Marlo's gone crazy, Dad," said Tamara. "He tried killing me."

I explained what needed to be known. "I've even seen her with this other boy named Timmy," I concluded. "If you don't believe me go check Tamara's room. You'll find his letters there. You'll even see her window wide open."

Everything went quiet. No one said a word. Rarely had I ever been a tattletale. Rarely had I ever accused anyone of anything.

Fear filmed Tamara's eyes as she tried to find a way out of her speechless moment. She appeared absolutely helpless.

"Is this true?" Dad asked calmly. Mother stood silent.

"Yes," she said wearily.

"Oh, can't this wait 'til tomorrow?" Mother stepped in.

Dad ignored her remark as calmness left him. The next thing I knew, he raised his hand and smacked Tamara across the face. I don't ever remember him hitting Tamara. In a way, I felt she deserved it, and in a way I felt sorry for her. For she was a girl, and how on earth could she ever stop being what Dad had professed all girls to be?

The photograph of the sandcastle I had built during my first days of summer rested on my desktop. I picked it up and observed its authentic appeal and promising grace. I forgot about the tides and waves for just a moment as my dreams took me to a different time and place.

"You didn't have to hit her," Mother's furious screams echoed over Tamara's cries.

"I don't want her being brought up like you were!" Dad bellowed.

With Dad's wisdom behind me, life should have been more bearable, things more certain and explicable, pointing to the male species as a most perfect entity—and the female species…a simple fall from grace. But could I ever truly turn one way and not ever look other ways again? Faith told me yes. My heart told me no.

Maybe there was another side. Maybe Mother knew of missing pieces to seemingly incomplete puzzles. Maybe she could understand and help with some of my internal and external dilemmas…Maybe she wasn't evil. Maybe she did know all the answers to questions Dad could never answer—or I could never ask…All these maybes. It's a wonder how I managed to survive and overcome all the things I would naively overlook. And oh, how I wish I had spoken to Mother as Tamara often did. Maybe then, things could have turned out better—or at least different.

8

Tears flooded Miami Beach. I heard them bang on rooftops and saw them create large measureless puddles throughout every street. Gray rainy days engulfed the remainder of the summer, and again I lay trapped within the confines of my own bitter reality.

I was certain Danny had found out about Gracie and was out there somewhere, suffering from pierced wounds running straight through his heart. I had time to cool off and was no longer as angered. I wanted to talk to him and tell him everything would be all right, that I could accept his decisions even though I didn't understand them—that I could sense his pain even though I could not feel it.

He kept himself well enough away though, his answering system switched off and eventually disconnected. No one answered his door in the midst of heavy downpour. His home stood dark and lifeless. Walking through the dampness of the streets, swirling winds yet again whispered what Dad had said to be a fact of life. The worst of pains were present in every girl, and Gracie was just one of many roses with a multitude of pointed thorns. I certainly was not going to be manipulated by any one girl, I told myself, no matter how nice or sweet looking she seemed.

Thoughts soon seesawed, however, as dreamy Desiree continued to haunt my mind like the insides of a haunted mansion. I could not understand why—why I could not look past her. Perhaps her eyes had whispered she might just be this rare exception. For she seemed too pretty and sweet to sting of venom and thorns. Maybe I too could be just as blind.

Ivan went away to visit relatives in Los Angeles three days following the concert. I was more sad than happy the day he left. He was leaving for a month. Miami just wouldn't be the same. There was so much I wanted him to know—so much that had to be let out into the open. He said nothing about Danny before he left, didn't even bring up the fact that Danny hadn't reappeared to hang out with us as promised. I came close to telling him about Gracie and the tickets before he went away, but when I found myself with enough courage, I imagined he'd become upset and hate Danny forever. A month would be enough time for Danny to smile once again. I saw us all hanging out again and saw Danny's gentle-nature come to life as it always had. There was no real need to tell Ivan anything—unless, of course, Danny brought it up in the future.

My days crept by ever so slowly. Everything I encountered seemed to remind me of our friendship. Wistful trees swept me back to the third grade when the three of us had gotten in trouble for attempting to chop down a tree at the park. Danny had the idea of hunting for firewood for our overnight camping trip in his backyard. We picked out the smallest tree near the pond and pigeon grounds. We hacked away at it with one of Dad's hatchets. It didn't take long before someone reported us. A police car soon stopped us and drove us all home. We were grounded for weeks, our overnight campout not realized until a year later.

Little kids playing football out in the middle of the street with no respect for oncoming traffic reminded me of the times we played football on the street. We'd curse any car or bus that interrupted our play. Ivan was really good at telling off any driver who warned us of getting hit. Some drivers even got out of their cars and chased us away, but we never got caught.

Out on the porch I remembered nights when we and other kids from Danny's block sat outside telling old ghost stories under the shiniest of stars. We'd tremble in the dark. Sometimes, I'd be afraid to walk home alone. Danny would cover his ears to keep from hearing the scariest of morbid parts. Ivan was the bravest of us all, daring to break into an old deserted home at the end of Danny's street, which many had claimed was haunted by a cannibalistic witch doctor.

There were those unpleasant moments when we'd fought as kids and handled our disagreements by running to our own homes. But the very next day at school, we'd act as though nothing had ever happened. Danny would share his newest toy, Ivan his trading card collection, and I a portion of Mother's chocolate cake. There was always something to break the ice. We never brought up past scuffles or arguments. Unlike my parents, no futuristic fiasco stemmed from prior altercations—no fiasco, a grudge holding contest. There was never any reason to part our separate ways, no real reason to think we'd ever stop being friends.

I went on with the rest of the summer not knowing how things would turn out. My friends had disappeared longer than I ever remembered, and home was not as sweet as the television world claimed it to be. It was even worse with the imprisoning rain. Dad, whose business came to a halt, walked around the house expressing his negative feelings about some unclear past which kept his subconscious always battling and always bullying. Women were his answer to all misfortune, even the rain. I was only there to listen but never talk.

Tamara kept herself as far away from me as possible. There was nothing I could do about that. Besides refusing to forgive me for having been punished, we had nothing in common. She lived in a world all her own. She was boy crazy and dreamed of groups like *The Summer Boys* and *Empty Charms*. My dreams were of castles which never fell...of a girl named Desiree who didn't appear to exist and who was probably no different than all other girls.

Mother was only around to tell me when to clean my room or empty the trash, nothing more. We continued our distant affinity. Our intimacy was as apparent as a single grain of sand found lost in the midst of an endless desert. We continued our hellos and goodbyes, and as much as I would have wanted to share in this closeness she and Tamara shared, I just couldn't find it in me to give her the chance that she and I needed. Dad's professed cynicism continued to provoke in me a great ominous fear—a fear I believed to be nothing but certain.

School was to start in less than a month, and I hoped everything would be as it once was. I had the urge of going back to the hobby I'd abandoned months ago, since neither Ivan nor Danny were around to distract me. But as I held the first handful of sand, the rain had begun and the waves and blistering wind became all too powerful...There was to be only one sandcastle built that summer, the only sandcastle I'd ever seen fall.

Obscurity encompassed the tiny flickering flame of candlelight resting atop my dresser. It was the only light in the room, and it whipped my clumsy shadow gallantly up and down my walls and mirror, making the confines of my small room more of a sanctuary of undiscovered thoughts. The rain continued to beat heavily on my window. Every so often, a glare of light and a giant boom shot through the dark-black skies above. Broadcasters claimed this was one of the worst storms to hit Miami in forty years. Some streets flooded waist high. Many had to paddle boats through the worst inundated areas of the city. There were moments my transistor went dead, and the only contact with the outside world lay deep within my own thoughts.

For days I sat in front of the easel, staring at blank white sheets of paper. I struggled as thoughts tortured through a vacant, lonesome unconsciousness. Desperately I wanted to give up, as my mind lay chained within itself. Desire pointed me to the beach, sun, water, and sand—but that was an endless storm away. Careless strokes soon glided over blank pages as my memory brought me back to shore. Everyone was there: Danny, Ivan, Kelly, and her three friends. There stood Desiree, quiet and observant, with green radiant eyes so stunning. Her face was perfect in the sun, her hair dark and shiny. She looked at me with her gripping stare, and I turned away, made shaky by the way it had made me feel.

On and on I sketched, keeping her image focused at the forefront of my mind. I must have started the same sketch over and over again a hundred times, struggling as my mind slammed into major roadblocks. Things I imagined, irregular or misrepresentations of worldly objects or vivid made-up images were easiest to paint, draw, or shape. For I was the true creator when I imagined, and I was the only one with the power to include or exclude. I could leave room for imperfection and be completely accepting of those things which lived deep within my own mind. Real objects and scenery, on the other hand, demanded perfection. Desiree was real, nothing of my imagination—or so I hoped. I couldn't afford to leave out or alter any detail. To do so would make her appear like just another girl, and that was something she was not, at least not according to the strange feelings that were woven deep within my soul.

I worked tediously through most of the night, trying to recreate something Dad had always claimed did not exist. I used fourteen shades of charcoal gray and only a light shade of green for her eyes. A half tablet of paper later, what I witnessed was as close to Desiree as the real her. A part of me lay spent as I took long moments just looking at her image. The creepiest feeling manifested itself as she looked at me just as she had months ago. Her stare was just as beckoning, seeming to beam deep within me to discover who I was, what my dreams were. She had no smile—just a peaceful quiet look. Her hair was as straight and as dark as ever, her complexion smooth and delicate. Dark shades of gray covered the background, as though the world had been too easy and, at the same time, too complicated to describe that day.

The storm grew in intensity as the lonely night wore on. Wild winds soon blew me back to the present as weird, eerie noises shrilled through our upstairs attic. Lightning seemed to come closer and closer as thunder roared its fury. My window displayed only dark shadows roaming wet streets. Every streetlight was out of order, and not one house showed any spark of life. Another thundering boom exploded from the sky, followed by a few flashes of light. Frightened, I backed away even though I knew I was safe in my room.

Someone tapped on my door just then. I opened and found Tamara frightened and shaken. Her flashlight beamed right into my eye.

"What's wrong?" I asked.

She quickly threw her arms around me as more thunder crushed down heavily throughout every inch of sky. "I'm just a little scared," she replied, "that's all."

I held her until she was stable enough to sit on my bed alone. Happy I was to hear her acknowledge me once again. For her weeks of silence and avoidance had only made me regret having gotten her into trouble.

"I was in my room under the covers," she said. "It was so dark. The thunder and lightening was driving me crazy. I hate it when it rains."

"It'll stop soon," I said, trying to ease her state of mind. After a while, she fell asleep on my bed but woke up shortly after another series of thunderous explosions shot through the sky. "It's all right," I said. "It's only the storm."

She looked over at me with her flashlight. "What are you doing?"

"Just some sketching," I let her know. I was so astonished at how well I'd done, I couldn't even think of rest.

"Aren't you gonna get any sleep?" she asked.

"In a minute." I took a final glance at the sketch and then laid next to Tamara. Only when I heard her deep calm breaths did I blow out the candle. I tried to picture Desiree's face in the dark as I thought of her portrait. Suddenly, I felt her gleaming green eyes upon me and my sandcastle. She gave me a smile that no other girl had ever given me before. It wasn't wicked. It wasn't sad. It was slight, gentle—almost delicate, innocent looking. I didn't turn away from her overpowering stare this time. Rather, I looked deep into her eyes and saw a unique her and a perfect me. I was angered when I awoke later that morning to find I'd only been dreaming. Even in the darkness of the early morning could I still see the outline of the easel.

Tamara was up early. Rain still fell. However, intensity lessened as downpour turned into a tranquil splash of delicate droplets. When I opened my eyes, vaguely could I see her stretching in front of Desiree's portrait. I drifted back to sleep, as I felt my drunken state of exhaustion lull me away.

She later woke me that afternoon inquiring if I was going to sleep in all day. "Maybe you shouldn't stay up so late," she said in a voice much like Mother's. I ignored her and rolled over. "Hey, where do you know her from?"

I looked over at the easel and realized for the first time that I'd forgotten to cover it up. "Just someone I know," I let her know. I wiped at my dreary eyes.

"I've seen her before."

Like a blaring alarm clock, my sleepiness quickly vanished as her words woke me entirely. I sat up instantly. "Where?"

She looked at the sketch again, studying it some more. "I don't know, but I know I've seen her. I remember her eyes. They're really weird like."

"Are you sure you don't remember?" Oh, how badly I wanted her to remember. How badly I wanted her to acknowledge that Desiree was indeed real. But I soon stopped my questioning. I didn't want her knowing how enthralled I was...didn't want the world seeing just how weak I'd become.

9

Next to last days, first days of school were most fun. Beach High usually mandated a minimum day schedule as an informal introduction of things to come. Classes were shorter, and there was never any homework, being that teachers were generally too overwhelmed to conduct class or focus on any kind of curriculum. Bells were usually unsynchronized and rang on and off at the oddest times of day. Fire alarms too were often triggered as a prank, and an occasional stink bomb in the halls or in the bathroom was to be expected.

It was a joy to see what physical changes familiar faces had made over the summer. Returning sophomores grew an average of twelve inches or more over the summer. Girls tended to grow outward rather than upward and bloomed in their new stylish clothes and hot, stunning tans. Rebellious seniors often dressed outlandishly or displayed the wildest new hairstyles with the loudest array of colors. Some smoked in the parking lots even though smoking was forbidden on school property. Others showed off the coolest tattoos imaginable as well as other forms of body manipulation which drove most of our prior generation absolutely crazy.

As juniors, we saw ourselves superior over incoming freshmen seeking to find a sense of familiarity and comfort in their new surroundings. It was a relief knowing we had already walked down that long road which now awaited these clumsy, immature little bodies. We were older and wiser—experienced, and it felt good knowing we had a handle on survival and conquest of high school.

A few clouds still lingered throughout the sky as the first appearance of the sun's rays hit the wet gleaming grass around the school. It had been nearly a month since I'd seen the sun brighten the morning with such hope and a new beginning. Outside the front gates we stood as we watched people rush to different areas of the campus. Bicycle lots were filled to capacity as many chained their bikes to metal railings and trees.

Traffic clogged the front parkway where students poured out of buses and vans. Many of them embraced one another as they hung out in the halls and talked about summer and the upcoming school year. Others gathered in huge lines as they waited for new schedules to be handed out.

"L.A. sucked really bad," Ivan described as we walked up to line. "It was smoggy and sticky everywhere I went. Everything smelled like dried piss, and the water tasted really bad." Ivan was really good at descriptions, blunt when it came to describing places I'd never seen or events I'd not yet experienced. After hearing of his trip, I had little interest in ever visiting Los Angeles. "And the girls…they were stuck up like nothing you've ever seen before. They all walked like they had sticks up their asses, and Disney World is way nicer than Disneyland—I don't care what anyone says. What's everything been like here?"

"Wet," I responded. "It rained the whole time you were gone."

"That's what I heard. I guess going to L.A. wasn't such a bad thing after all."

We talked to a few acquaintances, many of whom we knew from class. All asked about Danny. In the crowd I spotted Gracie. She was with her friends who all dressed in the same skimpy pastel colored dresses, smiling as they projected an artificial kind of sweetness that caught most guys' attention. They talked and laughed as they enjoyed their time back on campus. I still had not seen or talked to Danny and could only hope he was well over Gracie's heart stabbing ways. I figured he was around, perhaps already waiting in his first period class or out on the track field talking to his coach.

A group of volunteer parents helped pass out schedules. I anxiously scanned mine, hoping by some miracle one of Mr. Parlante's art classes would be listed. But sadly, that was not to be. I had already taken all available art electives. I was aware my art career at Beach High was all but over but had not yet learned to accept it. The usual English, social studies, physical education, as well as a foreign language were listed as graduation requirements. My science elective, however, read: *Advanced Integrated Biology.*

"No way," Ivan said as he peered over my shoulder. "How'd that happen?"

"I have no freak'n clue. That's impossible."

"Oh, shit, and you got Mrs. Wardell," he remarked. "I heard she's really hard—and a real big time bitch. I heard if you miss any homework you have to come in on Saturdays to make it all up." He laughed. "And she's been known to use a whipping stick if you don't know the answers when she calls on you. You're really up a shit creek now."

It was said Mrs. Wardell was the hardest teacher at the school—and for many, the first step of getting through life. Everything had to be perfect in her class or nothing counted. I'd always heard she was extremely difficult to get along with. The harder you tried, the more she'd bring you down. The less you tried, the more she enjoyed flunking you. Many parents and administrators throughout the school district complained of her tough curriculum and rigorous ways, but there was no intimidating her. She had been at the school longer than any teacher or administrator. She ruled her domain, and there was just nothing you could do but fall into place.

"It's gotta be a mistake," I said. "Only straight A people take A.I. Bio. There's no way I'm gonna hang in that class. I was supposed to be put into Life Science."

"Forget about it now, buddy" said Ivan. "You're stuck with it. They're not gonna change your schedule just 'cause you're afraid of A.I. Bio. You have to come up with a better reason than that. I guess we'll be seeing Marlo in summer school next summer with a few scars scabbed to his ass." He laughed hysterically as he handed me his schedule. "Here, read it and weep. This is what a real schedule should look like."

We shared two classes together—English and U.S. History. That was no surprise being that he, Danny, and I had always shared at least one class together during our years at Beach.

"There's no way. How'd you get band, art, and two PE classes all in the same semester?" I asked.

"It's all about connections."

"C'mon, really, how'd you do it? What about math and science? You can't graduate without a second year."

"Forget it, man. I ain't no rocket scientist. You know that. Mrs. Canizaro said I could join the alternative program and still graduate. I don't need to take no A.I. Bio." Again he laughed.

The first bell rang, and we made our way over to first period U.S. History class. Our teacher was Mr. Bernard, a rather bulky man with a thick mustache and straight banged hair. He was a strict teacher who loved to teach and was determined to make everybody learn no matter what grade he or she received in his class. Unlike other teachers I'd known, he was pretty well organized for our first day. He managed to pass out textbooks, a course syllabus, and go over class rules all on the first day. When he read Danny's name off his roll sheet, Ivan and I glanced around the room. But there was no Danny. This was surprising, as Danny had never missed a single day of school in his life. His mother always drove him to school even on his sickest days. I suspected something must have been wrong and couldn't help but wonder if this had anything to do with Gracie. But that couldn't be, I thought, feeling I was over-analyzing things. It was only first period. Perhaps he'd overslept...or perhaps he'd gone off on a last minute vacation trip with his mother to a far-off place and had not yet made it back.

After first period, we walked by the display case that resided in Main Hall. The track team's runner-up trophy from a year ago shined in eternal luster as it presided over all other trophies. Danny's squad represented the only team in school history to ever compete for a state title. You couldn't help but feel proud being part of the school. "Danny's a smart kid not letting his talents go out the door by falling in love," Dad had remarked after the track team had competed in the state finals. "When you fall in love with a girl, nothing else matters anymore. It's only a matter of time before you start losing your friends, goals, and eventually even your own dignity. I hope you never let that happen, Marlo."

I wondered what he would say now that Danny had let Gracie crush him in the worst of ways. Did this make Danny any less smart? Unfortunately, Danny never had a father like mine to pass along his wisdom. His father had died very young, and his mother had brought him up to believe that you should treat others as you yourself would want to be treated. Truly, I hoped Danny was okay and hoped his absence had nothing to do with any kind of pain.

Ivan made his way to his next class. I bypassed second period Spanish and headed straight to the guidance department in hopes of dropping that third period biology class. But as I walked through the administration building, the doorway was crammed with parents and students all seeking Mrs. Canizaro's help on similar issues. The secretary was extremely busy and showed little concern for my problem. "I'm sorry," she said. "All classes are full. You'll have to keep the same schedule for at least the first few weeks."

"Yeah, but. . ."

"You can fill out a call slip if you want," she said as she handed me a blue slip of paper, "but I'm not sure if it'll do any good. When she has time, Mrs. Canizaro will have you pulled from class. You can discuss your problems with her then."

I cringed, as I did not want to go a single day in that biology class. I went along with the bureaucracy and filled out the call slip, requesting that I speak to Mrs. Canizaro as soon as possible.

By the time I left the administration building, second period was just about over. I headed straight to the science wing, promising myself I would not let this Mrs. Wardell teacher get the better of me. This was just a temporary thing I assured myself, one of those things I'd hate but somehow manage to survive. I'd be out of her class in no time at all.

The loneliest classroom on campus resided at the very edge of school, near the teacher's parking lot. It was well enough away from hall traffic—and well enough away for anyone not to hear you cry for help. I was one of the first students to walk in. A human sized skeleton dangled from a banister near the front entrance. The room was filled with black granite-top desks, each big enough for two students and each containing a stainless steel sink. Glass tubes and flasks filled shelves and cabinets throughout the room. Vials and containers full of yellowish liquid and dead, preserved rodents and frogs rested on oversized window sills. Pictures of whales, salamanders, birds, and insects hung on sides of walls and over windows. Two large bookcases filled the back area with every book you'd ever want to read on nature, anatomy, and physiology, and a great big poster next to the chalkboard diagrammed every unpronounceable body part related to human anatomy.

Mrs. Wardell stood high and mighty on a platform which separated her desk and projector from the rest of the class. She was a tall, lanky brunette woman—middle-aged with thick glasses that resembled magnifying glasses. She was rather well-dressed compared to most other teachers, wearing cotton knitted slacks with a conservative, deep-purple blouse. Her serious aura carried well into the quiet room. You just knew silence would follow you through the rest of the semester as she conducted her class with the utmost authority. Already it seemed she was preparing for battle, and already I could feel her intensity. The giant ancient chalkboard shadowed over her as she busied herself writing dates and times up on the board. She held one hand over her hip as her hand forcefully pressed the chalk against the blackboard. Her lips were straight and narrow, not appearing to have ever known a smile.

The overhead projector hummed peacefully and displayed names written inside small boxes which mapped out each seating station in the room. I looked for *Clemente* and turned to see which box matched my seat. I found myself way in the back. I didn't really like the back since it was difficult to see the board, but I loved the idea that I probably wouldn't get called on very much.

Other students soon found themselves in the room. Most were the nerdiest students in the school—ones who dressed out of style, ones who still found reasons to wear eyeglasses, and ones who always won all the honor roll awards. These were students I rarely saw in my other classes or at football and basketball games. They were the brains of the school, ones who got into all the prestigious colleges and universities, ones the school took pride in when being evaluated by the state department of education…ones who could undoubtedly survive in Mrs. Wardell's domain.

Not one person uttered a word as Mrs. Wardell continued her squeaky writing on the board. I was still the only one not seated next to anyone. Seats had apparently been assigned alphabetically. The name beside mine read, *Castillo*. It wasn't anyone I thought I'd know—at least not until that last person walked into the room, just as the bell sounded. All present thoughts went blank as images from the past flashed before my eyes. She was someone I recognized well and still as pretty to see as the first time I'd laid eyes on her.

Mrs. Wardell stepped off the platform and walked up to her. I was too far back in the room to hear their soft voices. It wasn't difficult, however, to determine that Mrs. Wardell was inquiring her name. After looking up at the projector, Mrs. Wardell turned and pointed over in my direction.

10

Infatuation...what is this strong physical attraction for another person that hides our true identity and makes the other perfect in every way?

Now I knew her full name, Desiree Castillo, and that was all that mattered. She wasn't someone I'd dreamt up or the apparition I believed her to be. It seemed silly to let my heart become prisoner to a girl I was now seeing for only the second time, but to be honest, I couldn't help it. Maybe it was those mysterious green eyes of hers which indeed assured me she was distinct—those beaming green eyes that intimidated me even when they weren't looking at me...*Was she unique?*

A mushy sensation I'd always associated with fairy love tales—with princes and damsels, dungeons and dragons, wizards, and castles told me she was. It didn't seem to matter that I sensed the kind of power she possessed, the kind of heartache she concealed...that I had been programmed by Dad to be wise and not let myself become a blinded slave to a girl who could very well bring me to my knees with one potent stare of her eyes. For already I felt I was hers—hers to do what she wished of me.

A hefty book bag hung clumsily over her shoulder. She tilted to one side to keep her balance as she uneasily walked towards me. Her faded jeans and white *Wish I Was Dreaming* T-shirt loosely hugged her tall slender figure. Her deep-olive tone still showed in her face, neck, and arms. Her perfect, smooth complexion displayed not one blemish and called for not one ounce of makeup. Her shoulder-length hair was banged and streamed straight down like that of an ancient image of an Egyptian pharaoh. She sat next to me and paid little attention to all wandering eyes that spied over her. I wasn't sure if she'd remember me. It had been months since that day at the beach when she learned I was the architect who'd built that illusive sandcastle.

Mrs. Wardell rechecked her seating chart and then explained her grading policy and class expectations. I paid little attention to her lecture, not realizing her standards went far above anything I'd ever encountered in any one class. Desiree wrote down every word Mrs. Wardell said, as did everyone else in the class. Right then and there I knew she must have been very studious, competent, independent—as well as confident. Again I had to ask: *Was she unique?*

Regularly, I noticed most pretty girls gave little importance to school, not because they had very few brain cells to play with or the inability to be studious. It seemed all they dreamed of was becoming famous runway models, or hanging with professional athletes or flamboyant rock n' roll superstars—or at the very least, simply settling to marry some rich doctor or lawyer who'd take care of them forever.

I surfaced from my reverie as Mrs. Wardell went over lab requirements. This time, I pulled out a pen and notebook from my bag, trying to make it seem like I too fit in. "Each and everyone of you," she stated firmly, "will be responsible for handing in a lab report at the end of each week. Some labs may take more than a day and will take at least two people to complete. I've matched you up with a lab partner and that, of course, will be the person you're seated next to."

Desiree turned my way. I carelessly met her eyes. For a split second, I found myself deep within her stare, just as I'd been that day at the beach. Her gaze seemed familiar, her eyes like the ones in my sketch—reflective and telling of all dark shadows only she and I saw. I quickly broke eye contact and focused back on Mrs. Wardell, failing to respond or smile a brief hello.

How stupid and foolish I felt—especially since she had turned and looked at me first. I was sure she'd remember me now. I was the same person who had turned his eyes away from hers months ago. Through my peripheral vision I saw her turn her attention back onto Mrs. Wardell. A cold feeling of regret struck me everywhere, hinting that she most likely thought the worst of me now.

"Through sickness or in health," Mrs. Wardell continued, "either you or your partner will be responsible for turning in a lab report every Friday. But that's only if a lab takes both your work. If not, then a separate report is required from each of you. Any questions?" On and on she went, making it very easy for all of us to turn our attention to another world other than the one we'd have to face for two long semesters. She spoke fast and left out none of her demands. It was only our first day of class, and already she made everything seem routine. Already I was overwhelmed and unsure I'd survive even this first day.

A girl with funny pigtails and shiny fork-like braces raised her hand and asked, "What if you're sick on lab day?"

Mrs. Wardell pushed her thick glasses closer to her eyes. The lenses made them magnify ten times over. "Good question," she remarked. "If you're absent on a day of a lab, you'll have to make it up on another day before school starts—or on a Saturday. But since most labs will take more than a day to complete, you should be able to catch up the next day or following week when we resume. Your lab partner should be able to help you catch up...I don't think I've ever had two same lab partners absent on lab day. That's because I take participation points off everyday anyone's absent...In other words, the more you participate the better it'll be for you. Don't be absent!"

Like Mr. Bernard, she too passed out textbooks. They were twice the thickness of my history book and seemed to weigh as much as a hundred bricks. She pointed to the board behind her. "You must read chapter one tonight. The chapter review is due by tomorrow."

This surprised no one, as not one complaint was voiced. It certainly was foreign to me. Homework on the first day. That was unheard of...but I guess I was now a minor leaguer trying to bat in a major league game.

Just before class let out, Mrs. Wardell showed us some of the caged animals she kept in a small storage area in the back. "I want everyone to treat all my animals very gently," she said, holding one of her hamsters in her hand. "I despise anyone who's cruel to animals. Don't ever let me catch anyone playing with my animals in any inhumane way. I won't ever forget a few years back when two boys started throwing one of my hamsters around like some sort of ball."

Everyone laughed except Desiree. She kept quiet while everyone else snickered and commented on Mrs. Wardell's story.

"You people think that's funny?" Mrs. Wardell snapped. "You're probably just as crude as they were." The class silenced as her serious tone echoed through the room and out into the lonesome hallway. "It's going to be a long year, and it'll be longer if I have to be tough on you kids." She looked at the hamster in her hand and began to stroke it gently with her forefinger. Slowly, she looked back up at the class with hard, squinting eyes. Even through her soda-pop bottled glasses, no one mistook her stare as a joking one. "Maybe I should finish telling you," she continued, "that one of those boys was standing by the window in the back when I caught them." She motioned her head. The class turned to the window. "He missed my hamster when the other boy tossed it. Not only did the poor thing hit himself hard against the metal frame... he also flew out the window."

I didn't see why some people still laughed. The window wasn't high for us, but it would be for a small helpless hamster like the one Mrs. Wardell held in her hand. She didn't say anything more. She appeared upset about reliving the entire incident—and at the same time, disappointed that people would even find such a thing amusing.

The bell rang just then, and everyone rushed out of the class like a stampede of wild animals. Desiree took her time getting up and organized her things very carefully. I remained seated, not knowing what to say or do. By the time she zipped up her bag and placed the strap around her shoulder, everyone had completely evacuated the class, except for Mrs. Wardell who was preoccupied preparing for her next class. Desiree eventually looked down at me. This time it was she who caught me looking first. She wasn't as ill-mannered as I was. She didn't turn away or make it seem like she had something against me. Instead, she gave me a slight smile which for the first time revealed a dimple on the right side of her cheek. She gave me plenty of time to react, but I stood in my chair like a motionless naked statue with no face, hands, or arms. When I found it in me to return her smile, she'd already spun around and headed for the door. I sat there, feeling like a helpless intimidated fool, trying to determine whether her smile had been one of recognition or just a simple hello or good-bye. Anxiously, I got up and rushed to the door to see if there was any way of changing how she may have seen me. I couldn't let her think I was rude, thoughtless, or arrogant. Most of all, I couldn't let her assume I was strange because I liked to go to the beach and play with the sand in the most remote of ways.

She had already disappeared into the crowds of people making their way to fourth period when I reached Main Hall. And just as waves and currents made castles disappear, my courage also disappeared. Again, I was too late. Again, my barriers were back in full force.

The rest of the school day went by rather rapidly. Desiree wasn't in any of my other classes. I kept an eye open everywhere I went, my mind saturated with only images of her. Before I realized it, I was in eighth period English class with Ivan.

"How was Mrs. Wardell's class?" he asked as we sat down near the back of the room.

"It actually wasn't too bad," I replied, forgetting about Mrs. Wardell and smiling as thoughts of Desiree continued to plague me.

"I think art class will be my favorite this year," he said. "Mr. Parlante seems really cool. Nothing seems to be right or wrong in his class."

"He's the coolest," I said.

"He has one of your paintings up on the wall."

"He always puts stuff up in his room," I acknowledged.

"No, I mean on the Wall of Fame."

There was a famous wall near the foyer of the school gymnasium. It was more of a large display case than anything else. Everyone referred to it as the Wall of Fame. This was where only the best art projects by Beach High students were placed for all to see, some dating back to the last century. Displayed within the glass were the most remarkable works imaginable—pottery, ceramic, sculptures, jewelry, drawings, oil landscape paintings, and portraits of Malcolm X, Martin Luther King Jr., Lincoln, Washington, and Chavez. There were even fine handmade garments from days when the school still offered costume-design courses. Hearing my work was a part of this array of priceless art was exciting— but above all, an honor. For I had not yet graduated, and the wall was seen as a shrine for the most talented artists who had long since left Beach High.

This day was fabulous. First, I found Desiree, the dreamy girl who had long since evaded my notions of reality. And now, I discovered that my work had been placed inside the Wall. Oh, what a joy! It was not one of Danny's giant trophies or the kind of attention Ivan received when he played in the band—but it was a start to an acceptance of being normal, special—and yet, eternal.

Why hadn't Mr. Parlante told me he would put my work up on the Wall last spring? Which one of my works could it be? There were several I had never claimed or cared to keep—paintings, drawings, and molded figurines. I could hardly wait to walk by the gymnasium. "The Wall of Fame," I uttered blankly.

"Yeah, pretty cool, huh?" Ivan said. "He took us out there as part of his class introduction."

The bell rang. Everyone quieted as Ms. Farren walked into class with a soft drink in one hand and a binder in the other. She had been our English teacher for the past two years. She was a rather short and heavy bodied woman with pale brown eyes, a somewhat pretty face, and short-brown wavy hair. Most students liked her because she was still rather young to be a high school teacher (still in her twenties). She always dressed in the latest hip fashions and, in many ways, understood what it was like to be our age, possessing a rare sense of humor not found in other teachers' dry classrooms. She had a way of making each class different, shying away from routine and familiar expectations. Her curriculum was geared towards including some of the most modern literature of our time, incorporating a wide variety of cultural and dramatic themes young teens in today's society could relate to. She liked her students to write and express themselves; so, like Mr. Parlante, in many instances, there were no right or wrong answers in her class.

After a brief introduction and handing us a list of books we'd be reading during the course of the year, Ms. Farren took attendance. She called Danny's name but, just as in first period, he wasn't around to respond.

"I guess he's sick, Ms. Farren," Ivan responded when she inquired about Danny's whereabouts. Ms. Farren was well aware of Danny's perfect attendance and success on the track field. "I'm sure he'll be in tomorrow. You know how he doesn't miss that much class." Ivan then leaned over to me and whispered, "I wonder what's really up with him?"

Perhaps this did have something to do with Gracie. Perhaps Danny was in some sort of trouble. Ivan would understand if I told him the truth now, I thought. He was the wise one, the one who said a girl like Gracie could make a guy do anything—even give up his sense of self-worth and self-respect. If he truly was Danny's friend, he'd find a proper way of dealing with Danny's so called blindness. Wherever Danny was, I knew he was in some need of understanding and acceptance. Ivan wouldn't let him down.

When class ended, everyone stormed out of class and into the warm bright day. Ivan and I met with Ms. Farren at her desk.

"What's on your mind, boys?" she asked as she put papers and books into her bag.

"What do you mean boys?" Ivan protested.

"Well, you aren't men yet—only high schoolers. Life hasn't slapped you in the face yet."

Ivan really didn't understand her comment. To be honest, neither did I. I thought I'd lived long enough to know about every last thing that stung like a bee.

"Okay, so we're boys," he acknowledged. "But remember, you'll be in a rocking chair before us."

"That may be true," Ms. Farren responded, "but I also get to enjoy rocking back and forth while I watch you guys get into one."

"We're screwed any way we look at things," Ivan remarked.

"Depends how you look at things. I wish I could be sixteen again so I could be wild and crazy, fall in love for the first time, get on my parents' nerves, and do all the things I never had a chance to do." We walked outside, and she locked the classroom. The afternoon heat hugged us all very tightly as we left the shadows of the enclosed hallway. Everyone still hung around talking, gossiping, and laughing of times treasured and times they would just as soon forget about. Although the day was sunny and pleasant, there were still a few clouds left over from those dreadful gray stormy days I'd thought would never end.

"I don't care how old I get," Ivan said. "I'll always get on my parents' nerves."

"You can still pass for sixteen," I told Ms. Farren. She loved it when she was told she looked young and cool, down to earth. "You still look young and alive."

"How sweet, Marlo," she responded, "but looking so young at my age can get me in trouble. How was your guys' summer?"

"It was all right," I said. "It would have been better if it hadn't rained so much."

"What about your art?" she exclaimed. "*The rain's a perfect time to paint*. That's what you wrote in your journal one day. I remember reading that. It stuck to my mind because I've always thought the rain's a perfect time to write."

"Yeah, but I'd rather be in the sun and on the beach, thinking and getting ideas."

"This school," Ivan butted in, "hasn't even begun to recognize or understand Marlo's art. You should see what he can do at the beach with the sand and the sun."

Ivan had never sounded so impressed before. Maybe the Wall of Fame had reinforced a side of me he'd always seemed to overlook. It hadn't been long ago that he'd been fed up with my always being at the beach.

Ms. Farren looked into my eyes just as Ms. Varian used to, always trying to read what I could never see was really there—this "gift" which could touch thousands of souls in special ways. "Is this true?" she asked.

"You can say that," I acknowledged awkwardly, not wanting to brag about something I didn't really feel was a talent.

"C'mon Marlo," Ivan persisted. "Tell her about all those awesome sandcastles you build all the time."

Perfection was something few could ever understand, even me. It seemed to grab you by the soul and demand every ounce of your being, never once resting, never once being quenched by even the highest of tides. I stood there in silence, wanting to keep my secrets and abilities to myself as I had for so long. Why would anyone want to hear about sandcastles? I had always appeared to be this boring person with not an ounce of excitement in him. I couldn't play the guitar like Ivan or run around the track like Danny. And never had I wanted to be seen as someone who could only play with the sand or move a paintbrush and paint pictures only I could visualize. I wanted to be a Mr. Macho…someone who could chill and thrill everyone's spine in more recognizable ways.

"You should see them, Ms. Farren," Ivan went on. "They're so exact and seem so real. He doesn't even use premolded buckets or boulders to build on like those experts on TV do. They make you wonder what holds them up. If there was only some way he could save all of them. Sometimes he takes pictures of them. Maybe he can show you some. Right, Mar?"

"Yeah," I replied faintly.

"That sounds really interesting, Marlo. I knew there had to be more to your talent than just those paintings Mr. Parlante displays in his room. As a matter of fact, I believe he mentioned something about the Wall of Fame at our faculty meeting yesterday. He seemed happy."

"You bet he's happy," said Ivan. "Who wouldn't want to say he's Marlo's art teacher?"

I didn't mind Ivan bragging about me. In fact, it made me feel good. But there was still this feeling inside that told me I really wasn't that good, at least not like he or Danny was.

"I really hope Danny's okay," Ms. Farren said as we headed towards Main Hall. "I heard we're supposed to have an even stronger track team this year, and of course Danny's a big part of it."

Ivan's optimism seeped out. "Ah, he's all right. He's probably running a few laps around the track right now."

"If you see him, give him our reading list." She looked down at her watch. "Oh, gosh. We have another faculty meeting this afternoon. I better get going."

We walked down towards the gymnasium. No one was around, and I figured now was a better time than any to tell him. "There's something about Danny I think you should—"

"Holy shit," he interrupted as we halted, "I forgot my guitar lesson was switched for early today. I'm due in twenty minutes. Damn…I better head out quick style." He let himself think for a moment. "What about Danny?"

I looked at him with no words to say, figuring it could wait another day. Danny would likely be back in school tomorrow as it was. Maybe I wouldn't have to say anything. "It's cool," I said. "It's nothing major. You better head on if you wanna make it home on time."

"All right then. I guess I'll see ya tomorrow. Let's get here early though so we can pick out some cool lockers. We don't want trashy ones like last year. I'll come by in the morning."

"Cool."

He headed for the front of the school and blended in with the crowd standing in the parking lot and others who stood waiting to board buses. I turned and continued towards the gymnasium. To the left of me was the track and football field. Although the football team was already in pads and practice gear, the grassy plain seemed empty, lifeless as I searched for Danny. I hoped I'd find him running his daily wind sprints, but there was no sign of him. I proceeded into the gymnasium. A few members of the girl's volleyball team took turns spiking the ball over the net. Others stretched and ran laps around the basketball court. At the opposite end of the gym, I pushed the doors open and walked out. There, beyond the lunch tables and ticket booth was the famous wall. The edges surrounding the glass were plated in brass, which stretched two stories high and thirty-feet wide alongside the east wing of the gymnasium wall. Etched on the brass plated borders were thousands of names of every student who had long since graduated Beach High. My eyes became intertwined with endless names, turning most of the black-etched letters into a massive swarm of frozen locusts ready to fall upon me as I stood enamored by this aesthetic monument. A giant glass frame covered the center portion of the wall. Mr. Parlante had mentioned the wall had once been an enormous aquarium full of exotic tropical fish, with real sharks and even an octopus.

The inside was now reconstructed and layered in red and black velvet, the floor covered with landscape stone and broken seashells. Inside was where the school's most prized works hailed. Beside the porcelain doll and small miniature of a handcrafted wooden piano stood the wall's newest addition. It was leaning up against the bottom portion of the platform, a painting I'd painted at the end of my freshman year. I remember Mr. Parlante had marveled as he shared it with all his students that year. *Weeping Prince* was what I'd named it. The foreground showed a picture of a rock, resting on top an abandoned cape and spear. The background displayed a picture of a great Mayan temple I'd once seen in my World Cultures textbook. The owner of the cape and spear stood alone in his colorful, webbed leather clothing. He looked upon the horizon silent in his quiet thoughts, perhaps afraid of his own songs of worship—perhaps unsure of certainty. A reddish-orange glow topped the landscape beyond as the sun slowly sank behind green jungle mountaintops. Atop the temple were two tiny faint images of a priest raising a pointed dagger high into the air. Long hair of another soul fell from one end of a stone altar as her screams forever called *his* name.

I stood for a long moment in awe as I admired my work and for the first time accepted just a bit of my true magic. Here I was, for all to see. Suddenly, I seemed not a naked statue without a mouth to speak or eyes to see—or hands to touch or feet to stand tall and mighty. I was Marlo and maybe I did not live up on the moon…maybe I did not have to sink in with each and every tide.

Others walked by as they entered and exited the gym, but I ignored them. It wasn't until Irwin Pacheco, one of Danny's teammates, walked by that I pulled away. Irwin was a tall black Cuban immigrant who, like Danny, was a great sprinter and a big part of Beach High's sensational track team. Danny was more of the star, but you could not mention the track team without also including Irwin Pacheco. He guzzled a bottle of water and tossed the empty bottle into the recycling bin. He was dressed in his gym shorts. His legs were as long as flag poles and thin like those of a flamingo, a perfect genetic match for someone who could undoubtedly run the daylights out of a cheetah, I thought. *Beach High Track* was printed on the front of his T-shirt.

"What are you doing out here?" he asked in his thick Spanish accent. He'd been living in Miami since grade school; however, his accent was quite distinct despite his proficient English skills. He was usually an outsider who tried his hardest to fit in and be liked at school, but he was constantly caught up in a culture clash very few understood. Many considered Irwin black. However, his Cuban background was quite different than those of most African-Americans at the school. He depended highly on his good nature and alluring appeal to survive in many circles of friends. He was one of the fastest runners at the school, and this too boosted his notoriety.

"Nothing," I replied, "just checking out the wall."

He stared on for a moment but soon lost interest. "Hey, does Ivan know about this new guy in school? He's supposed to be a really good guitar player."

"I don't think so, but I doubt anyone'll beat Ivan out. He's too good."

"That's true," he agreed.

Ivan's spot as band's lead guitarist was as secure as a bolted metal door. He was too popular—and not only could he play just about anything, he could win over a crowd as easily as liquor could win over a recovering alcoholic.

"Danny sure has been like a stranger," Irwin said as we treaded through the still wet grass leading to the main gates. Many still boarded buses, and others sped off in loud, roaring cars. "He wasn't in third period when the teacher called him, and I think he's given up on running. I never saw him once at the park the whole summer. I wonder what's up...I called his mother, and she told me Danny had disconnected his line. Then she said I couldn't talk to him because he wasn't feeling well. That was the last time I spoke to his mom. No one ever answered her line again...I don't get it, man."

"Irwin," I said in a soft serious tone, "have you ever been attracted to a girl—I mean really attracted?"

He looked at me strangely. He must have wondered why I would ask him that. It wasn't the kind of question you asked a guy—much less ask him out of the blue. After pausing momentarily to make sure he heard me correctly, his heavily accented voice said, "Yeah, but I've never gone crazy in love if that's what you mean."

"Oh, don't think I'm weird. I'm just curious—that's all."

"If being in love is like what my brother went through way back when, then I'd rather not know love."

"What do you mean?"

"I remember when I was in the seventh grade, my brother was about to graduate from Beach. He was crazy over this one girl, man. They were together for about a year, and in all that time my brother was kissing his money good-bye and wasting all his time for nothing. 'Anything to make you happy,' he used to tell her. I remember 'cause I used to think he was dumb. It turned out, man, when he had no more money to buy her things, she lost all interest in him and dumped him."

"Are you serious?" I thought back to Danny and Gracie.

"Yeah, you should have seen him, man. He was so down that all he wanted to do was stay in his room and talk to no one. My father tried talking some sense into him, but all that did was cause arguments around the house. He ended up running away but came back the very next day. My mother then tried talking with him, and that was a little better, since my mom isn't as impatient as my father."

"Your brother must have really felt like shit."

"Yeah, he was still feeling hurt, but it wasn't as bad. He said the way he hurt was enough to make him want to die rather than live with the pain."

Could Danny be thinking of dying rather than bear Gracie's poisonous venom? No, I assured myself. *There's always something to live for. These worst of pains weren't worth dying over, were they?*

"I wonder why your brother felt so bad. It wasn't like he'd known her his whole life."

"I don't know, man. I guess that's the power of falling in love. My mother kept telling my father when he used to get mad at my brother, 'Oh, leave him alone. It's his first.' But all my father kept saying was: 'I'm glad it happened to you, son. That ought to teach you to watch out which girl you marry. Don't you know that people your age don't know what love really is? There ain't no such things as Romeo and Juliet romances in the world—at least there ain't no such part about Juliet.' I didn't even look at girls or know who Romeo and Juliet were at the time."

"You must really be scared of falling in love," I insinuated, hoping someone else would share my same fears.

"Not really. I just have to make sure she's the right girl and not rush myself. My mother says falling in love doesn't happen too many times in someone's life. If it does, then it's just infatuation."

"Is your brother still feeling crushed?"

"No way, man. He's finishing up college right now. He's way different now. I don't think he ever had another steady girlfriend after what happened to him with that one girl. He tells me not to take girls seriously. Every time he comes down for vacation or spring break and we see a good looking girl, he says, 'no girl's worth the time of day.' That makes sense, doesn't it?" He looked at me more closely. "I mean, we don't want to fall in love with just one girl so young in our lives. Someone always ends up getting hurt because, at our age, we don't really know what we want. Take a look at how many new songs, clothes styles, dance styles, and hair styles fade away so quickly because we're sick of them so soon—or something else comes along that we think's better. Haven't you ever played a song on your stereo that's only been out a week and then have someone come up to you and say, 'Ah, that shit's old, man'?"

"Yeah, I know what you mean."

"Well, the same goes for liking a girl or a girl liking a guy. Before you know it, there's another girl that tops that other girl you liked before. Maybe in some cases that's not so. Look at Romeo and Juliet."

I hadn't seen one girl I'd rather look at than Desiree, and I thought looking at her could never get old. My eyes were as attracted to her as a magnet was to metal, or a bear to honey. Though this could have been considered weak in Dad's eyes, I was certain I could keep my distance as I had with so many other things.

Irwin seemed wise, and everything he said made sense, much like Dad did when he spoke. He also seemed to have a handle on those protective barriers I seemed to know so well. It seemed he would not be a fool and fall into the power of any one woman. How foolish to believe I wouldn't either...How foolish to believe there truly were no Juliets.

We came to the corner of the street, where the campus came to an end. He was headed right, towards Ivan's part of town. "Was that really your brother's first love?" I asked finally.

"I'm sure it was," he said as he crossed the street. "Before he went off to college, he told me to watch out which girl I love first—'cause that's the girl I'd always remember and love most—no matter what happens."

11

This was more than just an uninhibited sense of fascination. This was an undeniable, almost painful attraction as real as the sky, endless shoreline, and gleaming sun which promised never to fade amidst mountains or oceans. Certain I could never be. I'd come face to face with the unexpected and did not know whether I'd ever live in a blatant, recognizable world again. To think Desiree could ever be in my same science class fell well beyond any of my perfect dreams...and to be placed on the Wall of Fame—well, that just reiterated what had always evaded me in the past. *Was I special?*

Her portrait stared at me as she had that first day—as she had earlier today in Mrs. Wardell's class. So haunting, so mysterious, and so graceful they were. Her eyes saw no barriers—could decipher everything I was, everything I dreamed to be. Forced me to look into my mirror they did, to see if maybe I too could see this real Marlo. My mirror never lied—even when I wanted it to.

Who was this real Marlo? Who was I to think myself any saner or certain about anything? Even though I should have always felt special, the tendency had always been to see myself stranger than life. Danny, with his unbeatable speed, who'd managed to win so many track meets for our school—and Ivan, with his electrifying ability to play the guitar that riveted everyone off their seats during football and basketball games, had talents that were chilling, thrilling, and spine tingling. Art certainly was not something to cheer for. What many thought came effortlessly was sometimes as difficult as accepting sorry when "sorry" just wasn't enough of an apology. I'd work hours to perfect what might look like a moment's work. All those smudges of paint that formed the simplest images of real life looked all too easy. And the sand I managed to place together to form the most elegant castles simply appeared to fit together like some glue-together model. There was no excitement or intense emotion—only a sense of beauty and indirect meaning many would not think to scream or shout over for even a second.

I had not liked little league as a kid. Didn't like the boys club or the playground either. Oh, if it had only been sane to be lost in paintings or sand, to be lost in a world free from the present—to be in tune with a world that seemed too foreign and far from certain…maybe I too would have shined like the stars, diamonds, and sparkling water. Even now, I was not into Saturday night parties much. I had not yet tried alcohol, and to even think of injecting myself with some strange drug or swallowing down colorful exotic pills went beyond every nerve in my body. Being the only virgin at school was another embarrassing realization which loomed high over my head—enough to make me even less than special. It seemed that every girl at school had been touched, handled, mishandled, and done to what any guy could possibly think of doing to a girl. I suspected some locker room stories were over-exaggerated tales of conquest. But still, they couldn't have all been far from the truth. For some girls would do almost anything to get what they wanted, and I couldn't help but feel that every guy at school was a "stud," an experienced love junky and conqueror of women…while I was left to wonder what it was like to really be with a girl.

"Hey, guess what?" Tamara asked as she came into my room. She'd just gotten home from her first day of school. Though still immature in her naïve little way, she did appear surprisingly older and wiser, just as I had in the eighth grade.

"What?" I replied as I kept my back turned. Thoughts of today's school day continued to dwell within my mind. Aimlessly, I sorted my art supplies and tried best I could to reorganize what I could on my desk. I showed her very little interest. No news could top my day, certain she would not be interested in hearing about Desiree or about the Wall of Fame.

"I'm on the cheerleading squad," she said enthusiastically. "I just signed up today. The coach said I'd be perfect."

"They have cheerleading in junior high now?" I asked.

"Of course," she sputtered, as if I'd insulted her. "It's not like high school cheerleading though. We're just like dance girls, that's all."

I finally turned to face her. Tamara's shady-brown eyes were like Mother's, shaped like big droplets with eyelashes as long as those of a baby doll. Her brownish-blonde hair hung down her back and was full and swirly, like spaghetti with no sauce. Her figure was still rather slender, but every day it developed more and more like Mother's. She wasn't even in high school yet, and already it was evident she could snatch away any boy's heart at will, with the option of either breaking... or less likely, cherishing.

"Dad's not gonna let you be a cheerleader," I told her. I looked into her eyes with no fear at all.

"Yes, he will," she returned. "All I have to do is show him I can get good grades, and he'll let me do anything."

By now she had learned Dad was a softy when it came to sweet, appealing voices, never able to say no when she sat on his lap and filled his cheeks with hundreds of kisses as she pleaded for things like going to the movies with her friends—or for Friday night sleepovers at her friend Jenny's house.

"You've never gotten good grades," I said. "What makes you think you'll be able to change now?"

"Well," she stalled, her smile coming at me in all directions, "the only class I always have trouble in is math. If I could get through math, I know I could breeze through all my other classes. Do you think you could help me, Marlo? I'm starting pre-algebra this year, and I know you're pretty good at that stuff."

She was incorrect. I was not good at math. But I had somehow survived Geometry. Like Dad, I couldn't turn down those pleading eyes and cute little face that resembled my mother's so much. I agreed to help her. I did still feel bad for getting her in trouble that night, when all of Gracie's actions made everything seem so pre-ordained. It may have been a sign of weakness on my part to give in, but I felt I was in control of the situation. I didn't feel manipulated.

"I'll get through it on my own," she said confidently, "but you'll have to tutor me good."

"I will, little sis," I said gladly, turning back around and continuing to rearrange my art supplies.

"You're the best brother I have."

"I'm the only brother you have," I replied, sensing she was trying to compliment me only because I'd agreed to tutor her.

"Okay, fine. You're the best brother a sister could ever have."

Now I was sold, touched by a warmth I so much needed yet not always knew was missing in my life. I stopped what I was doing, shocked to hear her say that for the first time ever. *Does she really mean that, or is this just another one of her tricks to get what she wants?* When I turned back to face her, I saw a fairly genuine smile, the kind I'd seen around Dad many times. It made me wonder. "You really think so?" I asked, frightened that she would say she was just joking and take it all back.

"Of course. You're not like all my other friends' brothers who treat their sisters like shit. You're pretty cool even though you do get out of hand sometimes and I could just kill you...But nah, I could never kill you. I'd miss you too much."

By far, these were the nicest words she'd ever said to me. Maturity was the only explanation I could think of. Her last year at Beach Junior High and already she was acting like all there was left to do was give into sincerity. How would she act in a few years? I could hardly wait.

"You're just saying that 'cause I agreed to help you," I stated, hoping again she'd deny this accusation and affirm that she really meant what she was saying.

"No, I'm not," she said. "I care about you, and I know you must care about me at least a little, right?"

Now I really had her right where I wanted her. "Yeah, I care about you. I'm just kinda surprised to hear you say all these nice things about me." I looked at the painting above my bed then back at Tamara. "Hey, do you think I'm out of it...you know, strange—from a different world?"

"I don't know what you mean," she responded.

"I'm not like any other guy you've come across, am I?" I felt awkward asking her since she was still very young and had not come across too many guys my age yet. I figured any kind of feedback was okay at this point—especially while she was still in this delightful state of mind.

"No, you're not like other guys," she said, sitting on my unmade bed, "but I don't think that's being strange. You're just different, that's all. It's kinda weird sometimes how you like to stay in here and paint all day instead of going out and having a good time. You never go to any parties or like any girls. A lot of my friends' older sisters think you're really nice, ya know, but you don't have any interest in them...I don't see why not. I don't think it's 'cause you're gay or anything. It's just weird, that's all."

"Is that why I'm weird?" I asked, afraid she had sunk the thread straight through the eye of the needle, "'cause I don't date or go to parties?"

"Not that weird," she assured, "just weird to anyone who loves going to parties and who isn't a virgin." She chuckled. I remained silent, making believe I hadn't heard her last remark. As always, she knew how to put me into difficult predicaments—knew how to push all the right buttons. How could I defend myself when being a virgin was like having some kind of dreadful disease? I felt cornered and wanted to get off the subject before she started making a bigger deal of it. "Another thing," she added, "you take things too seriously and worry too much about the wrong things. You know, Marlo, you're getting to be just like Dad."

I didn't know whether this was good or bad. Dad knew the answers to everything, but then again, Tamara did have a point. Dad did take things too seriously. I never thought she'd noticed so much. She usually kept to herself, since she thought her problems were the only ones present in life. Of course, I also kept to myself—maybe even more so.

"You're not strange, Marlo. You're just your own person...Yeah, that's it. You're your own person, and no one can understand you 'cause there's no one else like you." She put that rather easily. I couldn't argue with her, knowing she was probably right. She looked at the painting above my bed and added, "You see what I mean?" she pointed. "Only you could understand what you painted there. Sometimes when you're not home and I come in here to borrow your coloring pens, I look at all these pictures, and I say to myself: 'I can't believe I have a brother who can do all this neat stuff.' It's strange 'cause the more I look at one of your paintings, the harder it gets to turn away. It makes me wonder how something so nice can be so hard to understand." She took a deep breath before continuing. "Sometimes I wish I could do stuff like this."

Here she was, admiring what I did best—and even wishing she had my abilities, this "gift." She was right. I wasn't strange, just different. For some reason, that made me feel so much better. I was good at something, and not everyone could do what I could. I wasn't really living on a place like the moon. I was a part of the same world everyone else lived in, of the same grain and of the same soul—only different in shape, size, and talent. I was beginning to feel the fame Danny must have felt on the track field, or Ivan on stage with his guitar—only there were no screams or shouts. But all of a sudden, that seemed okay.

"You must be really smart," she continued, "if you can make sense out of all these paintings that look so simple but still hard to figure out."

"You know what, little sis?"

"What?" her girlish voice asked.

"You're the best sister I have."

"Hey, watch it. I'm the only sister you have."

"Okay, so you're the best sister a brother could ever have. Let's keep it that way."

The front door opened and slammed shut just then, making our walls shake and windows rattle. Dad's deep forceful voice hollered away, "Oh, you can't fool me. I saw the way he looked at you. And I saw the way you smiled back at him through the mirror." Dad paused. "And you still deny your lowlife tramp ways."

Mother responded in the same loud tone, "You take that back!" Her voice broke as it screeched into an awful cry. "I'm tired of your insults, tired of you making me feel like I'm cheap."

"You are cheap. I'm sorry for saying it, but that's just the way it is. You go down there every day and make me out to be a damn fool—like I've never worked hard for you, like you've never loved me—like I could never be enough for you. You don't need to be having that job. And you don't need to be cutting no man's hair. Next thing you know, you'll be doing other things."

A sudden chill broke through my room. It was enough to freeze and cover up this day which, up to that point, had been picture perfect. I was sure Dad was only protecting himself against this pain women appeared to wield throughout the world, of this anguish that would never leave his side. Had Mother harmed him long ago as Gracie had apparently harmed Danny? Or had another woman broken his heart so badly that now he had to act so forceful to protect himself so not to allow Mother the chance of letting his hopes down? It appeared evident she was hurting him. But it was not like she was purposely trying to be mean and make his life miserable, was she? Oh, how I hated such moments. Despite this perfect day, more than anything, I wished for this pretend world that obviously did not exist, and if it did exist—to never disappear as it was now. Tamara and I stood in silence as their words wrestled in torment.

"Stop it," Mother yelled. She couldn't keep her voice from drowning. Her weeps were fast and deep, her breaths more like gasps. "I hate you. I hate you so much."

"Hate me?" Dad responded. "You think that's gonna solve anything? You know how much it bothers me to see you work there, to see you around other men. You think I'm being self-centered just 'cause I feel this way. You think hating me's gonna hurt me any more than you already hurt me?"

"I'm leaving for good," Mother said. "One day you won't find me around. I'll go somewhere where I can be free and do whatever I want— and have whatever I want."

"What don't you already have?" Dad exploded, pleading in many ways. "You have a house, a husband who loves you—although you may not think so. You've got two kids. You buy whatever you want. You go wherever you want."

Tamara and I felt that eerie silence continue to force its way through the house. "Don't you touch me," we heard Mother say. "I don't want your hugs. I don't want your bullshit anymore. I'm too cheap. You remember that." Her footsteps tapped a most familiar rhythm as they rushed out of the living room, her cries fading as her room door shut behind her.

"Damn! Why do I love that woman so much?" Dad remarked aloud, as if someone were there to answer. "Why can't she understand?"

Tamara turned her attention back at me and said, "God, I hate it when they fight."

"Same here," I said with no real emotion. By now, I'd learned how to swallow up the pain their fighting always induced, realizing I could never really hide from it—but rather just pretend it really wasn't there.

"I'm gonna go and talk to Mom," she whispered. "She feels kinda bad right now. I sure hope I won't have to go through any of this when I get married."

"Tam, wait..." She turned and looked at me from the threshold. "What do you and she talk about when you're alone in her room?"

"Nothing you should be interested in," she acknowledged. "Just girl talk, that's all."

12

"**D**on't we look pretty today," Ivan said when he walked into my room early the next morning. I had on my best khakis and a crisp, clean white-collared shirt, a bit nervous as I anticipated seeing Desiree Castillo in biology class again. I could not imagine anything going right. I had embarrassed myself the day before, and even the thought of facing her again made me question what little courage I had.

I struggled through the last bit of Mrs. Wardell's homework assignment. Most of the chapter review questions were right out of the book, but the answers were long, and I knew copying directly from the text would not sit well with Mrs. Wardell. Paraphrasing was even harder when I had a limited knowledge and apathetic attitude towards science.

"What's that smell?" Ivan asked.

"My Dad's after-shave," I replied.

"Smells like bathroom cleaner. Seriously, what's with the pretty boy look?"

I looked at him without any answer, trying not to let on, but as always, Ivan jumped to the right conclusions. He smiled. "Are we in love, little boy?"

The touch of humor in his voice caught me off guard. "It's not what you think." I closed the heavy biology text and stuffed it and my three-page chapter review into my book bag. I couldn't begin to explain about Desiree and how she sparked this side of me which had never before been touched or defined. Ivan wouldn't understand if I'd told him I saw something more in her than just her pretty face. That would have sounded too familiar, sounded like Danny.

"That's what I thought. So who's the lucky girl?"

"It's no one," I assured him.

"Sure, it's no one," he shot back. He smacked my right cheek hard a couple of times. His fingers stuck to the smoothness of my skin, further irritating my face as Dad's after-shave settled deeper into my pores. He laughed as he said, "Just don't let your heart get confused with your dick."

By now, most streets were free of puddles and as dry as desert sand. I felt this would be another good day, free of rain and full of bright sunny skies.

Beach High was lifeless as we approached, a bit eerie given the fact we'd never been on campus so early. The administration offices remained dark and lifeless, as did other offices and classrooms around Main Hall. One of the custodians had just unlocked the parking lot as the first car ventured onto the desolate expanse of the blacktop. An early-morning school bus was barely on its way for its first daily route.

"I brought an extra lock for Danny," said Ivan. We'd each had our lockers next to each other dating back to grade school and expected that this year would be no different. Again I refrained from telling Ivan about Danny and his obsession with Gracie. I had faith Danny would show up today and believed everything would be as it was—with no memory of there ever being a girl named Gracie.

I looked across Dance Hall and noticed Mr. Parlante's light on. I had not yet seen him since last term and had not yet thought of the right words to thank him for acknowledging my talent ever so extravagantly. "I'll be back," I told Ivan. "Make sure and get us some good lockers."

I crossed the grassy open field surrounded by tall trees and rotted-wooden lunch tables. Much of the grass was rooted in muddy dirt, and the trees seemed forlorn with fallen leaves around their trunks. I avoided some of the muddy sod by bracing myself against the lunch tables and the big stage which connected Chatter Hall to Dance Hall. Everyone referred to this stage as Shame's Fame. It was where the Drama Club performed some of its smaller plays and skits during lunch. Others used the stage for pep rallies, debates, Spirit Week, open mike day, and student body elections.

I knocked on Mr. Parlante's door as I turned the knob. The room was unlocked. He was seated quietly near the large windows overlooking the field and stage, dipping dirty paintbrushes into water and a soapy-brown solvent. Soothing classical music softly caressed my ears, and a slight repugnant smell of turpentine pinched my nose. The usual twenty wooden tripods surrounded the two large worktables in the center of the room. Bombarding images of artwork dating back decades before my time chanted their glory in every way. Handcrafted wooden figurines and sculptured miniatures made of stone and pewter seemed to jump at you from surrounding shelves. Ceramic dolls, ashtrays, and pottery lay forgotten on upper-top, overcrowded compartments, yet still clamored for undivided attention. Walls resembled those of my bedroom as images of water and oil colored paintings blitzed my vision and took me into another time and era when art was truly defined by a limitless inner heart and soul. Splattered-stained paint passively decorated the old, worn discolored linoleum beneath me. The ceiling above was covered with spray-painted images of old, outdated graffitied mascot insignias, emblems, and school logos. Paint bottles, colored pencils, and other art materials enveloped Mr. Parlante's desk. In the glass compartments behind the desk were more art supplies and fleshly washed rags and towels. I couldn't help but feel so at home.

He turned to see me, his eyes squinting as he looked over his black-framed bifocals. The thick mustache above his broad, dried lips matched his shoulder long gray-streaked hair. His many years of teaching were clearly noticeable. Deeply etched wrinkles outlined most of his face, even before he smiled to say hello. He stood up, his untucked checkered Pendleton dropping over his waist, making his stumpy build seem even shorter. His casual appearance was deceiving, though his intellect and eloquence showed whenever he spoke. "Marlo," he said as he stuck out his hand, "I hope your summer was a good one."

"The rain was a pain," I said as I shook his dry callused hand. "I just wanted to thank you so much for having me up on the Wall."

"You have no one to thank. Your painting *Weeping Prince* is quite unique and simply defines a great talent. Rarely do I get a true genuine artist such as you anymore. Most take my class as a way out of daily routines. I welcome that. But most are lost, lacking vision and sentimental feel of a true artist."

"You're one of few teachers I've ever had that's understood my desire to express myself the only way I know how, Mr. Parlante."

"There's nothing to understand," he said as he shook his head. His eyes left mine. "What you are is a reflection of the world around us. Most people are simply common and live in a world devoid of the real beauty, horror, sadness, and joy as it really exists in this world of unlimited boundaries and possibilities. It's only people such as yourself, through your passion and delicate feel, that remind us all of the world we seem to take for granted—or simply overlook altogether."

"I express myself in other ways, too," I told him. "But not many people understand or seem to connect. I not only spend hours in my room painting, I also spend hours on the beach, building sandcastles. My friends think it's a waste of time. They say why waste time on things that fall and do not last forever."

"I haven't seen your sandcastles," Mr. Parlante responded. "But I'm sure they are as magical as some of the work I've seen you do in class." He looked around the upper walls. I too looked around the room and again marveled at all the works of talented painters who had long since stepped through Mr. Parlante's room—talented impressionists, abstract expressionists, realists, and liberal and conservative detailists who all viewed the world differently, who held different passions—who all told different stories.

"Look out at the trees," Mr. Parlante said as he pointed to the windows. The once green leaves I remembered before summer break had now turned reddish yellow, a reminder that autumn was just around the corner. Some floated off branches and onto the ground. Some parked themselves carelessly onto the lunch tables and the stage. "The leaves fall and die just as the sandcastles you build. Soon the seasons will change and more leaves will grow back. What we will always have, however, is the memory and hope of new beginnings and endings. Remember that you possess a talent no one can ever take away. You have the ability to touch souls—to enchant…and this, Marlo, lasts forever."

He lifted up a printed sheet of fine thin paper. "This is a work a student gave me from one of the graphic arts courses." The picture was that of a man's face surrounded by brightly colored objects made to resemble different faces in the background. The colors were amazing— ones I'd never seen before.

"It's really good," I exclaimed.

"Oh, don't let yourself be fooled. Yes, this is a good artist—but not a true one. His talent can be taken away. These are shapes, colors, and images created by someone else—a programmer who believes there is a limited set of possible shapes and definitions—of limited feel and precision. This student was guided by someone else's limited vision and appeal of a non-existent limited world of possibilities. The world you live in—the one you recognize, the one you bring out into the open, is unending and striking to the soul. I'm sure your sandcastles do last forever, Marlo."

He was quite profound, made everything seem complex yet fit together like a simple puzzle I had yet to piece together.

"I'm sad to say, Marlo," he said as he turned back to the paintbrushes which were piled in the small sink below the window, "that one day there will be no more traditional art classes left to teach here at Beach—or any other school for that matter. With students drawn and flocking into these newly designed computer courses, my room will soon disappear."

Unlike other classrooms, this one had no computer or television monitors. Mr. Parlante still kept his attendance records by hand. He never believed in video demonstrations and had always preferred guest speakers and live demonstrations over videos and films.

"All that you see here will be taken down," he went on, "the tripods burned—the room renovated and reconfigured to make way for computers and programs which will further hide that which is truly limitless and real. You, Marlo, are of a dying breed, one of few who has discovered this limitless world. This is why you feel few around you understand…There are others like yourself—though they are not as fortunate to discover this magic that lies within them. Hidden is their power as it is taken over by others who claim a pre-defined technical world."

By now more students had descended upon campus. The first bell was still a half an hour away, though many were also early for lockers, books, ID picture cards, and library cards. I stumbled onto Ivan as many rushed to vacant lockers and endless lines outside the administration building and library. Ivan had managed to secure three usable lockers in Main Hall, a perfect location, as the proximity was adjacent to all halls and not far from the lunch area. We soon scrambled to the long lines outside the library and waited until finally a photographer digitally snapped our photos. Our library and school ID cards were processed in seconds.

We spotted Kelly as we left the library. I had not seen her since the night of the concert. She was dressed in a nice blue low-cut blouse that matched her blue-bottomed P.E. sweatpants. She handed us a colorful flyer to her upcoming birthday party.

"You guys better come," she said.

I looked at the rainbow-colored invitation. Printed at the top were my name, Ivan's name, and Danny's.

"We're there," said Ivan.

"You're parents are actually gonna let you throw a party?" I asked. Kelly lived in an extravagantly large home, not far from Danny. It overlooked the bay and was practically the only home on the street, as the property's extensive acreage took up most of the surrounding area. Ivan and I had ventured past it only once. It was one of few neighborhoods besides Danny's where we were allowed to trick or treat on Halloween night. The neighborhood also attracted many tourists during the Christmas season, as an incredible array of lights decorated every home and tree in the vicinity.

"My parents won't be home," Kelly responded. "They trust me. Besides, only people I know are invited. Make sure you let Danny know. I just saw him walking out by the field." She rushed to greet others in the halls, handing out more of the same colorful flyers.

"She's like the sweetest thing," Ivan commented as we headed towards the field. "I wish I didn't like her so much. It kinda hurts knowing she doesn't feel the same."

"You don't really know that," I said, surprised to hear Ivan be so negative. But then again, I couldn't blame him. Everything about liking a girl seemed dismal.

"Oh, I know she doesn't feel the same. I can feel it in her eyes."

Feel it in her eyes. Maybe Kelly too had Desiree's eyes—only it was Ivan who could see and feel their magic…But that would have made Desiree just another girl, and that was something my heart felt she was not.

The track field was a ways away, difficult to distinguish Danny from others who were on the field. As we trudged through the muddy gravel, I thought back to the track meet last spring which saw the school win its first league championship and enter into the state finals. Dade High School was highly favored to beat us and go on to win state. In only his sophomore year, Danny anchored the 4 x 100 relay race. He had lost the long jump competition and the one hundred meter dash by inches but managed to win the two hundred, his favorite race of all. The relay event was Beach High's final opportunity to win. Johnny Garza took a quick lead for Beach. Everyone cheered with excitement, including our principal and secretary who managed to take time off from their duties to watch the competition. Dade's second legman pulled ahead. Irwin Pacheco, Beach's third leg, evened the race, but when he handed Danny the baton, it slipped and fell to the ground. It was Dade's race to win. But unfortunately for Dade, Beach High did not have an all-weather track. Recent rains had made the track damp and slippery. Dade's anchorman lost his footing and nearly fell as he sped off. Danny caught up and pulled ahead to take the race. It was the biggest upset anyone had ever seen. Everyone on the bleachers went crazy, and it seemed the hurrahs would never end despite losing the very next week in the state finals to a team from Orlando.

There were no cheers or endless chants for Danny or the rest of the team on this day, however. He was seated quietly on one of the bleachers facing the field, passive and silent in his thoughts. He failed to acknowledge our calls as we approached. Instead, he got up and began to walk away. It was then that we noticed his definite change. He appeared pale in comparison to white sands or angels sent from heaven, his face as expressionless as a cadaver in the city morgue and his posture drooped like a flimsy sack of potatoes. The clothes that had fit perfect months ago now hung on him like loose window curtains blowing softly in the wind, and they too appeared soiled and dirty. His hair had gone uncut and seemed displaced in endless knots. Now I wished I had told Ivan. But I had hoped…hoped Dad and the rest of certainty could be wrong.

"Long time no talk," said Ivan as we caught up.

Danny didn't respond. He did stop but continued in his quiet trance. Red streaks pervaded his eyes, and dark rings encircled his eyelids. He really did look hurt and distraught, keeping his hushed gaze affixed on the field, apathetic and speechless to our presence, perhaps wishing we had not found him. Oh, to see Danny ignore us and appear almost dead made my heart nearly sink to the bottom of the ocean. As I thought back to the night of the concert and having seen her with that other guy, there was no doubt in my mind Gracie was to blame for my best friend's appearance and apparent misery.

"Hey, man, what's wrong? You all right? You've looked better." Ivan peppered Danny with more questions. "Where've you been? Why haven't you kept in touch? What's with your phone being disconnected?"

Danny simply turned and walked away, still deep in silence and still in his malignant trance.

I tried holding Ivan back, but he fought off my hand. He ran up to Danny and tapped him hard. "Wait. Where are you going?"

This time Danny spun around and pushed Ivan back. Ivan took a few steps back, nearly losing his balance. "LEAVE ME ALONE!" Danny roared as he continued on his way.

Ivan was more shocked than anything else. He stood there for a moment deciding whether to blow up or just stay disenchanted in his thoughts. He was not one to ever keep anything bottled up. He hated when things made no sense, hated the thought of being the victim or cause of anyone else's debacle. As usual, his temper got the better of him as he grabbed hold of a nearby garbage can which he flung in Danny's direction. It hit the ground and bounced past Danny. Danny did nothing more than keep his even stride. Ivan stormed after him. Luckily, I managed to grab hold of him with both my arms. Neither of them could afford to be suspended from school, I thought.

"Let me go!" Ivan bellowed, struggling to free himself from my grasp. "I'll show him."

"No!" I said firmly. He continued to struggle, but I held on as tightly as I could until I saw Danny was far enough away. Ivan was so much tougher than I was. I did not know where I mustered up the strength to restrain him. My arms burned as my muscles flexed feverishly.

"All right, all right. Just let me go." He finally calmed, his face dimming from its boiling red appearance.

"Leave him alone," I said. My arms were relieved as they relaxed and unknotted. "He doesn't want to be bothered."

"What the hell's wrong with him? I didn't do anything to him."

"It's nothing you did," I assured.

"That boy is sick, Mar. Did you see him?" He brushed down his T-shirt and looked back in Danny's direction, still tempted to run up after him and start a fight.

"Remember that girl Gracie?" I asked, not knowing how to exactly reveal what I knew.

"What about her?" he replied abruptly, seemingly uninterested in hearing what I had to say.

"What would you say if you knew Danny had tried getting back together with her?"

"Why would he want to do something like that for?"

"I'm not really sure if they really got back together, but I do know Danny fell for her again. But this time it was worse."

He gathered his thoughts as he turned and looked my way. Calmly he went back and sat on one of the bleachers. "You serious? He fell for that skank again after what she did that one time?"

"Yeah," I said.

"Figures. Didn't he learn the first time around, doesn't he know when to stay away?" He kept silent for a moment, perhaps remembering that Danny was just one of many blind fools Gracie could have hexed her spells over. His face tamed as calmness seemed to extinguish the last of his steam.

"I've only told you half the story," I let him know. I paused before going on, not knowing how to spill everything out and still make sense of it all. "Remember how Danny got Day on the Green tickets for Kelly?"

"Yeah, she told me at the mall."

"Well, he did end up getting tickets, but he never sold them to Kelly as promised. He gave them away to Gracie instead."

"Gave them away?" Again, he went silent. "He wouldn't fall that low."

"Somehow Gracie found out Danny had tickets. She came up to him all nice, with some story about a cousin of hers who was dying to go to the concert. I guess she must have made it sound like she wanted to be his girlfriend again and suckered him into giving her the tickets…But that's not the worst of it. The day of the concert I went riding by the stadium and saw Gracie waiting in line to get in. Only, she wasn't with no cousin. I saw her with that same guy I'd seen her with before—and she was kissing him, passionately like."

His eyes shifted as he moved his head side to side in utter disbelief. Disgusted, he said, "That's so low, man. Fucked, totally fucked!"

"The next thing I know, I can't get a hold of Danny anywhere. And I just know he's ruined because of Gracie," I said so sure of myself. "I don't think he could have helped it though. I mean, he would have done any stupid little thing for her."

"You're right. He would have done any stupid little thing. I should have known he wouldn't give up on her so easily. That's the thing with Danny. He thinks just 'cause some girl's nice to him and gets all lovey-dovey with him that she's this dream kinda girl." He got up from the bleachers and walked back onto the field. "She ain't no dream."

"Hey, where're you going?"

"I don't know," he said. "I'm just gonna walk around for awhile…I just don't know about losing a friend, if you know what I mean. See you in class."

I didn't know who was more shaken up—Ivan or myself. There didn't appear much either of us could do. Danny seemed lost, caught in an endless maze of pain. I wished for a bandage to put over his deepening wounds—or maybe give him some of that juice Mother used to give me when I'd hurt and scrape my skin as a little kid. But I realized this was no simple scrape or ache Mother could soothe with sips of sweet juice.

Again, Dad seemed flawless. Again he seemed right. Girls were the worst.

13

If there were any way of being certain about anything, it would not have been life and its implications we sometimes mistake as genuine representations of what we want, don't want, hate—love.

Danny didn't show to class. Mr. Bernard called his name and marked him absent for a second straight day. Ivan walked in late, well after the bell had rung. He handed Mr. Bernard a tardy pass and sat in a crouched position at the far end of the classroom, paying little attention to our lecture on early Colonial America. I thought he may have run into Danny and gotten into a fight, but that was unlikely since they both would have been immediately suspended.

"I feel kinda sorry for him," he told me after class. "I wish I would have known sooner."

"I was meaning to tell you, but I didn't think he'd go and take things so hard. I thought Danny honestly knew what he was doing."

He didn't say anything after that. He just made his way to second period.

An office aide brought in my call slip sooner than expected. Mrs. Hansell, my Spanish teacher, handed it to me right when I walked into class. My own writing on the slip read, *Mrs. Canizaro, please save me from A.I. Biology.* As I headed to the administration building, I regretted having written it, for I now desperately wanted to remain in biology. Although it seemed Mrs. Wardell would be a very hard and demanding teacher, I wanted no more than follow my instincts and be as near to this Desiree Castillo girl whose enchanting eyes told me she was different. If not for the entire year, then for just another day.

"Marlo Clemente," Mrs. Canizaro commented slowly to herself as she scrolled down her screen. "Let me see...how could this have happened?" Not once did her eyes slip away from the monitor. Her loud orange hair lit up the room. I had never come face to face with Mrs.

Canizaro before. My schedules had always been accurate and complete, and since I was not enrolled in the alternative program or the college prep program, I remained one of few who lingered amidst a predictable limbo. She appeared no different than any other overworked school staff member. Her job was quite stressful and demanding, her daily life accustomed to little or no one-on-one intimate interactions. She had little time for remembering names, and thus, I suspected I'd be no more than a simple number that popped up on a computer screen every so often to remind her that indeed I did exist, that yes I was real and of this world. I remained silent as I stood at the edge of the door. There was no place in her office to sit. The chair across from her desk was full of papers, and file folders were stacked a mile high. The floor was cluttered with boxes and more file folders piled above those. Her shelves were full of old law books and volumes of the state education code. Some of the books had even made their way off the shelves and piled up on the windowsill, blocking most of the sunlight and view from the only window in the office.

"I was hoping I could just stay in biology," I said.

"But you're not in the college bound program. A.I. courses are for students heading to four year colleges and universities," she explained. "There are prerequisites, and the curriculum is much more demanding." She continued to scroll up and down her screen. "Well…" She paused and for the first time looked straight at me. Her oily complexion gleamed as though it were covered with cooking oil, as did her neck and shoulders. Her hands were the only parts of her body which seemed dry, wrinkled, and overworked. Veins protruded thin layers of wrinkled skin, and her fingernails were yellowed and frail. "All lower level science courses are full. The only thing open is Computer Arts I."

"No, I wouldn't want to do that," I immediately let her know.

Her eyes went back to her screen, not once inquiring why I did not want to join those many artists who'd made computer arts their home. "There's still time…" she said after a long moment of studying my profile. "You could still sign up for the college bound program. Did your mother or father go to college?" She handed me some forms for my parents to fill out and sign.

"No," I replied, not knowing what my mother or father had to do with me going to college.

"Ah, well then. You can be the first in your family. You're grades here are not that bad, and you've already completed most general graduation requirements…"

"I don't know about college," I said. I figured my destiny had long since been set, conceding that I'd end up working for Dad and helping him build magnificent homes and buildings—buildings which would never fall. Continuing with school was not something that had ever crossed my mind, nor had my parents ever brought it up. All I wanted at the moment was to stay in biology and keep next to this girl whose eyes told me I should. What was I getting myself into? College bound? Never in my wildest dreams.

She handed me some brochures from the University of Miami, Florida State, and then I looked at the one from the Art Academy. The Art Academy. Wow. I had never thought about pursuing an art career. Even if I was as talented as Mr. Parlante (and Ms. Varian before him) said I was, I always thought my ability was *passé*—a hobby, nothing to ever take seriously. I thought I'd one day simply outgrow my paintings and sandcastles, just as I'd outgrown my coloring books and electric train sets long ago. Maybe this was it, my calling. Perhaps the Art Academy here in Miami could help me tap more into this "gift" that for so long lay hidden from the rest of the world.

"Thanks, Mrs. Canizaro," I said with a smile as wide as an endless shoreline. Barely could I keep my eyes off the brochures.

"Have your mother or father fill out those forms," she said. "And please do give them back to me. Yes, you will have to survive Mrs. Wardell's class, and you'll also have to take some other demanding courses this year and next. But at least now I'll have you on my list, and I can check up to see how you're doing every now and then."

I walked out in a daze and sat on the nearest bench outside the administration building. Fresh bright beaming rays of sun accompanied me as I flipped through the brochure. Inside were numerous art programs and art majors to meet just about anyone's ability and interest. There was even a traditional arts program. Reluctantly, I filled out my portion of the forms, left blanks where my mother or father would have to sign, hesitating with each page but somehow managing to find it in me to fill them out blindly—not really knowing if I would ever follow through. Mother wouldn't understand if I tried telling her about going to art school. She'd never before questioned my talents or dreams...We were distant, always like strangers on a subway. And Dad, well, he wouldn't even care. He'd never marveled over my artwork in the past. All he cared about was pride and certainty. He was certain I'd one day take his place as owner of his business, certain I would never dream past his accomplishments.

The bell marking the end of second period blared. In seconds, students crowded hallways and walkways as many rushed to lockers and vending machines and then onto third.

Aside from Danny, this had not been such a bad morning. I was so happy having met with Mrs. Canizaro. Not only would I stay in Mrs. Wardell's class and see Desiree again, never before had I been so sure of where I wanted to be—so sure of where my heart really lay. For the first time, I came closer to touching the real Marlo. For the first time…I could say I was an artist.

Mrs. Wardell sat at her desk. The classroom was quiet as again I was one of the first to arrive. She looked at me, and I nodded a hello to her, but she gave no reaction. Her serious face went back to her textbook. I sat at my desk quietly as I pulled my chapter review from my binder.

Desiree soon walked into the class. Again she stood out above the rest. She looked very pretty in her mauve colored skirt and blouse, her skin so immaculately smooth—as smooth as wet, untouched, sandy seashores. She sat next to me but didn't say anything. She pulled out her notebook and prepared herself for class. I sat quietly waiting to say anything, anything to let her know I was alive and real. Mrs. Wardell got up and commenced writing notes on the board as the rest of the class poured in. Desiree jotted down everything. I should have been doing the same thing; but instead, I looked down into her bag and saw a few other notebooks and a thick book, *East of Eden*. Not part of Ms. Farren's reading list, I thought. What was this girl really like? Suddenly, I imagined myself loving her, like Danny loved Gracie. Then I imagined what it would be like if she went off with another guy. I could see her laughing because I was such a loving fool. I could see her enjoying herself with her other boyfriend and only recognizing me for whatever materialistic things I had to offer. I could see her never really caring about me while I would be working hard to give her the world. And when I'd turn and look around me, all I'd find would be an empty fool's paradise. She wouldn't know that I'd sulk or hurt, nor would she even care if I drank her poison to show her my love. Was this what Danny was already going through? If it was, as much as I may have been enamored, it was best I somehow discard my feelings.

Class ended before I knew it, and I walked out without saying a word to Desiree. From the doorway, I looked on as she remained behind putting her books into her bag. I was perplexed, hating that I actually liked her so much—hating what Gracie had done to Danny, and hating that I could actually bring myself to ever doubt Dad.

I knew what I had to do next. Staying in Mrs. Wardell's class no longer mattered if I wasn't going to follow through with the forms. I waited for the perfect opportunity. Dad was usually home from work late on Tuesdays, and Mother usually busied herself in the kitchen during the early evening hours.

"These are forms you have to sign," I said to her as I handed her a pen and the first of five sheets.

As expected, she turned her attention from the stove and signed with few inquiries. "What's this I'm signing?" was all she asked.

"Just a permission slip so I can take some advanced art classes in school," I replied. She handed me back my pen and forms and turned her attention back to our dinner. The hardest part was over. All I needed to do now was go back to Mrs. Canizaro and hand her the forms. But it wasn't easy to turn and walk away. Oh, how I wanted to tell Mother about my wanting to continue on to art school, how I wanted to reach out and tell her about my passionate artistic side, of my induction into the Wall of Fame, and my dream of one day touching the world like no one ever had. I looked at her as she silently peered into different pots and pans. Was I really just a stranger? Did my existence not extend beyond simple hellos and goodbyes? Would I ever stand atop this world and say I had a mother who really loved me, and I her? Again, I nearly shed a tear, but my pride soon squashed this weakening inner calling I so desperately wanted to submit to.

She turned but did not notice I had been looking at her in quiet, teary thoughts.

"Food's almost done."

"I'm not hungry." My voice nearly broke as I left the kitchen. I disguised my discontent long enough to reach my room where I would dive deep into an endless night of biology homework. A tear did fall, but I had my dream, and that was enough to carry me until yet another empty sunrise.

By week's end, I already hated biology. Mrs. Wardell was assigning large amounts of reading assignments and annoying pop quizzes. I stayed up nearly all night that first week just to complete assignments I would later earn low scores in. I wasn't sure where I stood with Mrs. Wardell, although there were those students she seemed to like—and those who seemed to irritate her. Those who didn't do their assignments or those who didn't follow directions were the ones ridiculed and graded harder than all the rest. I tried to be as obedient as possible, finally paying close attention to all her lectures and doing all my assignments as instructed. I feared being on Mrs. Wardell's bad side. It was bad enough knowing I wasn't really supposed to be in her class.

There were days Desiree came into class not as bright eyed as I'd seen her. I could only speculate what may have saddened her so. Her eyes no longer gleamed with the same charming glare. Her book bag appeared heavy and hung by her side like a massive ball and chain. She appeared dazed, her thoughts hidden, lost, her eyes a bit saddened—and this after having received one of the highest quiz scores in the class, an *A-* (the next highest grade being a *C+*). On other days, she'd come into class reading her *East of Eden* book. A couple of times she did give me a quick look and smile before burying her face deep within its pages. She really liked to read and appeared to be alone in a world all to herself, much like I was when I painted or marveled with sand. We still had not spoken to each other. Nearly a week and not a single word. But it wasn't as awkward as it appeared. No one really talked in class. Mrs. Wardell forbade talking to each other when it wasn't necessary.

It no longer mattered that I was so infatuated, for I had very little time to be dazzled or enamored. I was too busy trying to survive class and caught up with this newfound hope of one day attending the Art Academy. Mrs. Wardell would be my first real obstacle to making all my dreams come true. I could ill afford to drown. Already I had failed my first two quizzes.

By Friday, Danny showed up to Ms. Farren's eighth period English class. Ivan and I were surprised. We thought he had dropped out of school and had chosen to forget about the rest of his life. He looked somewhat better, his face less gloomy as it'd been the other morning. Still, he did appear sick. His body was still frail from weight loss and his posture fallen, like that of an old withering tree—or a sandcastle that had been smacked by the largest of waves. He didn't acknowledge us or talk to anyone else in class. He chose to remain after the final bell and spend time with Ms. Farren catching up on missed homework assignments.

The sun was as bright as ever, everyone electrified by the start of the year's first weekend. Many headed to the beach after school, while others such as Ivan made their way to the field for the football team's first pre-season game. I gathered my books and made my way to the guidance office where I turned in the forms Mother had signed. I made my way off the school grounds happy that I was well on my way towards a definite goal, glad that I could now live and accept my passion and dream of one day being a full-fledged artist. I saw Desiree waiting for the bus, but she didn't see me. Her reading held her captive. I debated on whether I should say something to her, but I couldn't bring myself close enough to even say hello. Her eyes still intimidated me, could still very easily penetrate right through me. Her bus came, and she waited until everyone got on before shutting her book and stepping in.

I took the long way home, passing by the beach and strolling down Ocean Drive. City life never seemed to skip a beat. Restaurants and cafes were full, hotel lobbies and shops swarmed with tourists, cameramen, and businessmen. The shoreline was endless, with people seeming to be minute representations of this normal existence I'd always known as Miami Beach. I even spotted a small kid trying to piece together a sandcastle amongst strong currents and tumbling waves. I pondered over Danny, wondered if he was really doing better. Showing up to school for even just one period must have been a good sign. At least he was alive and combatant against these worst of heartaches and pain. I soon headed off Ocean Drive and made my way towards Danny's. I didn't know if trying to talk would do any good, but I decided on going anyway, to let him know I cared—to show him he still had a friend.

There was no response when I rang his doorbell. His mother's red Mercedes was parked in the driveway, but that wasn't always an indication of her being around. I myself had never seen much of her. Her airline job kept her away most of the time. Although she'd known me since grade school, there had never been any reason for our relationship to go beyond a hello or goodbye. She seemed distant like my Mother— although Mother was not a stewardess.

I tried the door once again. This time Ms. Skies answered. She had a bathrobe on, her hair wet and her face dripping with water.

"Marlo," she said as she smiled, her face much like Danny's and her hair the same shade of blond.

"Hi, Ms. Skies, is Danny in?"

"No. I don't really know where he is." She looked at me for a moment, hesitant to say any more. I felt like a cop investigating a homicide. "Actually," she said as I turned to leave, "why don't you come in for a minute. I'd like to talk with you…about Danny.

I waited in the living room as Ms. Skies went upstairs. The ceiling there was twice as high as the one in my home, and the furniture was of a fancy French or perhaps Spanish decor. Its design matched some of the frames holding up exquisite artworks on the wall above the marble mantel. A large crystal chandelier hung from the center of the ceiling, shooting off a colorful spectrum of light from its crystals as the sun's rays streamed through the large front window. Bookshelves covered the other tall walls around the room. They were filled with thick reference books, hardback novels, and leather-bound law books and encyclopedias.

Ms. Skies came down moments later dressed in a pair of casual jeans and a T-shirt. She was a rather large big-boned woman, at least five feet ten inches tall, not fat but rather husky around the thighs and shoulders. She was not as feminine as my mother, though her face displayed attractive features and Danny's same wide smile. She brushed through her heavy moistened hair as she sat across from me. "I'm sorry if I took so long," she said. "This shower did me good. I just came back from Egypt."

"Egypt?"

"Yes. It's hard to believe I can be in two different worlds all in one day. That's what's so great about my flying everywhere. If you're tired of one place, you can always look forward to another."

"The pyramids must be awesome," I said.

"From afar, they look like they're made of sand, like the rest of the surrounding area. When you're up close to them though, they look like giant works of art that took someone a lifetime to chisel away."

I loved what she was telling me. The pyramids had always fascinated me, for they were ancient and timeless, built to withstand withering elements and made to never crumble or ever fall.

"They're like the sandcastles Danny tells me you build at the beach," she said. "You can't believe they're actually there until you get close enough. And when you do, you wonder how they got there because it seems just too unbelievable to think that someone could actually build such things."

"Danny must tell you a lot," I said, wishing I could be so close with Mother.

"He does," she said calmly, "at least he used to—when he was still my son. I don't know him anymore...You know about his condition?"

"He doesn't look so good," I said reluctantly. "He's also been avoiding everyone and almost started a fight with Ivan when we tried talking to him. I never thought it was possible for a guy like Danny to ever know such grief." I felt like telling her what I knew of girls, of Gracie—how girls caused the worst of pains, how they changed your life, making you give up on friends, relatives, school, and other ambitious endeavors... But I hushed, as I realized that as a woman she would never have understood.

She didn't say anything. She looked away from me and turned her eyes to the great big window which displayed the bright perfect picturesque day. The garden outside buzzed with life. Butterflies, bumble bees, and hummingbirds danced and pranced from flower to flower. The pond in the front glistened as the light from the sun turned the water into majestic silver.

"He's also been missing school," I let her know.

"You really don't know what it's been like," she replied. Tears fell from her eyes as her gaze continued to focus on the window. "It started about a month ago. He didn't want to eat. Then he wouldn't come out of his room…He'd never acted this way before. I didn't know what was wrong with him. He wouldn't say anything to me. There was one night I thought he even died. He didn't want to open his door. I had to force my way in. I started yelling at him and carrying on like you'd never believe, but he just sat there in the dark with the windows and curtains shut, doing nothing. His mirror had *Gracie* written all over it with my red lipstick, and it was cracked from top to bottom. Nothing I said to him got through. He was like a dead wall." She stopped to wipe at her eyes.

I was quiet, not knowing what to say or do to make things better.

"After he had enough of staying in his room," she went on, "he started going out and wouldn't come home until very late. He stayed out the entire night one night. When I saw him that morning, he looked all beaten up, like he'd gotten into a fist fight…I didn't know what to do next." She spun her attention back at me. Her tears were real, her sobs felt miles away—perhaps all the way to Egypt. Broken she was, evident this had not been the first time she had cried over Danny's torment, had not been the first time she had tried to piece things together. "I just can't understand why he's stopped living life," she said bitterly, "not going on with his running, school, and friends. I wish his father were still alive. Why, he would have smacked sense into Danny by now. Danny's father was a strong individual, had a very strict upbringing. He was very successful in whatever he set his mind to. This kind of thing would have never happened to him."

Oh, the hypocrisy of it all. Why was she not mentioning anything about Gracie—the lipstick and the mirror? Why did she keep pointing everything at Danny? Naive my thoughts may have seemed—ignorant her tears were sure to have been…Could she not see Danny's pain was not anyone's fault but Gracie's? Sure, Danny was sensitive, a bit impulsive; he never had the father figure Ivan or I had. Surely Ms. Skies must have recognized the pain a girl could cause a guy. Surely she must have realized a girl could fool any guy—cause him to give up on friends, family, and everything else in life. Surely she herself must have busted some boy's heart apart in the past, a boy she'd left crying, aching—left hopeless as all he could do was cry her name in vain. Again I hushed, as I felt it would have been impossible for me to explain. I was not as bold as Dad, though I felt he'd already taken over most of my thoughts and dreams. "I tried calling," I said finally, "but there's never any answer or reply…Ivan and I didn't know he was in this bad of shape until he finally showed up to school."

"Danny dumped our phones into the toilet," she said. She blew her nose with tissue and wiped her eyes dry. "He hasn't wanted to see or talk to anyone. I finally decided to call a psychiatrist even though I don't believe in any of their work. I knew it would have been impossible to drag Danny down to a shrink, so I managed to get one to come to the house…At first, Danny wouldn't listen to anything the doctor had to say, but somehow the doctor got Danny to open the door and communicate. Since then, Danny's been eating and has had the courage to go back to school. The doctor says it'll be a while before Danny recovers from his depression and returns to his normal state."

"Danny should try and not talk to Gracie anymore," I suggested out of the blue.

"Oh, but she seems like such a nice girl," she commented. "She always seemed to make Danny happy. She was all he ever talked about, all he ever smiled about… She probably doesn't know Danny's been hurt."

"Ivan and I suspected she wasn't any good for him," I said, again trying my best to implicate Gracie as the source of Danny's pain. "We tried warning Danny about her, but he wouldn't listen. All he wanted was to spend time with her. It was Gracie this, Gracie that. I guess that's why he won't talk to Ivan or me. He's kinda afraid to admit we were right about Gracie being bad for him…I came over to see if I could talk to him and tell him that he's still our friend no matter what happens."

"That's so nice," she said smiling. "I hope you get to tell him that when he comes home, if he comes home…Some days I just think he won't ever show up anymore." Her tears fell again. She didn't say anything more about Gracie or suggest girls could be evil—nothing about why Danny's mirror may have had Gracie's name written over it, or why it had been cracked like a broken heart.

I stayed awhile longer, but Danny didn't show.

14

I did not look forward to the countless hours of homework which would crowd my weekend. To make matters worse, Tamara was having a sleepover. Boys, teen magazines, talk of clothes and music television were not part of my worldly focus. Privacy would be lost, nights coupled with loud music and endless giggling and snickering.

"Why don't you knock?" I blurted as Tamara stormed in and stripped the old discolored sheet off my easel. She and her friends had been at the mall all day Saturday. With Dad quiet and lulled in front of the television and Mother off to the salon, the day had proved most peaceful as I struggled to keep pace with Mrs. Wardell's homework. "Hey, be careful."

"Marlo," she said, oozing with excitement. "We saw this girl today." Her three friends stood by the doorway in silence, seemingly puzzled by her sudden need to rush my room.

I focused in on Desiree's sketch, my mind still convoluted with terms such as *amniocentesis* and *metamorphosis*.

"I knew I had seen her before. Remember I told you?" Her eyes never broke away from the sketch. "She works at the mall, in the bookstore. I knew she looked familiar."

She couldn't have been making it up, though I always had my doubts whenever it came to her accounts on anything. "Are you serious?" I asked, wondering if that's where Desiree had been hiding the entire summer. I was enthused, eagerly wanting her to divulge every last detail.

"Yeah, I remember I was with Mom at the mall one day. Mom wanted some book about oceans and deserts. She was the one who helped Mom find the book."

Everything began to fall into place. When I saw Desiree at the beach that first day, she had been with Kelly. They must have met at the mall where Kelly also worked. Both the cookie shop and bookstore were adjacent to one another.

"We went in to look at magazines today," Tamara went on. "And she was there. She looks dead on like this drawing...She's got some *bad* looking eyes."

"You didn't say anything, did you?"

"No. I just looked at her for a while. Who is she?"

"She's just someone I know from school," I said. I couldn't really say whether I knew her for sure, but I liked to think that I did. After all, she was my lab partner.

We sat on the steps leading up to *Shame's Fame* early Monday morning. The school was still empty and desolate, yet the bright September morning sang songs of yet another promising day.

"Why'd you do that for?" Ivan asked in an icy tone when I told him I had gone to Danny's.

"I thought maybe he'd want to talk. He looks better."

He said nothing as he opened his history book to our assigned weekend reading.

"You sound like you don't give a shit."

"Screw him," his voice swelled as he looked me dead in the eye. "You shouldn't even waste your time. He's the only one who can dig his way out of the hole he's in. Besides, he deserves what's happened to him. He put himself in this no win situation...He chose to learn the hard way. We warned him, remember? He wouldn't listen."

"Doesn't mean we have to stop being buddies."

He didn't respond. His resentment seemed beyond me. We'd all been friends too long to let anything get in the way. It didn't matter that Danny may have been weak or too inexperienced to avoid Gracie's spells or venomous stings. "Wait a minute. Don't even tell me you're still pissed 'cause he pushed you that other day," I said.

"You don't get it, do you? Danny'll never get that stupid girl off his mind. He doesn't want us around. As long as that bitch whore has hold of his good sense, he'll continue on with this crazy heartbreak shit. He'll go on and let her screw with his mind and emotions. He's lost, man. Face it." He looked away, staring off into the grassy green lunch field just below the stage. "The same thing will keep on happening—just as it happened the first time, the second time, and the third time—and a fourth time, if it hasn't already happened...Things will never be like they used to."

I hated when he got all repugnant, yet I must admit...I loved that he could be so strong, so wise, like Dad—so certain everything would always fall into place like a row of neatly aligned dominoes.

"I bet if she wanted him back right now," he added, "he'd go running back at the first sound of her voice."

"No he wouldn't," I rebutted firmly. My temper was on the verge of letting loose, but I managed to keep myself under control, knowing he was probably right.

"Just forget it." He grabbed the rest of his books and quietly left the stage area.

I continued to sit there alone in my thoughts, frustrated as all I could think was: *Danny can't be completely lost. He'll snap out of it and remember how meaningful our friendship really was. He's strong in other ways. He can run anyone off the field. He can be the nicest of persons, possess the kindest of hearts.*

When Danny didn't show for first period, confusion set in even further. Should I have been like Ivan and just accepted that Danny was ruined, hopeless—never to be the same again? Was it really possible for one girl to truly impact all aspects of a guy's life in the worst of ways? Oh, how badly I wanted there to be an exception to the rule; how badly I wanted my father to be wrong just this once—if not for this girl Desiree who I so much liked, for Danny—whose friendship still meant lots to me.

Desiree walked into biology in one of her quiet, droopy moods. She kept her attention on *East of Eden*, a movie she could have easily downloaded on the cyber network. She raced through as many pages as she could before Mrs. Wardell called our attention. Her mystery only intrigued me more. Why was she so quiet? Why did she like reading so much? What was it she wrote down in her notebooks when Mrs. Wardell wasn't lecturing? Who were her real friends? They certainly were not in this class…and why was she so distressed and sad-looking on most days? As much as I wanted to voice even one of these questions, a side I knew so well restrained even my strongest of impulses. For fear and uncertainty told me I could ill-afford letting her know how enamored I was…I so much believed it would have been my downfall.

Ivan didn't bring up our bitter conversation come eighth period. Unlike that morning, he was back to cracking jokes and even tried talking to some of the girls in class. I caught a glimpse of Danny alone in the back. He didn't talk to anyone, nor did he look our way. He busied himself with various make-up assignments Ms. Farren had assigned. Seeing him there put a little hope back where Ivan had said no hope existed. It didn't matter that he was first to scurry out when class was over. It was evident he was battling, and that just had to be a good sign.

Ivan headed to the band room after class, claiming he needed to find some guy who was looking to challenge his lead spot in the school band. "I heard he's pretty good," he told me, "but I'm pretty sure I can blow him out—watch. I'll catch you later."

I continued down Main Hall, towards my locker. That's when I spotted Danny standing by the fence which surrounded the front corner of the school, a remote area full of trees, brush, and a few recycling dumpsters—an area you would not venture to unless you wanted to hide away from campus security. I kept with the large crowd of students before creeping up. Through the trees I watched as he observed Gracie approach down the front walkway. Like a big-shot celebrity she carried on like a giant spectacle for all to see, waving at friends and even others she did not know. Opening his car door was that same guy I'd seen her with before. Again he stood confident, his smile never an evasive one, his black attire still matching the stunning luster of his sports car, and his cool sleek-black hair still flawless as it beamed in all directions like a spinning strobe light. As they drove off, their silhouette showed them pressing lips for long endless seconds. Her head then dropped to one side as she rested it on his shoulder.

"She's not worth it, you know," I voiced at last.

Danny spun around, startled that I'd been there the whole time. A dead eerie silence followed as he stared at me with blank, hazy eyes; no expression or signs of wanting to say anything. He turned the other way and sped his steps.

I caught up and matched his steady pace. "Can't you just look away and pretend she's never existed? Can't you see you've been blinded beyond belief?"

He stopped and faced me, no longer able to ignore me. "What's it to you?" his voice sparked. "Why don't you just leave me alone and mind your own damned business?"

I was relieved to hear him speak. At least now he was communicating. He continued on his way again, but this time I pushed my way up in front of him. "Are you just gonna let everything be flushed down the toilet, gonna let everything you are go to waste over some girl?"

"Get out of my face. What do you know?"

"She's poison—nothing but a heartless wench. I bet if you cut her open, her heart would be made of nothing but ice, her blood nothing but sewer water." I wanted to say anything to get his attention, anything to make him respond and say more. I continued to impede his way. "I can't believe this—all this over some heartless girl. Look at yourself. You're losing it, man. Everything…your running, your grades, and even people who care about you."

"I said leave me alone!" he flared, grabbing hold of my shirt and spinning me hard against the chain-linked fence. My head snapped back and my back sank into the metal webbing. Disoriented, my strength grew weak as I looked at this person who was now a total stranger, someone I'd never known—someone who'd long since stopped being my friend. Where had the Danny I'd known gone—the quiet good-natured guy with the warm heart and big happy smile? Had this girl Gracie changed him so much that now nothing mattered? Yes, perhaps Ivan was right. There was no hope—perhaps Danny was lost and would never be the same again.

His eyes were perplexed as his reddened face met mine. He seemed unsure of his emotions, unwilling to let go of his confusion. His intensity soon left him as he slowly released his strong grip and left me there to rest against the fence. "What am I doing?" he said as he turned away and grabbed at his hair in anguish.

I didn't acknowledge or move an inch. I was still shaken up, and only now did I really begin to feel the sharp pain spiraling up and down my back and head.

He dropped to his hands and knees and fitfully cried his heart away. "It wasn't my fault," he wailed over and over again. "It wasn't my fault. I really did care, ya know. I really did care about her. I didn't do anything wrong."

I looked at my friend with a kind of sympathetic pity I'd never known. He remained crouched on the ground and cried even louder. I remembered him falling off the monkey bars when we were young. He cried back then, but this was different, like a raw burn that would not heal. *Oh, this was the worst, damn it…the worst.*

After a long moment, he slowly got up. "I'm sorry, Marlo." He still had tears in his eyes and tears in his voice. "Really, I am." He then put his arms around me, continuing to smother his words, "I'm sorry, I'm sorry."

I thought of all men throughout history who may have had their hearts ravaged by women. There must have been some survival mechanism which overcame even the worst of heartaches and pain. Else, how would we all have made it this far? How would Dad or *Abuelo* before him have learned how to heal and eventually be so wise? "It's all right, Danny. Things'll change. You'll get over her. You will."

He pulled away, sniffling as he choked back his sobs. "My life feels like it's ending though. I don't know why. I just can't seem to help it. I feel dumb and ache all at the same time. Nothing seems to help."

So many times I had felt dumb for feeling a certain way that didn't seem to make any sense, times I didn't like myself—times I felt my world would never change. Perception and actual interaction seemed quite an opposite realization even back then. Like my art, everything and everyone was difficult to define. I had many definitions. Danny too had many…the world, an impossible definition in its own variable right. I now felt like I was beginning to understand him better, though it was still very difficult to comprehend his attraction and obsession with Gracie. Yeah, I did like this girl named Desiree, but would I ever allow myself to fall into such torment? I liked to think not. For a perfect world I could paint. A perfect world I could dream. A sandcastle I could build.

We headed off campus and walked to the nearby quick food mart. "She told me she didn't want to speak to me shortly after the concert," Danny went on. By now his tears had subsided, his voice free of rasps. "She said she needed her space again."

"You do know who really went to the concert with her, don't you? Who she gave that other ticket to?" I sipped on an ice-cold soda, as the day was still at its hottest.

"It doesn't matter any more."

"Jesus, Danny, I saw her with that same guy at the concert. They were both waiting in line and…"

I did not regret telling him everything I'd witnessed. The truth was what he needed to hear, the only thing I felt would finally let him come to terms and deal with his anguish. As much as he may have been surprised by my revelation, deep down he was no more shocked to learn the truth than he would have weeks prior. He could no longer hide away from the depths of her coldhearted ways. Maybe that's why it all hurt him so. Keeping himself blind had provided a false sense of hope, made him avoid a most painful reality. He cried more as he opened his eyes and took in everything around him. All I could do was tell him it was all right—that everything would be okay. Useless I felt, as it seemed I was ripping away a bandage that had long since kept him from bleeding to death.

We didn't get home until late. Ocean skies had already begun to dim when we reached his home.

Many thoughts went through my mind when Danny didn't show for Mr. Bernard's class the following morning. Maybe he needed more time to think things over, or perhaps he still could not handle all social aspects related to school. Whatever the reason may have been, I did not let my negative side get the better of me. There was life in Danny yet. I strongly believed he would soon find a way out of the dark endless tunnel he'd been stuck in for quite some time—that he would soon see the light which would brighten all of our days and bring things back the way they were.

Social Darwinism was a term Mrs. Wardell lived by, though according to her, it was not a term directly associated with biology. Survival of the fittest was the only way she knew how to conduct her class. Even the brightest students trembled and stressed as they struggled to earn even passing grades, their perfect reports cards in danger of being blemished for the very first time. It was extremely frustrating knowing I was on the borderline of failing even after spending hours upon hours of study on her class alone—even neglecting my other classes altogether. At times, I felt like running back to Mrs. Canizaro to let her know I could not handle it. Perhaps being in the college prep program was too ambitious, my dreams too impossible to attain. Maybe the Art Academy could do without me. Maybe I'd just so much as settle working for Dad and become one of his journeymen—and perhaps later, one of his foremen.

"Tomorrow someone in each group must bring in a pair of tweezers for our first worm dissection of the year," Mrs. Wardell informed us. The class grimaced at the word dissection. "Any group without tweezers will earn a zero. There's no way you'll be able to participate without them. That's all for today."

Everyone left the room at the first sound of the bell. I trembled, as I knew Desiree was only a few words away. This was a better chance than any to finally exchange words. As I sat there contemplating, I felt a delicate tap on my shoulder. My confidence felt jerked in all directions as I found it in me to meet her deep green simmering eyes. Again, they paralyzed my every thought. Her complexion was so smooth and clear, her lips tender like and perfect. She was so pretty. "I can bring tweezers," she said, her voice soft and gentle, like the calmest of sea breezes. She had trouble pronouncing the word *tweezers*, making it sound more like *tweeshurs*. I wasn't too fond of lisps, though hers seemed to add more to her already perfect aura.

"You don't have to," I said awkwardly. "I can bring them."

"Don't even bother. I have tons of them at home."

I was stuck, didn't really know what to say next. "Okay…I'll just bring whatever we need next time."

She nodded as she stood up and pulled her bag onto the table. She slipped her notebook and text in and pulled out a set of headphones.

"You like *Empty Charms*?" I bravely asked when I noticed she was listening to *Empty Charms*' latest hits collection.

"Yes." Again she lisped. Instead of *yes,* it was *yeshhh.* "Don't you like *Empty Charms*?"

"In a way...I kinda like *Casual Lullaby* better though." I stood up. She was pretty tall compared to all the other girls in class, nearly meeting me eye to eye. "They were also at Day on the Green."

"You were at the concert?" Her eyes lit up.

"No," I said, wondering if I should have just lied just for the hell of it.

"I couldn't get tickets either," she let me know.

I calmed, though in the back of my mind I hoped I would not foul things up by saying something like: *How many hearts have you broken? How many guys have you made love you and then sent them off crying in eternal tears?* She looked at me closely, as if questioning things she would never dare ask aloud. Maybe she remembered me from that first day at the beach, remembered my quiet nature and my wishful sandcastle. I turned away, my confidence again shaken. Our conversation quickly dried.

She soon broke my silence. "My name is Desiree by the way."

Daringly I looked back at her, shaking her creamy soft hand as if I'd never met her before. "I'm Marlo."

"I guess we're stuck with each other."

"Yeah," I replied lackadaisically. "Oh, yeah, right. Lab partners." I broke a smile to hide my foolishness.

She placed her headphones on and returned my smile as she walked away; couldn't quite tell whether or not she'd felt my inner hostilities. It no longer mattered though. A sigh of relief I breathed, for a moment feeling free of fear, of imperfection, of uncertainty...free of Dad. So visible this world now appeared, having no flaws like the sandcastles I'd always dreamed. For once...I felt a part of this great perfect arena.

I was in tune with the rest of my classes for the remainder of the day. For once, I sat through them without being sleepy or bored. I said hello to everyone I knew around me instead of waiting for people to greet me first.

"Why are you in such a gay mood?" Ivan asked as we sat down at our usual lunch table. "Did Mrs. Wardell die without anyone else knowing?"

"No," I laughed. "What's wrong with being a bit perky?"

"Only little girls are perky."

"What's up with that musician dude who wants to duel you?" I asked with my mouth full. Even the cafeteria food tasted good.

"I still gotta find him. Our game against Dade's only a week away. I don't want anyone thinking they can place me."

"He won't place you," I assured.

"I know. I just wanna make sure he knows that."

Danny sat quietly in the back of Ms. Farren's class when we walked into eighth period. Ivan did not acknowledge his presence. I felt no need to tell him I had confronted Danny, as I knew he'd only say I was wasting my time. We sat near the front. I turned and smiled at Danny, glad to see he had made it to class. He looked so much better than yesterday. His ironed clothes, combed hair, and, for the first time in a long while, a smile made all the difference in the world.

Ms. Farren called me to her desk as I readied to catch up with Danny after class. Ivan had walked out with a group of girls, letting them know how badly he would skunk the pants off his newly rumored nemesis.

"Danny's looking much better today," Ms. Farren said stooping over a stack of ungraded book summaries. "He told me he's really sick. Is there something more I should know, maybe something he's not telling anyone?"

"No, he's just really sick, heartsick."

"He's too young to have heart problems, isn't he?"

"Not those kind of heart problems," I explained. "He broke up with his girlfriend, and he's been feeling hurt—hurting worse than a heart attack even." I made it sound all so very simple, not quite getting across that Danny had been subjected to the worst of pains—caused by no other than a girl.

"Well, I'm glad to see he's recovering and coming to class," she said. "I'm worried about you too. You haven't been turning in your book summaries."

"I know, Ms. Farren. I've just been really busy with biology. I have Mrs. Wardell, and she doesn't seem to understand I have other classes."

"You must find ways of budgeting your time. No television when you get home. No staying up late talking to girls on the phone."

Like that was a real issue, I told myself. "I know," I acknowledged. "Getting a good grade in your class is just as important as Mrs. Wardell's. I'm hoping to attend the Art Academy when I graduate…if I graduate."

"If you want to see all your dreams come true—whatever they may be, it'll cost. The cost is hard work, and facing up to things that may seem scary and impossible along the way. I was in your shoes not too long ago, so I know what you're going through—what Danny's going through."

"You'll have my chapter summary tomorrow," I promised.

I stepped outside, still hoping to catch Danny before heading home. But the halls were already vacated as I made my way down Main Hall. Only a few still lingered at lockers and vending machines. I searched my locker for additional books I'd need for another grueling night of study. From afar, the vastness of the field saw the football team practicing for the big upcoming game against Dade High. A few people were running laps around the perimeter of the field, and the cheerleading squad was busy doing amazing flips and somersaults on the grass. I lazily scanned the bleachers when suddenly I caught sight of two distinctive people. By the hair length, slim body posture, and guitar strapped to his back, I knew one to be Ivan. The other wore a bright-blue letterman jacket, distinguishable because it was covered with stars and prestigious patches that were only awarded to the school's top athletes. He appeared to be doing most of the talking, while Ivan just stood there motionless with his arms crossed in front of him. I wouldn't have been surprised had I'd seen Ivan just walk away. After all, he was known to hold endless grudges when it came to his manhood.

But he did not leave. He remained motionless as he listened to whatever Danny had to say. They were not too far off for me to see Ivan eventually rejoice, his face and smile lighting up the day beyond the glowing sun. They shook hands as we usually did when meeting or parting. Then it was Ivan who stepped up to Danny for a quick embrace. They started to walk off campus. I caught up, so happy to be alive and so hopeful the rest of our days would be as bright as the one we now lived.

Of course I was letting one picturesque day create the typical storybook ending, like the ones in the fairy tales my mother used to read me as a little kid—when angels from Heaven came down and lifted me up to take me away to other worlds I could then only dream about. If truly this were a fairy tale, I guess it could have stopped here. But I now know that fairy tales only exist in one's imagination, like in paintings, where I could capture any perfect sight and preserve it for all eternity.

That day ended like any other. The sun set. The sky darkened. The night danced.

15

We continued speaking only on occasion, in between lectures and in between bells. Sometimes Desiree did smile, and that usually made my day something to look forward to. But mostly, she kept to herself, as I did—reserved and a mystery to all. Her eyes went on expressionless and dreary, almost vacant—her character out of sync from what I had imagined it to be during my summer days when I thought she was just a perfect figment of my imagination. I wanted so much to speak on deeper levels and find which things made her happy…which things made some of her days seem so dark and bleak, like a painting with no bright or lively colors. If only I could have shared some of the brightness I saw and felt, I would have given it up in an instant—would have given her whatever joy and warmth I felt every morning when I walked into class just to see her there.

She did bring in *"tweeshurs"* as promised. She and I performed quite well on our gruesome worm dissection. I insisted she cut, while I held down the dead swirls of worms which resembled undercooked gray spaghetti. I tried impressing her by letting her know I was never afraid to bait my hooks whenever I'd gone fishing with *Abuelo*, but she didn't seem too impressed by that. She only smiled and kept her polite thoughts to herself.

Our next lab assignment focused on instinct and behaviorism—something having to do with a guy named *Maslow* and hierarchy. We worked with some of Mrs. Wardell's caged mice in the back. I was responsible for bringing in some cheese from home. Old wooden mazes would test our white furry rodent to see how fast it could race through each corridor. I was time keeper, while Desiree recorded our findings.

"A minute and seventeen seconds," I announced. "Not bad."

"Good, mousie," Desiree said. "He's so adorable. I hope Mrs. Wardell doesn't feed it to that snake of hers back there."

"She wouldn't do that," I said as I picked up the mouse and cuddled it in my hand. It had already devoured all of the cheese.

"Mice like these are used to feed snakes—or worse, used for horrible laboratory experiments." She pinched off another piece of cheese and set it in the maze. "Okay, let's have him try again. According to our reading, he should be able to beat his last time."

The mouse scuttled through the maze. This time, it found the cheese in nearly half the time, as though each turn and corner were now second nature. "Wow," I said. "That was pretty cool."

"I'm sure we humans couldn't tackle a maze in the same way," Desiree commented as she jotted down a new record time. "We'd start to think and analyze too much. We'd get lost in our own thoughts."

"No you wouldn't," Mrs. Wardell interjected. She had been watching us from a distance the entire time. "Don't think of intelligence—or that we posses intellect. Just ask yourself, do you ever forget when you're hungry...or cold, or thirsty?" Her eyes were barely visible as they fought to focus through her thick, impenetrable bifocals.

We didn't reply, amazed by our observation of this mouse who finished the maze faster and faster each time. When we switched to a different maze, we noticed the same pattern.

Desiree volunteered to write up our lab report over the weekend. A reluctant perfectionist she was, hating mediocre scores on exams and quizzes even when hers were tops in the class. When she wrote up our mouse report, she turned in twice as much information as anyone else—even attaching additional outside sources and detailed charts and diagrams. I must say she was an inspiration to me in many more ways than one. I found myself working harder, even on dark late nights when I thought I'd finally give up and fail—certain that I'd have to pay Mrs. Canizaro that loathsome visit regarding my broken dreams. I hung in with as much resiliency as I could muster, stretching that extra mile, breathing that endless breath—and at times, crying that senseless sigh.

"Have you finished your book yet?" I asked after glancing into her bag.

"My book?" Desiree asked, uncertain as to which book I was referring to.

"*East of Eden.*"

"Oh. No, not yet. I'm almost done though." She promptly packed her bag and turned her way to the door.

Her need to sometimes cut me off bothered me so, though certainly I should have been able to understand more than anyone, being that I too detached myself so readily in my struggles through this world. Maybe she knew I liked her. Maybe she was trying to spare me pain. Or perhaps her cutting me off stemmed from that first day at the beach when I'd failed to make eye contact with her—as well as all the other times I'd failed to acknowledge her presence…Maybe she'd been insulted, let down or frustrated that I too could be so mysterious. Even now, it was difficult for me to lock eyes with her…I guess I too feared being discovered—of being seen for who I was and what my dreams and wishes really were.

I felt nothing could come between us now—not even the prettiest of girls who roamed from one foolish heart to the next.

"All right, guys," said Ivan as we approached my home that Friday. I sensed he was happy as I to see Danny had not been forever doomed. "Next week you're gonna see some butt kicking. I finally set a date with that guy who thinks he can place me." He laughed. "Get this. His name is Sebastian Cuddles. He dresses like a cowboy and even wears a hat and leather."

"Why's he even bothering?" asked Danny. "He doesn't stand a chance."

Ivan displayed not one ounce of modesty in his voice. "That's what I'm saying. I tried telling him that."

Tamara raced out of the house at the first sight of Danny. She flung her arms out and gave him a great big hug. "How come you haven't been coming around?"

"I don't know," he replied as he returned her hug. "I've been feeling kinda sick."

"I wanna go see your first race."

"Have Marlo bring you down."

"I don't think Marlo wants to baby sit," Ivan commented.

"Go to hell, Ivan."

"You better watch your mouth, little girl," he countered, "or I'll feed your little butt to one of my neighbor's pit bulls."

"Hey, why don't we get together tomorrow?" I suggested as Tamara subsided. "I'm gonna be up all night tonight catching up in Ms. Farren's class. I'm game for anything that gets me out of the house."

"Let's head to the beach tomorrow morning and hang out," said Danny.

"That sounds like a cool idea." It had been a while since I'd walked the white sands or stepped into the sparkling beach water.

"Yeah," Ivan agreed. "Let's hook it up tomorrow."

"You can't go anywhere tomorrow morning," Tamara shrieked. "Mom wants you to drive her shopping tomorrow."

Mother had to be at the Salon by noon on Saturdays. I agreed to meet Ivan and Danny at the beach by mid-afternoon, where we planned on spending the rest of the day. I couldn't pass on a chance to drive. My driver's exam was just around the corner. Experience behind the wheel was just what I needed.

The following morning, I drove Mother's green sedan (a much smoother ride than Dad's old beat-up truck) and got to the mall just as the stores were opening for business. Mother went into a men's apparel store to see what she could buy *Abuelo* for his upcoming birthday. From afar, I noticed the bookstore, remembering this was where Tamara had claimed she'd seen Desiree. I stepped to the opposite side of the mall, behind the balcony and the escalators. There, I saw a heavy-set lady in her mid-forties come out of the back room with wads of money in hand. Desiree followed, wearing a faded orange *Beach Books* T-shirt, over-washed blue jeans, and a pair of aerobic sneakers. Her displaced hair was in a ponytail and her face appeared shallow and dull, as though sleep had evaded her most of the night. Even in her worst of appearances, my attraction did not fray.

Her boss motioned her to the back where she laboriously shelved newly-arrived books. I watched as Desiree worked her heart away, trying best she could to please that lady who appeared very demanding and picky about everything. Once finished, she came back to the front and offered help with the money and register. She was definitely a hard worker. There weren't too many individuals I knew who worked all day Saturdays— except maybe Dad and Mother, but they didn't have Mrs. Wardell during the week to haunt their every dream. Watching her there only filled me with more admiration. I knew she had to be different, had to be true.

I watched a while longer but then left, feeling as though my presence would soon be discovered. Mother later dropped me off near the outskirts of South Beach. I found Ivan and Danny near the small hot dog stand. They were sitting in sunglasses and smiles, trying to look as cool as possible. We ate lunch there and spent the rest of the day on the beach tossing Danny's Frisbee around. Later, we swam in the warm teal-blue waters of the Atlantic. I hated to think Desiree had to work on such a day. *What a waste*, I thought.

Nearly half the school scurried over to *Shame's Fame* the day of Ivan's big showdown with Sebastian Cuddles. Even those who'd never heard

Ivan's stellar play packed in, as if awaiting a highly anticipated prize fight or sold-out rock 'n' roll concert. Mr. Richards, the band teacher, watched alongside Mr. Parlante and other teachers whose rooms were just outside Dance Hall. I thought they'd break up the entire thing for sure and make everyone go home. The challenge was not an official school event, nor was it something the principal would consider extracurricular. They did not intervene, however, choosing to stand instead with the rest of the crowd, eased perhaps by the security monitors who stumbled by at the last minute.

I pushed my way through the tight crowd and found Danny near the front. A set of drums had been set up towards the back of the stage. Huge speakers nearly eclipsed the sun as they towered at opposite ends of the platform. They shrieked an annoying piercing sound as Sam Ticas, the band's drummer, tested the amplifier.

Ivan sat in one stool with guitar in hand, his poise tapping everyone on the shoulder to let us know he was ready to begin. He was wearing his lucky *Led Zeppelin* tank top and a pair of shredded jeans. His old sneakers were spray painted rainbow colors, matching his tie-dyed bandana which he strapped around his head.

The sun also shined bright on his opponent, Sebastian Cuddles. I had not seen him around school, yet I don't know how I could have missed him. He was hefty, more on the heavy side, his arms thick but with no muscular definition whatsoever. His style of clothes was most unusual. Ivan was right. He looked more like a cattle wrestler than anything else, wearing a cowboy's hat with brown corduroy pants and a brown leather vest which hugged his entire upper body tightly, like the plastic wrap Mother used to bundle sandwiches. His long curly-fluffed hair matted and stuck to his sweaty forehead underneath his hat. He seated himself on another stool next to Ivan, readying his immaculately polished guitar as he plugged his jacks into the sound system. The speakers shrieked once again.

"What will it be?" Ivan's confidence boiled over and smothered us all.

"How 'bout some Ozzy?" Sebastian's rough voice proposed.

"Name the tune."

"*Diary of a Madman.* Let's try the very beginning and then mix into the middle, just before the solo."

I hadn't the faintest idea what they were referring to. Ozzy Osbourne rang a bell, an ancient old hard rock musician of some kind, but I'd never heard any of his music. I often heard Ivan mention Ozzy whenever he spoke of his favorite guitarist ever, Randy Rhodes, but that was all.

"Okay, you go first," said Ivan.

We stood frozen in time as Sebastian tipped his hat up with his forefinger and repositioned himself on his stool. He held a gold plated pick which shined like a heavy orange flame of fire shooting throughout the far distant sky. His large husky fingers edged slowly over all six strings as he began the beginnings of an eerie, eccentric melody that seemed to chill everyone's spine. It went from its slow steady stage to a quicker, more intense pace. His talent became most evident, displaying incredible skill—handling his guitar as well as I'd ever seen Ivan. No one could deny his play was anything less than spectacular. He concluded, leaving all of us astonished—still frozen.

This did little to intimidate Ivan. He expected Sebastian would be very good, as had been the case with the others who had challenged him in the past. Anxiously he waited his turn, discreetly picking at his strings as he repositioned his strap around his shoulder. With only an ordinary plastic pick, music soon slipped from his fingers. He sunk deep into his play, showing incredible passion and depth. His head remained lowered, his eyes entranced in encompassing darkness as he wove this story with only his play to guide our ears to the very end. When the solo became so intense and quick, he moved his neck along with his head to the rhythm of this most haunting tune. Everyone watched without a blink, awestruck and tantalized by amazing consistent play. When he stopped, he raised his head slowly and finally opened his eyes—but did not focus on anything. He continued in his trance, still lost in another world. Seconds later, the audience went wild.

Danny kept hollering, "C'mon, Ivan. You're the best."

Others remarked, "You kick ass, Ivan. Show him who's boss."

Sebastian was left quiet and motionless on his stool. I couldn't tell if he was stunned or simply unimpressed.

"Let's go again," said Ivan as the crowd quieted. "How about some Van Halen...*Eruption*?"

Mr. Richards and Mr. Parlante were still standing in Dance Hall. By now other teachers had joined the crowd. It seemed even they wanted to hear more, as this was music which probably sparked back memories. This was not the computer-generated, artificially-synthesized, or digitally-mastered music I was used to hearing from groups like *Empty Charms* or *Casual Lullaby*—"bubble gum" music as Ivan liked to say. This was music from a different time, different place and era.

"We'll need a drum roll," Ivan announced. He signaled Sam Ticas who'd been seated quietly behind the drums.

"You go first this time," said Sebastian.

Sam Ticas raised both drumsticks into the air and struck them together before banging down hard on the drums. Ivan made his guitar explode into a loud jittery uproar. His quick agile fingers danced along each guitar string like a spider over its own spun web. Unlike the previous piece, this one intensified rapidly. It required the quickest and most accurate fingers to make the sound come alive. Once settled, he shut his eyes and again his natural instincts took over. Just when it looked as though he might falter, he repositioned his fingers and kept his poise. He struggled towards the finish but made no blunders. I cheered as loudly as I could with Danny and the rest of the crowd. Everyone behind me jumped up and down and pushed me forward. I squished into a short girl who was already pressed as far as she could go against the edge of the stage. Someone behind us yelled, "Sounded just like the record."

Sebastian said nothing as he had the last time. He raised his guitar, ready for play. When everyone quieted, he signaled Sam to begin. Sam hit the drums. The same authentic uproar exploded from his fingers, striking everyone frozen as had Ivan. Despite the rugged and intense play, he held strong and would not let himself stumble or slow, gripping his guitar as though he were firing a powerful machine gun. He kept his concentration every inch of the way and looked as though this would be yet another stellar performance. But that was not to be. His fingers tensed and slowed, barely able to keep up with the rapid demands of the climactic finish. Distortion reached everyone's ears as he faltered. Silence soon loomed everywhere.

Ivan jumped off his stool and stood tall. There was no question in anyone's mind who still reigned king at Beach High. He bowed, then raised both arms high into the air, welcoming the crowd as we all cheered his name, "Ivan! Ivan! Ivan!"

Sebastian kept a straight face as he quietly packed his guitar. He shook Ivan's hand as he stepped off this most shameful stage.

16

An aura of ticklish joy would soon become her. A foreign song she'd sing as gladly she spoke and gestured abundantly; talked about how she looked forward to the simplest of things such as her English class, payday, and her Steinbeck novel. And if I called her name, she'd turn attentively, dreamy eyed—whispering of secret tales outside my own little realm.

Everyday I'd see her walk his side; saw them at lunch together, always laughing and talking, as if they'd known each other for the longest time and had a whole life of things to share. She'd tilt her head to one side and watch him speak as he'd crack jokes and describe his tales of victory both on the field and on the court. His infamous macho image would dwindle away for a time as he too broke in smiles—his posture, walk, and stride softening altogether as he'd accompany her down the main walkway after school. She'd walk to her bus stop while he'd get into his old beefed-up coupe and speed off the lot. A big tender smile would draw her face as she'd wave most passionately, as though a smile and soft "goodbye" just wasn't enough.

Gerard Medina was one of the most popular seniors at school, a big-time jock—perhaps standing even grander than Danny. For he was a football, basketball, and baseball player—an all around athlete in three of the most popular sports. Being named *Sports Athlete of the Year* in the state of Florida made him a hot prospect for many top college athletic programs across the country. He was good looking—muscular, with a perfect shade of skin and an almost irrepressible gallant appeal that shadowed him everywhere he went. All the girls at school always talked about him—even Kelly. And I knew he wasn't one of those fake kind of studs who had to lie about the girls he'd been with. For he could have had any girl he wanted, and every girl it seemed would have jumped at a chance to be with him.

I couldn't deny I was left broken, a bit empty—wishing for a moment that I too could be so popular and macho, fearless on the field or on the court—fearless when it came to women…or maybe not.

I felt my confused heart sink into sobs—not big sobs, yet sobs. I dared not think what I might see of those two in a month—or maybe even a week. Jealous I was, yes. But what made it all worse was that I hadn't yet told her how much I liked her; hadn't yet told her she made me want to smile all the time, just as her smiles now strayed Gerard's way.

More than ever, I had to let sink in what he'd always warned, *"…every girl's like a wasp. They'll sting you and suck everything you got till your heart stops beating—send you off in eternal cries, scar your soul for life."*

Yeah, think of Desiree as just another girl was what I had to do—an insignificant, futile bystander playing a role in Dad's most predestined world of evil women and poor, victimized men…Oh, but if only it were all that easy. For every time I saw her, my insides turned to mush. Quickly would my thoughts vacate my uttering blockades, rendering all defenses weak. No longer could Dad keep me in his tight grasp I'd known my whole life. It did not matter that I had been programmed and predestined to believe in one-sided coins. Crushed and confused I remained, forced to keep my most passionate and intimate feelings locked away in this metal chamber I'd always known to be my heart.

Certainly, I wasn't first to feel like an empty pot of gold with only colors of a rainbow to guide his fair way, was I? A complex world I tried not to dwell. For what was—was, and what used to be…a set of predestined determinants appearing beyond anyone's control. I had my friends. I had my dreams…and there just had to be other girls who could be as heavenly as she.

I continued to work vigorously in Mrs. Wardell's class, spent whatever time I had left on my other classes; wanted more than anything to succeed and make my dream of entering the Art Academy a reality… Then, maybe then, could I paint over all skies and shores that ruled this world over.

"I'll help finish our lab this weekend," I told Desiree. "You can have a break for once."

"Are you sure?" she asked as she gathered her things.

"Don't worry. I won't foul up your grade." That would have been impossible. She was the note taker and a splendid one at that. Pages and pages of notes filled her notebooks. All I'd need to do was make her words presentable for Mrs. Wardell. Tamara could help me with the computer at home.

As I stuck her notebook in my bag, she noticed my sketchpad I often zipped away from all other eyes.

"Oh, let me see. I've always wanted to be able to draw by hand."

I stiffened, hesitant about revealing my most prized and private thoughts. For this was like a diary of many years past—of stories and tales only I could tell, of different worlds only I could paint. I relented, however, knowing if I had any chance of touching her with my magic, now was a better chance than any. I handed it to her, trusting her as I had few in this predestined arena.

"Wow," she said, studying doodled drawings and detailed representations of buildings, strangers, and landscapes that filled pages upon pages—just a glimpse of a talent and persona which for the most part had been hidden away. "These are really good. I've never met anyone who could draw without a digital divide."

I smiled at her pretty face, glad to see she wasn't in any rush to meet up with Gerard out in the halls. She flipped through more pages, intrigued and caught up in my web of dreams—almost as though she were reading an interesting news article—or even that Steinbeck novel. She finally looked up at me with a silent glazed look in her eyes, as if pondering a sudden touch of *déjà vu*. It brought me right back to that first day at the beach. She'd stood so peaceful and innocent behind her friends…she hadn't said anything when she found out I was the one who had built that deceiving sandcastle. Only then had she looked my way, penetrating my every disguise, looking deep inside my soul—that same exact stare I had somehow managed to recapture on my easel.

My eyes broke contact. Silent I became. *Now do you remember? Can your eyes really see right through me? Have you discovered all my hidden secrets I myself have not yet discovered?* Oh, the thought of her remembering I was the guy she had seen at the beach—that same guy who'd been playing with the sand like a lost little child.

"How long have you been drawing?"

"Ever since I was two," I stumbled as I met her gaze once again. "I always thought I'd grow out of it or turn digital soon after starting school. But I never have. It's the only thing I'm good at and the only thing that lets me keep in touch with who I really am."

She glanced through more of my drawings before handing them back. "They're fantastic."

I offered to rip out her favorite sketch of all, a drawing of a man looking into a computer only to find someone else's reflection. But she wouldn't hear of it. "They're like a poet's most sacred poems—priceless verses never ever to be tarnished or forgotten. I can't, really."

She turned towards the door where Gerard stood waiting. Aside from being big man on campus and having looks that made every girl water, I dared not ask what he had that I didn't. For that was easy...he had Desiree, and he was making her heart sing and skip beats, making her eyes dance an endless waltz.

"She's got some freakin' nerve," said Ivan. No question he shared my same disgust. It did not matter that he may have been over her—or that maybe she could have had some good in her and wanted to apologize when apologies just did not seem to fit these kinds of circumstances. Danny had been working so hard to get over her and bring his life back to a stable norm. He certainly did not need her coming back into the picture. Was he walking around with sightless eyes again, so weak at heart that he could possibly think of forgiving her and perhaps getting back together again?

"Wait," I suggested as I held him back. "Let's see what happens. Let's see if he's still blind." This was indeed Danny's war. We really could not help him in his battles—no matter how grim they may have been.

We sensed his growing strength, yet it was quite evident he was still weak. He looked down at her, quiet as she spoke up at him. He didn't walk away or hint that he wanted no part of her, almost accepting her tempting voice and devouring smile. She even pressed up tightly against his body. It appeared he'd fall for sure. For it was her sweet embraces, sweet talk, and false promises that were at the core root of her power.

He finally turned without any words, walking off to join the rest of his teammates for off-season practice—failing to respond to her pleas. She stomped her feet on the ground, demanding his return, seeming not to believe that he (or any other guy for that matter) could ever leave her there in the cold.

We rejoiced, happy such strength could exist to override this power and venom all girls appeared to wield. A powerful antidote Danny too did carry, an instinctual mechanism that had let all guys before him survive this most tumultuous of realities.

"Hey, wait up," we yelled as we ran past her. It was a mild hot day, yet she stood there skinless and bloodless, shivering among cool breezes that whipped Danny's name over and over again in vain.

"What happened?" I asked.

"You sure showed her," said Ivan.

"You guys were watching?"

"We couldn't help it," I said.

"What did she want?"

A look I had not seen in weeks plagued Danny's face—a face which had known only heartache and pain, a face without smiles or joys. His downcast eyes and thoughts silenced, apparently not wanting to share any details. "You guys know I wouldn't fall for her shit again." His eyes reached up for ours blankly. In a low pitched tone, he voiced, "I'd rather be dead." He went on with his warm-up stretches before joining the others in a lap around the track. His eyes ventured Gracie's way one last time.

We didn't see Gracie around school as much after that day. Rumor had it that a gang of girls from a different part of town were after her—something having to do with that guy she'd been seeing.

17

Counterculture his entire life, it was a sight for sore eyes to see Ivan dressed in what elders would have considered sociably accepted attire. His hair hung neatly down, combed and shiny to perfection—as were his rarely-worn dress shoes. The pleated khakis were his own, but the crisp-red polo shirt he borrowed from Danny. "You gotta come," he pleaded. "You can't just leave her hanging."

I pulled out the invitation Keliana Rubia had handed us the first week of school. Our names filled the top portion of the card and rainbow colors formed a big happy face.

Danny read it over, but his sulky demeanor went unchanged. "I can't go—not after what I did to her."

"She doesn't even know what you did," said Ivan. "You're still her friend. Besides, I'm sure if Kelly really knew why you did what you did, she'd find it in her heart to be understanding. She's cool. C'mon, even Marlo's going. You know if Marlo's going, it's gotta be a cool party."

It was true. I had not gone to any parties in the past. Now more than ever, I felt like I should go; felt a little of this world—felt as others should feel. "Yeah, you know it's gotta be a bash when Ivan's all dressed up for church," I shot back.

"Shit, you know I'll be stripping these clothes off as soon as I leave her house."

Danny looked out his window, still quiet and indecisive.

This time I pressed on, "C'mon, Danny. Just forget the past. Look towards the future and try to live it so you don't make the same mistakes over again. What's happened has already happened. Now let's go." I never liked to say what was easier said than done, but I said it anyway. Peer pressure was always easiest when one was the perpetrator. For my own personal reasons, I wanted him to go badly. A comfort zone I sought, as having both my friends there would make socializing a lot easier.

He turned from the window with a reluctant smile. Sullenly he muttered, "All right…but only for a while."

"You'll see" said Ivan, excited by Danny's response. "We'll have a cool time once we're there."

"And you don't even have to worry about a present," I remarked, showing off the small music box Ivan and I had purchased at the mall. A tiny porcelain boy on a piano popped up to play an eloquent melody. The man at the store said it was the theme from *Summer of '42*, a classic movie from way back when. "We already added your name to the card."

"Start prettying yourself up, boy," Ivan ordered. "We're already late."

Stars above us never shined brighter as patterned clusters formed our hopes and dreams. If I looked hard enough, some did sparkle my name, and some even gathered to form a sandcastle which would never topple among waves of glimmering glitter. Blocks seemed like miles as we strolled through streets which had no city lights or paved walkways. Elegant homes we encountered were more like giant wedding cakes compared to my cupcake of a home. Even Danny's home shrank in comparison. The deeper we ventured into this most affluent part of town, the more I wondered why on earth Kelly would hold a job at the mall. Her family was beyond rich, and surely there was no need for her to work a day in her life…Maybe she had parents who were trying to teach her the fine art of working hard for her money—wanting her to experience economic reality so that one day she wouldn't go and blow her inheritance on broken toothpicks, secondhand trophies, rundown casinos, or distorted computer-based art…Or perhaps she was unique and did not want to be carried by her parents the rest of her life. Maybe she didn't want to be rich. That was a possibility…But who didn't want to be rich? Who didn't want to live in a house as big as chocolate covered mountains, surrounded by perfect emerald landscapes, quiet whispering winds, ruby chromed cars, gold plated toilets, and windows made of diamonds?

Darkness swiftly engulfed last bits of light coming from the far distant horizon as the enormous two-story silhouette crept upon us like unexpected rainfall. Its outline transcended high upon the dark canvas sky, appearing more like a medieval castle lost on its own enormous slope—protected by this moat known to us all as Biscayne Bay. We stared up in awe as Miami's humidity stroked our skin from all angles. Tantalizing tropical breezes told us to hush as silence echoed every corner, nearly concealing the booming music faintly heard within this most magnificent of palatial estates. Two enormous palm trees grew on each side of the stone paved walkway, like two giant pillars leading to an exotic ancient temple. To the right of the path stood a pristine fountain of blue neon water trickling into a small pool which drained into a stream leading to the nearby bay. Several wide steps led up to a veranda as wide as the entire mansion. A light post to the left of the house shot enough light to find our way. Music grew louder. Faint sounds of people sharing in laughter and in voice echoed through the side windows.

"I've never seen such a sickening display of wealth in all my life," whispered Ivan. He pushed the glowing doorbell, sending off a loud authentic chime. Above the doors read, *Rubia Residence.* I turned, ignoring Ivan's remark. For a sight such as this should have made anyone wish they were a rich shining prince. The lush garden, trees, stoned carved walkway, and blue glowing fountain made it all seem like we were standing outside a royal palace awaiting entrance to the princess' annual ball. It really was some kind of paradise. "If this is sickening," I voiced, "then I wouldn't mind being sick."

Kelly swung open one of the two heavy doors. She stood in a long beautiful white dress that matched the glamour of the garden and the mansion. Her eyes widened and face glowed as she smiled, happy we were here. "You guys made it."

Intrigue captivated me as never before. I handed her the colorful bag with card and present as my eyes strayed past her. There were expensive handmade rugs on the floor, huge prize-winning paintings on the walls, priceless looking vases on antique tabletops, and a gigantic crystal chandelier hung high from a pointed domed ceiling above. The loud music came from a huge dimly-lit living room to the right of the doorway. Elegantly dressed people I did not recognize walked by constantly. I felt out of place for a moment, a bit intimidated as I had felt all those Halloween nights when we'd trick-or-treated past her home.

"It's beautiful," said Kelly as she heard the music box chime. She reached over and kissed us on the cheek. "It's great seeing you again, Danny. It's been ages since we've last talked."

"Yeah, I know," he responded shyly.

She introduced us to some of her other friends. They looked at us differently than they did each other, some exposing what seemed like fake hellos and shallow smiles. I did not recognize any of them and suspected most were from rich yuppie private schools on the outer part of town.

"There's food in the kitchen," she informed us as she pointed to another doorway to the left of a large spiraling staircase. "If the bathroom near the pantry is too crowded, there's another one upstairs to your left. If you guys need me, I'll be around." Her hospitality was far from rude, heading quickly to greet other guests at the door.

"What now?" I asked as I scanned what I could of the tall walls and ceiling. "This house is big enough to host the Olympics, and there're enough people here to watch 'em."

"Let's go home," Danny suggested. "I feel like a sore thumb on a hand full of broken fingers. I don't know any of these people."

"We can't just leave," said Ivan. "We just got here. Let's at least eat some of that food and get our money's worth on that present."

"I'm not hungry," Danny said.

Neither was I, but I didn't mind staying as long as Ivan did. He always had a way of making any place his home.

We entered a splendid gourmet kitchen surrounded by several stainless steel refrigerators and sinks. Spacious granite top counters it seemed could house an entire culinary school—or perhaps used to prepare meals for an entire royal army. We helped ourselves to some of the enticing hors d'oeuvres and succulent foods. A giant triple-decker birthday cake stood high on its own table ready for that one edible blemish. "You know," Ivan added with his mouth full of crackers and cold cuts, "this party sucks, but the food's all right."

"I wonder who all these people are," whispered Danny, staring at those who came in and out of the kitchen from a different entrance on the opposite side of the buffet tables.

"I haven't seen anyone I really know," Ivan said. "Not that I'd want to. I hate stuck-up people."

I picked at my sandwich but didn't eat much of it. Danny didn't try any of the food. He stood quietly with hands in his pockets.

"Having good manners is nothing but a bunch of bull to begin with," Ivan remarked as he continued stuffing his mouth. "Watch this." He squished in as many small sandwiches as he could, obnoxiously chomping down with his mouth open and sipping fruit punch until it spewed down his chin. Once done, he purposely made himself belch. Everyone in the kitchen looked his way but said nothing. "See," he added as he wiped his mouth. "I was just acting like they all would like to act—or already act when no one's watching."

Continuous intrigue drew me closer past a spacious pantry to a second entrance leading to the dimly-lit living room. I peered in for a better look. More golden framed oil paintings and mirrors hung on walls. There were elaborate fine furnishings. Exquisite sculptures and statuettes rested on spacious mantels and pedestals. Other finely handmade Persian and Oriental rugs stretched across glossy wood floors wide enough to house a basketball gymnasium. Mixed perfume and cologne fumes clogged the stuffy air. Groups of people talked and danced amongst each other as music blared from a stereo inside a giant glass-case entertainment center. Someone in the room soon caught my eye like a puddle of water sitting in the middle of a hot, dry desert. She stood near the other entrance on the far side of the living room, wearing a one-piece red dress that clung to her body's svelte figure—her hair full and as free as the wind.

How silly I should have felt to have my breath swept away. For I'd always associated "breathtaking" with eye striking paintings, inspiring sandcastles, exciting athletic competitions, or exquisite musical performances. But silliness stirred me not. For her beauty called my name more than ever, and an unfamiliar warming sensation poked my heart as she stood looking so delicate and immaculate in that pretty red dress—dreamy, yet alive.

The loud thumping music soon halted. My attention drew towards Kelly as she cued a slow ballad and requested that everyone find a partner. Quickly did my eyes swing back Desiree's way only to find Gerard approach her with hand extended. Like a gallant prince in one of those storybook fairy tales I'd always dreamed to be, he stood confident and poised in a flashy tweed jacket with matching trousers. Gently he took her by the hand and led her to the dance area where other couples swayed as one. Her soft green eyes gazed up in fondness. Gerard too locked eyes and became lost for long endless seconds. I thought I had been the only one who could be so lost. His face then moved slowly towards hers, placing a tender kiss over her lips. She returned his kiss and broke away only to rest her head comfortably on his shoulder.

A part of this world I now may have been—a part of this universe I may have claimed, but it was all so bewildering and overwhelming to even try and comprehend. Voiceless cries bounced silently in my head. A most intense feeling of agitation filled me top to bottom—a sense of losing something I so much wanted but could not have, a senseless hurt and yearn of wanting her to know just how much I liked her—yet knowing that I would never have the chance to let this side of me known. For only in dreams could she ever be mine.

Perhaps this was just a glimpse of the pain Dad had always described—inescapable, unavoidable, worst of torments—pain like fire. Oh, I wanted nothing more than to go home and sulk in front of one of my paintings where I could pretend and make believe I was in another world far away from this here reality. It was a mistake having come here, I thought. I should have expected to find Desiree here together with her dream guy in this here dream house.

I backed away and turned towards the kitchen. Ivan and Danny were gone, nowhere near the food table. Had they not noticed when I walked away? I scanned the living room again. Maybe they'd gone back to the other entrance and entered there.

Too many people stood and danced in the way for me to spot them, including Desiree and her companion who both danced with delighted eyes until that love song came to an end. Crowds of people then stormed the kitchen. Desiree looked all the more glamorous in the light. Her gleaming eyes sparkled like bright city lights, and her red dress made her beauty shoot out like a falling star on a clear summer's night. I stood tableside, calm as could be, trying best I could to hide my uneasiness as I sipped from a flat soda. She looked past me at first but soon gave a closer look, smiling as she picked up a soft drink off the table. "Hi."

"Hi," I said blandly.

"I didn't know you were coming."

"Kelly's a good friend of mine," I let her know. "We go way back."

Blank her out of my mind was what I had to do, like the one wave I'd seen wash away my illusive sandcastle that first day at the beach. But that was near impossible…for how on earth did I turn off that which seemed so natural, normal—of this world and of this universe?

Gerard stood in the background, his handsome face studying mine— as if trying to place where he'd seen me before, or perhaps sensing what secrets veiled deep within my heart. "What's up?" was all we said to each other.

"Well, you have a nice time, Marlo," said Desiree as they walked back to the living room.

"You too," I replied, wanting to vanish even if it meant leaving without Ivan or Danny. They'd understand if I told them I was a victim of the worst of pains. Ivan would. I knew Danny certainly would.

I stepped out of the kitchen and into the foyer. Again there was no one I knew there. The front door called my name, though I hesitated as second thoughts told me Ivan and Danny could still be somewhere around. I moved closer to the main living room entrance to have another look. Only more of those rich people stood chatting and dancing. Behind me the huge staircase spiraled up to the second floor. The bathroom upstairs, I contemplated.

The stairs were wide and layered with a plush royal-red carpet. As I climbed, I peered down and dizzied, as heights often made me nauseous. Finally, the corkscrew steps came to an end. The wall in front of me displayed a giant plaque which read, *Rubia Empire. March 2nd, '26.* Rather enchanting, I thought—epic, of a time when princes truly were princes and kings truly did reign over eternal empires. Beneath the plaque was a large array of light switches, likely controlling every bulb in the house.

For there were dozens and dozens of them. Some were switched on, many of them off. The corridor to the right of me went unlit and seemed as dark as the deepest of oceans. Left was where I proceeded, being there were lights and being that was where Kelly had mentioned the second bathroom would be—where Ivan and Danny were sure to be.

All was dead and lifeless—quiet, as a midnight cemetery. Noise evaded my approach. Had I not been downstairs, I would have never imagined a party on the lower level. The left corridor too was covered in the same red carpet and soon joined another corridor to the right. This next hall was also lit and extended down the full length of the house. Many doors claimed the walls, reminding me more and more of a hotel. The first door I tried was locked. Only when I reached the midway point did I find the only door left open. The lights were off, but I was certain it was a bathroom. The floor was covered with glowing white tiles similar to the ones my parents had in their bathroom. I groped for a wall switch but instead hit an object which came crashing to the ground. It sent a loud echoing noise throughout the entire length of the hall. I stood frozen as I wrestled with my thoughts. If I'd broken something, it would sure to cost a bundle.

None of the doors opened, nor did I hear anyone draw near. Relieved, I tried the lights once more. A metal shaped bird resembling others on the wall lay in the middle of the floor. I picked it up and tried refastening the clip which had broken off. It would not stay. Quickly I shut the door and scanned the room, finding myself surrounded by mirrors, even on the ceiling. A large pink porcelain tub sparkled one side of the room, the matching toilet and vanity another. Towels, expensive soaps, fancy decor, and several newly wrapped toothbrushes were set on a marble sink counter. I shuffled through several drawers and medicine cabinets, finding only a safety pin in the midst of more toiletries and towels. It was not a perfect fit, but it did do the job. The ornament hung as good as new.

It wasn't long before I heard someone pound the door. A small girl with blond hair stood waiting. The way she rushed in, I knew she had to go bad. She shut the door and the next thing I heard was the same loud crash I'd experienced when I first tried the lights. I felt so foolish, having worried so much about an ornament that would never break, no matter how many times it fell. It was that girl's problem now.

Again I stood in solace with only curiosity to keep me from a vacuum of stifling solitude. No, there was no half naked statue as there had been in the museum way back in kindergarten; simply a calling of wanting to search the unknown—like a person in therapy trying to uncover the scary realms of his unconscious. I moved on, passing other locked doors.

A window at the end looked down on a swimming pool that stretched the entire length of an immense backyard, seeming void of tides or currents—a pleasant ocean to greet you as you swam. A white gazebo stood far right where people gathered and chatted. A manicured lawn stretched poolside from one end of the yard to the next. Beyond the lawn was a stone wall covered with luscious vines and vegetation, and beyond the wall was the bay. It too sparkled in calmness as this most precious of November nights claimed perfection.

I turned right again, my eyes drifting into yet another seemingly endless red walkway. More doors punctuated the walls, except that only half of this next hall was lit. The other half was left in darkness like the one which had greeted me when I first reached the top of the stairs. I stole midway. A few stairs separated me from the rest of this most eerie expanse. They led up to a small upper level, where a grandfather clock stood tall to my left, its pendulum swaying back and forth like a hypnotizing crystal to remind me that time had not stood me by. To the right was a set of retractable doors for an elevator with its own pushbutton controls. Beside the controls were more light switches similar to the ones I'd seen by the stairway. I tried one of the flicked up switches. Immediately the hall I'd ventured went dark, even the one leading to the bathroom. When I tried another, the dark hall before me lit up. More doors still cluttered walls, and more blood-colored carpet led way to yet another corridor that would branch right. In the corner, at the end, stood an ancient set of medieval armor. *Just what this house needs,* I thought. *But what about the dungeon, or the princess who lay trapped in the turret awaiting rescue from her beloved prince? Perhaps this prince lay prisoner in one of these locked doors looking to escape so he could fulfill the most perfect of never-never land endings…But maybe the princess is really an evil sorceress casting evil spells, making all this just an imaginary illusion, a limitless impossible labyrinth where this prince would have to roam for all eternity, lost in thought and lost in broken dreams.*

I flicked off the switch flicked another back on. The corridor beyond went dark again. I thought of backtracking, but I was too drawn not to want to see where the rest of this maze would lead. Audaciously I stepped down. Silence ruled everywhere and darkness echoed my name as it threatened to swallow me up and send me to the bottom of the deepest oceans. Walls too reached out and spoke to me, somehow reading my mind and tapping into the deepest, darkest fears I'd ever come to know. The motionless set of armor sat in shadows from another window ahead, appearing as though it would grab at me if I did not speed my steps. Doors on either side of me could have been bedrooms or display rooms, but tonight they seemed they'd open at any second to reveal the ghastliest of ghostly ghouls. Or perhaps the walls would slide apart and unleash an ancient old dragon that stood guard over a fortune in lost magical treasure, waiting to devour anyone who dare spy his lair.

Light of day never seemed further in my mind as finally I reached the end with my trepidation intact. All seemed timeless, forgotten—untested by certainty. Chivalrous I should have felt as I stared into yet another vast dark corridor, though I felt more like an unwarranted thief stealing away the many secrets which lay within this grandest of homes. I looked back at the half lit hall behind me. It awaited my return. The girl had probably already come out of the bathroom and left that annoying ornament for someone else to deal with. No one would know I was here if I just turned back. I still had time to preserve my innocence, still had time to feel the safety in what had always been despicable certainty.

But no. I couldn't. I'd come this far, and so too did the faint light at the end of this next corridor welcome my approach. As I drew near, I noticed a door on my right cracked halfway open. A small bedside lamp dimly lit the entrance. Gripping intrigue and curiosity which had guided most of my way did not allow any hesitation. I stepped in for a better look.

Fresh scented rosy potpourri filled the air. Above the center of the room was a large skylight window. Moonlight beamed into my eyes to remind me of a familiar sky that still invaded much of the heavens. A giant king-sized canopy bed dominated most of the room. Snow white dresser, vanity, and night stands resembled the same extravagant design of furniture I had seen down below. A giant wall-sized television and digital player-recorder stood elegant across the bed. Neon colored tropical fish swam peacefully in a tank in a lonely corner of the room. Magazines, books, and stuffed animals were piled neatly in another corner above a pink hope chest. On the dresser I saw an array of different colored nail polishes, makeup, expensive jewelry, and pictures of Kelly with family and friends. A desk with a computer and glowing globe overlooked a window in the northern part of the room, next to the closet. *A window overlooking what?* I pondered, for this was not a room situated near the exterior of the house.

I crept towards the dim meandering light penetrating through the thin white blinds. What I saw was the most spectacular open courtyard ever. Beyond were dozens and dozens of windows embedded in the southern, eastern, and northern wings of the house. Below were stone paved walkways surrounded by flush green vegetation that seemed to grow every second I stared. The moon above shined on various stone chiseled benches and statuettes. Mesmerized was I by the elaborate waterfall which continuously splashed water into a pond of glowing water. I could only imagine live, swimming fish and a collection of wild tropical birds by day as they claimed refuge to this most heavenly of paradises.

I spun from the window as faint muffled voices drew near. My heart beat frantic thumps of panic as I waited to be caught and asked what the hell I was doing in here uninvited. Certainly no one was supposed to be in this section of the house, and certainly I had no right to steal away its secrets.

The closet. It was my only choice. I opened and shut both retracting doors just in time.

"What if we get caught?" a soft voice whispered.

My eyes squinted as they struggled to squeeze a peek through the thick wood blinds. I should have been relieved to find that it was not Kelly or any other denizen of this house. But who I saw was far from relieving.

"Don't worry," replied Gerard as both sat on the bed. "No one's even supposed to be up here."

Adrenaline rushed my body like the strongest of river currents as I held my breath and gulped down my fear. My forehead grew wet and sticky, though I kept as still and quiet as could be—as hiding would only make matters worse if I were discovered.

"This is Kelly's room, isn't it?" Desiree looked around the room, even towards the closet but had no idea I was behind the doors. Then she glanced up at the window above. The glowing beam of moonlight shined right through the thin canopy covering. Her complexion came alive as the light outlined her magnificent aura.

"Looks like her room," Gerard said as he uncapped a bottle of dark murky whiskey. He sipped straight from the bottle. "Here," he offered, wiping his mouth with his other hand.

"No thanks," she lisped.

"C'mon, take some. It won't hurt you."

"No, it's all right."

Gerard swigged another mouthful. She looked at him with less fondness than I had seen all night, the first time her eyes did not gleam his way, the first time they did not silently whisper his name—as though her image of him had suddenly tarnished.

He sensed her disappointment. "Sorry. I won't drink anymore. I didn't think it would bother you." He capped the bottle and let it fall onto the bed.

She was more at ease, relieved with an apparent forgiveness that allowed her to accept his apology.

"You know," he said softly, moving closer. "I kinda like you a lot, and I feel lots can happen between us."

"You think so?" she asked innocently, letting him place a small kiss over her lips.

He pulled away momentarily and delved deep into her eyes. Passion sizzled everywhere, even in this large oversized closet full of more clothes than anyone would ever want to wear. His lips pressed hers again, his hands caressing her hips and outer thighs—like switches or buttons he was trying to turn on.

How did I ever get into this? I asked as my body slid down against the side of the wall, not wanting to think what might happen next. *I should have just gone back downstairs when I had the chance.* A part of me wanted that darkness in those halls to swallow me up and splash me into the deepest of oceans where I could drown my feelings from existence. For ashamed and silly I felt as all my internal devotion seemed more like a passage out of some melodramatic romance novel or daytime soap—a bit fake and overly drawn to ever seem real. And still, this other side pled that it was okay to be this silly; that shame was only a part of an internal battle I would later regret having to fight. *Oh, if there were only a way of telling her she was the prettiest girl alive. If I could only voice she was the one who brightened my days far more than any morning sun…tell her I loved her eyes, her skin, her every movement…tell her that I liked her being so smart and liked it when I saw her read her books so quietly and peacefully…*

But what of Dad? He'd always been my stronghold. He'd probably say I was a fool to think she was unique, different from all pretty faces in a crowd, say all this was for the best, as whatever pain and discomfort I may have felt at that moment would likely be hundreds of times worse if she knew I liked her like I liked no other.

I stood to peep again. She lay with hair displaced and dress meshed over Kelly's pink ruffled comforter. Her eyes were glued shut and lips quivered in deep trance by Gerard's continuous kissing and fondling. His hand soon slid down under her dress—in between her legs, exposing for the first time her red lacy underpants. I grew cold as again I felt emptiness sequester me with the most bitter of agonies. Trapped I was as every second seemed like hours inside a million year old frozen block of ice. My eyes wanted to cry. My heart wanted to beat a final beat. *You see,* Dad's voice ricocheted in my head, *you never could listen—never could understand without having to question or doubt…Forget your heart. Be wise, wise like strongest of men, void of feeling and immune to darkest of evil spells and venomous bites…*

Helplessly I slid back down to the floor, thinking I should just walk out on them. But what would I say? How would I act? Moreover, how could I not be seen as this thief of deep secrets? Oh, how I wished I was back downstairs with Ivan and Danny. How I wished I was not the intrigued curious fool I'd always been. A foolish dead cat one could have called me, as I was the victim of this world only few could call reality—only a few would have dared stare nine, ten, a thousand times over. I bet Ivan and Danny were somewhere searching my whereabouts. Maybe they'd made their way up the stairs. Maybe they'd made it past the bathroom…They weren't ones gripped by countless doors, ancient armor, or dark endless corridors, however. They understood their universe—their world. And they were a part of this here certainty I could never on earth be a part of.

"Stop it," she suddenly muddled. "Stop it…Please Gerry, don't."

I got back up on my knees to have another look. "It's okay," he slurred, his face buried deep between her hair and neck, his finger beginning to edge slightly underneath her underpants.

"No," she murmured, her eyes still glued shut.

"Yes," he whispered back, bombarding her with more kisses.

As if snapping out of some powerful trance, she pushed his hands away and with all her might shoved him off her. "I said NO!" Her eyes popped back open. She stood up and rushed to button her undone dress. Clumsily she straightened out what wrinkled creases she could. Her face appeared troubled and her eyes as though they'd sob—ashamed it seemed for letting herself go so far.

"Hey, where're you going?" he spat, surprised she had refused his advances.

"Just stay away from me," her scratchy voice whipped back.

"You know you wanted it. You wouldn't have come up here if you hadn't."

She ignored his comment and scurried out of the room.

If it had been any other girl, I guess I would have been witness to one of his many conquests. This was, after all, Gerard—big man on campus, irresistible stud and true conqueror of women.

Eventually he rose and picked his whiskey bottle off the bed. "What a stupid little bitch," he grumbled as he left.

Unique and chaste she still stood—on a pedestal overlooking this world so desolate. I waited until I heard no one before stealing my way out of the room. I traversed the rest of the dark corridor and turned into the next adjoining hall. Darkness which had claimed me diminished. A familiar set of stairs welcomed my return.

18

She was not among the infinite faces I saw. The party had doubled in size in the time of my journey. Stuffy air steamed of heat and perspiration even in the confines of the capacious foyer. The living room too was jam packed, almost impossible to squeeze through the dancing crowd whose hands waved up and down freely to the sound of booming music. Some of the more conservative guys had removed their ties and had them strapped around their heads. The less conservative gents had ripped off their shirts as they danced and paraded like half-naked madmen. Wildly, everyone shoved and heaved into one another as they slam danced, making the entire room as rowdy as could be. Several times I was pushed into the dance area. A girl I did not know grabbed me by the arm. She appeared dazed and said nothing as she pushed up against me, inviting me to join her provocative dance. Her smile never wavered, and her eyes told me she couldn't care less whether or not she knew my name. Quickly I pulled away and shoved my way towards the back, where finally a set of sliding glass doors led me out to the yard.

The pool shot reflections of moonlight glimmer; my body welcomed and sipped in the vibrant tropical breezes. I followed the meandering concrete path leading up to the gazebo. That's where I spotted Ivan and Danny. Both sat on adjacent railings, joining others I now recognized from Beach High.

"Where'd you go?" inquired Ivan.

"You guys won't even believe the rest of this house," I said looking up at the one corner window where I had stood high above. It whispered in tranquil apathy secrets only my imagination would dare claim reality. Below were another streamline set of windows extending the full width of the house. *Another floor full of endless hallways and rooms,* I thought. No doubt the bottom floor surrounded the courtyard within, just as the top. No doubt there must have been just as much mystery and intrigue.

Ivan and Danny followed my gaze, but helplessly undisclosed my stolen secrets dwelled as both tried to picture my diluted depictions. "And there were great big palm trees and a waterfall—and pond," I said. "And moonlight shined right into Kelly's room from a great big window above, like a spotlight from a Broadway play. And there was armor, doors everywhere, and hallways like mazes."

"I've had enough of this place," Danny commented as he jumped off the railing.

"Same here," Ivan agreed. He too readied to leave. "You go out in my backyard and all you see is concrete, dead weeds, and wild alley cats waiting for you to drop dead for a free scavenging meal."

"Wait." I scanned the rest of the yard. Desiree was nowhere to be seen. "We can't leave now."

"Why not?"

"The party's just getting started," I replied awkwardly as I darted back towards the house.

"Hey, where are you going?"

Gerard was near the sound system when I reentered the barrage filled room. He had whiskey bottle in hand and shared it with teammates from the football and basketball team. Squeezing up to him, I thought of calling him a jerk off right then and there. But then I thought otherwise. For I knew he'd kill me in a fight any day of the week. "Hey, you seen Desiree?" I asked politely. "Kelly's been asking for her."

His dazed eyes looked right at me, but unfamiliar I seemed as alcohol by now had fogged the better part of his memory. "I don't know," he said. "I think she went home." I delved back through the dancing crowd but not before I heard him tell others, "Desiree's like the worst lay ever. She's got no skills. She just laid there like a sack of potatoes, and not once did she holler or even scream my name." Even through the loud music I could hear him and his friends laugh. Though only I knew his tales were nothing but egotistical lies.

When I reached the foyer, I looked back up the spiral staircase. Maybe she was still up there somewhere, I thought, lost in the midst of those infinite rooms and dizzying hallways; or, she could have come down and drifted her way into that exquisite central courtyard.

I would have thought nothing of the one figure I briefly saw out in the dimly-lit porch area. For there were many who entered and gathered there. But red was what I saw. I peeped through the side curtains along the doors. The obscured frosted glass blotched my view. Only when I stepped out did the distorted figure become Desiree. She was leaned up against the side railing, her back towards the house and her quiet thoughts seemingly affixed on the blue trickling fountain beyond. Lost for words, I nearly swallowed my tongue, fearing she would tell me to keep well enough away, as she had Gerard.

My reluctant stagnation soon washed itself away helplessly, not allowing me to shy away from wanting to reach out as a friend. Too long I'd waited for a real peek behind her eyes, for her to share reasons for her sometimes saddened and detached ways—to trust that I could be this comforting ear to hear her sullen weeps or joyous tales—and that somehow I would understand…It did not matter that I already knew what had transpired upstairs; did not matter that we were strangers to one another even though we were both lab partners in a class two days away from Monday. All I wanted was to share in her aura, to somehow reinforce that I was indeed of this world—that I really did care, and that I really could trust in such a female.

"Nice fountain, isn't it?" Only after my weak murmur did I reaffirm my inexperience in such quiet moments. Maybe I should have said something different, something out of Mother's Spanish romance paperbacks—or even in that old *Titanic* movie Ivan always referred to when trying to disprove the subtle essences of true love.

She did not acknowledge, I guess not realizing my voice was meant for her. She turned only when my presence drew near. "Oh, hi," she muttered, reluctant to look right at me for fear I would see her smudged tears or hear her sniffling voice. A silent moment combined with the tranquility of the night rushed us both. The fountain trickled its delicate appeal, and the sound of another soft ballad filled the interior of the house. Everyone else on the veranda rushed inside. I too readied to go back in and leave her be, as it seemed this was what she wanted.

She cleared her throat though. "I'm okay," she added, her voice still trying to cover up her hurt.

"I'm sorry you feel so bad," I responded, not knowing how far to push the boundaries. "I saw Gerard in the living room. This doesn't have anything to do with him, does it?"

"Not just him." She paused and dabbed at her eyes. "All guys. I'm sorry to say, but all guys are the worst. They don't care about a girl's feelings or emotions. They don't care about innocence or love. Physical sensation and attention is what they breathe—a girl nothing more than a feel-good tool."

Was she too lost in another world different than the one we all shared—out on the moon or on a different planet all alone for only the stars to shine and take hold of? Perhaps this was like that midday TV show Mother liked watching—something along the lines of men being from the desert and women the sea, a show I always figured was produced by women, for women, in order to justify the horrific actions they themselves transcended onto a guy's solace atmosphere. Were we all truly from different environments, caught up in our own inconsistent time and space?

"I don't mean to offend," she said. "I should be more careful with what I say."

"It's all right, I understand." But that was just it. I really did not understand. The male species suddenly seemed as one—a negative commonalty which struck me as odd and somewhat incoherent. How could she even begin to put down guys when girls were the heartless ones? Did she not know of a girl named Gracie—or Eve and the Garden of Eden? Was she so unaware of the pain women caused men, of the powers and spells—the torment and anguish that she too was capable of? This was the first time I'd ever heard of such talk. It surpassed anything Dad had made known to me long ago. For guys were supposed to be the caring ones, helpless fools subjugated by women's instinctual evil ways. Women could not care less for love or a guy's true heart, just so long as they got whatever materialistic things they all *breathed* for.

Indignantly absorbed she stood. I would have left right then, left her out on the portico alone with her apparent ill-sided views of oceans and deserts. But something inside battled to think her tender eyes could ever be like Gracie's, a devotion that still whispered she was this rare exception—this vast ocean of good and warmth waiting to spill over onto my cold-dry desert of a heart.

My thoughts simmered, almost motionless as I searched for an antidote to her misery. "Don't cry," I said gently. "I'm sure whatever happened will pass."

"Yeah, I guess," she agreed, "but helpless and certain things do seem—all guys the same in nature and in smile." She dried her embittered tears and hid her sullen gloom, soon changing the subject as quickly as her solemn smile gave way. "You've known Kelly long?"

"Since kindergarten," I said. "We were classmates. No one wanted to be her friend back then. That's obviously not the case anymore."

"I've known her since summer. We both work at the mall."

A touch of enthusiasm I did voice. "Wow, the mall?"

"Yeah, in the bookstore."

"Sometimes my friend Ivan and I go in there and read magazines, scan pictures, and laugh over childish ads." I dared not mention that sometimes we liked to browse through some of the girly swimsuit magazines. That would have just reinforced her image of my being one of many. We continued our talk. I even made her laugh a few times when I told her Mrs. Wardell was really a bifocaled alien from outer space.

"I moved here from Albuquerque with my mom. She designs clothes and is trying to open up a boutique so she can sell her own line of clothes. She thinks she can make it big here."

"I've never been to New Mexico or even traveled out of Florida."

"Mountains and deserts were all I ever knew before coming here. I'd never been to a beach or had it rain in the sun...It really is nice—like nothing I've ever seen."

"What about your Dad?"

"I've never known my father," she let me know. "He left my mom when I was very young."

Our conversation went dead all of a sudden. I wanted to say I could relate, but I could not. For my parents had always been together despite their constant tribulation. "Well, I guess I do take my parents being together for granted," I said, "though sometimes I do wish they'd split up. They've always fought and argued, never satisfied until the other decides to give in. And it's usually my father who does—although you'd never know it by his loud intimidating voice."

"You should be thankful though. Most kids with divorced parents are stuck between two worlds, forced to choose sides. You end up thinking everything's your fault—your fault for having a mother and a father who can't get along. My best friend had parents who were divorced. Sometimes I was glad to be in a single-parent home, never having known my father—although that wasn't easy either."

So many turns and so many corners of intrigue my drawings and paintings portrayed. Touched in every way one could be, many times leaving with a different eye to make me into a genius...yet still never heard or understood beyond my tideless dreams. And never difficult was it to choose from one of my two sided worlds. For I had always looked up to Dad who took away any notion his arguments with Mother may have been my fault (or his) by assuring that every imperfection and inconsistent sentiment stemmed from this one woman (all women). In a different light Mother stood—never strong or confident as Dad, always crying and making commotions about every little thing, yet always getting her way—and in the end, causing my father to rile his emotions which in the end scornfully tore at his precious pride...And then the worst of my complicated realities, this other tarnished side I could not completely run away from—this hidden neglected side that said I did love my mother in some indiscreet way.

I tried steering our conversation in a brighter light. "You know, not all nights are imperfect. The stars often make promises you can always smile at, and..."

"Hey, why'd you take off like that?" Ivan blurted as he and Danny stepped out onto the porch. "We went upstairs and got lost. We thought you might have fallen into the toilet and drowned." He looked at Desiree momentarily. "But I guess you didn't." He smiled. "Hey."

"Hi," she said, returning his smile.

"We're leaving," said Danny as he jumped off the front steps. "Ivan's spending the night. You coming?"

"Yeah, I'll be over in a while. She's just waiting for her mom."

They walked off into the blue-lit garden. Laughter tickled them, as they'd never seen me alone with a girl before.

Desiree's soft look traveled to see my face. Shadows crossed over her face but could not hide her pretty features and stunning eyes. Her stare it seemed could read my mind, even behind my unspoken thoughts— silently melting away every inch of me, taking apart my flesh and blood to vividly grasp sight of every complicated, simple, and mediocre composition my soul claimed. Could she read my thoughts? Could she really make sense of this speck of sand whose cries chimed, *Marlo*?

We soon forgot about the time and this grand old mansion which loomed over both of us. "What are your dreams, Marlo?" she asked. I felt no need to avert my stare, as I saw myself become suddenly welcomed, accepted.

"Dreams?"

"Yeah, what do you wish for more than anything in this world?"

I thought for a moment, not really sure how to describe my dreams. For how did I say I dreamed of sandcastles which never fell, or wished to be a part of a world that would accept my complications and true identity? So too I could have said I dreamt of spending an entire day with her at the beach, where we could talk and laugh all day...and maybe even kiss like she and Gerard had. But I knew I could never tell her this. Despite her probing eyes, she really had no clue I found her so dreamy and alive. "I'd have to say my biggest dream is to make myself be known—to touch people and show myself through art and craft."

"An artist," she said. "I should have guessed. Those drawings you showed me the other day were incredible. They remind me of something..." She stood quiet, looking away from me as she stared up at the sky, nearly stealing away some of the stars that seemed to spell my name. "Now I remember," she uttered slowly as she turned my way again. "Your friends. I've met them before...You were the one on the beach that day, the one who built that sandcastle."

My entire body felt it lost a blanket that had kept it warm and safe for an entire lifetime. Hushed I stayed as I tried to scrape away my frozen afterthoughts.

"I thought you looked familiar when I first walked into class—though I couldn't quite place you. You were the one who built it, weren't you?"

I nodded, forgetting how to say yes aloud.

"I've never seen anything like it before," she went on. "Something out of a fairytale book." She looked towards the sky again, as if she really could read my name high above the heavens. "It was more like an image out of a dream you don't want to wake up from. More than just magnificent...It was magical—mystical. I'm sure not many guys can do what you do, even in their dreams."

"I'm not that good," I said modestly, not mentioning the other countless sandcastles I had built over time—or the other works of art I had slaved hours upon hours during loneliest of nights when I thought my parents' fighting would never let up. I mentioned nothing of my induction into the Wall of Fame either, of being one of Mr. Parlante's finest pupils—nor being Ms. Varian's little prodigy who could create magic with chalk, paint, and colored putty.

"Oh, but you are good," she kept saying. "When I saw that sandcastle, I said to myself: *This guy must be special, unlike most people.*"

The spotlight never burned brighter. I wanted to quickly bounce away as I always had when faced with a little fame and glory. "What about your dreams?" I asked, concealing a bit of my discomfort. "Do your dreams stretch beyond mountains and deserts, beyond this world?"

"I'm not quite the same artist you are," she responded, "but my dreams are similar. I write poetry and stories—very long stories. I dream of touching this world with a key that unlocks doors to darkened rooms. I feel a need to reveal—say things everyone holds true in their hearts, yet fails to acknowledge because society seems to shun away certain realities. If people think I'm an outcast, fine. If they think I'm from the moon or another planet, then fine. So long as I spark any kind of emotion—good or bad, it doesn't matter. Having magic, magic like your magic, is what I dream."

"You want to write books?" I asked, loving the passion and feel of her words. Her views of the moon and world seemed genuine, yet not on foreign grounds.

"Yes, I want to paint the world with my words."

"That's really cool. I know you'll do well even though I don't know what you write about."

She smiled, but I really didn't know what to make of it. Was she really captivated by my tideless dreams—of my desire to someday touch this world as she dreamed?

A car pulled up in front of the white gates and beeped its horn. "I gotta go. I'll see you Monday." She stepped off the porch and waved goodbye. I remained on the veranda lost in my thoughts, glad I'd mustered enough courage to share the stars and speak of clandestine dreams. I'd even made eye contact, and so too did she admire my sandcastles.

"What's her name again?"

"Desiree—Desiree Castillo," I told Ivan.

"Yeah, don't you remember?" said Danny as he sat on the floor randomly flipping through various TV and web channels. "We met her a long time ago with Kelly."

"Oh, yeah, now I remember. She's kinda weird. Doesn't say much and has those crazy looking eyes, the kind that possess you when you look into them. I've seen her alone a few times at the beach. She's always by herself and sits in the sand with a notebook and pen. One time, I even saw her crying as she sat there alone with her own written words."

I pictured her there on the sand writing her stories and sentimental poems, just as I often sat building my sandcastles along the shore—or painting my endless paintings perched on lonely easels.

"That is kinda weird," Danny agreed blandly.

"She's not weird," I spat, annoyed they could not understand her hopes and dreams. They met my face as it turned a bit red; not from anger, but from an almost unwarranted shame I did not quite know how to push away.

"You like her a lot, don't you?"

Revelation seemed a far foreign cry from anything I'd ever known, an obstacle which impeded my every notion of normalcy.

"Yeah, you like her," Ivan stated as he smiled. "Just don't lose sight and get all crazy. It's easy for girls to get you to like them—easy for them to make you all weak in the heart and mind. Soon they have you under this dizzying spell that just blinds your every move and smile. They know they can leave and come back to you whenever they want—and know they can fool you into thinking they really taste like honey, right Danny?"

Danny gave no reply, and I knew not what direction to steer my feelings or desolate eyes. An upside-up picture I'd struggled my life to paint, though the world as always displayed me one upside-down. How familiar and safe that moon suddenly felt—if only I could say I was still really there.

Just what would happen if she found out how I felt? She might say she likes me. We'd fall in love, if that was at all possible. I'd buy her whatever she wants, do whatever she wants, say anything she wants—anything to please this girl that would mean the universe to me…And for what? I shivered just then. She'd see how much I like her and know I can't live without her because she'd infuse me with this false sense of security that makes all men feel like men. Then she'd use this same power to crush me and make my life miserable. She'd say, "I'm sorry Marlo. I'm just not into you anymore. You bore me, and you're no longer as cool as that guy over there. He's exciting and challenging—he's got a nice shiny car, and bracelets and late night concert tickets…But don't feel bad. His challenge won't last forever. I'll come back soon enough—to use and bite you with my false love. We can start all over again, okay? I promise I won't ever leave you again…unless of course that other guy over there buys me that rock diamond I just love…or this other guy over here takes me on a three month cruise to the Bahamas."

Ivan was first to doze off on the couch by the window. I rested on the other couch. Danny remained on the floor. He looked up at me but didn't know I was still awake. Even in the dark shadowy room could I make out his boyish face crying silently as it struggled to surrender into a peaceful slumber.

Sleep evaded me for quite some time as I stared up at the ceiling. I thought about Kelly's party and her house which claimed so much majesty. I too remembered all I had learned about Desiree on this very night. I later fell into dreams—but not before I asked myself once again: *Was she unique?*

19

She did not smile as I would have liked come Monday—nor did she glow or gleam the same exuberance I felt. Rather, her days gloomed for weeks to come, growing even worse when autumn swamped the city with tempestuous rainfall. Her coughing and sneezing was as regular as her breathing, and her nose became a continuous runny mess. Lackadaisically she struggled through lectures and labs, finding nothing more important at times than staring off into her own little world. And when I'd try cheering her up with foolish silly jokes, she'd only give me forced struggling smiles, displaying less and less of her dimples I had come to know. A twinkling of sadness overcame me to find her so distraught and apathetically inclined to forget those dreams she had so vividly described the night of Kelly Rubia's party.

Mrs. Wardell did not help Desiree's condition any. Her dictionary of words and ways were colored black and white, clear cut—open and shut. Expectations were high and rigorous, the class painstakingly competitive. Pop quizzes continued daily and could not be made up if one missed class for any reason. Homework assignments which could have easily been answered in one or two sentences fell short of any norm, as Mrs. Wardell expected outside resources from books, magazine articles, and reference manuals to back up page long responses. Many of us would live in the library that first semester, and it seemed improbable that we would ever breathe an ounce of apathy again.

There were those who did eke out *A*'s that first quarter—but at great cost, and even then, the highest grade in the class had been no higher than an *A-*. Desiree's grade had fallen to a *B*. I was barely surviving with the lowest passing grade. My dream of art school appeared a dismal world away. More than ever, I thought of visiting Mrs. Canizaro in the guidance office to ask for a drop slip.

"There's no sense in killing yourself," I said dully. "She finds ways of making it impossible—even if you're doing the best of all possible work. It doesn't pay to try and survive here."

"Oh, but it does pay," Desiree responded as she looked up at the posted grades with sulking eyes. The rain was spattering all around the hallway. Water had even found its way into the classroom through the cracks underneath the door. Mrs. Wardell hurried to mop the area dry. "Everything has a cost," Desiree went on softly. "No matter what you want in this world, those famous paintings you so much look forward to—or even that sandcastle you hope will never fall, it all comes at a price that only seems impossible." With those words she turned and quietly made her way to her next class. Rain drenched her body in seconds as she crossed over to Chatter Hall.

No matter how sick she became—no matter how dreary she may have appeared or felt, she refused to give in. It was then that I decided to hold strong—to put on my war gear and try even harder to raise and maintain my grades for the admission committee at the Art Academy. Yes, I did have that dream of art school and one day touching the world with my magic. And yes, I too, like Desiree, did have that sense of perfectionism which would make my talents shine. I gave up painting and even drifting off into late night television or midnight sleepovers with Ivan and Danny. So too did I give up my daydreams of sandcastles and endless summer days in sun and delight.

"And then there's *Weeping Prince*," I later revealed. "You just have to see it. It's near the gym; the Wall of Fame they call it. *Weeping Prince* is there." We walked and stopped in front of the glass-cased tank that seemed could swallow up the entire world. For that's what it was, an entire world full of every artistic expression you could imagine. The glass sparkled with an immaculate shine. Thousands of engraved names around the glass came alive and whispered endless tales of school history.

"I've walked past this wall several times and have noticed all its art," said Desiree. "Is that it?" She pointed at it, hesitant to take her eyes off the glass. "*Weeping Prince*?"

I nodded.

For a long moment she stood and looked on with glowing eyes and with lips slightly parted, speechless and stricken with a quiet look of admiration—as though she'd been lured into a never-never land that would never escape her. "What on earth made you paint such a scene?"

"I was flipping through my history book one day and fell in love with pictures of Mayan pyramids. I read passages about their temples and ancient rituals and thought of this scene. There's a whole story behind it, though I have no idea what it is. I thought I would just capture a simple scene and let all other eyes tell the rest."

"You really are gifted, Marlo. Your work would have never been placed in here if you weren't."

I looked away. "I'd like to think so, and I hope that one day I can share with the world what is now only shown for this school to see."

I was just as eager to share in her own articulate works. She was reluctant at first, but I assured her I was no critic of literature and that I was certain to feel the magic in her lengthy penned journals. Her poems flowed with a rhythm I had never picked up on in Shakespeare or Byron. Her stories were strange and difficult to understand—like Poe's work, but quite vivid and serene, putting the reader right into the scene. The more I read, the more I found her creative mind meshed with mine. It was amazing. She had a poem about graffiti, the moon, the stars, a sad child, and an open plain that was covered with tall grass and a single tree that stood alone in the midst of a desolate plain. *Nothing around*, she wrote in a poem called, "Paradise and Be." *Only wind, sun, and all that which makes us free and be.* It rendered me weak, with the same solidified solitude I had always felt in my own real universe.

She looked up at the sky. The sun we had not seen in days seeped through the clouds and hit her face. A splendid vivaciousness sparked her; the first time her smile had shown in weeks. "Oh, I hope to be the great artist you'll be one day, Marlo. Writing is the key to everything I am, everything I feel—everything I like and dislike. I don't really know my true self until I reach deep down and spill everything out on paper. Letting out what I feel is the only way I know how to breathe." She took a deep breath. "You know, I've never met anyone who likes to paint or who's even good at it. It seems all painters and artists have all but disappeared...Tell me more about those sandcastles you build."

"My father introduced the art to me when I was very young," I said, "though he's not much of an artist. Since then I've been hooked. But I think I really became inspired by this one guy I came across when I was nine years old. My parents had gotten into a huge fight at home. I had thoughts of running away because I was fed up with their fighting. I stopped by the beach, not knowing where I was headed. I thought of just disappearing into the ocean and sunset. But I soon spotted this one guy all by himself near the shore. He had built this huge amazing sandcastle that left me spellbound. He looked sad, as though he had lots on his mind. He asked me not to destroy it as he left. I stood alone for the longest time—just me and that sandcastle. Eventually it grew dark, and I went back home because I was hungry and afraid to be out after dark. When I arrived back the next morning, the castle was gone...I never saw that guy again. And then that's when I really began to build—when I really began to dream."

"That's an incredible story, an incredible dream to dream," she commented.

My eyes fled her deep, searching stare. "You know, I really liked your poetry a lot," I said, handing back the notebook she had lent me in exchange for my sketchbook of charcoal sketches she had asked to see again.

"Oh, stop. You're just saying that to be nice."

"No, I really liked it a lot." I found her eyes once again. "It totally touches me like nothing I've ever read. I mean, it reminds me so much of some of my own work...I loved the poem about the towers and how they will never fall so long as their glory lasts forever. The one about the stars giving us wisdom and the one about the lonely tree really strikes home."

"I was going to tell you the same thing," she replied. "Some of your drawings strike up images I'd pictured long ago. The one sketch with the big mushroom growing over the world reminds me of my poem about the world being vaporized by an ion explosion after nations have all but banned the reading and writing of poetry. The one of the boy in the mirror reminds me of the soul who could not be because he could not see."

If truly I was blind, I welcomed it. This was not to say Dad's warnings about women did not still haunt me. I was still reluctant to reveal all my feelings to her, afraid to disrupt whatever close friendship we were building. For I had no idea what her feelings were toward me and was unsure whether or not she still had eyes for Gerard Medina who continuously presided over all the school. I kept my feelings of attraction a concealed puppy-love fantasy, a sort of passion and feel expressed in great romanticized paintings—or maybe even in romance novels and childhood poems. I didn't have the nerve to call her in the evening, even though she had given me her number in case I ever had questions on homework. Not always would I join her when I saw her in the library after school either. *Oh, if I can truly ever love, then let it be now. If I really am a part of this world, then let my passion be set free like winds that stand hidden in quiet storms. Let my touch and warmth be felt like the touch of wild flowers growing in bursting pastures. A tree barren to this common field, a fish lost among this abyss of ocean. No longer do I feel a need to flee...For true I feel to be.*

"What's up with you and Desiree?" Ivan asked as he and Danny spotted me with sketchbook in hand as I parted ways with Desiree.

"We're just cool, that's all," I said.

"You mean you haven't gotten all nasty with her yet?"

A giant magnifying glass it seemed loomed over me.

"Don't think she doesn't want a piece of you. Don't think her eyes don't undress you—especially now that you have her hooked with your cute little artwork."

Danny laughed, though I didn't think it funny. They obviously could not see the kind of girl I knew her to be—the kind of dreams she dreamed or the smiles she smiled. "She's not that kind of girl," I said stiffly.

"Sure she isn't. I bet she screams your name every time she wets her pants."

"Go to hell, Ivan," I responded as I turned and walked away, no longer willing to be the quiet naïve little soul who'd always fallen victim to his father's own benevolent words.

"Dude, I'm only joking," said Ivan as he caught up to me. "Don't take shit so serious."

I stopped my tread through the wet uncut grass. "I can't help it. She's really different—not like what you say."

"It's cool," he said. "Just know she's only human though—you know, 'she grunts when she takes a shit too' kinda thing."

Danny stood in the background quiet as could be. No doubt he must have felt as confused when Ivan and I had confronted him about Gracie.

Was I really going dangerously blind, or was my heart only making me see what had long since been hidden within the blank canvases of my tideless dreams?

20

"Twenty pages," she said as her stern look stabbed at us all. "Your team has four weeks before winter break. I would take this report very seriously and use every precaution to make sure you do a thorough job. Forty percent of your grade is a make or break scenario. Do not start the report a day before it is due. Do not copy directly from online material or from pre-printed books or text. I've read virtually everything on genetics and biotechnology and will know who has legitimately done their work."

It seemed impossible to think Mrs. Wardell could have read every article and news clipping on such a highly publicized subject. Yet no one in class doubted or dared challenge her wisdom. "Listed are the top fifty firms and universities involved in genetic research." She passed out a stapled set of addresses and phone numbers. "You may call any or all and have them send you material. Neither the library nor cyber space will be a sufficient source for your research…Note also that some of these firms will be reluctant to give out information. The genetics research industry is a highly competitive and secretive industry—even to this day."

Desiree and I met after school each day in the library to begin work on our lengthy project. I took on the job of contacting every company and university on our list. Most were helpful—but there were those that, as Mrs. Wardell suggested, were reluctant to reveal any new found advances in genetic study. I also embarked on hand sketching a chart of the most modern decoded human genetic diagram to date. Each one of my sectioned maps was meticulously detailed and color-coded, pointing to several links related to inherited traits found in human DNA.

While we awaited material to be either mailed or electronically forwarded, Desiree focused her energies on our introduction and thesis statement. "What do we really want to say?" she asked as we considered many possible topics.

"Let's just say that we'll one day be predicable," I said, "variety in the human species gone forever. You know, a master race as Adolf Hitler envisioned long ago. We'll have no disease or physical or mental inferiorities to speak of. In the process, we'll see all artists, poets, musicians, and philosophers become even more extinct to make room for scientists with great IQ's—and perfect athletes with flawless physiques. Mr. Parlante says advancing technology and tampering with the physical may do away with what we consider to be the "ills" of our society. But no one realizes that it's these "ills" or imperfections which make us all great, so capable of tapping into irreplaceable sentimental accomplishments which stem from human soul and vision."

"True creativity and gifted talents could be God sent," Desiree suggested. "In theory, we've read nothing that suggests artistic expression or vision is inherited. Perhaps all talent and ingenuity really is a gift sent down from heaven, and it does not matter what science does to thwart our bodies or our minds. Maybe we'll one day be great scientists, with perfect healthy bodies—and still be able to sing, dance, rhyme and paint perfect pictures."

We agreed to keep our research a complete secret and our thesis undisclosed, hoping we could spark a sense of surprise when we pushed our question onto Mrs. Wardell: *Can Artists Be Cloned?* Oh, such a brilliant topic which seemed to motivate Desiree and me into writing a most eloquent piece of work.

Packages of material from the University of California at San Francisco and Stanford University soon arrived as promised. With them and other electronic forwarded journals and articles, we had enough to compile a finished draft weeks before our due date.

Other classmates did not enter the library until after the first week. Most had not yet thought of a topic. And when asked what we would base our report on, Desiree and I discreetly told them, "Albino mice raised on Jupiter."

"We're going to show Mrs. Wardell," Desiree confided fervently. "Our report is going to be perfect—as perfect as a cloned artist."

We were careful not to let our enthusiasm get in the way of knowing we had chosen a challenging topic. We were taking an awfully large gamble focusing on "artistic cloning." Mrs. Wardell was just one of those teachers you had to be conservative with and never go out of your way to combat her points of view. There was no reason for her or anyone else to think we could not replicate another human with the same vision and ingenuity of a Rembrandt, Picasso, Mozart, or Shakespeare. Mrs. Wardell wasn't the creative type or one to hold importance in something unrelated to the true building blocks of nature. To make her happy, we included a lengthy section on genealogy, DNA & RNA reproduction in humans, and chromosomal composition as it pertained to human development.

"How about getting together tomorrow?" Desiree asked after another long afternoon in the library.

"Tomorrow's Saturday," I said sighing, suggesting we had already accomplished plenty in two week's time. "The library here's closed."

"That's all right," she said. "We can finish up at my house. I won't have work tomorrow since I agreed to work the late shift tonight."

There was still lots of work I needed catch up on in my other classes. Had she still not been such a mystery, I would have declined the offer.

She lived not far from school. Her address led to a large apartment complex that stretched nearly two city blocks. I chained my bike and walked down one of the narrow pathways which took me through a maze of apartment houses, where finally a wall map brought me to a heavy cast iron gate. A pleasant swimming pool and a few patio chairs and tables greeted me as I stepped through the swinging door. Dozens of doors surrounded the pool area. A second level with a surrounding balcony so too hugged the surroundings.

"Up here," I heard someone voice. Desiree was stooped over the metal railing, motioning me to come up.

"Cool place," I said as I climbed the stairs. I turned and seeped in a most peaceful vibe of tranquility. From above, the entire complex looked like a small city of elaborate walkways and structures. Palm trees encompassed lots and walkways, outlined by groomed green grass and a spectrum of colorful wildflowers. Not a soul walked the paths I had strolled nor did cars or trucks on enclosed parking lots ruffle the silence. All stood still.

"It's a little too quiet for me," replied Desiree. "I'm not really used to it. I like a bit of noise every once in a while." Her hair was wet. A long football jersey hung over her jeans. Sandals exposed petite feet and tiny toes. She was as plain as a plain bagel, though all I saw was a lovely unset gem, sparkling with priceless charm. "You're a little early," she said as she escorted me into her apartment. "I had just dipped into the pool for a swim."

Silver-white carpet appeared unblemished and virgin underfoot. Long vined plants and flowers hung from different corners of the ceiling. Lamp tables were of a plastic-metallic alloy which glowed with an array of different fluorescent colors, and lamps were the kind that would illuminate neon colors when switched on. Both couches were bulky and patterned with different checkered and triangular shapes. The artwork I glanced at was of a curious computer-based design, also patterned with squares and triangles. Nothing my eyes viewed was circular or cylindrical in form—not even the large sliding windows ahead which saw the bay off to the distance and the metropolis and its skyscrapers etched into the background to paint an embracing picture of urban life.

Desiree stepped through a dim hallway on the left and into one of the bedrooms. A door at the end partially concealed a bathroom. To my right was a small kitchen area with eat-in breakfast bar. I sat down on one of the patterned sofas, putting my book bag down and noticing the photo frame on the blue plastic-cubed coffee table. A woman sat in a chair. Desiree stood elegantly behind her. No doubt this must have been her mother. Both their features were strikingly similar, sharing the same dark-brown hair and the same dimpled smiles. Only Desiree's darker complexion and slanted green eyes separated the two.

She came back with book bag in arm as she struggled to brush the dampness from her hair. "You know," she said as she sat next to me. "I was thinking. We'll be finished with everything this week."

"We'll be the first ones done," I said. "No one's really gotten started yet."

Her eyes shut as she propped back and whipped her hair across her face to free some of the moisture. Again she brushed through her damp hair, looking so radiant in her perfect olive-toned complexion. A priceless portrait I could have painted, but to seize her beauty would have been something only a cloned artist could have done, for not even my most tickled of fancies could have captured but even a glimpse. "I have punch, juice, or soda," she offered.

"No thanks," I said, not wanting to make myself feel too at home.

She opened her eyes finally. "I've been here all bored. My mom and I usually spend very little time together with her boutique and all. She would never approve of having a guy over she doesn't know."

"Maybe I shouldn't stay long," I said.

"Don't worry. She knows I have to get this report done."

The next several hours saw us put finishing touches on the entire body of our paper as well as our conclusion, footnotes, and bibliography. Twenty-three pages. Never had I been a part of such a lengthy school project—not even in all my history or English classes where three or four page reports were considered overachievements. I felt as though I had ascended into a higher level of school never before thought possible—so glad I had thus far avoided Mrs. Canizaro in the guidance office and so thankful to have such a hardworking lab partner by my side.

"Snowball likes you a lot," said Desiree as her tiny white poodle wagged its tail emphatically, insisting that I keep petting him. He'd been out on the balcony the entire time I had been there and could hardly keep still now that Desiree had let him in. He licked my hand and forced it over his shaggy white head.

"He's so cute," I commented.

She kept her smile, glad to see my affection towards her dog. Snowball jumped onto the couch and climbed on Desiree, trying desperately to lick her face. She laughed hysterically and finally calmed him. Her gentle ways and affectionate demeanor made her even more of an alluring entity. Everything about her seemed to make my smile as bright as day, my heart as rich as sweet frosted cake. Was this love? Had Dad been as romantically enamored by my mother long ago? Had Mother warmed his heart as Desiree warmed mine?

"I have some movies I downloaded from *Movie Buster*," she said as she got up and switched on the billboard. The screen displayed titles: *Bloodbath High* and *Escape from Zombie Island*.

We had more in common than I thought. We weren't fond of buttered popcorn. We liked our popcorn cauliflower white, with enough salt to make our lips flame. And I too was a fan of low-budget horror movies which all seemed to be filmed in the director's own backyard—with actors chosen from unemployment lines.

We watched the first movie but stopped midway through the second. Instead, we sat and discussed the most creative ways of chopping people up. Not the most touching of conversations, but we did wonder why murderers never simply shot their victims with guns rather than axe bodies to pieces.

"They couldn't use guns," she said. "It would give all us younger generation too many ideas."

"Yeah, I guess hacking teenagers to death is a bit more mainstream."

It was definitely different spending the day with a girl—especially one I liked. Ivan, Danny, and I had always had great times. But this was such a change.

Orange twilight shadowed the fading sky into a dark, insipid-magenta overcast. "I really should get going," I said as I remembered the countless hours of other homework I still had at home.

"Marlo, you're so unlike other guys I've known," she stated at the door.

"Don't tell me I seem gay," I said awkwardly, trying to interject whatever humor I could. Little did she know I was trying to see what her true reactions would be. For deep down, I would have wanted to be like Gerard, macho and strong—stunning and irresistible to all females.

"No," she giggled. "I mean, I've never met any guy like you, and I'm not referring to your art. You actually looked like you were having a good time."

"Yeah, I really liked the popcorn, and the movies were great."

"Other guys would have been bored and would have preferred doing other things."

I looked at her blankly. "What things?"

"You know."

I grasped the doorknob tightly, trying to find some way of doing away with the awkward feeling I was getting. It was like me to be so naïve, so like me not to look past the little kid in me. Our glances welded like iron, and her deep simmering eyes spied right through me as though I were a wide open book. Unexpectedly and yet tentatively she moved closer and placed a gentle kiss over my lips. Her eyes looked back into mine as she broke away, her body close enough to feel her small, perky breasts poke against my chest. My hand slipped from the doorknob as I reached to clasp onto one of her soft silky hands. Again our tongues meshed, and our lips embraced an awkward dance. A burning sense of excitement soon washed over me as that bigger part of me began to swell. My hand immediately let go of hers, and my body drew away. Flustered, I turned the knob. I crouched forward as I continued to bulge uncontrollably, my heart throbbing and my hormones raged like burning brush. "I gotta go," I mumbled awkwardly.

"What's wrong?" she asked, her eyes a bit confused—let down as though there was still lots left unsaid.

"Nothing," I assured. I retreated down the stairs as though rain were upon me. Not once did I look back or wave a hint that I truly did like her beyond dreams. Oh, how could I ever face her again? How could I ever learn how to live with doors wide open? I was supposed to be her lab partner, her friend, different in her eyes—not like other guys who'd only see her as prey. What would she think of me now—if she knew I was so much this guy to have these urges which to this point had only taken place in the deepest reaches of fantasy?

She'd hate me.

Intimidated by her presence, feeling as though she had unlocked a door never before opened, I said very little come Monday—very reminiscent of the way I had been the beginning of the school year. I was quick and precise with replies to questions and comments, leaving no opportunity for small talk or giggling smiles. So too did I look the other way when her stare fell my way. She sensed my change and soon too only spoke and smiled when needed. I tried desperately to change my inept ways, but there was that familiar sense of moonly isolation I had not felt in quite some time.

Again we were strangers.

"Aren't you guys gonna study today?" asked Ivan as we spotted Desiree alone at her bus stop.

"We're done studying."

"What's the matter, you guys have a little quarrel?" He laughed and so too did Danny share his laughter.

I dared not tell them she'd been my first kiss. For they would have never let me live it down. I'd be seen as the only virgin left alive. Even Gracie had not been Danny's first kiss, and even Danny it seemed had great tales of virginities lost. Oh, why did I have to be so different—be so sensitive? Why couldn't I simply sip in the present and spit away that which was supposed to be certain?

Oh, Desiree, don't think your kiss didn't mean anything to me. Don't think I don't like you beyond dreams. I know you're different than all the rest—know you don't have fangs with poison in your blood.

Ivan and Danny headed towards the gym where Beach High readied to play its first home basketball game against Dade. Ivan was to perform at halftime and wanted both Danny and me to be there. Sorely, I withdrew, wanting no part of any spectacle. Instead, I grabbed my books and left for home.

It was then that I faintly heard, "You hate me, don't you?"

The halls and classrooms stood empty. Even the custodians had abandoned their wash buckets and brooms to go watch the big game. As I looked her way, there was no denying her words were meant for me. Her head was held low with eyes averted, sullen and dreary—a look I had not seen in quite some time.

Our principal and his secretary came out of the administration building, but they paid us no attention. They locked the doors and also headed to the gym.

"Hate you?" My voice trembled as I took a few difficult steps forward. I shook my head. "No way, not you."

Her voice cracked, but she held back her tears. "I've felt horrible this whole week, Marlo. I'm sorry I came on to you like I did. I thought that's what you wanted—thought that's what all guys wanted. I honestly wish I could take it all back. I don't want to lose our friendship."

I tried best I could to say the right things, again realizing I had not seen *Titanic* nor been well versed in paperback lingo. "Please, don't feel bad," I said. "I'm the one who should be apologizing for acting so dumb. I loved spending the day with you, doing our homework together, watching those movies and petting your dog. You don't even understand how much. I couldn't paint a more perfect day."

This time her eyes streamed into mine as they simmered in the sun. "Then why did you rush away like I'd done something so wrong? Many times I've tried reading your eyes, but you always turn away, like you're trying to hide something you don't want me to see."

Yeah, this is me. I now stand in this great mirror for you and all to see. Oh, to be...to be, be, be...

"It was nothing you did," I said finally. "I just...didn't expect you'd ever like me."

"You really are different from anyone I've ever met, Marlo. You're deep, sensitive, and you care about how I feel...You have dreams, magical dreams, and you touch me so much with your art. Maybe I'm a fool to think you could ever like me in the same way."

"But I do," I said, trying to find the right words to tell her she was my dream come true—but without actually telling her. For that foolish indecisiveness still feared the threat of pain—the worst of all torments. "It's just that you were—" I paused again as my eyes shyly eluded her gaze, feeling as awkward as I had when I first laid eyes on that naked statue in the museum long ago. "You were my first."

"First what?"

"Kiss."

If truly I was different, then it suddenly didn't seem all bad. Her smile told me so. And her eyes sparkled a familiar sense of satisfaction I'd always associated with blue skies and warm sunny days.

"No girl's ever liked me," I went on. "I'm a weird guy around here, you know."

"Not weird—special." She stepped closer and kissed me on the cheek. "I'll see you," she said. "I have to get to work."

"What's up with our report?"

"It's polished as can be," she replied as she made her way back to the bus stop. "It just needs to be inputted. If you want, you can come over tomorrow and help me."

"I don't know how to work a computer," I shouted.

"It doesn't matter. Come anyway."

I took a deep breath as I kept the biggest of smiles. She too waved in delight.

Oh, days truly could be bright, so very bright. A fool in love I was, feeling I could walk in circles and still arrive wherever it was I was headed; felt too I could swim in a desert and float on waves—never dying of thirst, never drowning of sorrow. A perfect sandcastle I now could paint, far away from this shore and far away from this world where walls went unblemished and towers forever wind free.

She was unique…and I was special.

PART III

Blue

21

Warm tingly Atlantic waters washed over our bare feet to remind me of all the dreams my sandcastles had whispered in years past.

"Everything was so perfect, so exact—like a real castle," said Desiree. She looked peacefully out into the horizon just as I. "It was inspiring, something I'd always wanted to write about...It must have been sad knowing it would not last beyond that day."

"I watched it fall into nothing as the tide rolled in," I replied. "The sand fell neatly into place, and the water became its blanket...I was held powerless as all I could do was watch."

She was making me see differently, making me look past my art for the first time to see a real me—this ordinary person I'd longed to be. She caused me no pain, no sorrow, no misery. We liked the movies, the beach, the park, and bright sunny days. We liked to laugh and sometimes look in each other's eyes and play teasing games or simply just lose one another in each other's sight. Yeah, we'd innocently kiss on the lips and hugged whenever we parted, but that was the extent of it. It never went beyond the most casual of affections which she and I always welcomed. For we were more friends than anything else, bonded like links to a chain.

"What do you think we'll get in Mrs. Wardell's class?" she asked.

"You'll probably get an A," I answered. "I'm up in the air."

"No way. My average was way down."

"Yeah, but our report kicked butt. She can't deny you a top grade."

I thought back to the morning of our presentation. It was the day before we were dismissed for winter break. Mrs. Wardell had motioned us next. Desiree was beyond nervous. "C'mon, you wrote it," I whispered. "The least I can do is present it. I promise I won't mess your words up."

I stood up in front of the entire class, at once regretting my courage. Public speaking had too much spotlight for me not to feel the nervous bite and vulnerability of swallowing anything I'd say. I settled behind the podium, a bit safer yet still internally swarmed with fluttering butterflies.

Mrs. Wardell looked on with a keen eye, grasping onto her grade book and opening our report to page one. *"Can Artists Be Cloned?"* she remarked to the class. "Very interesting. A bit ambitious and passive, wouldn't you say?"

I ignored her and cleared my throat, looking on at my audience who had been expecting a report on albino mice bred on Jupiter. My nerves continued on edge as everyone's eyes beamed on me with delightful anticipation.

"Have you ever wondered what it would be like to live in a world full of artists?" I began. *"Ever wonder what it would be like to be filled with dance, rhyme, charm, and vivid empowerment without ever knowing you had the power to rule emotion and touch spines? Countless patterns of genes rule our domain."* I motioned to our five-set diagram behind me. *"To pattern them and clone a perfect universe: would we want such a place? To rid this life of ills we so much loathe: would it not too undo an already perfect man in an imperfect world?"* I stopped and again referred to our diagrams. Briefly I elaborated best I could, going into tangents and describing our findings of various gene pools that were linked to cancer, heart disease, diabetes, and other widely known imperfections we had come to know. I made sure to stick to the topic at hand. Mrs. Wardell appreciated this. She listened and seemed to hold interest in our profound poetic prose.

"Perhaps it would be possible," I went on, *"to one day tap into an unknown set of genes which make some of us viewers and feelers of this here true world. But would we ever want to live in a world full of Picassos? Would we ever feel and touch his beauty if we were all just as insightful and magical? For if artists could be cloned, then so too this universe…and so too this here God who sends these unique gifts for us to discreetly share and touch hidden truths…No, we say. Artists cannot be cloned. Gifts are they—gifts tapped into hidden realms of this here universe… Create us blue, yellow, black, brown. Create us to be men and women who can dunk basketballs, men and women who can out equate mathematicians—even create us to rise above time and space. But do not generically recreate a man or woman who can see, feel, and touch truth. For there may never be any more greater truths to feel or touch. Generic and fake this here world would lie, for us to die and rest awake in bitter charm."*

Our report ranked up there with the very best, though Mrs. Wardell only smirked, questioning, "Do you not believe we could all be supermen and still be and feel different?"

No one in the class replied. Desiree stood up. "If we were all supermen, then there would be nothing to measure our super abilities against. Everything would be superficial and relative only to the new complicated miseries that will face this new world of superheroes. It is our imperfection which allows artists to be artists."

Mrs. Wardell gave no reply. Rather, she sat quietly at her desk and flipped through our project once more. "Okay," she said as she clapped her hands rapidly, "who's next?"

Waves rolled gently in about our feet, then receded. "You got to believe she liked it," I said. "It was well researched, and you had a chance to charm her with your words."

"Oh, but you know that lady. She'll hang us if we've left so much as one *T* uncrossed or one *I* undotted." She paused to dig her feet under the wet sand. "Maybe you're right though. I shouldn't worry...It's just that so much depends on me getting into a good college. I want to make my mother proud. No one in my family has ever gone onto college."

Again she looked off into the horizon, where water touched sky. I stood silently as I too watched the sun shine brightly over the silvery ocean. The sky overhead seemed to engulf us all, including sunbathers who settled in the sand.

"And you know what else?"

"What?" I responded

She shoved me unexpectedly toward the water. It was the second time she'd tried pushing me in. This time I lost my balance and fell. A wave crashed over my head and engulfed my entire body. She backed away as she laughed hysterically. "No!" she hollered as I reached for her feet. "Don't you dare." She fell back onto the sand as a second wave rushed in to drench us both. We were wet and covered in sand as we walked home, but that was okay. We'd had another fun day.

Come Christmas, I gave the greatest present of all—a piece I knew Desiree would prize. No, it was not an expensive bracelet or priceless concert tickets. She admired the idea of sandcastle dreams, so I tediously worked to capture that same sandcastle she had so much cherished. It took about a week to seize the image I remembered from early summer. Its towers mesmerized the entire canvas as it stood in solitary splendor, near a vast lonesome shore, accompanied by cloudless blue skies which offset the perfect blue-teal waters of the horizon. White-sandy dunes and shoreline stretched from one end of the canvas to the other, displaying heavy surfs and tumultuous waves. The castle stood untouched atop a high sandy hillside. This had not been the way it had originally been constructed—not the way it had actually been made mortal and tactile.

But this was how I had wanted it, an illustrious sandcastle never to fall, never to be victimized by countless tides rolling in and out like a constant stream of certainty eliminating all hope from this world. Not the highest of waves or the moon's detracting cries could remove its elegance—nor tear away at its heart and dreams…Forever it would stand. Forever its glory would rise and cry.

Desiree's eyes gazed over it like a magical book that transported her to another world where everything was indeed perfect. Her lips parted, and her smile soon glistened over the entire day. "I don't know what to say," she said as she tore away the rest of the brown wrapping paper. "It's absolutely beautiful."

And you're even more beautiful, I wanted to say, to somehow reveal my deepest of sentimental feelings. But I stopped myself from such clichés. Again, this was a side that terrified me so, a side I had not yet come to terms with. "I tried to get it exactly as I remembered it. I figured you'd like it."

"Oh, I do. You must have spent forever on this. I'll hang it in my room so I can look at it everyday for inspiration. Your pictures really are worth a thousand words."

I didn't know that it would quite fit in with the modern array of geometric computerized artworks already hung in her apartment, but that didn't seem to matter to her. "I'll write about it one day," she promised. "And I'll try my best to describe these sandcastle dreams you hold so dear to your heart."

She handed me a flat, colorfully wrapped package of her own. I thought maybe she too had painted me a picture, but the wrapping was from the art supply store at the mall. I tore at it knowing it must have cost a fortune, for most items in that store were beyond expensive. I stared at the bundled collection of fine art supplies I had always wanted but could never afford. I refused to take her gift at first, not ever wanting her to spend money on me. She insisted, however, hugging me tight and kissing me on the cheek—giving me a bit of that mothering sensation I had not felt in quite some time.

It was safe to say this was my most magical Christmas ever. As it was, my parents rarely fought during the holidays. Mother was usually in the best of moods, loving the scent of a fresh cut tree in the house and loving all the shopping and cooking that went along with Christmas. Dad too liked Christmas because he truly did like to see Mother happy. Yeah, he complained about Mother's spending, but he never went cheap when it came to putting a sparkle in her eyes. He usually bought her expensive jewelry or fine clothing from department stores Mother couldn't afford to shop at. In return, she would see to it that Dad got what he wanted—usually expensive hand tools, a workbench, or a tool shed to store his large assortment of building materials that cluttered our garage.

"Marlo's got a girlfriend," Tamara teasingly blurted as she childishly skipped through the house that year. "Marlo's got a girlfriend. Marlo's got a girlfriend."

"What's her name?" Mother asked as she smiled at me from across the table.

Awkward I felt admitting I had a girlfriend, as it sounded like a cute little phase a small child would go through when having a crush on a teacher...or maybe even a certain babysitter. Desiree was no phase.

"Her name's Desiree Castillo," Tamara blurted as she dug into her dinner plate, "and she's got these weird looking eyes."

"Why don't you hush?" I told her.

"Desiree," Mother commented to herself. "That's a nice name. Means desire." She smiled again. "Why don't you invite her over for dinner one of these days?"

"Yeah," Tamara agreed.

"Invite her over for your father's New Year's Eve birthday party," Mother suggested.

Dad finished the last of his rice, but he said nothing about his party or Desiree. In his mind, this was just a cute little phase, feeling, I suppose, that I would know better than to ever give my heart away so carelessly. For he'd always been the one to warn me of the pain associated with girls.

Desiree was hesitant at the invitation when I told her, afraid my parents would not like her.

"You have nothing to worry about," I assured. "My parents won't think badly of you." Of course, I did not mention anything about Dad and his views of women. "And you don't have to get him anything either. All you need to do is be there. My mother and sister really want to meet you. My dad's party would be a perfect opportunity...I'll admit, my home life is sometimes shaky, but my parents have always accepted my friends and Tamara's friends."

"I'll see what my mother says," she responded. "She may not want me out on New Year's Eve."

Our report cards arrived shortly after Christmas. Desiree's biology grade read *A-*, and to my great surprise, mine was a *C+*. "It's not the best grade in the world," I exalted, my eyes widening bigger than the sky that day, "but hell, it beats failing. And it does say I'm above average—above average in an advanced biology class."

"You'll have no problems getting into that art school, Marlo," Desiree said as I walked her home from another of her busy days at work. "Your grades are good. Combined, they boost your grade average to a *B*. Why, getting a *C* in an advanced integrated class is really like getting a *B* in a normal mainstream class. All colleges know this."

Yes, I had stepped a giant leap closer to my dream. Yes, I could survive. And yes, I still had a chance to share my magic with the world so long as I kept my focus. Oh, how could I ever not thank God for having Mrs. Canizaro put me in Mrs. Wardell's class along with Desiree who by now had been my newfound strength, my newfound hope? .

We reached the front gate of her unit complex and hugged and kissed goodbye. Just as she turned to enter the gate, a woman dressed in a conservative gray business suit stepped up to the entrance. Her hair hung limply to her shoulders; her makeup etched her face ever so immaculately. Familiar though she looked, I couldn't say I had ever seen her, though I should have recognized her by the gray bluish eyes I remembered from the photo in Desiree's living room. I would have ignored her had she not looked at us with such a sharp, demeaning stare, standing so motionless in her posture. "Who's this?" she asked in a broken Spanish accent.

Desiree's tone was soft and uneasy. "This is Marlo. He's the one who painted that painting. Remember I showed you? He's also the one who came by that one Saturday to work on our biology report."

The awkward silence and piercing glance her mother gave bit at me like an infested pool of hungry piranha. "Hi," she voiced.

"Hi," I replied politely, but not before her eyes swung back towards Desiree, demanding more of an explanation. I grew uncomfortable with each passing second—especially knowing she had been by the gate the entire time we had talked and kissed goodbye.

But why did that suddenly seem so bad? Why did everything suddenly turn into some kind of bad forbidden young love?

"I guess I'll talk to you tomorrow," Desiree uttered in a dead, disguised tone, showing not one speck of warmth we normally shared when we were alone. She did not turn back to acknowledge me either.

The gate swung shut.

Had Desiree not told her mother how special I was, how I could touch her and the world with my art—how I would some day touch everyone with my sandcastle dreams?

They stood inside the gate area as her mother's ridiculing voice echoed everywhere. I crept up beside a huge stone pillar that supported the surrounding cast iron fence. Their shadows beamed straight through the metal bars like dark black flashes from a ray gun.

"I do not ever want to see you with that boy again, *me comprendes*?" her heavy accented voice stated firmly.

"But mom," Desiree responded calmly, "he's not like other guys. He's really nice."

"That does not mean you have to give yourself to him," she snapped back. "You think *ese niño* could ever truly love you?"

I couldn't make out Desiree's soft reply.

"Well, you're wrong. Don't make the same mistakes I made with your father, Desiree. No boy will ever truly love you. He'll only want you for your body. When you lose the shape of your figure and lose the color of your hair and the gleam in your eyes, you'll remember me and know how much the man of your dreams really loves you. I already told you no boy is what you think he is…You're one of the lucky girls to have the power to light any man's heart on fire. I bet just turning your eyes away from that boy's sight is enough to leave his heart in pieces."

"You don't even know Marlo. He's way sweet and very talented."

"Makes no difference. I know enough, and he's no different. All he wants is what's underneath your clothes. Your father was also handsome and talented. He could recite poems from memory and always say the right things to make me feel like I was special. And I always fell for it…My life was never the same again. Ask your aunt how it was next time you see her."

I was stunned, flabbergasted—unable to believe the things this woman was saying. I was already a spoiled image to her, and she hadn't even met me.

Desiree's tears gave way as her weeps spoke her dismay. "Mom, please," she pleaded. "You don't understand."

"No, you're the one who doesn't understand," her mother's strident voice shot back. "Can you not see I'm only trying to help you? You're giving yourself to some boy who's only thinking of getting his needs met. Don't throw your life away. Become something in life so you will never have to depend on any one man. Become a doctor or a lawyer. Maybe then you can make this family proud of you and also make every man around respect you."

Oh, what the hell was she saying? I never heard such a one-sided obtuse person in all my life. There was Dad, but he was Dad…How could she not think that I did not respect Desiree? How could she say that I was evil, seeking only to use her daughter for my needs? I felt worse for Desiree whose cries for understanding went unheard. She had so many hopes and dreams, goals and passions I could very well relate to. But in her mother's ears, it seemed Desiree's sincere pleas for understanding would never be heard. Perhaps this was why Desiree appeared so down and gloomy on some days. Perhaps this was why she rarely mentioned her mother or ever offered to introduce me to her, knowing very well that I would only be seen as one of many.

Desiree continued her wounded sobs. Her shadow withered like a pile of dry sand blowing in the wind, diminishing with each word that came from her mother's chiding voice. I wanted so much to pull that gate open and take her in my arms, alleviating those aching weeps and showing her mother that I was not what she presumed me to be. I really could be Desiree's exception, just as Desiree was mine. I really could be the Romeo…and Desiree the Juliet.

They climbed the stairs, her mother appearing apologetic as she put her arm around Desiree's shoulders.

Tears, however, continued to fall.

22

Glumly I stood, wishing she were saying something other than those words I never wanted to hear. Certainly I did not want things to change. God no. She was the biggest thing in my life, bigger than Ivan or Danny even. Oh, I should have known it would come to this, should have known she'd be so easily thwarted by her mother—just as I'd always been by Dad. Maybe I should have swung that gate open and carried her off into never-never land, saved her from this enclosed disheartened arena encompassing every inch of our free fall universe.

"My mom wants me to keep my grades up next semester."

"You got all A's," I said straight faced, trying my best to accept her bleak revelation.

"I know. It's just that I have to be a bit more focused. I almost messed up in Mrs. Wardell's class. I can't afford to slip up, not now—not ever."

I reached for her hand ever so gently. "We don't really need to stay away from each other."

"I think it's the best thing right now. We've been seeing too much of each other." She released my hand, her eyes expressionless as they stared off into the fountain that spewed endless water into a pool of countless coins and wishes.

"Are you sure it's 'cause your grades?" I pushed on, hoping she would just come out and tell me about the horrid things I'd heard her mother say.

"Yeah," she replied dully, her eyes still a spacey, voiceless gloom.

Shoppers swarmed in and out of the bookstore in disarray, many taking advantage of extravagant after-holiday bargains, while others formed lines to exchange or return unwanted books. Desiree's boss motioned her back into the store—her fifteen minute break all but over. I let myself collapse onto a nearby bench as she made her way back into the store. It would not have been so crushing had I not suddenly felt like I'd never meant anything to her. A sullen shadow washed over every inch of me, not only making me feel as though a part of me had been torn away—but so too a tremendous sense of being misunderstood, of not being seen for who I really was. She'd said I was special, said I was unlike any other she had ever met…Yeah, there were those moments when I'd find her in her swimsuit only to wonder what it would be like to see her fully unclothed, just as I had with Daisy long ago. But I wanted to think that was normal, an innocent kind of momentary awakening that couldn't truly be evil—just a simple fantasy made harmless and personal. I was simply of this world, in tune for the first time with feel, touch, passion, happiness, and now…bittersweet sorrow. Was it this innocence and natural instinct to *feel* what made Desiree's mother think me bad—what made Desiree now feel I was just one of many, or all? Her mother had it all wrong if that was the basis for her cynicism. Boys weren't the ones who were evil; girls were. If she only knew who Gracie was—who Danny was…why, she wouldn't say men were evil at all.

For days I did nothing more than watch television and doze off with constant nightmares that I would never see her again. I left the house only once to buy Dad's birthday present, trying hard to bypass the bookstore only to find myself spying through the store window. She was not there. A different girl worked the register. All I could do was ponder whether Desiree was home or at the beach feeling any of the ache and loss that accompanied my every turn.

"It could have been worse," Ivan commented as he chewed his dinner over the phone. "She could have waited until you were really hooked before she let you go."

He was right. It could have been worse, though I felt like things were already worse. For I missed her smiles and the soft touch of her hand so badly.

"The foolish romantic thing to do," Ivan went on, "would be to go to her and do the flowers and candy thing. But I wouldn't do that. If she really is genuine, she'll know in her heart you're no jerk."

"That's really too bad," said Danny. "I know you liked her a lot. Why does she want to break up?"

"I don't know," I responded. Really, I did not—at least not a justifiable reason. How did I make sense of her mother and explain her in a way that would not sound so outlandish? "She says it's because of her grades, but I don't know. I think she thinks I'm gonna do something bad to her."

"Like what?"

"Use her for her body, I guess."

"Use her for her body?" he questioned. "You should just call her. Let her know different. Tell her how you feel."

It was so like Danny to display this hidden side of me so willing to fall into impulse. Repression and inhibition had always jailed me, and I wondered if I'd ever be so fortunate to break these walls which had always been made of rock solid certainty.

"She told me it was best we not talk."

"It's okay," he remarked. "You'll get over it. People always get over these kinds of things."

That must have been true. He'd gotten over Gracie, something which at one point had seemed impossible.

Mother struggled to ready the house for Dad's birthday party. Tamara helped out but complained about me not doing more to lend a helping hand. "Marlo's already mowed the lawn and helped with the balloons and decorations," replied Mother. "And he hasn't been feeling well."

I spent my time straightening out my room and remained there for most of the day. Later, I forced myself into my old dusty blue suit I only wore on those rare family occasions. My mirror humorously displayed an innocent child who still had not rebelled against his childhood, showing me in these pants which were too short and this jacket which was snug enough to make my eyes bulge from their sockets. Tamara eventually ventured out of her room wearing a glimmering gold dress that hugged her developing figure. She had her hair pinned up and looked more like a woman of twenty than a pubescent girl of thirteen. To my surprise, Dad said nothing about her makeup or Mother's high heels.

Family and friends arrived shortly before dark. Aunt Trinidad gave me her usual big hug and kiss. I couldn't really handle being around her too long. Not that I didn't love her. She just liked to talk too much and never let anyone put a word in edgewise. She also wore considerable amounts of perfume that made me and Mother's pet birds nearly croak from asphyxiation. She was nice though, never forgetting my birthday and always saying I was a good boy.

I assisted in handing out drinks and finger foods. Dad sat in the living room with *Abuelo*, my uncles, and co-workers. They were all dressed in the same solid sky-blue shirts with black or brown polyester slacks. *Abuelo* was the only one who wore a short-sleeved silk shirt. His white hair webbed his head but wrinkles did not etch his face as did some of the other older men. Speaking mostly Spanish, Dad and the men lost themselves in their laughter and heated debates on World Cup Soccer and the endless world war on terrorism. Mother and the other women were layered in one or two-piece dresses, fastened by white, red, or black belts to match the color of their shoes. They conversed in the dining room, their talk geared more towards gossip and vanity than anything else. Focus stressed on what one neighbor had done to the other or styles of clothes and cars people wore or drove around town. They too spoke dreams of being young again, wishing they had never aged past twenty. For that was the age they claimed one felt timeless. Aunt Trinidad's voice was the loudest, her boisterous, annoying laughs blaring throughout the house—bumping all other conversations off track.

I was soon overcome with boredom, sitting quietly with my sister on the couch—refusing to lend an open ear to any more of this senseless talk. For no one around knew or seemed to care about my sandcastle dreams or my other artworks I hoped would one day touch everyone. Eventually, I retreated to my room and watched the New Year special on television.

Ivan arrived later that evening. Danny was also supposed to stop by, but he fell sick and remained home.

"What'd you get your pops for his birthday?" asked Ivan as he shut my door.

I handed him the watch I'd purchased at the mall.

"Where did you get the bucks for that?"

"I had some cash stashed away," I replied.

The doorbell clanged countless times in the background. Aunt Trinidad's voice shrieked loud cries as she greeted more guests. Moments later, Tamara hollered my name.

"What?" I shouted from my room.

"There's someone here to see you."

I poked my head from my doorway and could hardly believe my eyes when I saw Desiree standing in my living room. She had a brightly wrapped gift in hand as Tamara eagerly introduced her to my mother.

"Unbelievable," I told Ivan.

"What?"

"It's Desiree."

"No way."

"Yeah."

He poked his head out to have a peek. "See," he grinned as he spun around, "she must have come to her senses."

I looked in the mirror. Shady images of my flimsy balled-up suit reflected back at me. I looked through my closet but didn't have enough time to change. Tamara tapped on my door.

"I can't go out there," I told her when I let her in.

"Why not? She's waiting for you."

"Look at this suit." We both eyed each other through the mirror which had never lied to me or anyone. "I didn't think she was coming."

"Aunt Trinidad's gonna drive her crazy with her annoying questions if you don't go out there."

Ivan laughed as he pushed me along behind Tamara. "You look fine. She'll understand it's one of those family things."

Desiree really did look stunning in her low-cut lavender dress, strapped together with a black-knitted belt. I could only imagine her mother had designed it, as it fit her as perfectly as a glove to a hand. She met my eyes, dimples teasing in and out of both cheeks as she smiled—continuing to keep one ear on Aunt Trinidad and Mother who would not stop talking.

"I thought you weren't coming," I whispered softly.

"I convinced my mom to let me come."

"Oh," I responded, a bit perplexed as only days ago she'd been told to stay away. Now she was here in my home, looking as ravishing as ever and smiling as if nothing had ever come between us. Was it these unexpected moments which made Dad swear he would never in a million years understand women, or why there were shows on TV about men being from the desert and women the sea? Regardless, a joyous smile fluttered over my face. For a moment, I even forgot about my ill-fitting suit. And she didn't seem to notice, or at least didn't say anything about it.

"There's plenty of food for you kids," Mother said. "Eat all you want."

"Thank you, Mrs. Clemente," Desiree replied graciously.

"Make sure you eat plenty," Aunt Trinidad added. "We can't have you growing up weak and malnourished. You might get ulcers or cancer."

Desiree was extremely shy and too polite to eat much, though she did eat most of what Aunt Trinidad had served her. We sat in the living room, next to Dad and his guests. At times, he glanced over at Desiree whose alluring dress and face glowed with enough elegance to light up our dim-lit living room…Maybe she reminded Dad of Mother when she was younger. Oh, but Mother didn't have Desiree's eyes, nor did she have the radiant complexion and tender aura that went along with her slender figure. Mother was fair and her beauty a bit more electrifying, as she possessed more of those curvy attributes which made all heads turn.

"Your sister's such a cutie," Desiree whispered. "She came up to me and gave me a great big hug, like she already knew me."

"You can have her if you want."

She laughed. "Why do you say that?"

" 'Cause, she's a pain."

"Don't be mean. She's gonna be such a beauty when she gets older, like your mom."

"You shouldn't have bothered getting my dad anything," I said as I reached for her gift wrapped tightly in bright-yellow paper with a soft-colored pink bow.

"I couldn't come over without getting your father something." She took a closer look at Dad as he went back and forth with *Abuelo* about the construction business. "You know, he looks a lot like you."

"That's what the rest of my family says. I don't know if that's good or bad."

"He's really handsome and so young-looking, almost like a brother of yours."

"Talk about making a blind man see," Ivan greeted as he approached with a second large serving of Mother's chicken with rice. "You look absolutely gorgeous." He grabbed Desiree's hand and kissed it like the gentleman he had never been.

"Thanks," she said shyly.

"Glad you could make it." He seated himself next to Dad, near the corner of our largest sofa. Ivan had no problem blending in with Dad and my uncles. In fact, he was the center of attention as they all ate from their plates.

After singing a short happy birthday, Dad cut Mother's baked cake. It was lightly frosted with real scrumptious strawberries to make everyone crave seconds and thirds before it had even reached our taste buds. The frosting spelled Dad's name as forty lit candles showed his age. I handed him his new dressy, metallic watch, hoping he would wear it even though it was not the rugged digital sports kind he was accustomed to. Tamara gave a varnished wooden toolbox she had crafted in her woodshop class at school, while Mother got him a dark red bathrobe that was as thick as a dozen woven towels. And as usual, Aunt Trinidad came prepared with generic dress shirts she liked giving to all the men in the family. I must have had an entire closet full of the same light-blue long-sleeved shirts, all still pinned and stuck together in their awkward packages. She looked pleased, in her mind satisfied with her vintage selection of birthday and Christmas gifts.

Desiree smiled benevolently as Dad opened her gift, a blue tie striped with streaks of gray. "It's very nice," he told her. "I'll be wearing this with Marlo's new watch. You didn't have to, but I'm glad you did. Thank you."

"I still haven't given you my present," blurted Ivan. He surprised us all, as he had already mentioned he didn't have a present to give. He retrieved his guitar by the front door and sat across everyone. He played a pleasant song for my father. He didn't play long, but it was enough to make everyone, even the oldsters, admire his incredible, delightful talent. Dad thanked him and asked him to play another song.

Right at midnight, loud explosions protruded through the peace and quiet of the lonesome sky. A sparkling display of fireworks lit up the dark atmosphere overhead as we all peered through the living room window. Everyone embraced the new year, and when I hugged Desiree, I held on as long as I could, wanting never to let go. She later called her mother to come pick her up. The lines were jammed, and it took a while before her call went through. Mother and Aunt Trinidad collected dirty plates and silverware as everyone else staggered home, including Ivan, who hitched a ride home with Uncle Chico.

"Tamara's been telling me about your room," said Desiree as we waited in the living room for her mother to arrive. "She says it's an art lover's dream."

"It's not much," I said modestly as I helped her up from the couch and led her to my room I was no longer as reluctant to share, at least not with her.

Her eyes widened in amazement as she inspected every one of my works. "Wow," she remarked. "These are all yours?"

"Yeah. Some I painted when I was six."

"This is impressive. You should really think of showing your work at art shows. I bet there'd be lots of buyers."

"Hardly anyone paints oils anymore," I said, remembering what Mr. Parlante had said about dying breeds.

She walked along my huge mirrored wall. "Did you have this put in?"

"My dad said it came with the house long ago when my grandfather bought it. I can remember being a kid and looking right into it as you are now."

"It looks like it's dug into the wall," she said as she ran her hands over its reflective smooth surface.

"I don't think it's breakable either. I've thrown so many things at it, and it's not cracked once."

After looking out my window, she stopped and eyed my easel. The usual stained sheet hung over it like a deformed ghost.

"That's where I do most of my work."

"Ah, like a writer's most prized word processor or voice recorder," she responded as she unexpectedly lifted the cover to find her sketched portrait of long ago.

A discrete vision I had made of her, only to share on those rare occasions I had forgotten her image or wished her to be near when my heart yearned because she was not. I'd meant no one else to share this priceless piece—meant no one to find out just how much she meant to me, how much I truly did like her.

She stared as though she were looking at her own reflection for the first time, mesmerized—though she gave no praise or critique. She turned and her eyes met mine already looking quietly at her, no longer able to hide what for so long had been my secret alone. I breathed somewhat deeply, debating whether I should go on. "I painted it a long time ago," I dared to say, "shortly after I first saw you."

"You mean at the beach?"

I nodded.

"Is this the way I looked, the way you saw me that day?" She scanned my face deeply and extensively. Again I nodded, letting myself sit back on my bed as I saw myself in the mirror. A frightened little child I appeared. "You only saw me once. You didn't know me...How could you have drawn me so well?"

"I felt you were different when I first saw you," I stammered softly. "Everything about you. I couldn't get you off my mind. It was like something in me whispered you were this unique girl found nowhere else on earth. I've never felt like this about anyone..."

Her eyes said no more about what she was thinking than did her speechless thoughts. They only stared at me through the mirror, looking at me in her hushed, quiet tone. *This is me, everything I am, everything I've longed to be...* As difficult as it was, I went on, figuring there was no longer a reason to refrain from letting her know everything. "I sketched this so I could always remember you; thought I'd never see you again. Ivan and Danny said they knew who you were, but I never asked them about you. They're so used to accepting the fact that I've never had any feelings for a girl. They would have teased me, never taken me seriously. When you came into Mrs. Wardell's class that first day..." I paused for the right words, "that was like a dream come true."

Her eyes grew sulky and moist all of a sudden. "I always thought I was just another girl to you," she murmured. "When I first sat next to you in class, it felt like we were miles apart. You seemed frightened, as if I were going to do something bad to you."

I stood up and came closer to her, putting my arms around her. "You don't need to cry. I don't like it when I see you sad."

"You've got to know that I'm so sorry I said we should stay away," her voice broke softly as a tear streaked down her cheek. "It was all a lie.

My mother was the one who didn't want me spending time with you. To her, you're just another guy. She thinks you could never be one to care about me—that you're only out to use me and ruin my life."

Relieved I was to hear her come out into the open. At least now, there was honesty where before there had only been senseless perplexity. We sat on my bed as she went on, "You see, my mother has always believed there isn't one guy in the world that will ever care for who I am. And I've always believed her. I don't know what it is about you that makes everything she seem so wrong. Maybe it's your sincerity…or your sandcastles, I don't know." She turned from me. "Do you care for me, Marlo? I mean, you just don't like me because you think I'm pretty or because you think I'm an easy kinda girl, do you?"

I put my hand on her shoulder, wanting her to turn around though feeling a bit more at ease with her back to me. "I care for you a lot," I uttered, "and I do think you're so pretty, but not in a bad kind of way—just in a beautiful kind of way. There wasn't one thing I wanted more than your friendship when I first met you—anything to be near you, even if it was just to share in smiles or sip down flat sodas at the park."

She laughed as she spun back around, sighing as her tears stopped their dripping.

"I wouldn't have sketched you," I assured, "wouldn't have ever wanted to speak to you if I didn't feel you were different."

"I've always known you, Marlo," she said. "Yup, you're that guy who only exists in dreams. I've never thought I'd ever meet or feel like this about any one guy. My friend Misty and I always told ourselves there was no such thing as a perfect guy…and if there were, we'd only wake to find we were dreaming."

"What about Gerard?" I asked. "I thought you liked him."

"Gerard's a jerk," she responded bitterly. "He was the first guy to approach me when I arrived here. I did like him, but only for all the wrong reasons. I should have known he would turn out to be a jerk. You're nothing like him…Why, when I first saw you on the beach I knew there had to be so much behind those sandcastles you build."

Gerard was the all-around athlete, big man on campus—popular and liked by all the girls at school. For the first time it felt good not having to wish I were him. For I was Marlo, and I was special to the only girl that mattered. I held her tight, my arms letting her know I'd hold her for all eternity if that's what she wanted. We sat and rested quietly until Tamara stepped into the room. "Desiree, I think it's your mom. She's out on the driveway honking for you."

We kissed a simple goodbye and briefly made plans to spend the next two days together before school resumed on Monday. We were happy, and it seemed I could sing a thousand mushy love songs despite my horrid singing voice.

Oh, to be…to be, be, be. For the first time I can see this me who has always longed to be…

"Desiree is such a sweet girl," Mother commented as I walked into the kitchen.

"She certainly is," Aunt Trinidad added. "She's got the loveliest eyes too. But she's too skinny. Needs to eat more. You tell her I said that."

"She's from New Mexico," I said, figuring they would want to know more about her. "She recently moved here, and her mother designs clothes."

I helped Mother and my aunt empty some of the collected bags of trash. I heard clamoring in the garage as I stepped alongside the house. Dad was doing pushups on the pavement as he counted to himself aloud. He stopped when he reached forty.

"What are you doing, Dad?"

He stood up, surprised to find me in the doorway. "Just something I do every year, a pushup to go along with my age. Last year it was thirty-nine. Next year it'll be forty-one."

"You're not even old," I assured. Clearly age had not caught up to him. His physique was as I had always remembered, broad and muscular. His hair evaded gray, not yet turning like *Abuelo's*. And not one wrinkle marred his bronze-chiseled face.

"I just fear I won't be able to count my age without croaking one day." He chuckled to himself as he buttoned up his shirt. "That Desiree girl is very pretty. How long have you known her?"

"A few months," I said proudly, feeling he could not ever say she was like Gracie, nor say she had qualities that would prove harmful.

"You know," he said, "I had an old uncle who died way before you were born, and he used to tell me never to spend money on a girl or waste time getting serious unless I got a piece of ass. *'No girl's worth the money, or the time,'* he'd tell me. *'Women are only to be used, just as they use us.'* I didn't know what the hell he was getting at. I was only your age—and not very wise either. Now don't go taking this girl seriously, Marlo. You never know when she'll decide to turn her back on you and bring you down like you've never been brought down before."

"She's all right, Dad," I told him.

"Yes, she appears very sweet. But don't let that fool you. Those are the worst types; the ones with the pretty faces, the nice bodies—the ones with the great smiles. They don't care about anything. They live for the present and couldn't care less when they leave you for another who may sweep them off their feet just as you or any other first guy did. It would be too easy for her to break hearts just by making those eyes of hers look away. You need to be careful. Like her, but don't love her. Give her anything, but don't give her your heart. You'll only regret it if you do."

But what about the warmth she shares, the sincerity she exhibits in her gentle eyes that never lie or soft touches which never sting—or the enthusiasm she exudes as she listens to my sandcastle dreams? And what of her magical dreams of painting pictures with her words? What about the tie she gave you for your birthday? Oh, I wanted to say all these things, but I knew he'd only laugh and think me unwise to deny his ruthless world. It all seemed so hopeless. No way would he ever see my world. For a different kind of certainty I'd always felt, one which said my pictures were indeed hung upside up, one which said I could be free to feel and expose myself in this spotlight which for too long had cried my name.

He stepped out of the garage, but not before reminding me of the trash bags I'd left sitting on the walkway.

23

Second semester was an endless storm I weathered. I earned my place on Mrs. Canizaro's list of college bound students. Excited and confident I was, though I realized I was taking on more than had ever challenged my wits and courage. I was dropped from mainstream math and placed into a higher-level trigonometry course where I was surrounded by most of the same students from biology. My mainstream history class was also dropped and switched to an advanced-standing history program. "As long as you maintain your grades," Mrs. Canizaro announced as she peeled her eyes from her computer, "you'll have a great chance at most colleges, including that art academy you so much dream of."

Biology continued to be the most painstaking of courses, but in many ways, it paved the way. "I'm switching your seat," Mrs. Wardell said bluntly when she called me to her desk. The rest of the class had emptied into the hall, including Desiree who rushed to her next class.

"Why am I being moved?"

She didn't expect I'd question. I was one of her quiet forgotten souls, always humble and bowing to her every wish. "C'mon now, you and I know Desiree's been holding your hand this past semester." She aimed her heavy magnified glasses up at me for the first time. "But that's not the real reason you're changing seats. I see how you and Desiree look at one another—see how both your eyes lose themselves in each other's stares. That's cute, but we can't afford lovey-dovey games in here. Mrs. Canizaro mentioned you were accidentally scheduled into my class. Every so often I get a student or two who stumbles in with your same background. They usually survive no more than a day before they drop. I'm very impressed with your focus and determination. I want you to keep working hard, to do well—and not suddenly give up on class. Tomorrow you'll be sitting in front, right next to Billy Wise. Vivi Inez will move next to Desiree."

Her grading system seemed like a losing game to many, her stern harsh ways far from ever being sympathetic to the most studious of youthful souls. I guess I had her all wrong. She did care, cared about bringing out the best in all her students—even me.

"Oh, but Billy Wise is very smart," Desiree said when I told her. "He's in my English class and writes very well. Besides, I don't think you sitting next to me really matters anymore. You've been handling most of the class on your own. I'm sure Billy will be counting on you just as much as you'll count on him."

"I know," I responded, smirking to hide a bit of my let down. Perhaps Mrs. Wardell was right. Desiree had held my hand. But it wasn't all in a negative way. She was, after all, the only one who made my moments in biology tolerable. "What can I say, Billy's just not as pretty as you are," I added jokingly.

"Oh, come off it," she teased in response.

No more did we write those cute little notes in class or whisper in each other's ear how sweet we thought the other was. As our schedules grew more intense and our classes demanded more of our time, Desiree and I saw less and less of each other. The bookstore kept her busy on most days, and others she set aside for her writing. Five minutes between bells was all we shared on some mornings—our lunchtime usually cut short, as there were either tests to make up or study groups to attend. My mind did focus more in class, and Billy Wise was indeed very smart and a hard worker. I passed all of my courses with that illustrious *B* average that wouldn't get me into Harvard but would certainly suffice in my aspirations for art school. Never had my grade average soared so high.

Come late spring, Danny led the track team to a first place finish in league competition. The team did not win state that year, but Danny alone medaled in seven final events, four of them being first place finishes. He stood alone as our high school's only athlete to ever become a state champion in three or more track and field events. His coach had convinced him to focus on multi events, with hopes of one day becoming a successful decathlete. Even with world class speed, Danny was not one to dominate the competition. He could ill afford to put all his eggs in one basket. With his sprinting ability, combined with jumping, leaping, and shot putting skills, he was sure to excel at the next level.

That summer, Dad insisted that I join his workforce and learn a little of his construction operations. But I refused. I dared not tell him I had no aspirations of following in his footsteps. He still did not know my plans for college and the application I would submit to the Art Academy in the fall. Instead, I secretly chose to work my first summer job at the beach, renting out waterboards and snorkeling equipment. That made me most content, given I was in South Beach, near the water, the sand, the cafes, the shops—with tourists, surfers, skaters, beach bums, and incredible summer days.

With school out, Desiree and I found more time for low-budget horror movies, shopping, the beach, the park, and even art museums. We also registered to take our college entrance exams on the same morning and location. Surprisingly, I too had a chance to meet her mother. Desiree had arranged for the three of us to have dinner at her home. I was a bit anxious the night we met, imagining her mother would bite my hand as I graciously shook hers.

Ms. Rencor was a quiet lady, much like Dad was when you first met him. She was very young considering she had a daughter Desiree's age—dressed in stylish attire of her own fashionable design and still retaining much of her youthful beauty and figure. Desiree said many nice things about me that night, describing some of my paintings and illustrious sandcastle dreams— and so too the good times we shared whenever we were together. But Ms. Rencor took very little interest in hearing this, changing the subject at once by reminding Desiree of chores or errands that needed doing by week's end. The stifling atmosphere she created really did keep me repressed, feeling almost like there was some way I should have been acting...only, I did not know what that way of acting was. A sense of her disapproval sent my confidence spiraling way down, but Desiree later reminded me that this was how her mother always acted around men. She too mentioned how lonely she got sometimes, never having her mother around being that Ms. Rencor was at her boutique most of the time. And when Ms. Rencor was home, she was usually too tired or moody to interact, often negative or unconcerned about her own daughter's troubles or thoughts. She had no clue of Desiree's passion for writing or how hard she worked at school to stay among the top of our class. In all, Desiree had no one to look up to. She knew nothing of her father nor had any close contact with other family members who could make a difference in her life.

I, more than anyone, understood lonely moons, desolate worlds, and wishless dreams. Dad never acknowledged my artwork. As a child, when I was at my neediest, when I thought I could reach out, I'd run up many times to show him drawings and sketches I'd made in Ms. Varian's class—ones he'd never even seen at parent-teacher night. And oh, how I longed for his approval, his acceptance and his willingness to love me for who I was—what I was...But he wouldn't flinch a bit. "I'm sorry son, I'm not much into art," would be all he'd say, with eyes I knew would only chastise me later on for frittering away my time on meaningless walls of canvas. I knew then he would have rather me be like Danny so he could brag to all his friends that he had this amazing athlete for a son…and now, more than ever, he wished for the same things—wishing I would be the great builder of homes he was so that one day I would take over his construction business here in Miami…And Mother? Well, what could I say? I never thought she would understand. It seemed too late to reach out. After so many years of being indirect strangers, I was nothing more than a long-lost son she thought simply too shallow and serene. Never would she know that even now this son of hers wished for just a second to hug and truly say, *I love you, Mom. This is me, your son I've always longed to be. This is who I am…this dreamer of tideless dreams.*

Our senior year arrived more quickly than a two-minute dream. It was the best time of my life, and I didn't want to wake from my perfect world I truly did believe could only exist in dreams. I had Desiree. I had direction, and my dreams were just a high tide away. Confidence became a part of everyday life, and anxiety towards surviving school was no longer an issue, as I had now developed valuable study skills which allowed me to survive courses like Chemistry, Calculus, and fourth year Spanish.

Desiree and I saw each other as much as possible, though school still came first. Getting into the colleges of our choice was at the forefront of both our minds. Since we had little free time for anything else, we met in the library after school when she wasn't working. She studied harder than I did, her class schedule even more intense than mine. Sometimes I had to leave her behind in the library while I went home for dinner. It was difficult at times to care for a girl who had such big dreams. I wasn't always on the top of her priority list. With school and her writing, I sometimes came third…But I never let her dreams get me down. She made me feel I was very important in her life. Always would I be the first she'd contact when faced with tough times at home, with work, with her tedious class schedule, or when writing blocks made writing seem so impossible. Often, I eased her mind, and when I was around her, I made her smile whenever possible. I don't know how many times we had to tell each other that everything would work out in the end—that our dreams were far too big to let big or small setbacks keep us down. And that was the biggest thing, the pinnacle of the strong relationship we had built: I believed in her, and she believed in me…and we both felt there was nothing we couldn't do, a moment that couldn't be happier as long as the other was in our lives—even if it was only minutes a day.

I tried keeping my close ties with Ivan and Danny, but it soon became difficult for any of us to keep our tight-knit friendship alive. Our worlds were turning in different directions, and we no longer turned the same corners.

Danny was a hundred and ten percent immersed in his running, focusing on intense competition as college scouts ventured onto campus to view his spectacular performances on the field. Seen as a top track and field prospect, Danny received thirty-one athletic scholarship offers from colleges and universities throughout the country. He finally signed an intent letter to attend the University of Oklahoma the following year. Undoubtedly, this was stepping on foreign grounds—two giant leaps closer to his hopes of one day competing in the Olympics.

Ivan busied himself forming a rock group with other musicians from the school band. He began touring and playing gigs in garages, school parties, and bizarre, underground eighteen-and-over clubs that attracted all those who imagined themselves vampires or "children of the night." He welcomed his new lifestyle of fast women and fast cars, living by night and sleeping by day. He'd never done well in school, and graduating from high school was more than enough of an academic accomplishment. College was definitely out of the question. Faced with dead-end menial jobs the rest of his life, Ivan decided on the Marines. That decision made him happy, since his father had served a couple of years in the service before he was born. He enlisted that fall with written intent to leave for Texas two days following graduation.

When the holidays were over, uncertainty wrestled my every thought more than ever. I had submitted my application to the Art Academy, praying to God I would be one of the fifty applicants accepted to enroll as a freshman next fall. A lot was riding on that one application. For I had not applied to Florida State or the University of Miami, instead taking an all or nothing approach toward my big passion of going to an elite art school. I had Desiree pick out the painting she thought would best give the selection committee a true representation of my artistic ability.

"Oh, *Weeping Prince*," she said. "By far. That's more than just a painting. That's a tale, a story that makes any onlooker cry and feel...feel what, I can't even tell you."

"I can't. That has to stay in the Wall as long as the Wall continues to cry fame."

"Then, I guess it'll have to be the one above your bed—the outer space one, the one with the boy on the moon."

Ah, yes. How could I not? That too told not just a tale, but also cried out all my lonely dreams of years past.

"You know, though," she added, "you are taking a big risk submitting an oil painting, Marlo. What if they only want printouts or graphic designs on virtual memory, you know—computer-based art?"

"I called and asked about that. The school has one of the only traditional arts programs in the country. That's why everything depends on my getting in."

My first two letters of recommendation came from no other than Mr. Parlante and Mrs. Canizaro. The third letter was a bit more challenging to get. For I had to face Mrs. Wardell, the intimidating force who had touched my world in many more ways than one. She was actually quite gracious when I approached her and told her my plans. "A letter of recommendation," she commented as she looked at me briefly. A new class of biology students she had inherited, and I did not envy them in the least as I watched them storm out of her room. I was, however, proud to say that I had been one of her intrepid students who'd managed to survive her class. "Of course I will. The Art Academy…I must say, I can't remember having had too many artists come my way. I don't suppose you'd ever want to be cloned." She smiled.

"No ma'am."

With Tamara's help on the computer, I intercepted our electronic mail every morning before school. There were no replies. Then, to my surprise, the mailman hand delivered a certified letter to Mother one morning while I was off at school. It was from the academy. She didn't say anything at first but later did inquire about it. "Just some note from school," I replied.

Nervously I held onto the envelope, resisting the urge to open it until I was with Desiree later that afternoon.

"Well, aren't you gonna read it?" she asked. We sat with a couple of sparkling sodas at the nearby café, overlooking the vivid scenery of the teal-blue ocean and white sandy beach that could have made a thousand artists famous. "Oh, for God's sake." She snatched it from my hand and tore it open, reading it silently as she sipped from her bottle.

"What is it? What does it say?"

"Don't feel bad," she said. "It's not the end of the world. Hopes and dreams like yours never die." She handed me back the letter, straight faced—without the slightest twinkle of expression in her eyes.

I unfolded it and reluctantly read the first few lines: *Congratulations, Mr. Clemente. We are pleased to inform you of your acceptance into this institution's fall semester. Your talents speak beyond any words can describe, and we here feel that you will add to our wonderful tradition as you embark on a most powerful and expressive mission…* I stopped reading and let my head and arms fall to the table, as for a moment I felt I no longer knew how to breathe.

Desiree leaned over me and ran her fingers through my hair. "You're no longer a dreamer, Marlo boy," I heard her say. "You'll now share and touch the world with your magic."

Never before had I cried tears of joy. Never before had anything been so decisive as to who I was or where I was headed. For certainty now carved and sculpted its way into a different horizon. I couldn't care less of the barriers which faced me now—the cost of tuition or the demanding four years that would come my way. I too thought little of what Dad would say when he found out I was headed to college and would not spend my life running his company. I smiled and dabbed at my eyes as again I breathed freely—happy Desiree's eyes could look my way...and happy that dreams could come true.

24

Desiree's academic accomplishments towered over many at school. She received acceptance letters from Georgetown, Columbia, University of California at Berkeley, and Princeton. She was one of five seniors accepted into an Ivy League school, one of only three to earn a perfect grade point average her senior year.

"My mom doesn't want me to be a writer." She put her arms around me, embracing me ever so tightly, as a child would when faced by a night alone in a dark empty room. "She says I'm crazy to let opportunities go to waste with foolish dreams of wanting to write."

"So what?" I replied. "You can do anything. You no longer need her approval."

"You don't understand. I don't qualify for financial aid. She makes too much money. I couldn't afford Georgetown or Princeton—not in a million years."

"It doesn't matter," I said, so sure of myself. "I still haven't told my parents my plans. My Dad thinks I'm gonna go work for him after graduating. I know he won't think twice about helping me if he finds out I'm going to that art school. No doubt I'll have to do it on my own."

"Princeton's so far away. It seems like such a difficult road ahead, and I can't just do it without her approval or her help. She wants me to major in science or computers, so I can be a doctor or computer engineer. What good are words when it's more prestigious to be a doctor or computer scientist, she says."

"But even you've said that her dreams aren't yours…" I stood up and leaned up against the railing overlooking the ocean. "My whole life I've looked for just an ounce of my father's understanding and approval. But not a single drop of recognition has ever come my way. I now see it's hopeless to base my hopes and acceptance on him. You also have to break away. It's not like you don't have anyone who cares or believes in you…I believe in you, and I do care, care more than anything."

"Why can't she understand me? Why is she so caught up trying to be so independent, free from men and void of love?"

I wanted to say anything that would make her feel different, but I knew just the kind of influence her mother had on her. For I'd lived the same perplexity my whole life. "It's okay," I assured weakly. "I'm sure she'll come to her senses. She can't force you to be a doctor if that's not where your heart is. This is Princeton we're talking about. She won't let you throw that away."

"You don't know her, Marlo," she said bitterly, brushing at her eyes to focus on me a little better. "She won't force me. She'll just make my life unbearable. She'll never support me, and I'm not just talking financially either...Like your father, she won't want to share in my accomplishments—or think that they are any more genuine than graduating from medical or computer school. She'll never admit I can be successful—even if my novels and poems do end up touching the world over." Her voice was on edge, her breaths deep and inconsistent. "I can't live with that, Marlo. I just can't. I've lived with her my whole life. I've never had anyone different stand by my side. I've always done everything she's wanted, counted on her for everything...To make matters worse, she says we may be moving back to New Mexico after graduation—says her business is not doing as well as expected."

My attention drew back to the water, my thoughts silent as they usually were when faced with situations over which I had no control. A ship tugged steadily along. Another stood afloat, appearing lifeless and abandoned. Going off to college and accepting departure was one thing, but her leaving Miami would mean maybe never seeing each other again—or seeing less of one another to eventually lose this special bond which had grown miraculously strong. "So you're just gonna head back to New Mexico?" I asked, irritated that she would even consider the option of losing her dream. "What then? Princeton's all you've talked and smiled about. That's big time."

"I don't know about Princeton anymore," she said as she shook her head side to side. "I can get the same education elsewhere. What's in a name anyway? At least I won't be mortgaging my life away. One year at Princeton can buy me a dream home— or many trips around the world. I'll just enroll at a local state school when I get back."

Deep down, I sympathized with her dilemma. Princeton did seem worlds away with insurmountable costs I couldn't even begin to comprehend. It just seemed like nothing should keep her from making her dreams reality. This time I breathed in deeply as I took in the salty, moist air. "You'd be looking past your heart...You've worked so hard.

You don't need your mother's approval. You can do this. Do whatever it takes to go." I sat back down and grasped her hand tightly. "I just hate to think you won't be going ahead with what lives in your heart. I wish you could somehow stay here and find a way of going off to Princeton—knowing I'm here and that I care about you more than anything."

Her eyes were smudges of deep green as they dazzled in the sun and looked past mine into the deepest reaches of where the real Marlo stood and hid. "Don't think I haven't dreaded the thought of leaving." She reached for my face and gently stroked my cheek. "I can still come to Miami during summers and holidays, just as I would if I were at Princeton. And I'm still following my heart. I'll just be doing it at a different school, closer to home and with far less financial burden." She looked at me with no other words, as if looking for my approval for something she herself, deep in her heart, didn't really approve of. She sighed to catch her breath and break from her tears. "I thought I would hate Florida when I first arrived. It was all new to me. I was so used to living in New Mexico, and I thought I would never make friends or fit in anywhere…Then I met you. You've made such a big difference in my life, Marlo. You, more than anyone, understand my dreams—and believe in them. I can't imagine being away from you. I've never been in love or believed that such a thing exists…All I know is that something inside just kills me to think I'm not going to be around you anymore."

If this love thing only did exist in romance novels—if Romeo and Juliet were the only ones who could experience what I was experiencing, then life was nothing but a work of fiction, a priceless collection of classic prose written to stand engraved for all eternity in one's heart. I too felt something inside almost die at the thought that I would no longer have her with me in what had always been my barren little world. Was I in love? Most definitely. I wasn't going to lie. I had fallen into a trench I myself never thought would trap me ever so helplessly. "I love you too, Desiree. I always have and always will." We hugged and held on oh so tight, rooting ourselves in the present and slipping into a painting that captured a flawless image we didn't ever want to let go of…this priceless prose—this most enchanting of melodies…this timeless sandcastle we'd never see fall.

Mother lent me her keys to the sedan. I was honored, as she had never let me go past pulling it out of the driveway. Since passing my driver's test with perfect scores, I had to settle for driving Dad's miserable old truck on short errands to and from construction sites. This was definitely a step up, reinforcing that I truly was older—a bit more responsible and independent to make my own turns down any boulevard I so chose.

"Be home early," Dad told me as I readied to leave, though he didn't say what "early" meant. Desiree was already in the car, waiting for one of our most magical nights ever. "And remember, prom night's not a night to go out and start a family."

"Oh, stop pestering," Mother chided as she straightened my tie. "Why must you think our son a pervert or Desiree some domineering bimbo trying to ruin our son's life?"

"I think Marlo knows what I'm talking about." He gave me one final glance of approval from his chair before his attention went back to the television.

Our prom was not held on the boat that year due to terrible weather. Instead, it was held at one of the hotel halls off Ocean Drive. Desiree looked so beautiful in her long pink dress and white fluffy shawl which made her float in and out of heaven. The money I made at the surf shop came in handy. I'd bought her a nice pink corsage and rented a black and white tuxedo with a pink tie and cummerbund to match her dress.

Ivan rode with us in the car. His date was Pilar Domina, a loud Puerto Rican girl who had her opinion about every little thing. She was dressed in a solid black dress, her skin pale-white and her hair dyed jet black to match the dark color of her lipstick and blush. Danny had no intention of going to the prom. He hadn't dated any girl since Gracie and was too shy to ask anyone even though most girls would have gone with him in a second. Ivan and I urged him to come along, even if he had to ask Vivi Inez, considered one of the nerdiest girls at school. "C'mon," Ivan persuaded, "she could never break hearts, only shatter mirrors." Danny remained reluctant but did end up going. He took a very pretty girl from a different school, a daughter of his mother's best friend. Ms. Skies had even allowed him to drive her convertible Mercedes.

It was definitely a night to remember, a night never to be cheated out of if you could help it. We ate dinner at an expensive restaurant, and somehow Ivan talked our waiter into letting us have several bottles of sparkling champagne which made our noses twitch as we drank. Desiree had three glasses, and liveliness followed her everywhere. We danced all night, never once losing sight of each other's eyes as we swayed and paraded into another world far from the one that would rule our lives in months to come. We took pictures and then went out for fast food, being that our fancy dinner had not entirely filled our stomachs. Ivan insisted that I lend him the keys to the car while Desiree and I went in to order burgers and fries. He and Pilar had been necking and fondling each other in the back seat the entire time I drove. His neck was stained with love bites and his tuxedo shirt was wrinkled and creased beyond recognition. A leftover bottle of champagne from the restaurant also dangled from one hand. I could only imagine the worst as Pilar stood near the car awaiting Ivan's return. "No way, dude," I whispered. "That's my mother's car. If you stain anything or make it stench, it's over for me."

"What do you think I am, some kind of animal?" His speech slurred and his eyes fought to see me.

I didn't answer. I simply tossed him the keys as any good friend would and walked back to Desiree.

"Aren't they coming?"

"They'll be in later," I told her as I quickly tugged her through the glass doors. Though Ivan never made it in. Pilar rushed in to let us know Ivan had passed out sick. He was laid flat on his stomach when we arrived, his neck, head, and arms dangling from the rear door as vomit surrounded the back left tire.

"We better get him home," Desiree suggested.

Pilar helped me carry Ivan into his apartment building. Fortunately for him, I found his keys in his coat pocket and was able to let him in quietly. His parents never woke, and he was able to sleep away the champagne by morning.

After driving Pilar home, I drove Desiree to her apartment. Stubbornly she held onto the last of the champagne as she insisted I come in. Ms. Rencor was not home which was good. She was spending the night at a client's house, making last-minute alterations to a wedding dress for later that morning. Desiree poured herself another glass, and I was tempted to join her but realized I had to drive back home and could not risk getting a DUI. Other schools were holding their prom that same night, and there were sobriety checkpoints everywhere.

"Marlo, wait," she said as I readied to leave. "Don't go yet." She grasped my hand and pulled me back down onto the couch.

"My parents'll get pissed if they wake up and find the car still gone."

"I know. I just want to tell you that this night was very special to me. I'm gonna keep this corsage forever." She unstrapped it from her wrist and placed it on the coffee table. That's when she stood up and kicked off her shoes and jumped on my lap. I felt that usual twinge of excitement I usually experienced when her body was so close to mine. It spilled over me like a giant waterfall.

"It was a special night for me too," I acknowledged softly. I was foolish even then not to look past my innocence. She turned to reposition herself in front of me, her legs pinning me to the sofa. Her eyes were shapeless smudges of desire, lost in a blur of passion I was now beginning to be taken by as I felt her heated warmth underneath her underpants. She looked even more beautiful with her hair displaced and her shawl slipping behind her to expose her narrow shoulders and thin-set neck. The thought of making love was something always tied to my mind, but I had respected her too much to even dare consider it. We had never gone further than simple wet kisses.

I reached up to kiss her gently, though Desiree pressed down on me, forcing my mouth open. A jolt of electricity hit me as moments later I found myself nibbling up and down her neck, hungry for more—more of what…I could only imagine. Her breathing became harder as she began to thrust and brush her pelvis over me, the rest of her quivering vibrantly. My hands went around her slender waist and made their way underneath her dress which was already pulled up. It was the first time I'd ever placed my hands on her buttocks. I felt the fine silky texture of her thin, lacy panties as I caressed and squeezed just enough to make her quiver more, almost helplessly. One of her dress straps fell to one side as she shrugged her shoulders and forced my head into her breast area. Her nipples protruded through the soft-knit material of her dress, and her crotch area moistened and burned even over my pants. I looked up at her, her eyes closed as she appeared lost where only eternal ecstasy resided.

The champagne, I thought…As much as I wanted her, as much as I was throbbing and pulsating to have that part of me satisfied, I knew I couldn't. Something inside didn't feel right. What about the big wedding—the white dress, that unforgettable wedding night? I couldn't take that away despite all the burning passion generated through the room. "I can't," I said as my hands fell free from her waist.

"What's wrong?"

"Nothing," I said, looking deep into her eyes. "We've had too much to drink. Look what we're doing."

"I do know what I'm doing. I want you to satisfy this love I have for you, of making you a part of me."

I had second thoughts as she said that, as she continued to thrust up against me. "I just pictured you wanting to be married, with someone you really love. If we did this now, what would we have to look forward to later on?"

"We may never get the chance if we wait. And it's not like I don't love you so."

"When you leave," I said, "we probably won't see each other for a long time. We might not even see each other at all again. You might find some other guy in Albuquerque." It hurt to think that, but it was a possibility being that she would leave and be forced to live her days without me. Why there may be others who could cross her path with more flawless and grander sandcastle dreams than I. "What then? He might turn out to be special, and you might regret we ever did anything."

"No way," she responded. "I can't. There's only one Marlo—and I never intend on forgetting him."

"You think we could actually continue to be so close?"

"Yes," she said. "I'll send you messages everyday. I'll call every chance I get. I'll save every cent of my money and fly here on holidays. I'll even move back here after I finish school…My mom won't be able to tell me what to do once I can make it on my own."

"Then will you stay with me forever?" I asked.

She did not reply just then. She looked at me with a hushed blank stare I had not seen in quite some time. "Yes," she said finally.

We did not make love that night. We set our passion aside, as strong as it may have been, and talked and fantasized about how our lives would be the day we were married. Again we let ourselves slip into this most picturesque of dreams, where waves were nonexistent, winds never hummed, and sand was never touched.

She dozed as I picked my keys off the table. A notebook filled with endless penned pages nudged me to read past the first few lines: *Long before the Spanish Conquistadors came in search of vast riches and wealth—in much of what is today Guatemala, Belize, and Honduras, there lived a Mayan prince...*

Mizolitlo was the son of the great emperor, Toclán, whose empire stretched for many miles. Though he was to succeed the throne, Mizolitlo had no intention of ruling his father's vast empire. An artist and architect in his own right, Mizolitlo was more interested in building temples and pyramids that would stand for as long as the sun god, *Kinich Ahau*, shed light on the land. In love with the daughter of his master foreman, Dixotlalt, Mizolitlo defied the social order that prohibited royalty mixing with peasantry. Only after discovering the actions of his son did emperor Toclán order Dixotlalt to be sacrificed atop the great temple of *Chac*, the great rain god that had always saved the land and crops during the worst drought seasons. Powerless to avert his father's wrath, Mizolitlo fled the land to avoid witnessing the sacrifice and death of his beloved Dixotlalt. Mizolitlo never resurfaced and became more of a nomad along the beautiful coastal shores of Central America.

Many myths have shed light on this most magnificent weeping prince, Desiree concluded. *Legend has it that Mizolitlo lived the rest of his days building the first and finest sandcastles the world had ever seen. Sadly, most of art, his temples and pyramids constructed for Kinich Ahau, perished at the hands of the first Spanish explorers during the early part of the 16th century. Many still speak Mizolitlo's name. To this day, some have mysteriously found immense structures of sand constructed overnight near the water's shores. Some claim to have even heard faint cries during the brightest of moons and tranquil of nights as the name Dixotlalt echoes throughout the land.*

I was enthralled from beginning to end. I looked over at her as she slept peacefully in her dreams of greatness. It seemed almost incredible to think anyone could write such a story, a story I could paint but never imagine ever being told. No one could ever say Desiree wasn't a good writer. She'd brought me face to face with Mizolitlo's subconscious, making him seem so real and so lifelike. I felt I was present to feel his struggles and pains of coming to terms with his passion to build and the pressure of confronting his father's rule—and in the end, losing his dear, beloved Dixotlalt. Oh, and what about that sandcastle, the first sandcastle ever?

Daylight rays were on the verge of engulfing dim, starlit skies when I got home. Everyone was still asleep. Dad mentioned nothing of my being home late when I awoke later that afternoon.

25

Slipping into that blue satin cap and gown made me feel like a prince. But, oh, I did not weep. Big I felt as I stood atop the highest of plateaus. With everything I'd gone through—the courses, teachers, projects, exams, Ivan, Danny, and Desiree…how could I ever feel small again? Grown I had, grown into this giant who could now stand next to mountains.

Dad was happy but not as warm and sentimental as mother. Education was nothing he'd ever valued, nor could he conceive that my graduating would ever surpass or meet up to the successes he'd experienced as a self-employed contractor. Physical work was all he'd ever known since the age of fourteen, working at the very same company he would eventually inherit from *Abuelo*. He never saw school as an important or necessary part of life. In his mind, graduating high school had become a simple accepted norm—but only because I was joining all his other co-workers' sons who by now had graduated from high school. And like all these sons, he expected that I would join his illustrious workforce and see college as an unnecessary, incomprehensible luxury.

I suppose it was not so much my graduating that made Mother's smiles sparkle and her tears fall as she snapped photos of me, Dad, and Tamara together. Unlike Dad, she had graduated from high school—had not dropped out at a very young age never to return. No, this night was more significant than the event itself: a realization—a realization that I was now stepping into manhood. No longer was I the dependent little child who needed to be by her side for every little hug and kiss we'd never shared. Perhaps that is why she cried. For when she hugged me and told me she was happy for me, I could only return her hug without the same tight squeeze of affection. And that was sad, sad because she was not a bad woman as Dad had made her out to be all those years—sad because I did feel love and wished for just one single second the ability and instinct to express it…But how, how did I go about suddenly replacing so many years of missed affection—real affection? How did I look past all the years of hidden emotions neither of us had shared or expressed—forever trapped in a vacuum full of benign neglect?

Hundreds of spectators swarmed the bleachers and folded chairs near the outer portion of the field as I stood atop this stage overlooking clouds and mountains. A sea of eyes looked my way, my entire life seeming to flash before everyone. Emotionally, I was only certain that all things around me were only uncertain. The Art Academy was only a summer's blink away. Who was I? What was I? If I could have cried out, "Marlo," I would have. But all I knew at that moment was that I hated spotlights—that art was touching to the soul, and sandcastles were surreal and mystical but supposed to always fall...and girls were supposed to be evil—but not a girl named Desiree. My friends were also leaving...and I was supposed to be special.

I shook our principal's hand and proudly walked off stage with diploma in hand. All my teachers, including Mrs. Canizaro, sat in the front row. Mrs. Wardell's expressionless demeanor told me I was a survivor. Mr. Parlante's smiles said I was great. "Congratulations," he'd told me before the ceremonies, "I'm sure you'll do well at the Art Academy. Know that you'll be just one of many great artists at the school, but no need to worry. Remember, you are of a dying breed. Many will look down on you because you still hold true a craft which is all but gone now. Computerize you they will try...and those teachers who are still of the old tradition may not always see the magical visions you hold."

Applause from the audience sprang a thousand fold. In the midst of everyone I no longer felt alienated from a greatness I should have felt so long ago—this greatness Ms. Varian had shed light on as a tiny little kid. In this world I stood. Missing pieces of my life fell to the forefront like never before, this giant jigsaw that had always been muddied by countless tides along the shore. In this vast array of different spectacles my art shined, faintly echoing that it would one day take this world by storm. Like breathtaking views from a window a mile high, my eyes strayed as I felt my soul, embodied talents, and persona become an entity unlike no other—special and grand, yet not distant or strange.

Danny got the most applause of anyone. No one could help but admire him—not because he had done so much for the school, but because he was Danny, quiet and sincere—successful, yet modest. He was definitely a star, someone who shined above the stars. You also couldn't help but cry your lungs out for Ivan when he went up on stage. With his low grade average and apathy towards school, graduating was a huge accomplishment. He kissed his diploma and bowed to everyone.

Desiree made top honors and even won an English award for best essay and poem published in our school journal. She wasn't the popular athlete or the flamboyant musician or class clown. She wasn't prom queen or class valedictorian or the type to look for more than just a few acquaintances at a time. Yet her smiles were full and bright when she stepped up. Strong and smart she was—filled with vivid dreams and flames which seemed could never fade.

Caps and tassels flew up in the air. Danny and Ivan threw themselves on me. Just like little kids in a sandbox, we wrestled away our joy. Parents rushed in and scoured the field for their beloved graduates. Ivan and Danny disappeared as I scanned infinite faces come my way. Elbowed and pushed I was. A familiar sense of being this stranger in a strange land crept in like never before. As big and as confident as I had stood moments earlier, I now faced this inkling of being back on my own barren little world. Gradually, I floated into the farthest reaches of space, just me and whatever greatness I had claimed. Everyone's voices whispered echoes of splendor and grandeur. None came my way. Lost I was as I focused to find anyone who could understand my blank masked smiles.

I soon spotted Danny as he stood to one side, his mother, aunts, and uncles surrounding him like a renowned celebrity. They soon disappeared in the crowd. I saw Ivan too stand joyously praised by his mother and father as he proudly showed off his diploma. They too faded in this sudden breeze of fame that seemed almost too unbearable to face. What was happening to me? Why suddenly could I no longer claim mountains, say I was here…say I was Marlo?

"Marlo," I suddenly heard as I sucked in my fears. Desiree fought her way through the crowd, her eyes tearing with joy as were the eyes of many of the other girls. She too nearly disappeared in the crowd even as she fought to reach me. But she didn't as I stood frozen and lost. Her arms went around me, and suddenly I was back. We hugged an eternal embrace, not wanting to ever let go. And we talked so fast, as if we'd never have time to speak again. We hadn't seen each other in over a day. We had been seated in opposite sections of the ceremony, and I had also arrived later than expected to rehearsals.

"I'm so happy," she said. "What happens now is like a new beginning."

"But you'll be leaving soon," I awkwardly voiced over the loud crowd.

"It doesn't matter. You're in my heart, and wherever my heart goes, I'm sure you will follow like my everlasting shadow."

She spotted her mother who'd not been too supportive days before graduation. She'd been upset with Desiree's talk of still wanting to be a writer. She had even threatened not to come to the graduation if Desiree continued her "silly little dreams." She approached with a rare smile. The touch of satisfaction in her voice was just as rare. For she was much like Dad, life simple and certain in both their eyes. Oh, certainty...a thing which had always seemed so elusive and deceptive to ever think it real. What would it be like to live in certainty? Would I too fail to smile if my eyes were so prone to see such a conspicuous world? Would I too live in cynicism and fail to smile or be touched by the simplest of things—a child's painting, delicate prose, or symphonic harmonies? More importantly, would I ever be able to have sandcastle dreams?

A lady who resembled Ms. Rencor stood nearby. In fact, they could have been twins. Her hair was dark, her skin fair and her smile quick and reluctant. She had the same almond shaped eyes, and her stare seemed so sure about everything around her, as if most things were also so undoubtedly certain. She congratulated Desiree and then another girl came into view to share her embrace. She was much younger than the lady and resembled Desiree so much I thought I was seeing exact clones. A long-lost sister, I contemplated. But why hadn't I ever seen a photo? Why hadn't she ever been mentioned?

Predictable this girl seemed, though this was only a sense that tingled somewhere deep inside me and was nothing I could ever call certain. A touch of irresistible femininity and sophistication surrounded her aura which left me a prisoner of a discreet excitability, remembering glimpses of a time when Daisy had caught my eye as a child. She was older, seemingly out of high school. Shorter in posture and hair longer and lighter than Desiree's, she had the same enriched olive skin color and the same dimples when she smiled. Her figure was sensual—not slender or lanky like Desiree's. Her tight-knit dress fit her snug and short, making her bosom and curves swell out in every direction. Her eyes too beamed the same shade of green as they looked my way. Invite me they did as I gaped quietly in the background, though she didn't know who I was or even suspect that I was in any way acquainted with Desiree.

"Smile!" Tamara hollered as she stuck her camera in my face. The flash left me blind for a moment. As soon as I regained my vision, Mother and Aunt Trinidad were by my side. They each gave me great big hugs and red lipstick kisses. "I'm so proud of you, son," Dad said when he and Uncle Chico approached. A handshake was all he gave me for such an accomplishment, but I understood this was all he knew how to share. An envelope full of money accompanied his strong grip. It was the most money I had ever held at one time. Mostly fifties and hundreds, but they added up to several thousand dollars.

Tamara kept taking pictures. I didn't know whether to laugh or cry. Everyone around me was happy. An anchor was dropped for the moment, and there I rested again above clouds and mountains, no longer feeling myself float away into my own recognizable world. I smiled and felt good.

By the time it was all over, a few caps and tassels lay abandoned on the open field, from which I could see the courtyard and the Wall of Fame faintly lit in the loneliness of this vast, open campus. I wondered if our newly engraved names would be long forgotten like all other names that now only brought faded memories of a once enriched Beach High tradition. *Marlo Clemente, Desiree Castillo, Ivan Cantón,* and *Danny Skies.* Forever we would be spelled for the rest of the world to see. Forever the wall would cry our names. Forgotten? Maybe not.

Desiree came over to say goodbye. My family and I were headed to Danny's for a small get-together. I asked her to come along, but she hesitated as she turned to her family halfheartedly. They were waiting.

"Just ask," I pleaded, wanting her to come along badly. It would be one of a handful of nights we would spend together.

Her twin soon approached us. "Your mom's ready to leave," she said. Her voice was deeper and didn't carry the familiar lisp I was so accustomed to.

"This is Marlo," Desiree said when she realized we had never met. "And this is my cousin, Divina."

Our introduction was not intended to be a memorable one. And it wasn't. We simply smiled at each other casually, without voicing any words.

"Tell my mom I'll be right there."

Divina walked back to Ms. Rencor.

"I kinda expected you'd say she was your sister."

"Not quite."

"Why haven't you ever mentioned you had a cousin who looks so much like you?"

"I don't know. Why would it matter?" she stated blandly as she ran back to her mother.

Divina eventually looked my way as though she could feel my gaze tap her on the shoulder. She knew my eyes were meant for her, and I didn't know quite how to break the spell I by now could not help but be in. I forced myself to turn and pose as Tamara took a final family snapshot.

"My mom says I can go with you," Desiree glared with a big warm smile. "But I'll need a ride back home later on."

"That's no problem," I said as I shared in her smile. As we left the field, I looked back. My eyes met Divina's once again, but she only watched as Desiree and I joined hands and walked to the parking lot. She stood like an immovable statue never to melt away and make me forget I was still this most curious kid tampering with forbidden taboos and overflowing with innate, insatiable curiosities. You couldn't really call it sin, though I did feel a bit guilty that my eyes had been so submissive. For I did love Desiree so and the inconsistency of finding her cousin so desirable made me feel all the more like a Romeo burdened by his own relinquishing inhibitions.

Danny's get-together was nothing like the all night crazed parties other graduates were throwing. Both my family and Ivan's spent a quiet time talking with Ms. Skies about how happy they were we had graduated and had managed to stay friends for so long. Desiree and I sat alone up in Danny's room as Danny and Ivan were out in the hall singing the national anthem off key. Alcohol had gotten the better of them.

Desiree described in detail some of her family's past. Her mother and aunt were twins as I had suspected, and both had married two men who were twins themselves. Her mother divorced her father for reasons unknown to Desiree. "My mother says he simply got up and disappeared out of our lives, as if he never existed. I was too young to remember him."

"So that's why your cousin looks so much like you."

"My mother claims she's never kept photos of my father," she went on, "but I'm sure I know what he looks like. I saw my uncle once when I was very young—my father's twin. My aunt and he also got divorced. I remember him being tall and dark, and he was very nice to me. I remember him giving me a dollar for candy. He always came by wanting to see more of Divina, and sometimes he would even ask for me. But my aunt would always make him leave. Then, I never saw my uncle again. I wanted him to come back when I got a little older so I could ask him about my dad, but he never did."

"Why did your aunt and uncle divorce?" I could only imagine continuous arguing and endless torment as I thought of my parents and how they had always fought. Only during the worst of Mother's over-dramatized tantrums did she threaten to leave Dad, but it was never taken seriously given she was always so clingy and so melodramatic.

"I don't know why they divorced. My whole family is all screwed up. My mom never wants to talk about it. Divina and I grew up together back in Albuquerque. We've never gotten along. She can be really mean."

She kept quiet after that, not wanting to go into any more details. "Two weeks before I leave," she added. "That's all we have together."

"I know." I ached at the thought.

"I've really been thinking about Princeton, Marlo," she said as she turned and leaned her head on my shoulder, snuggling comfortably in my arms. "I'm thinking of going ahead. I called last week and reserved whatever loans I qualify for."

"It's the biggest decision of your life—and I think the right one."

"I know. That's where I belong…But I can't go off not knowing I have you by my side. I'll need your strength even though we'll be many miles apart."

"I've already told you I care about you more than anything, and I care so much about your dreams. I'll be right here every step of the way."

"I plan on coming down here on vacations and holidays, no longer making New Mexico my home. It's not like my mother will be at all supportive when she learns I'll go off to Princeton on my own."

"You could always major in science and still write," I suggested.

"Yeah, I could, but I wouldn't be following my heart. If I'm off to Princeton, it's to be a writer. I can't go on and try to achieve other fake goals while dreaming of others. Things will be tough as it is. You were right all along. If I don't go, I would only be looking past my heart."

"Why don't you just stay here until the end of summer?"

"I can't," she nodded. "I do have some money saved, and I could afford to stay a couple of months here in Miami, but I think the money could be better used when I get to New Jersey in September…Don't worry, though. I'll still send you messages everyday and try to call too. Maybe I'll fly back here a week before I go off to Princeton." She kissed me repeatedly on the cheek, much like Mother kissed Dad when he came home from a long hard day at work.

I could have said anything just then and not cared—not cared because it felt so right and so good to let her know what her eyes had only long since ruthlessly battled to see deep inside my soul. "I do love you Desiree. You can have whatever strength I have to make you go on."

"I love you too, Marlo boy—more than any dream I could ever have. And this is the only reason I can ever go on with something like this. I've always had dreams I wish could come true. Not many have. You're the biggest dream that could have ever come my way."

"What dreams should we accomplish before you leave?" I asked.

"Let's do something we'll never forget."

After a moments thought, I suggested, "Hey, let's build a sandcastle."

"Yeah," she said as she looked up at me. Her face lit up. "Let's build one we'll always remember, one that will never fall."

Ivan and Danny soon stumbled into the room. Their eyes clumsily focused on us as we quietly sat at the edge of the bed. "Hey, there's plenty of time for romance later," said Ivan. "C'mon, let's go out in the back and celebrate some more." He held up a bottle of Bacardi rum, something neither Dad nor Ms. Skies would have approved of. But it was our night, a night that would never fade in memory.

They left the room, and we followed. I couldn't help but notice the picture of Gracie Danny still had up on his dresser as I reached for the lights.

It was goodbye. The friend I had long since looked up to, the friend who for so many years had been my strength and confidence—this most flamboyant of entities, was indeed leaving Miami. It was a day none of us could say we had dreaded being that we had never conceived ideas of ever parting.

"Your hair," I commented, laughing as I rubbed the rough surface of his now shaven head. The change was drastic. For he looked more like a plucked chicken where once he had stood like a glamorous peacock.

"Ah, I figured I'd get a head start—not wanting to give them any satisfaction of seeing it all go. My dad helped me."

Danny and I loaded the last of Ivan's things into his father's old station wagon. The wind blew as the sun dimmed red rays across the sky.

"Hey, man," Danny said. "You take care."

"You know I will," Ivan replied as they slapped and shook hands tightly. "You just go on and kick some ass in Oklahoma? Write me so I know where you'll be."

"I will."

"And you better write too," he said as he gave my arm a hard punch.

"You know I will," I returned.

He stuck out his hand, and I shook it as strongly as I could. I didn't want to let go. "Good luck in art school, and don't be afraid to paint your own *Mona Lisa*. I'll be back some time during Thanksgiving." We gave each other a rare embrace before we let go of each other's hands.

"I gotta admit, I'm scared. I don't know what to expect. I think I've seen too many of those cutthroat military-sergeant movies—you know, the kind where you always see the private get broken down, roughed up, or blown away 'cause he can't keep up with the rest."

He was the ultimate survivor—beyond strong. "You won't have any problems," I assured. "If anyone's gonna have any problems, it'll be those other guys."

"I'll miss you guys." He got into the car and stuck his shaved head out the window as he waved. "Don't ever forget everything we've been through, 'cause if you do, then we'll never live to say we were ever friends."

His father drove off slowly. We waved until he was out of our sight. It was only then that Danny and I realized he wasn't going to be around anymore.

26

The surf shop was hectic and demanded most of my time, though I soon quit despite animate pleas from my boss. He even offered more money, but spending time with Desiree seemed more important. She had already quit her job at *Beach Books*, and it wouldn't be long before she too left Miami.

"Who's there?" a mysterious voice called out from within.

I didn't reply at first, checking to see if I had the correct door. The view of the quiet landscape painted a pleasant picture as always, and the railing behind me was a familiar deterrent from accidental plunges into the pool. It could have been Ms. Rencor, I thought, but Desiree had mentioned her mother would be too preoccupied during the day as she readied to close down her boutique.

"I have a big ferocious dog that'll tear your every limb," the voice called out once again, "so you'd better go away."

I heard Snowball's faint barking from the balcony on the opposite side of the building. He wasn't big, and the only thing he'd ever tear into was his dog food. "It's me, Marlo," I said finally, figuring Desiree must have been somewhere inside.

The door cracked open slightly, exposing the heavy security chain. Divina's face peeped through slightly. "Oh, hi," she said, surprised to see me as I was to see her. She unchained the door and swung it wide open, giving me the friendliest hug I'd ever received from any second time meeting.

"Hi," I returned awkwardly. Desiree had mentioned nothing of her cousin staying in Miami.

"Why didn't you say anything after you knocked?"

"I didn't recognize your voice. I thought I had the wrong apartment."

She invited me in and offered me something to drink. "If you're looking for Desiree, she's stepped out to the store."

"That's cool," I said, making sure she knew I could accept the situation. I was a bit ill at ease at first, being that I was alone with her in the apartment. But I was soon not as anxious to leave, wanting to talk and learn more of this cousin who looked so much like Desiree—who so too attracted me in her own unique way, with her innate ability of showing off her figure with almost little regret—of flirting with my most concealed inklings of libido, but still coming across as decent and debonair. It seemed she had been bathing in the sun, her skin enriched by a gleaming dark complexion which made her legs, face, and arms radiate perfection. Her soft-yellow skirt was thigh-high, and her white blouse revealed enough to let its thin straps tease and capture my most candid of thoughts. The casual way she walked around the house in her bare feet, the easiness with which she stroked back her falling hair as she poured us two glasses of soda, and the warmth with which she had hugged me hello made me feel as though I had known her a long time. Thoughts of Daisy came back to the forefront once again, though my thoughts were not as innocent as they had been when I was six. For my mind went beyond the point of undressing her with my eyes. Quick images of the most erotic fantasies crept to mind, naughty kinds of thoughts sparked by images seen in naughty magazine covers at the local liquor store. Force myself I did as I settled and stuffed these most unreserved of thoughts away to somehow ignore a part of me that could barely keep from crying out.

"Why are you still here?" I asked as she handed me my drink. "I thought you'd be back home after our graduation."

"My aunt asked me to stay. I thought it would be great to spend a week here. I've never been to Miami." She let herself fall onto the sofa, not far from me. She folded her legs underneath her, seeming so comfortable and carefree.

"I find it very intriguing how you and Desiree look so much alike."

"It's not like we wanted it that way," she said with a touch of dry humor in her tone. "I would have liked to look a little different, but that's all right, I guess." She sipped her glass. "Are you going off to college somewhere?"

"No, I'll be attending the Art Academy right here in Miami."

"An artist," she said as she paused to ponder the idea. "Artists seem so unlike other people. Aside from being so sensitive, they seem to hold secrets the rest of us often overlook…That's very admirable. Desiree told me you painted the picture in her room. It's really beautiful."

"I gave it to her for Christmas a year and half ago," I let her know.

"Wow. How long have you guys been seeing each other?"

"Going on two years."

"I don't ever remember Desiree having a boyfriend. She's never had a thing for guys. I can still remember her being this skinny little girl who never liked talking to any boys. Now look at her. She's finally wearing a bra and has a steady boyfriend who's not so bad looking. I would have never believed it had I not come down here and seen it for myself." Her eyes scanned my face as she continued to sip her soda. I felt I should shy away, but I didn't. Drawn I was as I felt her surge of flattery take over my senses. She didn't seem mean at all.

We talked a while longer until the front door opened and Desiree walked in with a small bag of groceries. "What are you doing here?" she asked me. Her puzzled look quickly jumped over to Divina who sat quietly with her glass.

"I told my boss I was quitting," I said as I stood up from the sofa. "I thought I'd surprise you."

She walked to the kitchen, not saying a word as she shelved away the groceries.

"Why didn't you tell me your cousin was staying over?" I asked as I joined her in the kitchen, hoping to break her awkward silence.

"I don't know," she blurted brokenly, only to have her eyes rage my way. "I guess I forgot. You can go back and have a seat." She could barely keep a steady voice as she stormed out of the kitchen and headed to her room. "I wouldn't want to disturb you guys."

"Oh, stop it, Desiree," Divina butted in. "He just got here. I'm sure you didn't want me to make him wait outside. You're being ridiculous."

Desiree paid her cousin no attention and slammed her door shut. This was the first time I'd seen her so angry. It wasn't the first time I had come over without her knowing...But I guess if there really was animosity between her and her cousin, I had stepped on forbidden grounds.

"Leave her be," Divina remarked as I walked towards Desiree's room. "She's just in one of her bitchy little moods. She'll get over it. She always does."

I ignored her comments and proceeded to knock on Desiree's door. When there was no reply, I tried the knob and gently opened the door. Her room was small—much like mine, but hers was clean and well kept. It had a touch of Tamara and Kelly Rubia's room. Posters and cutouts of her favorite music bands blended in with the soft-pink finished walls. Magazines, paperbacks, and reference books were compiled and arranged in an orderly fashion across two levels of bookshelves. My painting hung proudly above her bed, along with the award plaque she received on grad night. A small window exposed the same view of the city skyline as seen from the living room. "I'm sorry I overreacted," she said as she sat on her bed, unwilling to expose more than just her back. "It wasn't anything you did. I just didn't like the idea of you being near her."

"I didn't know she'd be here. I was expecting to find you here alone."

"I know; I shouldn't be mad." She turned, revealing those tears I so much detested to see in those glamorous eyes of hers. "You should be able to do whatever you want."

"I wasn't going to do anything," I said.

"You just don't understand how much I hate Divina. Ever since we were little, she's done terrible things to me—things I can never forgive her for."

"Why is she here if you guys don't get along?"

We heard the front door open and close. Silence soon descended on the apartment, yet Desiree still kept her delicate whisper, "Because my mom loves her. Divina acts so good and convincing around her. My mother doesn't have the faintest idea how evil Divina can be. She's not as nice as she may seem. Every time she comes along, something always changes, and I don't want anything to change between us. I love you so much." She put her arms around me which made me feel good. I was touched by her jealousy, feeling as though I was the only guy this world had to offer, the only one who could make her heart skip beats and her eyes dance eternal waltzes. "I know I can't tell you to stay away. That wouldn't be right. I just don't want to lose you."

"You could never lose me," I said convincingly, trying to ease her insecurity. "I don't know what's really gone on between you and Divina, but you shouldn't let it get to you now. She seems like she's being nice enough."

"What about when we get back to New Mexico?" she asked. "She's one of the reasons why going to Princeton seems much easier than staying in Albuquerque."

"You should be thankful, then. Just stay away from her when you get back," I advised. "It'll only be for the rest of summer. Besides, aren't you going to spend most of your time writing and calling me?" I got her to smile, finally—but it wasn't enough to cheer her up completely. I continued as the wise one, the one who could be so certain about everything, assuring her that everything would be all right. I promised to stay away from Divina, not fully understanding why she and her cousin could dislike each other so much. I thought of all the fights my sister and I had gotten into over the years. We had disowned each other so many times only to realize we were of the same blood.

"That's my friend Misty Showers," she said as I picked up the only photo frame in the room.

"I really like that name," I said as I studied the pretty girl of about twelve or thirteen standing next to a tree with a great big smile pasted over her face. Desiree had mentioned Misty had died young. It was a shame to think she was gone—how someone who looked so normal and without a worry in the world could no longer be around to share this world many would dare paint perfect and certain. "You never told me how she died."

"I'd rather not," she shot back.

"Why not?"

"It's not of your concern."

Even though I was supposed to be special in her eyes, there were times such as these where her guard seemed impenetrable. A page out of her mother's book I thought. But I guess I couldn't blame her, being that I had always subjected my life to many pages out of Dad's book. "Why would you say it's not of my concern?" I challenged, a bit hurt that she would not confide in me. "Aren't we past that point? Why must you insist on keeping certain things a secret? Everything about your mother, your father, your cousin, and now your friend…You make me feel like such an outsider, like I'm somebody who isn't going to try and understand."

She didn't say anything at first. Hushed she remained as she looked at me with her simmering green eyes. "You really want to know why I hide certain things?"

"Yeah."

She stood up and opened up her closet door to expose a large hope chest that rested on the floor. A treasure chest of secrets was what I thought when she unlocked the top to reveal dozens of old notebooks and piles of typewritten pages. She pulled out a stack of papers which were tied together with a gigantic rubber band. "This is why I keep everything such a mystery. I write better than I speak. Most of the time I don't have anyone to listen to me, you know that. This is the novel I told you about way back when, the one I wrote long before we met. My first ever. It's not the best literature in the world, but it is special. A part of me and Misty hides in these pages, a story true to life and too painful for me to ever reread or edit."

The giant stack of typed pages overflowed my lap. Her talent seemed to pour from every page, and I just knew she would be a great writer one day—and that she would be read by all, for she too held secrets only few knew how to reveal to this world which often turned its back on truth and uncertainty.

"Names and places have been changed to make it fictional," she said.

I looked at its title, **Blue**. A strange title even though it was one of my favorite colors. For it was the color of the sky, a seemingly endless abyss that could take anyone who knew how to dream anywhere. And so too had blue seen many cloudless days make hopeful promises of castles that would never fall.

No doubt it would take me weeks to read, maybe even months. I did want to read it, though I knew she wouldn't let me take it home especially if it was her only copy…and especially if she were leaving in a week.

"You really want to know why I hate Divina?"

I nodded but did not give her my full undivided attention as I continued flipping through pages of this thousand page manuscript. Finally, I did look at her, finding her alone in her thoughts, as if refraining from a past too painful to recount. "Let me start by saying that everything that has ever been given to me or earned by me has either been taken away or shaded by Divina. Ever since we were kids, she would take away my dolls, my candy, my friends, and even my mother's love. She used to beat me up for no reason and always tell me I was good for nothing and ugly. She'd get on my mom's good side and manipulate her into believing whatever twisted things she wanted my mother to believe. She told on me whenever I did something wrong, and eventually made my mom feel I was nothing but a troublemaker…You might think that's impossible to do, but she managed to take my mother's love and respect away from me.

"Back when I lived in New Mexico, Divina didn't always live near us. She lived in Las Vegas with my aunt, so we really didn't get a chance to see each other very much until after I had turned ten. We'd go a long time without talking to each other, and then she'd show up out of nowhere, looking for some part of my life to mess up. Whenever she heard I had something good, here she would come to see if she could have a piece of it. She can be so convincing at times, making herself seem so nice—so sincere. She'd ask for forgiveness all the time, and I'd actually forgive her all the time for the ugly things she would do to me. Before long, just when I felt I could trust that her vendetta against me was over, she'd do something else to hurt me.

"Divina and my aunt eventually came back to New Mexico to live with us. One day, a teacher at school had told me how pretty I looked. Divina heard about it. On my way home, she grabbed a rock and threw it at my face as hard as she could. I hated her then, but I can actually remember her saying sorry. I forgave her. The next day, she went on and did something else that was equally despicable. I could never tell my mother anything. She never saw Divina as anyone who could ever do any wrong. Divina was always an infallible saint in her eyes…I've never wanted to tell you how or why Misty died, figuring you'd never believe me." She paused as though all words she'd ever known were too foreign to pronounce. "She killed herself." Tears streaked her cheeks continuously, and her eyes then swelled into inflatable cushions.

"You don't have to go on if you don't want to," I said. "I know enough now."

"You don't know everything," she replied, taking Misty's picture and putting it back on her desk. "Misty was the greatest friend a girl could ever have. She was always there when I needed her. She was always smiles and nothing but jokes. She was the one who inspired my writing when being a writer was only a far-off dream. She used to tell me one day I would be famous. She too had dreams of one day being an astronaut and visiting all the stars she had gazed at as a little child. She had high hopes and was even religious. She never gave up on anything. She was definitely someone I always wanted around. We shared everything together. She was the only one who liked me as a true friend, and I guess this was why Divina hated her. She saw how well Misty and I got along and simply could not stand it. One day, when Misty and I were thirteen, a boyfriend of Divina's came by the house. He started taunting and harassing Misty for no apparent reason, calling her a witch. Misty defended herself and told him and Divina to screw off, which was not at all like her. Now that I look back, I wish Misty had kept her mouth shut."

I held her as tightly as I could, letting her know I was right next to her, to ease her tears and, if at all possible, ease her anguish. But the tears kept coming, and her pain seemed too endless. "A week later," she continued weakly, "Misty called me up crying. She told me she had been raped—raped by four older guys, one of them being Divina's boyfriend. She said three of them had held her down while each had their way with her. It was terrible, Marlo…Somehow, I just knew Divina had something to do with it."

It sounded horrible, and it must have been even more horrible when it had all transpired. I looked back at the photo and saw Misty's smile suddenly tarnish by this most horrid of pasts. It almost made me want to cry along with Desiree.

"Misty was so scared. I was the only one she told. She said she was too ashamed to tell her family. She couldn't go to the police because those guys told her if the police were to ever find out, her mother would be next—and that they'd find some way of doing in her father. God, how I hated Divina. There was no other person I would have liked to see disappear from my life, from this world...I wanted to go to the police, but Misty wouldn't let me. And how did I, a thirteen year old, go about proving rape if Misty wouldn't even think of testifying?" Her voice trembled, and her eyes continued to stream rivers. "I tried to do my best for Misty. I cried with her and talked and listened to her over and over again. I begged her to go for help. I saw how depressed she was becoming. She would no longer smile or gleam of talk of the future. I was foolish to think she would get over it. She never did. At school, she talked to no one, and if a boy came near her, she'd start to scream her lungs out and go into hysterics. The last thing Misty told me was that she was pregnant, and then she cried even more. She made plans to get an abortion, something she was morally against but had no choice. I broke open every piggy bank I had and even stole some money out of my mother's purse just so I could come up with enough to pay for it...The abortion never happened. I got a phone call from her mother one morning before I left for school. Misty had killed herself. She had taken three bottles of valium. She made sure there was no chance of being saved. I almost went crazy when I found out. My best friend had left me. And it was exactly what Divina wanted, gone forever—and there was no way of bringing her back." She looked up at me, almost pleading to make her pain stop. "I tried, honest. I tried to make her go on living. There were many occasions where I wanted to join her, but every time I look at her picture, I know she would want me to live on and find a way of making all my dreams come true—to touch the stars as she had so much dreamed."

"What happened was awful," I said as I tenderly stroked her back. "It wasn't her fault, and it certainly wasn't yours. I know Misty must have been a great friend."

"She was," Desiree said as she sighed for the first time. "She would have liked you too, would have liked your paintings—and your sandcastles."

We heard the front door again. Moments later, Divina stormed into the room and said, "Desiree, my *tía*'s coming." She looked at me, ignoring that Desiree and I were deep in thought and that I was holding her with my soul's every might. "Marlo, if you don't want to get Desiree in trouble, you'd better leave her room, or maybe just leave. My *tía*'s not in a good mood. Something about her boutique getting broken into last night."

She could have said nothing and let Ms. Rencor walk in on us—could have made up stories that Desiree and I were alone in her room being bad...But she did none of this and again did not seem as evil as had been implied.

"I'll call you tonight," said Desiree before I left. Her eyes were deeply reddened and still caught up in distant sorrow.

I looked down at the pool area and saw Ms. Rencor coming up the stairs. I thought of stopping and greeting her on my way out, but I thought otherwise. Instead, I used the opposite set of stairs and walked back to Dad's truck.

27

How innocent we are growing up in a world full of fear and uncertainty. How naïve and artless we stay when learning only one side of the coin.

Desiree did not call that night. When I dialed her line, it had been disconnected. It was then that her imminent departure became most real and no longer deniable. It wouldn't be long before she'd be off to a faraway state where beautiful mountainous landscapes stretched as far as the eye could see—and dry barren wastelands washed over souls in loneliest of ways. I dreaded the thought of her leaving. For a part of me would be gone, empty—Florida too a deserted isle where I would loom in solace as I tackled my never ending tideless dreams.

The following morning I had Dad drop me off at the mall. The money-filled envelope he'd given me on grad night had grown bulkier, as frugally I had saved all of my earnings from the surf shop. I had enough for my first year's tuition and figured I could work while in school and borrow the rest if need be. It was tempting to go off and blow all my money on a car or on expensive new art supplies. But I remained focused and peered in only on my number one goal of surviving the academy.

Some of the money I did use—but not foolishly. Desiree didn't like jewelry much. She wore only a ring and a bracelet her grandmother had passed down to her. No, I did not buy her a diamond bracelet or concert tickets as Danny had done for Gracie. Instead, I picked out a simple gold locket and chain—something she could wear near her heart and remember that I was close by her side—if not physically, then in mind and spirit, in heart and in soul. There was room inside for a tiny picture where I planned on inserting our miniature prom photo.

"Must be someone special," the heavyset sales lady commented as she wrote up the receipt. "What would you like to have engraved on it? You can have up to thirty characters put on the back."

She handed me a pen and paper. I thought for a moment as I scribbled down several ideas. *Marlo and Desiree forever…* sounded just right. She glanced over it and copied it down on the order form. "It'll be ready by tomorrow," she let me know. "Do not lose your receipt. It has a lifetime guarantee. If anything happens to it, we'll replace it free of charge."

From there, I rode the bus to Desiree's. I figured we'd go see a movie or spend the rest of the bright shiny day on the beach. We could hold each other in eternal embrace and maybe build that sandcastle we'd promised each other.

I approached the gate and spotted Divina in the pool. I watched quietly as she swam to the far end. She pulled herself out and climbed up on the diving board. Her orange neon-colored bikini bottom barely covered her rear, and the top portion was almost too small to conceal her swelling bosom. Her skin was dark like brown sugar and enriched by the sun as gleaming wetness dripped down every curve, peak, and valley. She whipped her soaked hair back and closed her eyes. I myself would have thought twice about jumping off that diving board, but not her. She calmly flung herself up and down and cleaved the water ever so perfectly. She swam the length of the pool underwater and finally came up gasping for air. I continued to watch from the shadows of the trees as she pulled herself out once again and reclined on one of the tanning chairs. She then leaned back and closed her eyes. "Are you gonna come in," she voiced suddenly, "or are you just gonna sit out there and spy on me all day?"

I remained frozen as I felt caught off guard. I quickly looked around to see if anyone else was present, but everything was silent. The pool water was the only thing which moved as the sun's rays of glimmer shot all around the surrounding walls and windows. The balconies were empty, and all the apartment doors were closed. I debated whether or not I should flee, but that would have been foolish. It was obvious she had spotted me, spotted me admiring her every which way possible.

"Is that you, Marlo?" she asked as she sat up and scanned my way.

Gawkily, I walked through the gate. "I just came to see if Desiree was here."

"Nah, she ain't here," she said as she leaned back and closed her eyes once again. "She and my aunt went to the airport to get their flights squared away and do some last minute shopping. You should just come back tomorrow. I don't know what time they'll be back today." She didn't say anything else. She let herself rest back peacefully under the bright morning sun. Somehow, I felt she could still see me staring at her. I could have told her I thought she looked good in her swimsuit, but it seemed she already knew that.

For the rest of the day I thought of nothing but Divina, and that did make me feel a bit guilty. For it was Desiree I loved, so pretty, innocent, wholesome, and proper…Yet, it was Divina who seemed innately provocative, cunning—malevolent. And that I found exciting. This had nothing to do with love. In my mind I had stripped off that revealing swimsuit Desiree would never think of wearing. An ugly part of me seemed unleashed, a part of me I never thought existed…What was worse was that I liked it. Was I normal—a hormonal crazed eighteen year old, or was this indeed just some sort of blinding spell? It felt safer to think I was being victimized, but deep down it was my own internal thoughts and infernos which could no longer simmer as they brewed to the point of explosion.

The next morning it rained. Soggy skies turned dullish gray, the water a continuous splash of warm vigor. Again I hitched a ride to the mall with Dad. I mentioned nothing to him about the locket, figuring he would say it was stupid to spend money on a girl. He had no idea what I saw in Desiree, had no idea how different she was. In many ways I felt wiser than he was, certain about things he could never be certain about. For Desiree was unique…and I was special.

"I heard you've taken a job at the beach," he said before I exited the truck. "I want you to start at the company when the rain clears. You can't start throwing your life away, son. You've been avoiding this too long. You've graduated now. You must start on your future."

As usual I remained silent, afraid to tell him my dreams of the Art Academy. I shut the door and, for the time being, avoided having to confront this man I had always looked up to—avoided having to tell him that my dreams were not his.

I took one last look at the locket before I rode the bus to Desiree's. I knew she would love it, especially the elegant engraving which seemed to be inscribed in both our hearts: *Marlo and Desiree forever.*

I splashed through puddles as I walked along the endless walkways leading up to the small gate. The pool was covered and the only sound heard was the whispering wind and rainwater pelting from railing to railing. Curtains in every apartment window were drawn—balconies emptied and lifeless, almost ghostly.

I hadn't seen Desiree in over a day, and I could hardly wait to put my arms around her and kiss her gently without ever stopping. But when the door opened, Divina was the one who stood in the threshold.

"You're not going to believe this," she said, "but Desiree went to the store again. I told her you'd been by yesterday and would be back sometime today."

I looked at her indecisively, questioning her story even though I had no reason to doubt her, except for all those ghastly things Desiree had revealed about her. I was reluctant to go in being I had promised Desiree I'd stay away. But I went in anyway, feeling as though being daring had always been a part of my nature.

"She'll be back any minute. I'm sure she won't mind this time."

Most of the small furniture had been cleared and personal belongings boxed. All coziness seemed lost as the walls were bare white and the floors invaded by endless space. Again I was struck by Divina's pretty features as she closed the door behind us. Her long and narrow emerald eyes latched onto mine and seemed as though they would never let go. She wore a white pullover dress. It resembled a big T-shirt which hung down near her knees. Her hair was wet, just as it was yesterday out by the pool. She must have been out in the rain or had just gotten out of the shower.

"You want anything?"

"No, that's okay," I responded.

There were boxes on one of the couches, but I cleared enough space so I could sit alone on the sofa opposite her. I figured it would make Desiree feel better when she returned.

"So what's so important that you want to see Desiree?"

"I haven't seen her, and I kinda miss her," I replied.

She didn't say anything. She only got up. I followed her smooth strides into the kitchen. She returned with a lollipop in mouth. "How come you won't sit next to me anymore?" she asked in a smothered voice as she enjoyed the sweet taste of her candy. "It's not like I'm gonna bite."

"I always sit here."

"You didn't last time."

I was too strong for her twisted games. I was wise, wiser than Dad, I thought confidently. I loved Desiree too much and couldn't imagine doing anything behind her back. I pulled out the locket from my shirt pocket. "This is why I want to see her," I said as I handed her the sparkly gold box, wanting her to know that I cared for Desiree very much.

She opened the box and dangled the locket in the air, as if hypnotized. She even read the back and popped it open to look at our prom picture. She handed it back to me but made no comment whether she liked it or not. "You know," she said, "you shouldn't be fooled by Desiree. She's not as innocent as you think she is."

"What do you mean?"

"I caught her the other day with a guy who lives downstairs."

I grew tense even though I knew what she was saying could never be true. "What guy?" I demanded as I put the locket back in my pocket.

"Some guy who lives downstairs," she responded calmly. "He had her shirt unbuttoned and was kissing her breasts."

Why was she telling me this? It just couldn't be true. Desiree would never do anything like that. She was lying, and I felt myself fill up with immediate hate. But not so much at her. As farfetched as it seemed, jealously strangled me to the point of actually believing everything she was saying. I could not help but feel betrayed—almost sensing this pain I didn't want to think of feeling if this was indeed true.

She came over to me and moved the surrounding boxes out of the way. "Are you mad?" she questioned as she sat next to me, continuing to work away at her lollipop.

"I don't know. What you're saying can't be true."

"Well, it is. You just don't know her."

My eyes weakened and my body kindled as I took in the scent of her fresh body spray and cherry flavored candy.

"She doesn't know what she's doing at times," she commented. "I felt so bad for you when I saw her with that guy. I thought, God, why on earth would she want anyone else when she has Marlo?" She leaned her head back, resting it against the headrest. Her neck was flawless and delicate like Desiree's, her face so relaxed and poised. "She made me promise not to tell you, but how can I ever keep such a thing from you?"

"It just doesn't seem true."

"I know," she said, not moving an inch. She remained calm while I sat tense and crinkly. "It's hard to admit those things which seem impossible. I've had to do it all my life, believe me."

I drowned in my jealous thoughts.

"Marlo," she said suddenly, raising her head back up and looking into my eyes again, "do you find me attractive?"

I felt trapped all of a sudden, caught in a question I really did not know how to answer. For it was Desiree I'd always thought prettier than all the rest—the one I found to be unique. "Yeah, I think you're pretty," I responded weakly, though I don't know why I answered her. My eyes averted her poignant gaze.

She stuck her lollipop back in its wrapper and set it on the floor. "I think you're very attractive too, and very sweet," she said. Her hand went up to caress my arm and shoulder area. "But I think you find me more than just pretty. I see the way you look at me, see the way your eyes undress me when we're alone."

I said nothing as her straightforwardness made me feel even more uneasy, for it seemed she too could see right through me with her burning green eyes. I pulled away from her touch as though each one of her fingers were powered by electric sparks.

"To tell you the truth," she said, moving closer to me and gently pressing her body up against my shoulder, "you turn me on a lot. Sometimes, I just sit around here and just think about you...Desiree tells me you and she have never done anything. That's pretty hard to believe." She took my hand and put it on one of her thighs, softly caressing it against my will. Our eyes clashed, and I too slowly relaxed. I could have even started to stroke her leg without her help—but as much as I wanted to, something inside me retaliated. I remembered Desiree and her charming smile and glimmering eyes. I remembered how unique she was to me, realized how special she thought I and my dreams were.

"No," I said, taking my hand back and pushing hers away. "I can't do this. I love Desiree a lot." I stood up, showing her I was not going to fall for her seductive games. I used whatever inner strength I had and managed to overcome whatever instinctive impulses were weakening my better judgment. "Why are you doing this? I'm your cousin's boyfriend."

She looked at me without saying anything. When she saw I had nothing else to say, she exclaimed, "I'm not doing anything. I think you're making a big deal over nothing. I'm leaving in a few days. Who knows, we'll probably never see each other again. I think you're a nice guy, and I'd be lying if I said I didn't want at least one kiss from you."

Oh, but it seemed she wanted more than just a kiss. I could feel it in the warmth of her touch—the passion streaming from her eyes. She stood up. She was much shorter than Desiree. "I don't think a kiss is asking for too much." She jerked my arm by pulling on one of my fingers. "Desiree doesn't even have to know."

"But she's gonna be here any moment."

"No she won't. Today's the day she and my aunt went to the airport to take care of our tickets, and they'll be gone all day. I just told you she went to the store so you'd come in."

I couldn't believe how easy it was for her to lie. For the first time, I sensed the evilness Desiree had struggled to describe. She was likely lying about her story of Desiree and the guy downstairs as well. I let go of her hand and tried to shake off her entire spell, but I couldn't. I had fallen in too deep to pull myself free from this ravenous desire begging to erupt. There was something about her wickedness and cleverness that made everything inside me come alive all at once. Even if I could have turned away, I no longer wanted to. Everything else seemed forgotten, unimportant...even Desiree.

She tiptoed and pressed her lips on mine, forcing my mouth open as she sucked on my tongue and tugged on my lips ever so fervently. I tasted the sweetness of her candy and grew mushy all over except in one place. For a long moment our lips joined and our tongues intertwined. Her fingers ran through my hair and eventually went down my chest and underneath my T-shirt. She stroked my stomach area and started to undo my belt buckle. I pulled away just then but didn't say anything. Her eyes looked up and fastened onto mine. She sensed my doubts. "It's all right," she whispered. She pulled off my T-shirt, and we kissed again. That was the final blow. She continued down my neck and gently kissed my chest until she was on her knees and undoing my buckle once more.

I could not believe any of this was happening. I shut my eyes imagining I would wake up any moment with messy stained sheets. But instead, I looked down in shock as I saw her eagerly devour every inch of me, hungrily kissing and polishing me until I felt myself ready to explode. "Don't you dare come yet," she said as she stopped and looked up at me. Standing, she quickly shoved me back onto the couch. She didn't bother taking off her dress as she stripped off her panties and climbed on top of me. Slowly, I felt myself penetrate her wet resisting flesh. Her eyes shut and her face grimaced as though in anguish, easing herself all the way down until I filled her completely. "Oh, Marlo," she then said with a weak devilish smile, "feels so good and BIG." She pulled off her dress, and her breasts hung freely. Effortlessly I raised myself and buried my face between her breasts, not caring if I'd ever breathe again. If this was heaven, then I had known hell, and if this was hell—this being the worst of sins...then I wanted no part of heaven—at least not at that moment. She screamed as though she'd die any second. Moments later, without further warning, I erupted inside her, feeling the life of me almost drain completely. My body jerked repeatedly as if I'd been stabbed with an ecstasy I had never known. It was only then that I looked over at the cluttered boxes and suitcases only to notice the painting of the sandcastle I had given Desiree a Christmas ago, the girl of my now pitiful tideless dreams, the only girl I could now say I shamefully loved.

I said nothing as I lay motionless. Divina insisted on continual kisses—not wanting me to let go of the moment. But I did let go as I let myself fall aimlessly into quiet dread. Instead of being happy that I had now joined the ranks of the machoest of men, a member of the best locker room stories ever told, I closed my eyes, hoping I'd wake and that the locket and all the happy memories I'd had with Desiree would be forever preserved...But all seemed lost now, meaningless as my eyes opened to see the rain-washed windows and stormy gray skies. The photo of Desiree and her mother rested unpacked atop one of the boxes. Desiree was holding her mother and smiling at the entire world. I guess I wasn't so special after all...Blended I did with all other grains of sand this planet seemed to claim.

I was still without words as I quietly put my clothes back on. The smell of our lovemaking still clogged the air. Looking at the painting once again, I remembered how lovely the original castle had been under the warm shimmering sun. Then I remembered how awful it was to see it collapse into a shapeless muck as the tide rushed in like an invading army. "You can't tell Desiree about this," I said, knowing it would destroy her.

"I won't," Divina said, slipping back into her dress. "Why are you so concerned if she finds out anyway?" Her voice grew abrupt, irritated that I would bring up Desiree.

"I could never do anything to hurt her," I let her know.

She laughed to herself. "Oh, I wouldn't know about that." She looked at me sharply. "You just slept with her own cousin."

I couldn't say anything after that. In the worst of ways, she made me wonder if I truly did care for Desiree. I had a locket in my shirt pocket that said I did, and my heart still called her name...yet it was my conscience that poked me of my actions. Oh, why did I do it?

28

"Marlo, don't you get too close to those waves," Mother warned as I treaded towards the water. My tiny sister was too young to come along and had to stay behind, underneath the shaded umbrella. The day was warm and the water just right as I dipped my feet and felt the gentle rush of surf enchant my tingling toes. Stepping in deeper, heavy surf slammed against my waste line. I wasn't at all scared, not as I was of the dark. I grew bolder even as waves enlarged and swarmed to eventually knock me off my feet. When I tried to get up, I felt the force of the current pull me in. I grabbed fiercely for the sand behind me, but all that did was scar the shore. Panic rushed me when the next set of waves smacked me right in the face and forced my body to tumble underneath the water. The undertow pulled me deeper, and I could no longer feel the ground underfoot. I coughed profusely as I swallowed large amounts of salt water and sank in even further. When my eyes focused, all I saw was the top of the water high above me. I thought I had died as I felt darkness take over all my senses. The next thing I recalled was being pulled out of the water by a local lifeguard. Dad stood and observed as water was pumped from my lungs. It felt as though I was being killed with each of the lifeguard's thrusts. Lackadaisically, I looked over and saw Mother crying frantically. "Mom," I cried out in broken gasps. "MOM!"

I woke up in a deep sweat, realizing I was only dreaming about an incident I had never wanted to recall because it was one of few family outings we had ever had—an outing I was responsible for ruining. Mother and Dad fought the rest of the day, each blaming the other for what had happened. It was the very first time I wished the ocean had swallowed me up…Now there was a second.

I couldn't close my eyes without having another nightmare, and reality seemed no better as I thought of my actions. I threw up several times the next morning, regurgitating it seemed the ugliness and guilt fluttering my insides. I was no better off when Desiree unexpectedly showed up later that afternoon. The cowardly side of me thought I'd just avoid her and never see her again. I had no intentions of ever going back to her house again, not with Divina there, and not with her mother's eyes which always seemed to suggest I was no different than any other guy, even if I did have sandcastle dreams.

"Why haven't you come by?" she asked, her smile big and wide, elated as she hugged me tight. "My line's been disconnected." She looked so pretty in her pink shorts and white top. Her dreamy expression softened her skin as the sun shined bright on her even through the dark sulky sky above. The rain had subsided, but it appeared stormy weather would be with us for weeks to come as gray dense clouds lingered overhead.

"I know, I tried calling but couldn't get through," I said as I now realized more than ever the extent with which Divina had gone to make sure I'd slip and fall. She had never told Desiree I had showed up looking for her, nor had she been honest about Desiree's whereabouts either. I wanted to kneel and come out into the open. I really did. As horrible as my actions may have been, however, I smiled along with Desiree and returned her tight embrace. Dad, who was camped in front of the television, paid us little attention. We stepped out into the porch. I tried my best to make it seem all was as it had been, forced my mind to see things differently. I would never have to see Divina again, I told myself. Desiree would never need to know my terrible actions, wouldn't have to be hurt so long as I kept my newborn skeletons in the deepest of closets. I had never been one to think, *What you don't know won't hurt you*. But it now seemed like the only alternative—the only way of preserving whatever was left of our relationship. I held strong, growing in confidence, falling deeper into my mask of deception.

"Is something wrong?" she asked.

"Nothing's wrong," I said as I stared off into space—solemn, distantly quiet. My stomach then turned. A gust of wind blew our way. Trees overhead ruffled to remind us of another nearby storm. Usually, I liked to sit and gaze at her as she spoke, but my eyes fled her long searching look, afraid she just might see right through me.

"I've got both good and bad news," she announced. "Which one do you want to hear first?"

"The bad, I guess." No news could be bad, or good—not at that point in time.

"The bad news is that my plane leaves a day earlier than I thought it would. That means we only have two more days together…The good news has to do with Divina. She won't be living in Albuquerque with us. She'll be moving to a small town about two hundred miles away, so that means I won't have to deal with her anymore. I'll only have to deal with confronting my mother when I tell her I'll be off to New Jersey in September—with or without her blessings."

Her smiles still filled the day and her beautiful eyes seemed to turn even the driest of lawns green. I listened intently but had no reaction. "Here," I said dully, handing over the locket I had bought her.

She opened up the box and her eyes lit up. "Oh, my Gosh! It's beautiful! You shouldn't have." She feasted her eyes on it for the longest time, reading the back and looking at our photo inside. "I'll never wear it because I'll be too scared I might lose it," she added. "I've never had anyone give me anything like this before."

"You deserve it and all beautiful things, Desiree."

Her smile again conveyed there was nothing I could ever do to make her sad. In this world I was perfect. Even in her eyes there appeared to be certainty.

"I think I should tell you something," I said as I helped her put it on. "It's something terrible." She spun around once it was around her neck, though she wasn't too concerned about what I wanted to say. She clasped onto the locket and held it tight. I looked at her again but there was no way I could tell her. I wasn't man enough, couldn't take away that big smile that spread across her face. "I—I just want you to know that I'll never forget you."

"Why is that so terrible? I could never forget you either." She kissed me, but not the kind of kiss Divina had given me. This was soft and gentle, not with the same kind of ardent fervor that made me forget myself. "I love you, Marlo. I really do."

Maybe it was best that she was leaving. As much as I didn't want her to leave, she would be better off if she never saw me again. The words, *Marlo and Desiree Forever*, just didn't seem true anymore. We sat on the porch a while longer as she talked of her dreams. "I've sent out one of my manuscripts to an agent in New York. It's a long shot, but I figured I'd get started with my dream earlier than expected."

"Which one did you send, *Blue*?"

"*Blue* is dear to my heart. But no, the one about the weeping prince, the one you weren't supposed to read yet…the one about the first sandcastle ever. Do you know what it would be like if it gets published?" Her eyes widened. "Why, it would be like you building a sandcastle that would never fall. It would be something so great…I think I'll dedicate my first book to my favorite guy in the whole wide world—you."

She couldn't stop talking, and I couldn't help but continue to drown in my guilty thoughts as I dared not look her way.

Despite the weather, Desiree and I made plans to meet the following day so we could finally build that sandcastle she and I so much wanted to see stand forever. But there was no chance of that, not on this day. Clouds overhead turned darker and darker by the minute, and forceful gusts blew loose debris in all directions.

I was feeling much better. I'd slept long hours with no waking nightmares, a bit relieved that Divina would fly to her new home—and even more relieved that I'd never have to hear from her again. Like many of my other experiences, what we shared would only be a distant memory. Desiree and I would start college many miles apart. We would graduate and hopefully one day get married and spend the rest of our lives together. She would write her breathtaking novels, and I would build sandcastles that would never fall.

The sign near the sand read, *DANGER—SURF WARNING*. Only a few people braved the elements near the shops and cafes, and an occasional car cruised down Ocean Drive. From afar, I saw Desiree drooped motionless over the metal railing. Her windbreaker waved in all directions as the wind refused to subside its fury. As I approached, she turned and displayed me eyes which were red and engorged, as if all her tears had been sucked dry. Everything in me grew suddenly cold—extremely cold, as now I sensed what I had feared most.

"Just answer me one thing. Did you or did you not do what my cousin says you guys did?"

For a long moment I just stared blankly at the ocean. I couldn't deny my actions, yet this ugly part of me fought to come up with some explanation, anything which would somehow erase the pains of my deed. She knew me better than most, could read my eyes and search the deepest part of me. I didn't need to answer, though lamely I said, "I can explain." She continued to stand there so motionless. A lifeless mannequin she could have been. How did I explain desire? How did I explain passion—the difference between the physical and the sensual? How did I explain stupidity to the point of intoxication?

She nodded many times in disbelief as she took a few steps back. "Oh, Marlo, how could you? How could you do this to me? If there's one person I've ever cared for more than anything, it's you!"

I remained silent just as she had wanted me to, and my eyes began to sob. I don't remember ever crying too many times in my life. I had always cried only because of broken bones or bruises on my body, but never before for a broken heart. Foreign this pain seemed, as before I could only imagine—where as now I was living.

"I didn't believe Divina when she told me. I was hoping she was lying." This time she stepped up and pounded my chest as hard as she could. "Why did you do it?" she screamed hysterically. "Why? Huh? Why? Why?" She continued to punch me profusely, and I stood there hoping her anguish would subside long enough for me to say things could still be as they were, that our dreams together could still live beyond even the most horrid of fallen skies. "You said you loved me. You said you would never do anything to hurt me."

"I do love you, more than anything," I said. "You got to know I don't want this to be happening, honest. If I could go back, I would. I—"

"No, you don't love me. You slept with her! You know how much I cared about you, how much I believed in you. How could you do something like this—especially with *her*?" Her voice screeched beyond recognition. She paused and sighed with the raging wind. "Divina told me you were just like any other guy, and I was a fool to think she was full of it. I told her you were different, that you knew how to love, and that you loved me—and could never love anyone like her. That's when she told me that you did know how to love all right."

Divina had promised, but how could I have been stupid to think she would never say anything, especially when she and Desiree had so much contempt for one another? What better way to put a dagger straight through Desiree's heart than reveal I had broken all trust we'd had for one another?

Droplets began to fall, turning the beach into a mushy wasteland. "I'm so sorry, Desiree," I said sounding more like a rhetorical recording of excuses which had no validity. "You gotta know I ache, gotta know I just wanna vanish far away, like in your book—never to be seen again." I was better off remaining quiet, for the more I talked, the worse my actions seemed to be—the more I wanted to sulk and hold my head down for all eternity.

"NO!" she fired, her eyes hard and belligerent. "I thought you were different, Marlo—special, one of a kind. You just don't know. I turned away from my mom and from everything she's raised me to believe. Now I know..." She sprang away and staggered to turn around only to tell me never to speak to her again. Her bellowing cries echoed above whipping gusts, leaving me to stand so alone with my own salty tears which would soon join this ocean and this rain. I debated whether going after her would make any difference. What else could I say? What God awful story could I tell which would not sound as though I had a locker room audience?

Oh, God, it wasn't supposed to happen. I wasn't supposed to hurt her—wasn't supposed to be evil. Why did I fall? Why did I get too close?

29

It stood tall, with enough might to make any dream come true—even those that were tideless. I remember. I was there. I had not forgotten how the water took its place only to leave behind shapeless thawed memories of what should have been a timeless relic.

Last remnants of what had been so promising conquered this scene as no other painting I could ever imagine. Half the night I had slaved as I reached the bottom depths of what could have never been deemed certain. The sun beamed an off orange glare. Ocean waves were near—black and ominous, with no ships or swimming barriers to make you feel you were anywhere near any kind of existence beyond your own doubts of certainty. Dark shadows encompassed the surrounding shore, even from way off in the distance. The sand too appeared dark, with enough mystique to hide that it was indeed white and bright. A silhouette of tumbled towers emanated through last dim rays of hope. Without repair these uneven walls would become one abundant shore—the staircase a slide of sand falling ever so neatly into a once glorious dream.

Fallen I had into what seemed eternal doom. The cup I'd been drinking from smacked my mirror hard. It was the first time the mirror had ever been broken.

"Marlo?" Mother asked as she entered the room.

"I hate myself!" I said as I put my hands to my face to hide my hollering cries.

"My God, what have you done?" She picked up some of the broken pieces of glass and examined the cracked gash that seemed beyond repair. Who cared about bad luck when nothing in this world seemed certain? All along I'd always thought there was someone behind its reflection telling me what to see and feel. But there was no hollow space for anyone to hide behind, only dry rotted plaster.

"I'm sorry," I said finally. "I just can't take it anymore."

"What's wrong? You've never done anything like this. Why are you saying you hate yourself?"

"I don't know."

"I've never understood you, Marlo. You remind me so much of your father. You keep everything inside and never talk to anyone about what you feel. That's not good. Makes you hate the world."

"I just can't talk to you," I shot at her, not knowing if my reply was geared more towards making her feel bad, to further extend our distance—as that had been our way.

"And why is that? You've never even tried! All I ever see you do is paint, paint, paint. Never have you come up and told me, 'Mom, I feel bad. Mom, I feel good. Mom, I hate you. Mom, I love you.' "

"I do love you," I replied with forgotten haste. "It's just hard for me to tell you. I don't know why. It's like I can't trust you, though I know I should." My head lowered. Not since a little kid had she seen me cry— not since my loneliest of dreams where I was indeed able to experience this subtle necessity of humanity.

"But, Marlo, I'm your mother." She came up to me and put her arms around me, squeezing me with all her might. Like a magical ointment, my tarnished insides turned to gold. "I love you so much, more so than any words can describe or any of your paintings can show. For the longest time I've wondered why I lost you. I remember we were so close. You'd come running to me every time you cut yourself or fell off your bike. When that stopped, it broke my heart. I lost a part of you I no longer thought existed. I thought it was only because you were getting too old to be hugged and loved."

It was a wonder how I had not starved in everlasting gloom. I hugged her back and cried on her shoulder—cried like a baby, as for the first time I felt this love I had somehow known, yet knew not how to express or accept.

"Cry all you want," she said as she continued to comfort me as only a mother could—so warm and with no conditions. "It's all right. I'm here. I've always been here. I thought I had lost you in one of your paintings, thought I'd lost you behind those quiet thoughts of yours. Tell me why that painting you're working on is so sad and dark. Tell me why it is you cry. I want to be someone you can trust—just as you did when you were little…Did something happen between you and your girlfriend? I know she makes you very happy."

"I'm not evil, am I?"

She forced my chin up with her hand. Her eyes seemed to plead with mine, almost begging me to accept her sincerity. "No, Marlo, you're not bad. When you really get a closer look at yourself, you'll realize you're no different than any other person. We all go through good times and bad—our ups and our downs. You're an angel in my eyes. I don't ever worry about you getting in trouble with the law, doing drugs, or skipping out on school."

It wasn't easy letting her know why I felt the world was coming to an end, why I could never think of painting a happy picture or even think of looking into any mirror again. I started telling her about Dad and how he'd always made all women out to be evil. The more I talked, the more Dad's views of certainty seemed even more foolish, bringing me face to face with more uncertainty than I ever thought possible. For deep in my heart, Desiree was different, the exception—perhaps one of many, perhaps one of few...but certainly not evil. "Desiree was unique...not like Dad had said all girls were," I told her. "She was far different than Gracie. Never once did her eyes show any signs of brewing spells."

I thought she'd acknowledge my foolishness for letting myself be thwarted by Dad. But she didn't. Mother remained quiet and listened, never once doubting I was still a genuine soul—never once convinced I could be so wicked...not even when it seemed it was I who had inflicted these worst of pains. I briefly told her how I had hurt Desiree, though I did not go into details, my eyes in total downcast as I said, "There was her cousin, Divina—and we kissed...kissed all over."

I sensed her uneasiness, as if her eyes wanted to question but at the same time refused to think I was any less innocent than the little boy who had depended on her so long ago. "We all make mistakes," she said. "Some are hard to live with, some we learn to hide and forget. We later understand the true fact that no one is perfect. You can't expect that you, much less anyone else, is perfect. It seems you've hurt Desiree pretty bad, and you should feel bad. What you did was wrong. She may stay angry and resent what you did for quite some time, maybe forever. But again, you're not perfect—and neither is she. In time, she will realize that both of you were young. She seems like a smart girl, not one to ever lose sight that the world is an irrational place."

Why wasn't she saying I and all other guys were evil like Desiree's mother would have said? Why did she not agree with Dad that girls could be evil? Everything she was saying seemed to be caught in the middle somewhere. Ugly I felt, but hopeless I was not—not after speaking and listening to her side of certainty...or perhaps her side of uncertainty. It seemed wisdom became her, wiser than I had ever imagined, for all along I had seen nothing but weakness, a clingy female who ultimately got her way from Dad—but always too frail to break free of his harsh, forceful ways. Never had I felt so comfortable and so understood in all my life. No, I was not an angel…nor was I the devil in an artist's mind or soul.

I would have talked with her all night long, but Dad soon came home. He pouted about dinner.

"I'm glad we had this chance to talk," she said before scurrying off to the kitchen. "It really means a lot to me. I just want you to know that you can talk to me about anything. Let Desiree cool off, then try letting her know you're sorry—but when you do, don't expect anything. She has a right to remain broken for as long as her heart chooses—has a right to move on with her life. Let me know what happens."

"Thanks, Mom." It had been so long since I'd called her that. For the first time in a long time, it felt right.

She didn't let Dad know what really happened to the mirror. He would have gotten furious. And I know he wouldn't have understood why I broke it. He would have blamed me because it was I who had fallen for a girl with pretty eyes—and never I who could inflict hurt in the worst of ways. When he examined the mirror later that night, I told him I had slammed my closet door and it accidentally cracked. He had no pleasant comments, only that I would have to pay for it with my own money—money he said I could earn quickly at one of his many construction sites.

The rains subsided the following day, the day Desiree was supposed to leave for New Mexico. I thought of a thousand excuses why I should not face her and ask for whatever forgiveness her heart would allow, but when I thought she'd leave Miami without ever knowing how truly sorry I was and how much I truly cared for her, I forced myself out of the house at the break of dawn—unsure what time her flight would leave. It did not matter that I might run into Divina or that her mother would tell me to leave the premises after having learned of my actions. I figured as difficult as it was, this was the right thing—the thing which would leave all stones turned and leave me with the kind of peace necessary to relinquish this seemingly never ending anguish.

When I arrived at the apartment complex, I spotted Ms. Rencor getting into her car. The engine roared as she pulled out of the carport.

"Ms. Rencor," I shouted as I got off my bike. She stopped the car. Her face appeared distressed. Dried mascara streaked her cheeks as she struggled to focus in on me through the window. "I'm sorry I'm here so early. I was just hoping to catch Desiree before you guys left."

"Desiree isn't here," she said in her usual broken English. "They took her away to the hospital."

"What?"

"Desiree's in the hospital. She took a whole bottle of sleeping pills last night. They just took her away to have her stomach pumped."

I froze in what seemed an eternal ice age. I doubted my ears as I let my bike fall to the ground. Desiree's eyes and hopes had always shined above the sun, the moon—the stars. This just couldn't be happening... But then, something slapped me back into the moment, remembering her hurt—that it was I who she had been counting on to make her strong and continue on with her dreams.

"Oh, God," I exclaimed as I thought of Misty Showers and the fate she had suffered. "No."

"What am I going to do?" Ms. Rencor voiced, putting her head on the steering wheel and letting herself roar in tears along with the engine. "Desiree's my only baby," she shrieked. "I know I treated her badly *a veces*. I know I am to blame. Her dog kept barking, going back and forth from her room. That's when I found the empty bottle. She would not wake up, Marlo. My poor baby is going to die." She banged her head on the steering wheel several times, finally letting go and opening the car door. I remained silent and still as she flung her arms around me, desperately wanting me to wake her from this horrific dream that seemed too unreal to be true. Obviously she had not known what had transpired—had not yet known that I was really to blame for her daughter's desperate act. I could not return her tight embrace as I delved into a motionless state far away from the present, much as I did when I was six painting lions, bears, and space monsters—wishing again that my sandcastles could for just once stand forever.

She had me drive her to the hospital. I shook the whole way there, quiet voices echoing as they whispered that I had been Desiree's dream come true—that I was different in her eyes, unlike any other guy she had ever thought existed—and that because of meeting me, she no longer had those dismal thoughts of joining Misty to escape this dreary world. *Why, Desiree? Why? You're so beautiful and gifted. You don't have to die to be happy or escape everything that seems unbearable. God, please don't let this be happening. Let it all be just another nightmare; let this be just a simple awful painting I can paint over and make right.*

Ms. Rencor rushed into the emergency entrance while I parked the car. When I walked in, she continued her hysteric shrieks in front of the reception counter.

"You found her just in time," a doctor with white hair said as he reviewed the medical chart. "She's in a deep coma. Her heart rate is extremely low, and other vital signs are also critical. All we can do is hope her heart does not suddenly stop beating."

"Please," Ms. Rencor begged. "You have to save her. She is my only child, my only baby." The doctor tried calming her, but all that did was make her more distressed. She fainted and fell and was carried away into one of the empty rooms across from the ICU ward.

When I called home, my mother picked up. I told her what had happened. She and Tamara rushed to the hospital, and we spent grueling hours in the waiting room. I rested on Mom's shoulders and kept telling her I was sorry for causing these worst of pains. "There's no doubt I'm to blame," I kept saying.

Tamara put her arms around me too and told me Desiree would be okay. "God won't let her die."

We prayed.

The unfamiliar sun had set by the time the same doctor approached us. "She's in stable condition, but she's still in a coma. We're still uncertain when or if she'll come out of it."

We were not allowed to see her, so we went home for the night. Ms. Rencor remained in the hospital, calmed by sedatives as she rested peacefully in the waiting room.

"You can't cheat life," Dad stated when he learned Desiree was in the hospital. "The world's a hell full of temptations and pain we all have to survive before we get to this other place. You can't cheat and cut in line."

Oh, if I could only tell him that it was I who'd crushed her—that it was I who had wreaked these worst of pains he'd always associated with women.

I didn't sleep that entire night, and neither did Tamara. We spent the entire night in my room as I told her everything. It did not matter that I thought her too young to understand.

"Marlo, you should go back and visit," she said, "even if Desiree told you to stay away."

I knew she was right, but I didn't want to go back, not because I didn't care—but because the emotional anguish was almost too unbearable. I was to blame, the reason why she now lay near death. How could I think of ever showing up there again? If I showed, she might never pull through. Why it seemed only yesterday Desiree had stumbled onto me and my sandcastle, seemed only yesterday that she had strolled into Mrs. Wardell's class with her immaculate aura of sweetness...only yesterday we had laughed with each other in good times—dreaming and embracing in what seemed eternal young love.

I wept that night not because of pain—I cried because I hated mirrors and my shadow in the twilight of that fallen day. *Desiree, you have too much to live for. Don't you dare die—even if it means never seeing me again. Oh, if I could take your place—if it could be me to lie in your endless sleep...*

The following morning we drove back to the hospital. Doctors and nurses whispered amongst each other—perhaps speaking of me and the fact that I could cause enough pain to make even the biggest dreamers see death. My paranoia only swelled as the aroma of death lingered throughout every inch of that ICU ward. The sound of beeping machines hummed as we walked past a room with an old man who lay dying while a woman wept by his side. Partially drawn curtains of another room concealed a boy who lay covered in a cast from head to foot. He sipped his meals through a straw as a nurse adjusted his tray. We walked down more white, bland halls, plain pictureless corridors with not one picture frame or hanging ornament to make you feel you were any place but a purgatory on Earth. Anxiously, I pleaded with God that she be okay.

When I walked in, I was stunned by a motionless Desiree, a pale almost ghostly-white Desiree. Her chest moved up and down as she breathed peacefully through a mask which supplied a lifeline of oxygen into her nose and mouth. Tubes coming from several machines penetrated her arms. One machine beeped slowly as a wiggly line zigzagged lifelessly across a screen, confirming that her condition was indeed serious. If I had known grief prior to this moment, then I would have welcomed it in place of this impossible pain that repeatedly mashed my heart. I was still calm when I walked up to her, but when I saw her body so listless—her eyes closed with the possibility of them never opening again, I screamed and fell to my knees. Would I ever see those green eyes sparkle again, or ever hear her flawless lisps and talk of perfect dreams—or feel her warm breath against my cheeks as I lay next to her on those perfect sunny days at the beach?

"I'm sorry!" I shouted hysterically. I put my arms over her covers and cried for what seemed eternity. "Please don't die. Please." Mom tried pulling me off of her, but I held on to Desiree's now motionless body as it seemed to rest in lifeless sleep. Ms. Rencor had entered the room, and she too listened as I wailed on, "I'm so sorry, Desiree. Hate me all you want, just don't die. Just don't die. Don't die...please, don't die."

"I have asked God to take my life instead of hers," I heard Ms. Rencor tell Mom and Tamara. "He has always given me everything I've ever wanted except happiness. Maybe He will grant me this." I turned and saw her holding a dangling rosary, every bead securely wrapped around her fingers. Dried mascara still streaked her cheeks, and her hair stood tangled and displaced in all directions.

My face fell back down onto Desiree, wishing I could somehow drown in this sea of covers. After long moments alone with her, I joined Mom and Ms. Rencor in the small hospital chapel. For the first time since I was a little kid kneeling in front of my bed at night, I asked God for what I wanted most. I asked for forgiveness—and more than anything, asked for Desiree's eyes to sparkle as they had when I first met her…to again show her smile and again have her speak of splendid dreams.

30

Who is Marlo? Who is Desiree? Who's Gracie? Divina? Who is anyone at all but a pile of flesh with many questions and a few wonders left to ponder?

I did not return to the hospital until a week later, avoiding the realization that Desiree may never recuperate. To my relief, a nurse informed me she had miraculously awakened and checked out of the hospital two days after I had knelt and prayed. I knew then that her eyes would gleam again and her lisp would one day voice her dreams come true.

So foreign was this sun which no longer seemed to shine so bright over Miami. The sight of my own reflection only tortured me with a tremendous guilt and shame, knowing I was the one who had shattered everything Desiree had come to trust. Days grew gloomy and nights filled with endless nightmares of Divina biting me with her sharp fangs and slithering tongue. And I would see Desiree's dead corpse in the background, I holding a long wooden stake that I had used to stab her right in the heart.

Beach High was now only a reminder of our days in Biology with Mrs. Wardell. The beach only brought back all those Sunday afternoons when we'd walk hand in hand along the shore. The sight of the apartment complex whispered reminders of our first and last kiss. I walked its now lackluster pathways one last time. As expected, Ms. Rencor's parking spot was vacant. I stopped to look at the pool where Divina once swam, and that only made me weep at the empty balcony above where Desiree stood countless times waving her bright hellos and goodbyes.

Talking to Mom did not change much of my dreary state of mind, but it did help to communicate and express more of the love we'd begun to share. "You cannot make her the victim," she went on to say. "Desiree too was wrong. Even though she may have been hurt and depressed, she should have never tried to take her life." She seemed right, but this only lessened my guilt and shame slightly. I could not deny that it was I who'd fallen into uncertainty, I who'd caused the worst of pains when it had always been made certain that girls were supposed to be at the root of all evil. I could have made myself the victim and blamed all my actions on Divina. But I did not want to grow up to be like Dad and seek safety in cynicism. I turned and faced my actions. A man I could have been called for confronting my fears, but if this was being a man, then wisdom I could not share, for I felt no more a man than the little boy who'd wandered off to look at naked statues.

Weeks passed before a package arrived addressed to me. Inside the brown coated wrapping were several folded sheets of stationery that had something small wrapped inside. As soon as I unfolded the first piece of paper, out fell a painful shiny reminder of squandered happiness. The inscription still read, *Marlo and Desiree Forever*, and the note inside revealed writing I recognized all too well:

> *Dearest Marlo,*
>
> *By now, you know I am no longer in Miami. If I've made you feel bad for what I did, I want you to know that I am sorry. I honestly thought I loved you more than life. When I learned what you and Divina did together, it just made every heartbeat too unbearable—every breath too painful.*
>
> *I was weak, and I don't want you to blame yourself for what I tried to do. I don't know if you'll ever understand what I felt during those last days, but one thing's for sure: I hope you know I was wrong. I feel much better now and find it hard to stop remembering you. I know you were in the hospital. I just could not wake up to let you know I could hear your cries.*
>
> *I'm giving you back this locket because it's the only thing that makes forgetting you so difficult. I don't think I can ever say I'll be over you. My pain still lingers, and I think it best that we simply move on with our lives and our dreams.*
>
> *I wish you well, Marlo. I never believed everything my mother said about you. In many ways, I've come to realize that no one's perfect. You'll always be that mysterious boy from the beach—the one with magic power of making sand come alive.*
>
> *—Desiree*

I wept with every word, knowing I had betrayed a love that still lingered more than anything I had ever known. I wanted to reply in some way and tell her she still had my heart and that I still loved her so. But she left no number or address where she could be reached. She meant it to be like this, and I can't say that I blamed her. Attached was another page. It read:

Machiavelli's Weeping Prince

Oh,
to be loved. . .
to be cherished. . .
A foolish fantasy?
Perhaps an agonizing reality.

The misery I know knows no one
as it knows me:
Quiet weeps do to keep deep reign
across the land. . .
Casting everlasting shadows alike,
though profound for a crowd's
demeaning gleaming stare;
building shielding castles ashore,
never standing dancing beyond a
moon's mellowing, bellowing tide.

Unspoken cries of pride
mirror not my silent sighs.
Only lonely realms
echo my unseen
tideless dreams.

I stared at Desiree's portrait all night long. Hours seemed like minutes as time passed me by. I couldn't see myself going on with life. Yes, a part of me wanted to die, while this other side screamed to define uncertainty in this world I'd never shared. I looked out my window and eventually saw the sun slowly rise as birds chirped and flew from tree to tree. It was a weekday. A few people got into cars and prepared for another routine day. Street cleaners burrowed their sweepers from block to block, perhaps not ever imagining the sun could rise without ever shining.

I can't say what made me go out that morning. I hadn't slept and could have collapsed with one shut of my eyes. Perhaps it was the waves. Drew me they did as they dared me to prove I indeed could be this prince to reign magic and make even the most impossible of dreams come true. Dad was already up and in the kitchen, ready for his routine day. I dressed and gently covered Desiree's picture, placing her letter and locket into one of my desk drawers. I went into the garage and grabbed my bucket, shovel, and skateboard.

Not a seagull scavenged the serenity of the beach. Hotels stood silent—shops, restaurants, and cafes gated and lifeless in the earliest of morning hours. I picked an empty spot near the vast, serene shore. There I sat thinking of the past, present, and whatever there was of the future. The sun was barely above the water as it appeared like a floating ball upon the horizon. My hands dug into the sand as I put all energies and feeling into a most familiar dream. Buckets and buckets of sand piled my domain. From dawn until early evening hours, I shaped, smoothed, expanded, and created from within—as this was how it had always been, an innate, magical sensation not felt anywhere on shore. Visible only to me this talent spoke—and I to share with this world these loneliest of dreams.

When finally I had the chance to look at what I had accomplished, I took a deep breath and almost fainted with exhaustion, letting myself fall into the shallowest part of the water. The most remarkable of sandcastles soared high over the beach. Mountains of sand became its resting place to emanate an impenetrable plateau. It stood five feet high, surrounded by a three-foot deep, fortified trench to divert all threatening tides. Multiple towers stabbed clouds high above as its turrets screamed everlasting glory.

The smell of salty air and the sound of crushing waves soon invaded my senses as my detachment dissipated as quickly as it had arrived. As usual, a gloom of darkness began to shadow over my creation like a falling sun, my magic all but gone now. Emptiness and abandonment encompassed the castle like dancing tides that would soon become its cover of doom. Only echoes of lost voices roamed its empty staircases and corridors—much like the streets and hotels had been early that morning. There was no sense of life or any signs this castle would not ever fall like the many falling stars I saw dwindle from existence on crystal clear nights. It did not matter that it was massive and fortified. Only in a fantasy world would this lonely prince rule—a world with no danger of enemies or misfortunes such as earthquakes, hurricanes, falling comets, or great big tidal waves...For in reality, surrounding my tideless dream was an entire world full of mystery and uncertainty waiting to come crashing down.

I sat listlessly as I stared from the water. The last of the sun's rays gave little enlightenment as now only silhouettes sang my magic dreams. People walked by and gave compliments of many sorts, but I did not blink their way. Lost I was, and it seemed that only a world without tides could make my magic reign forever. A weeping prince I had become, and soon it seemed I would lose all my dreams to make way for this world I now called home.

I rolled out of the water and let myself fall into deep sleep. A familiar voice eventually shook me awake.

"Hey, Marlo...buddy. Hey...hey, c'mon, wake up. You okay?"

I slowly opened my eyes and focused onto Danny's face which hid behind the darkening sky. Everything was fuzzy, and I felt so tired and weak. Go away I thought as I dazed into his eyes.

"You okay?"

"Yeah, I'm all right."

He helped me up and said, "Your mom's been worried. She didn't know where you were. I drove by and then saw this big thing sitting by the water. I had a feeling you were around here somewhere."

"I was just building."

"More than just building," he said. "Man, this is incredible. You can even see it from the street—this huge castle that just draws you in." He stepped inside the trench and could hardly let go of his awe. "You've never built a sandcastle like this. You must have been out here a while."

"Took all day."

"You okay though? You don't look so good."

I didn't say anything. I merely looked at the castle once again. Unblemished it stood in shadows—its walls and cliffs still untouched.

"Your mom told me in about Desiree."

I looked at him so helplessly. I was wet and sand covered my shorts and most of the skin around my arms, legs, and face. I almost wished he hadn't come along so I could just fall along with the sandcastle and forget about everything, though I looked at him and realized he was Danny, my dearest and closest friend ever. How could I not cry in front of him and not be glad he was around to share my moment, any moment? His big arm wrapped around my shoulders as he held me up.

"I want her back."

"I know she meant a lot to you."

"I just ache so much right now," I said as I blinked back my tears. "I can't say it'll ever go away."

"It will," he said. "Only time can heal this kind of brokenness. There's no pill or ointment that can take it away. You remember how I was."

"She was so special though," I said as I managed to stand on my own and stare my way down the shoreline. There was barely enough light to see the entire length of beach. I sensed waves nearer than they'd been all day.

It was not easy to come out in the open and explain everything Desiree and I had shared, including how I had managed to hurt her. But somehow I sighed and began my long story, from the beginning—this story I could not ever imagine penning on endless pages—but only painting on shredded canvas as I had all stories in my past and in my dreams. Danny listened intently as we walked away. I turned and looked back at the sandcastle one last time. The further away he and I walked, the less concerned I became with its fate. The past was something that just had to be left behind in order to face a future that was not always so certain. We walked towards a new kind of beginning where I'd try to face whatever came my way in a more insightful manner. Danny would be off to Oklahoma in a few weeks, and I would have the Art Academy to conquer in the fall.

There was just no simple explanation why things worked out the way they did, no way of defining a perfect or imperfect world—or a moon which sometimes holds us prisoners of certainty. I would never speak to my father as I had in the past—not that I'd ever done much of the talking to begin with. Mom and I built our relationship. I only regret that we started so late. She understood so much I didn't and always made it known that there would always be gray…and so too rays of sun to enlighten and make hopeful a perfect day.

I don't think I ever got over this girl named Desiree Marie Castillo. Who ever does? There were others…but none like her. As I now sit quietly in my chair and watch my grandson play out in the yard, I worry over what to tell him when he encounters every obstacle of life that rolls his way. He is already aware of uncertainty and fear around every corner— just as I was at his age. "Trust your feelings and don't be scared—no matter what happens," is all I can tell him. His pale-green eyes look up at me, and I know he questions his feelings and whether or not they are legitimate. I can do no more than just hug him after that.